A Kiss to Remember

As the band began another waltz, McClanahan slipped his arm around Emily's waist. He chuckled at the sparks he saw in her amber eyes.

Matt was a good dancer, so she relaxed and enjoyed matching her steps to his. She leaned back against his arm, wanting this dance to last forever. He lowered his lashes seductively, and as he held her closer, she could smell his leathery cologne. When her head stopped spinning from their quick turns, she realized they were in the dim, curtained alcove between the ballroom and the hall. The music went on but Matt stopped dancing. His face was shadowed and handsome as he leaned her against the wall.

Emily raised her face for the kiss she knew was coming. Matt nuzzled her ear, running his tongue along its sensitive shell, and she felt all sense of reason slipping away. He pulled her closer, and her protest sounded weak even to her own ears when he kissed her deeply. He pressed into her, his lips seeking out her secret desires, moving hungrily over her face. His mouth lingered on her cheek and behind her ear, then returned to her eager lips. He moaned and eased away from her.

"That's how a lady should be kissed," he whispered.

FIERY ROMANCE

CALIFORNIA CARESS (2771, $3.75)
by Rebecca Sinclair

Hope Bennett was determined to save her brother's life. And if that meant paying notorious gunslinger Drake Frazier to take his place in a fight, she'd barter her last gold nugget. But Hope soon discovered she'd have to give the handsome rattlesnake more than riches if she wanted his help. His improper demands infuriated her; even as she luxuriated in the tantalizing heat of his embrace, she refused to yield to her desires.

ARIZONA CAPTIVE (2718, $3.75)
by Laree Bryant

Logan Powers had always taken his role as a lady-killer very seriously and no woman was going to change that. Not even the breathtakingly beautiful Callie Nolan with her luxuriant black hair and startling blue eyes. Logan might have considered a lusty romp with her but it was apparent she was a lady, through and through. Hard as he tried, Logan couldn't resist wanting to take her warm slender body in his arms and hold her close to his heart forever.

DECEPTION'S EMBRACE (2720, $3.75)
by Jeanne Hansen

Terrified heiress Katrina Montgomery fled Memphis with what little she could carry and headed west, hiding in a freight car. By the time she reached Kansas City, she was feeling almost safe . . . until the handsomest man she'd ever seen entered the car and swept her into his embrace. She didn't know who he was or why he refused to let her go, but when she gazed into his eyes, she somehow knew she could trust him with her life . . . and her heart.

Available wherever paperbacks are sold, or order direct from the Publisher. Send cover price plus 50¢ per copy for mailing and handling to Zebra Books, Dept. 3284, 475 Park Avenue South, New York, N.Y. 10016. Residents of New York, New Jersey and Pennsylvania must include sales tax. DO NOT SEND CASH.

Colorado Captive

CHARLOTTE HUBBARD

Zebra Books
Kensington Publishing Corp.

http://www.zebrabooks.com

ZEBRA BOOKS are published by

Kensington Publishing Corp.
850 Third Avenue
New York, NY 10022

First Printing: January 1991
10 9 8 7 6 5 4 3 2

Printed in the United States of America

Chapter One

Matt McClanahan strode into the Angel Claire Mining Company's tiny office building and looked around. The walls were bare, except for a photograph of two middle-aged men shaking hands, and a portrait of a woman whose eyes held an ethereal beauty that almost made him shiver. The room was only big enough for a plain wooden desk, and the slender clerk sitting behind it seemed well suited to poring over his ledgers. McClanahan noted a rather girlish face beneath the brim of his dusty hat, and could imagine the whistles and catcalls these hard-rock miners tormented the young bookkeeper with.

"I'd like to see about getting work here at the Angel Claire," he said quietly. "Is this where I talk to the manager?"

Emily Burnham nodded, and without looking to see who belonged to the easy-going drawl, she pushed the registration book toward him. His hand was well formed and unusually clean for a miner's, and his script stood out from the illegible scrawls and X's that preceded it . . . Matt McClanahan. When she glanced up into his tanned, handsome face, she knew he'd never swung a shovel in the dark belly of a mine. But when he focused his bottomless blue eyes on hers, Emily couldn't have questioned his application for work if she'd wanted to. She'd seen those eyes before!

"E. R. Burnham's manager turns one of the biggest

5

profits in Cripple Creek," McClanahan said with a matter-of-fact smile. "You must be a sharp young fellow, to be doing his bookwork."

Emily grinned nervously. The man seemed to be looking right through her, yet her dust-caked overalls and oversized hat had him believing she was a boy—a common mistake here at the mine, and it suited her purpose. She tried to remember her usual questions about previous employment, but before she could open her mouth, a reedy voice came through the window.

"Do yourself a favor, pal. Go to work for Tutt and Penrose across the Gulch, at the C.O.D."

Emily grimaced, knowing quite well who'd made the snide remark. Sure enough, Nigel Grath was grinning in at them, his eyes beady and a little too close together under eyebrows that met in the middle.

"Why do you say that?" Matt asked. He sensed the gangly miner was a troublemaker, and the last thing he wanted right now was trouble.

"Hey—this place is *haunted*, by Angel Claire herself," Grath replied with a high-pitched giggle. He pointed to the woman's portrait with a dirt-blackened finger. "Ain't you heard about her? Ask Eliza there. She's so scared she ain't hardly said boo since she's been here."

"I'll take my chances." McClanahan glanced curiously at the clerk, whose hand was shaking badly, and he finished signing in.

But Grath wasn't ready to give up. "You'll be sorry," he jeered. "Everybody knows Silas Hughes is a slave driver. He's just like E. R. Burnham was—too damn rich to *care* that we're bustin' our butts in his hellhole. He pushed for a longer day with no pay raise back in '94, and he'll do it again."

McClanahan rolled his eyes, irritated by the scrawny miner's incessant whining. "Is that true?" he asked the wide-eyed bookkeeper.

Emily shook her head so hard her hat almost slipped off. The wiry miner taunted her every chance he got, but when Nigel Grath accused her murdered papa of dealing unfairly with his employees, it was more than she could stand.

"You gonna believe that little tomboy, pal?" Grath challenged. "Why, she's so odd she don't even like boys, if you get my meanin'."

McClanahan moved toward the window, but Emily beat him to it. She slipped in front of him to slam down the sash as Grath loped away, laughing at her. Then a loud *pop* ricocheted in the little room, and the window-pane shattered in a puff of smoke. She shrieked, lurching backward into McClanahan's solid chest as pointed pieces of glass showered their feet.

"Jesus! Are you all right?" Matt exclaimed. When his arms closed around her, there was no doubt she was female, and the poor girl was such a bundle of nerves it was all he could do to stand her upright again.

"Dammit, Grath, I've told you to steer clear of my niece!" a voice shouted outside. "Your shift's over. Go home."

Thank God Silas was here! Emily crammed her hat farther down on her head, avoiding McClanahan's stare as she stepped away from his steadying grasp. Fragments of glass were scattered across the floor, and the window was now a jagged hole with a splintered cross-piece at the bottom.

"This'll come out of his pay," her father's partner was muttering as he entered the office, but his scowl relaxed somewhat when he saw they had a visitor. "I hope you'll excuse the commotion, sir. Mr. Grath has a nasty habit of baiting Eliza with his blasting caps. I'm Silas Hughes, manager of the Angel Claire."

"Matt McClanahan." He smiled confidently as he shook Hughes's cool, slender hand. "I was hoping to find a job in your mine. I've heard you're the best manager to work for here in Cripple."

"I like to think so." Silas appraised him quickly and adjusted his black hat. "I start my men as muckers, at three dollars a day, unless they bring me some experience."

7

"That's fair enough."

Silas nodded and glanced toward Emily. "My niece isn't usually so tongue-tied, Mr. McClanahan. She's just recently come to work for me — but Eliza's smart beyond her years, so don't think you'll fool her as to how many hours you've put in, or how much pay you're due." He gestured toward the door, and the blue-eyed man tossed Emily a smile before he preceded Silas outside.

She'd never seen such a handsome grin, but Emily had watched Matt McClanahan's compact physique in her nightmares a hundred times, recalling his swift, powerful movements from the night Papa was shot. This was the moment she'd been waiting for — the reason she'd come to Cripple Creek! Yet now that her number-one murder suspect had shown up, Emily Burnham was suddenly afraid to go through with her plan. What if he remembered *her?*

Her hands were trembling so badly she could barely hold the broom as she swept the broken glass into a pile in the corner. Fortunately, the only person close enough to notice her agitation was Silas Hughes. As he entered the office again, regally tall and slender in his black suit, Emily saw amusement crinkling his crow's-feet.

He glanced behind him, then leaned on the door jamb to block the view of any passersby. "If you don't keep those eyes in their sockets, you'll give yourself away, young lady," he teased quietly. "Just because McClanahan's the best-looking — "

"It's *him,* Silas!" she said in a strained whisper. "It's the man who shot Papa!"

The manager's gray eyes sobered. "How can you be sure? It was nearly midnight, and you were awakened by the gunshots and — "

"But the lamp was lit in the parlor," she insisted. "When I saw him dragging Papa in from the porch, he looked up toward where I was peeking through the stair railing."

Silas scowled. "You'd better be certain about what you're saying, Emily. If it's true, we just hired a killer."

She glanced nervously toward the ore house, where the miners were changing shifts, filing in and out like busy ants—too far away to realize the new payroll clerk wasn't who Silas claimed she was. "It's him," she repeated quietly. "I'd recognize those eyes anywhere."

The mine manager sighed as he looked at the pile of broken glass, and at the window that gaped like a toothless mouth beside him. "You're upset about Grath. I think you'd better head on back to the house."

"But I haven't finished—"

"I'll check the day's records myself," Silas replied firmly. "Now scoot! The men'll be curious enough about McClanahan without my *niece* staring after him."

Emily leaned the broom against the wall, vividly recalling every detail about McClanahan and the way he'd studied her with his startling blue eyes. "He doesn't look much like a miner, does he?"

"No, but with the shiftless types who're drifting in from Creede and other mined-out towns lately, I'm not complaining." Hughes gave her a businesslike nod, dismissing her. "Tell Idaho I'll be dining at the club tonight."

Silas turned and walked briskly away, and Emily knew she'd better be gone when he looked back. She shut the ledger with a thump, and after a last glance toward the buildings of the Angel Claire Mining Company, she followed the dusty, downhill trail into town.

It was a crisp September day, and the intense sunshine made her squint. The air around her vibrated with the roar of the mines, while ahead of her the crystal-blue sky made a brilliant backdrop for groves of golden aspens, with a hazy Pike's Peak standing watch behind them. Below her, Cripple Creek bustled like a hive of bees preparing for winter. Only two years ago one fire had followed another through the original collection of clapboard buildings, but now, in 1898, the city had risen from its ashes to rival Denver and Colorado Springs.

Gold fever had settled into a steady, heady wealth for

men fortunate enough to own the mines and the businesses that supported them — and Emily's father had been one of those men. But the new brick buildings and streetlights standing proudly along Bennett Avenue failed to impress her. Not even the invigorating breeze made her smile as the stately Victorian mansion north of the business district came into view. Her father had built the house for Silas, and as a place to stay when he came to Cripple to supervise his businesses here. But without Papa, no place would ever feel like home to her again.

Emily walked around back to the kitchen entrance, pausing to collect her thoughts, because Idaho would know something was bothering her the moment she stepped inside. And when he heard Papa's killer was in town — the same man who shot Idaho's wife as she'd carried Papa's toddy to the porch that evening last May — the old housekeeper was likely to wither up and cry.

She took off her hat, letting her braid uncoil down her back. As Emily opened the door, a sweet cinnamon scent greeted her as cheerfully as the black man who was pulling a lattice-crusted pie from the oven.

"You're early, missy! Did you smell Idaho's apple pie all the way to the mine?"

Emily inhaled deeply, still trying to think of the easiest way to break the news. The old cook was her dearest friend now, and the last thing she wanted was to upset him.

Idaho set the steaming pie on the windowsill. Then he glanced at her and shuffled back to the oven, this time for a pan of golden biscuits so high and light they had splits around their middles. "Wish you'd let me wash those clothes, Miss Emily," he said crisply. "If your papa would've seen you looking so gritty — "

"He's here, Idaho. Came to the mine today."

The metal pan clattered onto the stove top as the housekeeper stared at her. "I don't need any of your teasing, child," he said in a wavery voice. "Your papa's been gone four months, but I still feel his — "

10

Emily smiled sadly and picked the stray biscuits from between the stove burners. "Not Papa's ghost, Idaho. It was the man I saw dragging him into the parlor."

The old cook's breath caught in his throat. "The man who . . . who shot my Viry?"

She hugged him fiercely, seeking the same comfort Idaho needed as he crushed her in his muscled arms. His chest heaved with silent sobs as they rocked each other for several minutes. Then Emily pulled away slightly, stroking the coarse black hair that was sprigged with white. "Did — did *you* see him that night, Idaho? I have to be sure he's the same man."

The colored cook shook his head, taking a shuddery breath. "No, child. All I saw was my Viry lying there beside Mr. Elliott, with their blood soaking into the parlor rug."

Emily shuddered against him as she recalled the gut-wrenching sight of their lifeless bodies. Alvira Pearce had all but raised her, from the day Mama died of birthing complications. Those gentle black hands had coaxed her to eat and combed her hair — and occasionally warmed her bottom — and now they were still, along with Papa's.

Idaho wiped a tear from her cheek. "Guess we'd better dry our eyes, missy. Mr. Silas means well, but he doesn't know how it is to lose his family. He'll be wanting his dinner soon, and —"

"He's going to the Club tonight."

"Oh. Well, then." The furrows in Idaho's broad brown forehead relaxed as he loosened his hold on her. "You and I'll eat mighty high on this baked chicken, Miss Emily. And we can discuss this piece of news between us. What name does this gunslinger go by?"

"Matt McClanahan." Emily wondered why an outlaw's alias would roll so easily off her tongue, and how such a heartless man could come in such a handsome package. Then, when the old cook backed away as though she'd named the Devil himself, she frowned. "What's wrong? What'd I say?"

11

Idaho passed a hand over his brow. "Is this McClanahan a dark-haired fellow? Good-looking?"

"Yes. Why?"

He cleared his throat anxiously. "During those months you were mourning your papa and wouldn't see anybody, he came to the ranch, must've been four or five times. He said he wanted to talk to you."

Emily let out a short, humorless laugh. "Probably wanted to propose — wanted to save the Burnham empire from ruin, like the rest of them," she added wryly. She'd spent an endless, empty summer holed up at the Flaming B, running Papa's businesses and refusing callers through Idaho, while lawmen searched the mountains and ranches around Colorado Springs for her father's murderer. When they found no clues, she decided to hunt the killer herself, allowing the rumor that E. R. Burnham's daughter was on the verge of collapse to continue its course among Papa's friends and associates. The fact that McClanahan was applying at the mine confirmed her plan as a good one, but how would she snare him without endangering. . . .

Idaho's quiet voice interrupted her thoughts. "So now that he's here, what're you going to do?"

"I'll see that he gets what he deserves, by —"

"Now don't you take one of your wild notions!" Idaho warned as he shook a gnarled finger at her. "He's a dangerous —"

"But he doesn't know who I am — or that I'm here!" Emily blurted. "If McClanahan saw me up on the stairway that night, he didn't recognize me at the mine today. He'll never guess we're plotting to —"

"I don't want any part of killing." The old Negro gazed sternly at her, crossing his arms.

"Who said we'd kill him? I want to see him *suffer* for what he did to Papa and Viry. For what he did to *us*." Emily took his leathery hands in hers, challenging him with her eyes. "You've got to help me, Idaho. Silas thought we were crazy to come here, hoping Papa's killer would believe the rumors about me and try to worm his way into one of the businesses. And now that he's in town, I can't let him get away."

Idaho sighed and shook his head wearily. "You be careful, child. You're all I have left in this world to love."

She hugged him tightly, and then put the warm biscuits in the napkin-lined basket he'd set out by the stove. "I'll change into my uniform, and then we'll see how much of that chicken and pie we can stuff ourselves with before I go to the Golden Rose."

The housekeeper took two plates from the cabinet and set them on the small kitchen table, watching her uneasily. "What if McClanahan shows up there tonight?"

Emily smiled. "I doubt he'd recognize me in clean clothes, and with all the bawdy houses on Myers, there's not much chance he'll choose ours. It's too refined for his tastes — and too rich for his wallet, if he's got to earn his pay as a mucker."

Chapter Two

McClanahan paused inside the double doors of the Golden Rose, struck by how a whorehouse could be so opulent without looking overdone. The parquet floor and stairway were decorated with rich Persian rugs in a gold rose pattern; the walls, velvet draperies, and parlor furnishings were the color of cream and trimmed in gold. Ornate gilded mirrors reflected a magnificent crystal chandelier, which hung from the parlor's vaulted ceiling. A young colored man played softly upon the grand piano — a somber piece for a bordello, Matt thought — as a few of the ladies conversed with their clients. He smiled at an exotic Indian princess, who winked as she ran her tongue across her lips.

"What's your pleasure, sir?"

The voice came from his left, where a burly Irishman stood behind the carved bar. His thick auburn hair defied its center part; he stroked his beard, studying Matt with suspicious eyes.

"I just got into town, and I've heard the Golden Rose is the best place to find an evening's entertainment," McClanahan offered.

"It doesn't come cheap, mister."

McClanahan reached for his wallet as he approached the massive bar. "I'd like a bottle of your best whiskey, and a black-haired beauty with a taste for adventure. But first I'd like a bath. Let me know when this runs out." He laid one hundred dollars on the counter.

"Keep goin'."

Raising an eyebrow, Matt added another fifty. "This better be the best roll I've ever had, Mr. —"

"Donahue. Clancy Donahue." The barkeep stuck the money in his cash drawer and slid a brass token across the bar. "I always charge first-timers a little extra. We're a high-class establishment, and it's my job to keep it that way."

Matt nodded, watching the bouncer reach for a bottle and a glass. Donahue was built like a buffalo, and the buttons on his stiff white shirt strained across his belly as he moved. "Is it always this quiet on a Saturday night?"

"It's early yet," the Irishman replied. "And you know how women are — one day you can't get two words out of 'em, and the next you can't shut 'em up."

Matt poured some whiskey. "It wouldn't be because one of your girls got roughed up today, would it?"

Donahue's catlike green eyes bored into him, and he snarled, "You some sort of inspector, Mr. —"

"McClanahan." He shrugged and took another drink, wondering if Clancy Donahue always answered questions with such defensive ones of his own. "I overheard the barkeep at the Imperial saying—"

"Well, Frankie's mouth always was bigger than his brain." The Irishman leaned closer, looking McClanahan in the eye with a confidential smile. "The girls're pretty shook up — stuff like this usually happens at lower-class houses. If you expect your lady to be at her best, you'll keep quiet about it. If you know what I mean."

"Certainly. Didn't pay that kind of price to watch a woman cry." Matt drained his glass, and then picked up his token and his bottle. "Now where do I go for that bath?"

Emily stopped outside the bathing suite to smooth the crisp, white apron she wore over her black uniform. When she opened the door, she nearly dropped her arm-

15

load of towels: the customers were usually dressed when she checked the supply of bath oils and linens, but this man was totally nude. Thank God he was facing the mirror, shaving, so he didn't see her staring at his body. His broad shoulders rippled as he scraped the razor over his face.

"Come on in, sweetheart. Shut the door." The customer flashed her a half-lathered grin. "You can't tell me you've never seen a man with his clothes off."

Emily flushed furiously and looked away. "Most of our guests are mine owners, or—modest, or—"

"A little softer around the edges, are they?" His drawl was teasing yet friendly as he splashed his face over the basin.

"I—I'm only seeing if you need anything before—"

"Got a bottle, got a girl. What else could I want?"

He turned, wiping his face with a towel, and Emily bit back a yelp. That perfectly proportioned body and those playful blue eyes belonged to Matt McClanahan! She set the towels on the vanity across the room and looked frantically around for something else to talk about. "Uh, that sure is a nice hat," she said, pointing to the chair where he'd folded his clothes.

"New Stetson. Got it in Denver this summer," Matt replied proudly.

She nodded, avoiding his gaze as she ran hot water into the tub and reached for the decanter of bath oil. "So what brings you to Cripple Creek?"

A bronzed hand covered her own, gripping the bottle. "If it's all the same to you, I'd rather not smell so pretty. That's *your* job, little lady."

McClanahan turned her in his arms, holding her lithe body firmly against his own. Then he smiled down at her. She was shaking like a rabbit ready to bolt . . . a vaguely familiar-looking rabbit . . . and he stroked the soft, stray hairs that had escaped her braid. "Came to town for the gold, like everybody else," he said gently. "Never expected to find it *here*, though. You've got the prettiest hair I've ever seen, honey. Go tell Donahue I've

16

changed my mind about that brunette—and be back soon, or I'll come looking for you."

It was the escape she'd been hoping for, and Emily rushed from his arms and out through the Rose's back exit. Never mind that he was the only man she'd ever seen in all his natural glory! He killed Papa!

Emily leaned against the house's cool foundation, trying to harness her racing thoughts in the darkness. This was her chance to quiz McClanahan—to find out why he was here, and see if he remembered her from the night he shot Papa and Viry—while he was relatively defenseless. It would take all the gumption she could muster to pretend she didn't know the awful truth about this man, but if she could keep him talking, whichever lady Clancy was sending him would eventually come to her rescue.

Emily took a deep breath, confident she could get McClanahan convicted with whatever facts she learned tonight. When she stepped back into the bathing suite, he was already in the tub, sipping his whiskey. Perfect, except he'd turned off the lamps and lit the candles the ladies used to create a more romantic atmosphere. And without any bubbles on the water, his rugged, masculine body was in clear view.

"Come here, sweetheart. Let me see your pretty face while I talk to you," Matt said with a patient chuckle. "This is a mighty fancy setup and I intend to enjoy every minute I'm here."

Emily stood like a statue beside the porcelain tub, not wanting to look into those probing eyes, yet not knowing where else to focus. Matt McClanahan had long, dark lashes, yet she doubted that any man dared call him effeminate.

He leaned his head against the back of the tub, smiling lazily. "I could swear I've seen you before—"

Emily's pulse sped up: he *had* spotted her that night at the ranch!

"—but the only places I've been are the Imperial Hotel and the Angel Claire gold mine."

17

She let out the breath she'd been holding, certain Mc-Clanahan could hear her heart pounding. "You—you saw me this afternoon. I keep the mine's payroll records for Silas Hughes."

"Eliza?" he murmured. McClanahan drained his glass and handed it to her. The girl's ivory complexion was flawless, now that it was clean, and the difference a dress made intrigued him immensely, but she was so scared she was shaking. "So Silas is your uncle? And he lets you work *here?*"

"I work both jobs to earn my keep," she hedged with a nervous laugh. "Here at the Rose I just do the house-keeping, though. The ladies'd have my hide if they thought I was horning in on their business."

He chuckled, gently grasping her arm as she set his glass on the floor. "I knew you weren't one of the whores, Eliza. You're too unsophisticated—too natural. That's why I asked you to stay."

Emily wasn't sure, but she thought he was paying her a compliment. With those eyes gazing at her, she couldn't be sure of anything right now, except that she couldn't break free . . . and that she was foolish to think she could outfox the man who'd murdered her father. But it was too late to stop trying.

McClanahan let his fingers trail down her sleeve until he was holding her hand, which felt frail and damp. "So what happened to your folks?"

"Mama's dead," she replied quietly. Then she braced herself, hoping her voice didn't give her lie away. "And Papa . . . well, he left me with Silas. Went prospecting, and I doubt he'll ever come back."

"He's missing a lot, not seeing what a beautiful young woman his daughter's become."

Emily felt herself flush. "Thank you. I—"

"Ever let your hair out of that braid, Eliza?" Matt asked as he sat up straighter. "Nothing I'd like better than to run my fingers through—"

"*No!* I—" Emily jerked her hand from his, stunned out of the spell he'd been casting with his low, hypnotic

18

voice. "Clancy would know. The ladies would think—"

"Some other time, then." McClanahan leaned forward, appreciating her innocence, yet wishing she weren't so damn jittery. "How about washing my back?" he asked in a low voice. "No harm in helping a man lead a clean life, is there?"

As Emily picked up the soap, she knew she was losing ground. *She* had intended to ask the questions, yet McClanahan was getting more information than she was, even if most of her answers were lies.

And the moment she touched his back, Emily realized she'd be better off letting him do all the talking. How could a man with muscles of steel have skin like velvet? McClanahan was hugging his knees; his eyes were closed and he was smiling sweetly.

"Scrub harder, honey . . . that's the way," he murmured. Her hands were small yet surprisingly strong as they eased the knots from around the base of his neck. "Lord, you feel good. Left-handed, aren't you?"

Emily stared at his frothy back. What else had he observed about her? That her eyes widened when she lied? That her hands were shaking and her breathing was shallow and uneven? Without warning, McClanahan leaned back and submerged himself in the tub. Soapsuds floated above his dark hair, and then trickled through his wet waves when he surfaced again.

He grinned at her, wiping the water from his face. "Can't remember ever having a woman wash my hair. Would you care to be the first?"

It was silly, but Emily felt as though he was honoring her with his request. And as she massaged shampoo through his thick ebony mane, she was glad she was standing behind him—her face would surely betray her apprehension. Yet after he ducked his head again, and guided her around so she was facing him, his expression was serious and . . . pleased.

"Wash the front of me now," he said in a husky voice.

She hesitated, knowing damn well she should run out and get Clancy or the marshal before he could pull any tricks. Then McClanahan drew her hand across his taut chest . . . small satisfaction that his heartbeat was as rapid as hers when she rubbed him with the soap. He was studying the braid draped over her shoulder, and then he caressed her face, giving her a blue-eyed gaze that made her knees go rubbery.

Matt guided her hand lower, not caring that he soaked the sleeve of her matronly uniform. Her breath was falling lightly on his damp forehead, and she was getting every bit as aroused as he was but she didn't know what to do about it. He decided it was time golden-haired Eliza found out what made the world go around, and that he was the man to teach her.

Emily was skimming the flat hardness of his stomach with the soap when McClanahan squeezed the bar from her hand, moaning as he curled her fingers around his rigid manhood. Her gasp was stifled by a kiss as he draped a wet arm around her, clutching until she had no strength to struggle. Then Matt stroked her cheek, and claimed her mouth again with a firm tenderness that made her want more, despite her best intentions. When he released her, she staggered backward to keep from falling into the tub.

"That the first time you've ever been kissed, Eliza?" he asked with a grin.

"Of course not!" Emily took a ragged breath, feeling foolish and terribly vulnerable. But again McClanahan's finesse made her wonder how he could possibly be a hardened killer.

"I've had all the clean living I can stand, sweetheart," he said with a soft chuckle. "Help me up now. And fetch those towels."

She went immediately to the dresser, to avoid being so close to his overpowering body — or worse yet, being pulled into the tub with him. When she turned, he was standing, watching her, looking taller than she remembered and majestically male even though he was dripping wet. As Emily handed him the towels, his expression told her exactly what he would ask for next.

20

But instead of saying anything, McClanahan rubbed his hair dry. Then he tugged the towel diagonally across his back as he continued to look at her with a casual grin. Damn, she was ready! Her topaz eyes glimmered with the first light of womanly fire, yet her face was flushed with innocent confusion. He sensed she wanted to explore his male contours, to discover what made his body so different, yet so like her own when it came to desire, so he left her no choice but to dry the front of him.

Against her better judgment, Emily grasped the towel he pressed into her hands. When she touched it to his rugged face, he stood stock-still, closing his eyes. He was at her mercy—she could strangle him, or hit him over the head with the bath oil decanter. But those foolish thoughts disappeared when he let his own towel fall to hold her hands: she could no more overpower McClanahan than she could control her galloping heartbeat.

Matt guided the girl's towel lower, across the plains of his chest and around his hips. He smiled warmly at her, then chuckled as he again closed her hesitant hand around his manhood. "You're not afraid of me, are you?"

Her eyes widened. "N-no."

"Good." McClanahan raised her hands to his lips and then stepped out of the tub. She was looking like a scared rabbit again, so he lifted her effortlessly, catching her under the bottom so she was straddling him.

How had she gotten into this hopeless situation? Even fully dressed, Emily could feel his damp warmth and arousal as he carried her to a chair beside the bed. He sat down, holding her on his lap as though she were a small child. His hands began to caress her back and follow the fullness of her hips. "Mr. McClanahan, I—"

"Call me Matt," he whispered as he felt all sense of control slipping away. "Touch me, honey . . . kiss me. I know you want to."

He nuzzled her ear, running his tongue along its sensitive shell, and Emily felt all sense of reason slipping away. She rested her head tentatively against his damp, tousled hair, trying not to notice the smoothness of his freshly-shaven cheek against her neck. McClanahan pulled her closer, and her protest sounded weak even to her own ears when he kissed her hungrily with his full, urgent lips.

Matt moaned, nibbling and teasing at her tender mouth as his hands found their way under her petticoats. He desperately wanted to explore the depths of her, and watch her eyes widen at the wonder of the love they'd make, but she was too precious to rush this first time. "Mmm . . . silk stockings," he murmured against her fragrant hair. "What other surprises does this prim little uniform hide, honey?"

Emily laughed, hoping to cover another lie. "The ladies let me have their old underthings sometimes. But what Uncle Silas doesn't know won't hurt him. All right?"

He'd molded his hands to her graceful hips, and he gripped them suddenly. "Damn you, little girl," he muttered.

He stood up, still holding her. Was he carrying her to the bed to make love to her? Emily closed her eyes, trying to think coherently. If McClanahan was so desperate for her body, she could use it to snare him, after she notified the marshal that he was Papa's killer. Losing her innocence would be a small sacrifice, if it brought McClanahan to justice . . . and now Matt was loosening his grip, dropping her playfully onto the bed.

But instead of landing on the mattress, Emily splashed into the tub of cold bathwater. She gasped and came up sputtering.

"Sorry to cool you off this way, sweetheart," McClanahan said. "But if Hughes found out I took liberties with his niece, I'd be out of a job."

"Why didn't you think of that *before*, you damn—"

"I did," he protested. "I only intended to kiss you, but when you felt so good, I couldn't—"

"Is that the first time you've ever been kissed?" Emily

jeered. She struggled to stand up in her heavy, wet clothes, slapping away the hand he offered her. "Don't touch me, McClanahan. Just get out of my way."

He choked on a laugh, noting her flushed indignation—but paying more attention to the way her wet black uniform clung to her curves. "The least I can do is bring you a towel. And when you're dry, we can talk about seeing each other someplace besides here."

But as he went to the vanity, Emily had other plans. She stepped quickly out of the tub, scooping his clothes and Stetson off the chair as she ran toward the door.

McClanahan turned, scowling. "You'll catch cold, leaving here all soaking—hey, what're you doing—"

Emily threw the door open. "I hope *you* get *pneumonia*, McClanahan."

He was coming after her, so instead of taking the back exit, Emily raced down the hall toward the main parlor. Her waterlogged braid thumped against her back, and her shoes squeaked with every soggy step as her uniform clung to her body, but she managed to stay just ahead of McClanahan's grasp.

"Dammit, Eliza, I tried to apologize!"

Voices were mingling above a spritely piano tune in the parlor as Emily burst through the crowd beside the bar. Gaudily-garbed ladies and their wealthy, well-dressed customers gasped, then laughed loudly as she hurried out the double doors. Emily was so angry she didn't feel the least bit embarrassed about the way she looked. She heaved McClanahan's clothes toward the nearest watering trough and kept right on running.

"Well . . . how nice of Eliza to get you all warmed up. I was just on my way in."

McClanahan glanced at the owner of the sultry voice—the Indian princess he'd noticed when he came in—and he hastily covered himself with his towel. Clancy Donahue and some of Cripple Creek's most prominent citizens were watching him, so it was no time

23

to argue that he'd canceled his request for her company. "If you don't mind rounding up my clothes, I'll wait down the hall," he said quietly.

"It'll cost you," the princess purred.

"I'm hardly in a position to argue, am I?" With a polite smile, he walked away from the crowd of curious eyes in the parlor. The last thing he'd wanted was to call attention to himself, and now this!

Once inside the suite, he flung his towel on the floor. Who would've guessed that golden-haired innocent would make such an ass of him? Yet he couldn't stay mad at her. He'd sincerely hoped to get better acquainted with Eliza, but under less questionable circumstances. He wanted her trust — her friendship — before he succumbed to her seductive young body. Damn few women could offer him any of those things these days, and he had a feeling he'd ruined his chances with the most fascinating female he'd met in years.

Matt knelt before the marble hearth and stoked the fire. The flames licked at the logs with a light that shone like Eliza's hair — God, he wanted to lose himself in its sweet-smelling warmth! But he'd be lucky if that amber-eyed little vixen even spoke to him again.

"Your clothes, Mr. McClanahan," the Indian princess crooned as she shut the door behind her. "But you can't pay me enough to fetch the hat. It landed under the wrong end of a horse."

He groaned and shook his head. "Thanks. Let's spread these by the fire to dry."

Matt took his wallet out of his pants, while the woman draped his shirt over a chair. She was slender and dark; ornate silver and turquoise combs held her blue-black hair away from her mahogany face. Her buckskin gown was fringed and beaded in a colorful design, so snug it covered only the flimsiest of underthings — if indeed she wore any. War paint accented her left cheek, making her smile exotic but extremely jaded.

"How much was that favor worth, Mr. McClanahan?"

24

she asked pointedly.

He sighed. "How about sharing my bottle? I'm not really in the mood—"

"I already live on whiskey. I need cash to keep Clancy in his place."

It wasn't the first time a whore had wheedled him for more money, but it was the most direct line he'd ever heard. "Donahue takes more than his percentage?"

"Every chance he gets. And he's a slobbering pig about it." She came to stand against him, running a fingernail through the curls on his chest. "You're the best-looking stallion I've seen since I came here, McClanahan—not old and overfed like most of these men. But your mind's on Eliza, isn't it? Princess Cherry Blossom doesn't stand a chance," she continued with an artful pout, "unless you pay her, and she'll show you some Indian tricks Little Yellow Hair will never understand."

"Princess Cherry Blossom?" Matt felt a laugh rumbling up out of his chest, and he draped an arm around her. "Sweetheart, you're about as Indian as I am. No deal."

Cherry Blossom's mouth dropped open. Then she chuckled until she shook. "H-how'd you know? Everybody else eats it up."

"You're wearing Blackfeet beadwork and Navajo jewelry. Guess these mine owners and stock brokers are too caught up in the fantasy to notice, huh?" He smiled down at her, sensing he could learn something much more valuable than Indian fakery. "But I'm taking up your time, so it's only fair to tip you. Something tells me you won't see much of what I already paid Donahue."

Cherry Blossom gave him a wry smile. "Between Miss Victoria and Clancy, most of the girls here are too indebted to leave. Would you like a cigarette?"

He shook his head, watching as she took a metal box and a small square of paper from the vanity drawer. "I take it you're better off than most?"

She studied him as she rolled her smoke, and nodded.

"So why do you stay?" He walked over to light her cigarette, noting the network of tiny lines around her dark brown eyes as he held the match.

"It's a living," she said with a shrug. "No decent man would have me now. My Indian getup's novel enough to attract a lot of generous customers, and this is certainly a tamer crowd than I worked in Denver. If it weren't for Clancy, this house would be the closest I'll ever come to Heaven." She walked to the bed, lifted her dress over her knees, and scooted back to sit against the wall. "So what's *your* story, McClanahan?"

Matt picked up his whiskey bottle and joined her. The Princess was comely for a whore her age—had the taste for adventure he'd requested, too—but after the stunt Eliza pulled, he decided to concentrate on conversation. "Just got into town," he replied as he poured whiskey into the glass she gave him. "Took a job at the Angel Claire— and from what I hear, you and I have the same boss. Ever seen E. R. Burnham's daughter, Emily?"

"Nope. They say she never leaves the ranch in Colorado Springs—wasting away, instead of taking care of her father's businesses." She blew a thin stream of smoke from her nostrils and looked pensively toward the opposite wall. "Spares no expense running this house, though. Good food, nice clothes. If anybody comes up wanting, it's usually her own fault."

McClanahan studied her as he drained his glass. "So how'd somebody get manhandled today? I thought it was Donahue's job to prevent that sort of thing."

Cherry Blossom's dark eyes narrowed. "You ask a lot of questions, McClanahan."

"Yeah, I guess I do." He handed her the bottle and slid off the bed to check his clothes. They were damp, but he could wear them without leaving a wet trail. He pulled a soggy bill out of his wallet, laid it on the vanity, and slid his arms into his shirtsleeves.

"I'm not used to seeing a man dress before he does anything," the woman behind him said with a low chuckle. "You sure we couldn't swap a few Indian tricks?"

Matt turned, smiling. "You've been very entertaining, Miss Cherry Blossom."

She snorted and butted her cigarette against the inside of his glass. "If you promise to come back and see me, I'll tell you my real name. But you've got to keep it a secret."

He stepped resolutely into his pants, wondering how many other men had fallen for that ploy. "Sure. I may need you to keep a few secrets for *me* someday."

The woman smiled, and the hardness faded from her painted face. "Grace Putnam," she said with a wistful grin. "Used to go by Gracie, but I haven't heard that in years."

McClanahan's wet belt creaked as he buckled it. Then he leaned across the bed to kiss her cheek. "Take care of yourself, Gracie. We'll do this again sometime."

As he opened the door, she cleared her throat loudly. When Matt glanced back, he saw a foxlike smile and long, shapely legs. He'd guessed right: she didn't wear anything under that buckskin gown.

"Next time, let *me* bathe you," the Princess said with a wink. "I guarantee you Little Yellow Hair'll be the furthest thing from your mind."

Little Yellow Hair . . . McClanahan chuckled as he turned toward the parlor. Then he thought better of it and used the back exit, circling the house until he saw the horses tied to the post out front. They were nickering quietly under the streetlight, cocking their ears as he approached. And there was his Stetson, half buried in a pile of fresh manure.

"Eliza, if you weren't so damned different, I'd—well, I don't know *what* I'd do with you," he muttered as he picked up his hat. She'd make some lucky man a helluva woman someday. But for now, Matt could see where Silas Hughes had his hands full just keeping her out of trouble.

27

Chapter Three

"Emily, that's the most preposterous idea I've ever heard!" Silas argued. "It's like putting the fox in charge of the henhouse."

"And what would *you* do about McClanahan?"

The mine superintendent glared at her over his newspaper and the clutter of breakfast dishes. Even though it was his day off, he wore his charcoal vest and and a white dress shirt, which made him look sternly autocratic. "He wasn't a problem until you made him one."

Emily stabbed her last bite of honey-drenched biscuit. "You just don't want to admit my plan's working! We came here thinking the man who shot Papa would infiltrate the mine, and we were right. Weren't we, Idaho?"

The old Negro looked at her, then glanced cautiously at the man across the table as he began to clear the dishes. "Miss Emily, I'll do whatever I can to help, but I've got no say about running the mine. That's up to Mr. Silas," he said in a low voice. "I'll be leaving for church soon. Are you coming with me?"

"Not today. I'm in anything but a prayerful mood."

"Time with the Lord may be just the thing to calm you—"

"I'll calm down when this thing with McClanahan's settled," Emily snapped. She was immediately sorry, and smiled apologetically at the housekeeper. Then she looked at Silas. "I still want you to put him in charge of the ore house. He'll think we *trust* him! And the promotion'll keep him from moving on before we can prove he killed Papa."

"Meanwhile the men will think I'm bringing in outsiders to keep the union from taking over." Hughes gazed intently at her, forcing patience into his voice. "You weren't here in '94, when the miners' rebellion forced us to close the town down."

"But the union won! Why will Federation members care if you bring in another supervisor?" Emily protested. "It's obvious McClanahan's no common laborer—he'd fit in perfectly as a manager."

Silas flattened his *Cripple Creek Times* on the table, pointedly tapping his finger on a column near the top of the page. "And what makes you think he'll take the bait, after the stunt you pulled at the Golden Rose last night?"

"He doesn't know who I am."

"The way you gawk at him, he'll soon figure it out." Her father's partner smoothed the white streak in his steel gray hair, sighing as he held her gaze with bulldoggish determination. "What were you doing with his clothes, Emily?"

"That's none of your concern."

"If it made the gossip columns, my *niece* will be the talk of the mines tomorrow," he countered. "Now what happened?"

Emily stalled as Idaho picked up her plate. The man across from her was a confirmed bachelor, discreet to the point of seeming prudish, so her best ploy would be to either appeal to his sense of decency or to embarrass him—or both. "He insulted me," she stated flatly.

Silas let out a snort. "And how could he do that in a parlor house, unless you were in one of the rooms with him? If your father knew you'd been—"

"It's not what you're thinking," she interrupted. "How was I to know he'd be standing there buck naked when I took in some towels?"

The mine manager's face paled, yet his gaze didn't waver. When the front door knocker clattered loudly, he gestured for Idaho to go answer it. Then he leaned across the table, and in a low voice he asked, "Did he force you to . . . or did you lead him into it, young lady?"

"Silas, really! If I had something to be ashamed of, I would've sneaked out the back — or hidden upstairs till he left." Emily crossed her arms and looked away, hoping her expression registered indignation rather than triumph. "McClanahan *deserved* to be made a public spectacle," she insisted. "I didn't ask him to chase me into the parlor without his clothes on."

Silas rolled his eyes and folded his newspaper with crisp, forceful strokes that told Emily he'd seen right through her. Her cheeks felt flushed — she was trembling like a schoolgirl, despite the fact that she'd won their sparring match — and all because of Matt McClanahan's outrageous behavior last night.

"Seven years ago your father put me in charge of the Angel Claire," Silas said tersely. "And until he died, E. R. Burnham and I were two of the most respected men in Colorado. I understand your reasons for assuming another identity while you hunt his murderer — for your own safety, if nothing else. But I'll be *damned* if I'll let your cockamamie schemes ruin everything I've worked for."

"But McClanahan'll be headed to prison as soon as we expose him," Emily replied earnestly. "In just a few days—"

"Why do you think it'll be so easy?" Silas stood, slipping his newspaper under his arm. "You're a very wealthy young woman, Emily Rose, and until yesterday I thought you were smart enough to take over your father's affairs. But mark my words — McClanahan's not who he claims to be. If I promote him to ore house supervisor, he'll take advantage of the position to steal us blind. Or if he doesn't do that—"

"Promote him, Silas."

"—he'll expose your identity, and every fortune-hunting drifter in the West will be pounding on this door, just

30

as they were starting to do at the ranch." The mine manager glanced across the dining room, to where Clancy Donahue was standing. Gesturing for the bartender to wait in the vestibule, he lowered his voice. "I won't—I *can't*—create a supervisory position for McClanahan, Emily."

She stood up, her eyes flashing. "Then we'll give him *your* job, Mr. Hughes."

Silas's mouth dropped open, but then his gray eyes narrowed and he pointed across the table at her. "I'm glad Elliott's not here to see that you've become as insolent—as impossible to reason with—as the mules at the Angel Claire."

As he strode across the dining room, Emily suddenly felt very childish for egging him on. Silas was her father's most trusted friend and partner; not always a likable man, but certainly a fair and decent one. And his talk of how Papa would feel about her recent escapades struck a sorrowful, guilty chord within her. "Silas, wait! I—I'm sorry."

The tall, black-clad figure stopped a few feet from the doorway, but he didn't turn around.

Emily approached him, steeling herself for the rebuke she knew she deserved. "I'm behaving badly," she mumbled. "And it can't be easy, having Idaho and me underfoot."

"It's your house now, Miss Burnham," he replied in a chilly voice. "I'd appreciate fair notice if you want me to find another—"

"No! I—" She walked around to face him, her eyes smarting with tears she was determined not to shed. "It's just that, well—Papa died so suddenly, and the lawmen found *nothing* to lead them to his killer. All I can think about now is avenging his death, and then I'll go back to the ranch. This isn't easy for me, either."

Silas looked down at her for a moment, and his rigid posture relaxed. "I know that, Emily. You're carrying a very heavy load."

"This plan seemed to be the best thing for all of us,

31

until . . ." She paused to get better control of her voice, and to compose her most eloquent, sincere appeal. "I'm not sure how long I can bluff McClanahan," she said quietly. *"Please,* Silas. Let's make him pay for murdering Papa as soon as possible, so things can return to normal."

For the first time in all the years she'd known him, Silas Hughes touched her. He stroked her damp cheek, sighing. "I'll see what I can do," he replied with obvious resignation. Then he glanced over at Clancy, who was sitting on a bench near the front door. "You wanted to see me about something?"

"Actually, it's Emily I need to talk to," Donahue replied.

Silas nodded, excusing himself to the study.

Clancy had obviously enjoyed eavesdropping on her scene with Silas — Emily could see it in the grin that flickered beneath his rust-colored beard. Did he, too, intend to lecture her about her behavior at the Golden Rose last night? "What is it, Clancy?" she asked brusquely.

He stood, gripping his hat with pudgy hands. "Sorry if I interrupted —"

"It's settled now. Is something wrong at the Rose?"

Clancy grinned as he looked her up and down. "No, ma'am. Bob's tendin' bar today, so I thought it'd be a good time to discuss some business — over Sunday dinner in town, if I may."

He was up to something; his slicked-back hair and cheap suit made that as obvious as the gold tooth shining near the front of his mouth. "It's not a good idea for us to be seen together," Emily replied carefully. "People might connect —"

"Even the whores get out now and again, so nobody'd think twice about a bartender and a cleanin' girl sharin' a meal. We'll go someplace quiet."

Emily sighed, still fighting a frown. "Why can't we talk here? I just finished breakfast —"

"So I'll come for you around one o'clock." He stroked

his bushy beard, eyeing her with pale green eyes that held intentions she couldn't read. "A change of scenery might do you good. And it'll let the gossips know you're not the type to hide from waggin' tongues."

Her dash to the trough with McClanahan's clothes had apparently caused quite a stir, and although it had seemed like a punishment the dark-haired outlaw deserved, Emily was now having second thoughts about her impulsive actions. The last thing she needed was for people to start noticing her, and asking questions about Eliza's sudden appearance in Cripple Creek.

But it would be a long afternoon, with only memories of McClanahan's caress — and regrets about how quickly she'd succumbed to it — so perhaps dinner with this cowhand-turned-bartender would be better than keeping her own company. "All right, then. One o'clock."

"I was hopin' to see one of the pretty dresses you used to wear Sundays at the ranch," Donahue said in a sly voice.

Emily looked up from the mashed potatoes she'd been dawdling over. Clancy's pomaded hair, suit, and white shirt bespoke his position at the Golden Rose — a far cry from the dusty jeans he'd worn as a cattle hand on the Flaming B. Had he not dug Papa's grave and then insisted on helping the sheriff with the lengthy, grueling search for his murderer, she would never have made this rough-cut cowpoke part of her deception. "I'm supposed to be Silas's poor relation, remember?" she reminded him in a low voice.

His eyes challenged her as he chewed a bite of steak. "Hughes can afford to deck you out as the belle of Cripple Creek. People must wonder why he doesn't."

"They surely know by now that he's not one to squander his money on women." Emily set her fork down, tired of this pointless chitchat. She *had* wanted to wear something nicer than a simple cotton frock, but the fashionable gowns Papa had bought her hardly suited her role as Eliza. Delmonico's was full of diners in their Sunday finery — people who looked quickly away when she caught them watching her. She'd never felt so underdressed or overexposed in her life.

And to make matters worse, here came McClanahan. His dark brown suit complemented his swarthy complexion; it was the exact color of his Stetson — which he wasn't wearing — yet he tipped an imaginary hat.

"Miss Eliza," he said with a playful grin. Then he nodded to Donahue and stepped between the linen-draped tables, to a seat across the room.

Emily's face flamed, because the people around them recognized her and Matt as the stars of all the local gossip columns. Even Prudence Spickle, the restaurant's hostess, threw her a disapproving glance as she seated customers at a table behind them. Emily looked over at Clancy in time to see him swallow a smile. "What was it you wanted to discuss?" she asked impatiently.

The burly bartender cut the last of his meat away from the bone. "I thought we'd talk after dinner. Maybe take a buggy ride, and enjoy this fine fall afternoon."

"Speak now, or it'll wait until tomorrow. These people are being unspeakably rude."

Clancy's gaze hardened slightly, and then he shrugged. "Business is so good, Victoria thinks we should hire another girl. Since Miss Chatterly doesn't know you own the Rose now, I told her I'd go see the reclusive Miss Burnham about it, to save her the trouble."

Although Emily had grown up expecting to take over her father's many responsibilities, finding new residents for the Golden Rose was a job she had no taste for. And keeping her true identity and her working relationship with Clancy a secret from Miss Victoria would be no easy task, either. "All right," she replied coolly. "I trust Miss Chatterly's judgment."

Donahue nodded, chuckling quietly. "Miss Victoria wants somebody exotic . . . maybe a colored girl. Other

34

houses have niggers, but Golden Rose clients would pay top dollar to indulge their fantasies with somebody fresh and excitin'."

Prostitution was extremely profitable—a necessary evil in mining towns, where women were in short supply—but it turned Emily's stomach to hear the ladies discussed as though they were so much horseflesh. "You and Miss Chatterly know more about men's tastes than I do. Just take care of it, all right?"

"Your daddy's business didn't seem to bother you last night, Miss Eliza," he replied slyly.

Emily glared at him. "I only spend time there to listen for something that could lead me to Papa's killer. When he's behind bars, I'm going back to the ranch."

The bartender's eyes narrowed, and he looked her over as though for the first time, letting his gaze linger on the braid that curved down across her breast. "Out of respect for your feelin's, I haven't mentioned this before now," Donahue said in a low brogue. "But seein' how you handled McClanahan makes me think I should tell you about a talk I had with your daddy."

What was he after, playing on her grief this way? Emily sat back and looked him cautiously in the eye.

Clancy cleared his throat. "You're a pretty young thing. Turnin' more heads than you did when your daddy kept you hidden away at the Flamin' B," the former hand purred. "He told me, not long before he was shot, that he wanted me to court you when you got a little older."

He might as well have punched her. Clancy had jumped at the chance to come to Cripple Creek because he and the ranch foreman didn't get along—and he was built like a bear, so he made the perfect bouncer for the Rose. But let him *court* her? She'd rather suffer Miss Spickle's spinsterish fate than feel those bushy cheeks rubbing hers as he pawed at her body.

"Shall we finish this discussion in the buggy?" he asked with a cocky grin.

"I—I don't think it's the proper time to—"

35

"I realize you're still in mournin'," he murmured as he leaned heavily upon the table. "But the men at the Rose don't know that. And the things they say about Eliza's sassy walk and her pretty little . . . well, it'd make your ears burn. And if the miners figure out who you are, they'll jump your bones before you have time to explain why you lied to them."

Emily's cheeks prickled with heat and she looked away. Donahue was probably right, but she refused to take the cow-eyed bartender's suggestion seriously.

"Darlin', this is no town for an unattached woman," Clancy continued earnestly. "It'll take time for your feelin's to catch up to mine, but I'd make you a good man. If you married me, you could get away from the whorehouse — come out of hidin', and take your rightful place in society. Haven't I proven I can manage your daddy's business?"

She knew from the ledgers that it was Victoria Chatterly who did the real managing, but she didn't dare say so. The barkeep's eyes were bright and he was stroking his beard repeatedly, as though working himself up for a more direct proposal.

"You could do needlework, and decorate the house, and raise the kids, instead of—"

"Clancy, I'm not ready for any of that," Emily replied in a strained whisper.

He let out an exasperated sigh. "But surely your daddy explained that without a man, a woman is—"

"Papa always told me I could take care of myself." Emily lowered her voice, because people were starting to stare at her and Clancy again. "I certainly don't have to marry for money. And I'm so spoiled, I don't see how any man could put up with—"

"I'm willin' to overlook a few faults—willin' to spoil you *more*, darlin'. I've watched you grow into a fine young lady, and now that I'm not just a common cowpoke, I intend to prove how happy I can make you." Clancy reached across the table to clasp her hands. "It's what your daddy wanted, Emily. Better think about it."

36

She jerked away from the huge paws that were holding her. "I think we'd better go," she said tersely. She looked away from him—right into the distant yet distinctly curious eyes of Matt McClanahan, which only flustered her more.

Clancy's gaze followed hers across the room, and he stiffened. "So *that's* it," he said in a low snarl. "Runnin' out with McClanahan's clothes was just an act, wasn't it? You were back there with him the whole time, lettin' him—"

"I'm leaving, Clancy. Are you escorting me?" Emily stood up, aware that the dining room had gotten suddenly quiet. The barkeep's only response was an icy stare, so she walked quickly between the tables toward the front door.

Then Donahue was behind her, his boots thumping loudly on the hardwood floor as he took her elbow. "We're not finished talkin'," he snarled when they reached the sidewalk. "You can't just walk away from me. I love you, Emily. *I'm* the one who thought up the name for the Golden Rose—after *you*. I bet your daddy never told you that."

Emily scowled at what she sensed was a lie, yanking her elbow from his grasp. "Papa didn't tell me a lot of things, Mr. Donahue. He didn't *have* to."

McClanahan paid for his dinner and strolled out to the sidewalk, grinning as he leaned against the front of Delmonico's. Eliza was staying a step ahead of Donahue, answering each of his remarks with an impetuous toss of her golden braid. It did his heart good to see someone else being made a fool of by such a feisty imp.

"Well—McClanahan! Didn't recognize you with your clothes on," a familiar voice behind him teased.

He turned to see Barry Thompson, who now wore a city marshal's star on his blue uniform. Thompson was sturdily built, tall enough that Matt had to look up slightly when he talked to him. "I should've passed the hat. Must've been the best entertainment in town last night."

"I see Clancy's not faring much better," Thompson replied with a chuckle.

They looked down the street, to where the bartender was trying in vain to step in front of the woman who was barely half his size. "I'm only thinkin' of your reputation," he was saying loudly. "Would you have people call you a *slut?*"

"Is this how you'll talk to your *wife?*" she retorted as she stalked across the street. "No *thank* you, Mr. Donahue. No man tells *me* what to do!"

"Amen to that," McClanahan murmured.

The marshal laughed. "You here on business, old buddy?"

"Yep."

"Don't suppose you want to tell me about it."

"Nope. Not yet anyway." McClanahan watched Eliza and the bumbling bartender disappear between the smithy's shop and the livery stable, then turned his attention to Thompson. "What do you know about Donahue, Barry?"

"Not much," he answered with a shrug. "Keeps the Golden Rose in respectable order. They say you don't want to cross him — especially when he's drunk — but there's a lot of men that way."

Matt nodded and glanced down the dusty street again. "Does Burnham's daughter ever come to check up on him? I hear she moved him off the ranch to get him out of the foreman's hair."

"Silas Hughes tells me Elliott only brought her here once, and she hasn't gone anywhere since he died," Barry replied. "And when Victoria Chatterly needed a big fellow to keep the peace at her parlor house, Silas figured it'd solve both women's problems if Donahue took the job. Seems to be working out, from what I can tell."

"What about the little blonde — Hughes's niece?"

Thompson's ruddy face creased into a smile. "You

38

watching her closer now, to be sure she doesn't run off with your clothes again?"

"A man'd have to be blind *not* to watch her." Matt stared as a dusty-gold palomino came up the street at a full gallop. Eliza was riding him bareback, her petticoats billowing out above her shapely legs as she urged the horse toward the edge of town. "Makes you wonder how Silas has kept an eye on her since her father abandoned her awhile back."

"Is that what she told you?" Thompson shrugged and adjusted his hat. "That could be, but I don't recall seeing her till a few weeks ago. Then again, maybe she just lately dyed her hair that color, so she'd get noticed."

McClanahan stepped off the sidewalk to follow the palomino's progress toward tree-studded Mount Pisgah, about a mile to the west of them. He knew damn well Eliza's hair was naturally golden-blond . . . just as he now suspected her story had a hole in it.

The marshal cleared his throat pointedly. "You tired of chasing shadows around the mountains, Matt? Ready to settle down?"

"Maybe. If the right woman comes along." McClanahan studied the lawman's weathered face, noting the same etchings he was seeing in the mirror lately — time lines he hadn't had when he and Barry last got together. "Say, you know where I can get a hat cleaned up? Mine's new enough that I don't trust it to a laundry."

"Funny you should ask," Thompson replied with a knowing chuckle. "I've heard Silas Hughes's new housekeeper — an old colored guy named Idaho something — is pretty handy with herbs and potions. That's who I'd try."

"Thanks, pal. I'm at the Imperial, but don't look me up," Matt teased. With a light punch to the marshal's shoulder, he headed toward the hotel with a plan already forming in his mind.

"Good luck with that little blonde," Barry called after him. "Looks like you'll need it."

* * *

Emily wrapped the reins around a low tree branch and stroked her horse's firm, warm neck. "Good boy, Sundance. We needed that ride, didn't we?" she crooned. She patted his muscled shoulder, and then wandered a few steps across the grassy hillside.

The view from Pisgah stretched forever in every direction. From up here, Cripple Creek and Victor looked like toy towns; the roar and smoke of the mines, and the noisy bustle of the business district didn't exist. There was only the whisper of the wind through the aspens, and the panorama of autumn's palette glistening in the afternoon sun: golden leaves, the subtle crimsons of sumac, and the deep green of Douglas firs that gave way to the misty purples of the Cascade Mountains. It was the closest thing to the open spaces of the Flaming B she'd found, and she came here whenever she needed time alone.

Yet the soothing scenery wasn't working its magic today. Emily sat down in the lush grass, running her finger over the petals of a pale blue columbine. How long could she play two parts without getting caught? To Miss Chatterly and the men at the Golden Rose and the mine, she was Hughes's abandoned niece; to Silas, Idaho, and Clancy she was herself, Elliott Burnham's daughter. Her deception had seemed like the perfect scheme: as Eliza, she could watch for Papa's killer without insulting the wealthy men who frequented his parlor house or making the miners at the Angel Claire resent her for suspecting there was a murderer among them. And her plan had worked—until Matt McClanahan showed up with those observant blue eyes.

He was more of a problem than she'd bargained for. Did he already *know* who she was? The way he'd watched her at Delmonico's suggested amusement, as though he thought she deserved the same sort of embarrassment from Clancy that she'd dished out to him. If McClanahan were ugly, or cruel, or discussed around town as a suspected criminal, her plan to get him convicted would

40

be much easier to follow. But the memory of his caress still made her shiver uncontrollably.

And now Clancy was complicating her life even more. The thought of kissing *him* repelled her—the ladies at the Golden Rose whispered about his insatiable appetites, yet she suspected they had little choice but to put up with him. Papa had *never* mentioned him as a possible match. Indeed, Papa had tried to avoid the subject of his little girl getting married, although they both assumed the day would come. But to Clancy? After a lifetime of watching her father pine for the one love of his life, she doubted Elliott Burnham would suggest a husband his daughter couldn't tolerate. Because Papa knew better.

And now poor Silas had learned about crossing her, too. She understood Hughes's dilemma: he wanted his partner's killer caught, yet he insisted on running the mine with his usual efficiency, as he had when E. R. Burnham was still alive. And Idaho meant well, but he'd been a hired man all his life. He was old and grieving and tired; not much help when it came to trapping the man who'd snatched away his reason for living.

Emily stood up, knowing the challenge of bringing Matt McClanahan to justice—without revealing her true identity—was hers alone.

"I'm not sure how I'm going to handle this, Papa," she murmured to the vast blue sky. "But somehow I will."

Chapter Four

The relative hush of early Monday afternoon greeted Matt as he stepped through the double doors of the Golden Rose with Silas Hughes. A few ladies lounged in the parlor, talking with each other or with the young pianist they referred to as Josh, but everyone else was upstairs. Once again McClanahan was struck by how this could easily be the home of Cripple Creek's most upstanding citizen—except for its brightly-plumed residents, who twittered and waved when they recognized him.

"Let's sit in the bar, back in the corner," Silas said as he gestured toward the small walnut tables. "Whiskey all right?"

"Fine. Thank you." Matt eased into a chair, his back toward the wall. He caught Clancy Donahue's suspicious glance, but the bartender was the least of his concerns. The mine manager had taken him aside this morning, whispered the request, and then walked on as though his newest employee were just another mucker shoveling shattered rock into ore cars. Hughes didn't impress him as the sporting-house type—and he certainly wasn't a boss who'd socialize with his crew. So why were they here?

Matt smiled blandly at Princess Cherry Blossom, who was descending the stairs in a feathered headdress and a fringed gown that left one shoulder bare. Was Eliza here? Was this a set-up, where the innocent housekeeper and her indignant uncle would confront him about his part in Saturday night's scandal? He doubted it. Silas was coming from the bar with a bottle, looking as supremely controlled as he always did. But McClanahan sat up straighter. A man in his profession stayed alive by keeping track of where all the players stood at any given time.

The bottle thunked solidly onto the table as Hughes sat down. "Cigar, Mr. McClanahan?"

"Thanks, I believe I will." He noted the label and smiled to himself. If Hughes was moving in for the kill, Cuban smokes and Irish whiskey were lavish last rites.

The mine manager poured their drinks, and moistened his cigar in his mouth before lighting it. He puffed pensively. "You'd think all the smoke and grit I eat at the Angel Claire would kill my taste for these. Must be the psychology of the thing."

Matt smiled, waiting.

"What sort of work have you done before, McClanahan?" the pepper-haired superintendent asked.

He lingered over lighting his smoke, considering his answer. "Managed a ranch and a smithy for several years. Most recently, I've worked for Wells Fargo."

Hughes nodded. "What brings you to Cripple Creek?"

McClanahan chuckled. "When the gold mines are turning men into millionaires every day, it'd be a shame not to try my hand at it."

"Ever killed a man?" Silas's eyes were gray and direct behind the thin stream of smoke he was letting out.

"Nope. I'd rather not carry a gun, except these days you never know when somebody'll decide he's got more use for your property than you do." The mine manager wasn't smiling or frowning, and Matt found none of his questions particularly surprising. Then he caught Princess Cherry Blossom winking slyly at him — just what he didn't need.

Silas shifted in his chair. "You seem like a stable, responsible sort," he said in a low voice, "so you'll under-

43

stand my concern when I saw my niece's name connected with yours in the *Cripple Creek Times.*"

"Yes, sir. And I take full responsibility—"

"The whole incident was overblown," Princess Cherry Blossom interrupted. She swayed up beside the table, refilling their glasses as she coyly widened her eyes at Silas. "I asked Eliza to take some towels in for Mr. McClanahan's bath, and the next thing I knew she was dashing out with his clothes. She was laughing—everyone knew it was a just a joke. And McClanahan spent the rest of the evening with me. Didn't you, lover man?"

"That's pretty much how it happened, yes." Matt gave her a grateful yet purposeful smile, and when she slithered toward the bar, he faced Hughes again. "Sir, if you're worried about my—"

"I figured Eliza had a hand in it," Silas said with a resigned chuckle. "Ornery as she is, it was only a matter of time before such a thing happened."

"Yes, sir." Matt smiled, recalling her tawny eyes and the eager, rosebud lips that had him so ready to teach her all she wanted to know. "It surprised me a little to find such an . . . unspoiled young lady working here."

"Oh, she's spoiled," Hughes said with a sparkle in his gray eyes. "Not the type to do needlework or help around the house, so when she's not with me at the Angel Claire, I have her work here, where Miss Victoria and Clancy can keep an eye on her."

Matt glanced toward the beefy bartender. "I imagine he does a fine job of it."

"As well as any man can. You've probably noticed that Eliza's got her share of spunk. Comes from never knowing her mother, and not having a father who cared enough to raise her, I suppose."

McClanahan flicked the ash off his cigar, thinking only a golden-haired gremlin like Eliza could make such an upstanding man as Silas Hughes ramble so indulgently . . . and even lie.

Then the superintendent scrutinized him over the top of his whiskey glass. "I'll make my point, McClanahan.

I've been wanting to hire an ore house supervisor for quite some time, but frankly, no one I've considered capable has come around. Would you want the job?"

Matt almost dropped his glass: the opportunity he was looking for had just fallen into his lap. But had it come too soon? He'd only worked at the Angel Claire for two days. "I — I'm not sure I'm qualified to —"

"If you've managed a ranch and worked for Wells Fargo, you'll do fine," Hughes stated. "You have a natural ability to get along with the men, yet you display more intelligence than a common laborer."

Was this a trap? Matt looked the older man in the eye, taking a long sip of his whiskey. It was time to make his move. "Well, everybody says E. R. Burnham was about the fairest boss there ever was, and you must be a man of the same breed, to be doing so well now that he's gone. I hate to sound presumptuous, Mr. Hughes, but I'd like to meet Burnham's daughter. I couldn't be a supervisor for a mine owner I've never seen."

Hughes sat back against his chair, staring. "Emily's still distraught about her father's murder," he insisted. "The last time I heard, she was —"

"Surely she'll come to Cripple Creek sometime soon. Her father invested a fortune in businesses here," McClanahan countered quietly.

The mine superintendent studied him, crushing out his cigar. "Maybe Clancy can tell us if she's seeing visitors yet. I'd regret losing you over such a modest request."

McClanahan poured himself another tumbler of whiskey, and from the corner of his eye he watched the whispered conference at the bar. Hughes had his back to the room, but Matt couldn't miss Donahue's pointed, wary stare.

Finally Silas came back to the table, clearing his throat. "I'll get in touch with Emily this week. May I tell her you've accepted the position? She'll be disappointed if she makes the trip for nothing — and Miss Burnham's not a young lady any of us likes to disappoint."

Matt grinned and stood up to shake his hand. "Yes, of course. Thanks for being so accommodating."

"I'd kick myself for letting a man with your qualifications get away." Hughes reached for his glass and drained it quickly. "And now I have another appointment. But please don't hurry off on my account—enjoy another drink, and another cigar. I'll let you know when Miss Burnham will see you."

McClanahan watched him stride to the door, and then splashed more whiskey into his glass, thinking it was going to be a very interesting week.

"Why on God's earth would he ask such a thing? And why did you humor him?" Emily paced beside the fireplace in the study, glaring first at Silas and then at Clancy. The unkempt bartender seemed out of place, surrounded by leather-bound books, gleaming walnut furniture, and the colorful mineral samples her father and Silas collected, but it was no time to be concerned about Donahue. "How's McClanahan supposed to talk to me without figuring out that we've all lied about who I am?" she demanded.

Silas looked at the painting of Elliott Ross Burnham, which dominated the room from its spot above the fireplace, as though wishing for his deceased partner's guidance. Then he glanced nervously at Clancy. "Emily, I've told you—I was stunned that he asked to meet you. Your hysteria is getting us nowhere."

"It was *your* idea for Silas to promote him," Donahue chimed in. He sank lower in his wing chair, smiling smugly as he clasped his hands over his belly.

Emily glowered at him. It had been her idea to let Clancy come to Cripple Creek, too, and she was starting to regret it. "All right. I'm sorry, Silas," she said with a loud sigh. "What have you found out about him?"

The mine manager rested his elbows on the massive desk and relaxed somewhat. "Like I said, McClanahan's run a ranch and a smithy, and he's worked for Wells

46

Fargo. Those references check out. And frankly, I have a hard time believing he's a killer."

"He was *there*, Silas," she replied firmly. "No doubt in my mind that he shot Papa."

Clancy shifted, crossing his legs. "Silas could ask him to come here, to pay Miss Burnham a call about the mine job," he said in a stealthy tone, "but he'll be answerin' to you about the murder instead. It's the trap you've been waitin' to set, Emily."

"McClanahan and me alone?" she demanded. "What can I *do* with him, once he's figured out who I am?"

The barkeep snorted. "You've handled him before."

Silas sent Clancy a warning glance and focused on Emily again. "You could keep him talking," he suggested tautly. "Coax a confession out of him, or press him point-blank about where he was the night of May seventh. We'll be waiting outside the door, and at the least sign of trouble. . . ." He pulled a .45 caliber revolver from the desk's top drawer. "Elliott used to brag that his daughter was a crack shot. Is that true, Emily?"

"Yes, but—" The sight of Silas's gun suddenly made her plan to bring McClanahan to justice a little too real. She'd practiced with a pistol dozens of times on the ranch, but she'd never aimed at a person.

"You'll only have to fire a warning, and we'll be in here," Silas reassured her. "He won't have time to retaliate."

Emily hesitated. "What if he doesn't confess? He'll know I haven't been pining away at the ranch since—"

"Lie to him! You're certainly good at *that*," Clancy muttered.

She looked away from the Irishman's nasty little grin, recalling McClanahan's handsome smile and blue eyes that were extremely observant. "He's a smooth talker, Silas. We could be spinning tales at each other all night, getting nowhere."

"We'll be listening outside. We'll know if you're having trouble."

"And then we'll be in here, *shootin'* him," Clancy added

47

gleefully.

Emily scowled. "You can't just open fire! The neighbors'll hear —"

"So we'll knock him out with our gun butts. Pile him into the wagon after dark, and finish him off out in the mountains." Donahue looked at her with a half-smile, stroking his beard. "Your daddy probably never told you, but we did that to a few rustlers at the Flamin' B. When you catch a thief — or a killer — the only sure justice is *your* justice."

She sighed, glancing up at Papa's portrait for inspiration. But the sternly-handsome man in the painting merely gazed back at her. "How long do I have to get ready?"

"I'll tell him to come tomorrow evening," Silas said quietly. He checked the pistol's cylinder and put it back in the desk drawer. "The sooner we get this behind us, the better."

"It's for the best, Emily." Clancy stood up, looking her over with a possessive smile. "Once McClanahan finds out who you are, he might try to kill you next. And Silas and I'd never forgive ourselves if he hurt even a hair on your pretty little head, darlin'."

Chapter Five

Emily carefully pulled a stocking up over her calf, savoring the silk's caress. A glance in her oval mirror gave her a heady sense of power . . . power over McClanahan. He'd expected her to *believe* she was the first woman to wash his dark, wavy hair — had coaxed and kissed her beyond the limits of her control! But tonight she'd show him a woman he'd never forget. A woman he'd want, but could only wish for as he suffered the consequences of killing Papa.

She took a deep breath and pushed McClanahan's face from her thoughts. This was no game: she was risking Silas's safety and reputation — everything he and Papa had worked long and hard for — not to mention her own life. Matt McClanahan was quicker and smarter than Donahue realized, and much more distracting than Emily cared to admit. Getting such a handsome, affectionate man to confess to shooting the two people she loved most would be the hardest thing she'd ever done. She'd stayed home all day, trying to anticipate every argument and trick the gunslinger would use to elude her.

Emily slipped into a gown of golden-brown watered silk that matched her eyes. Its fitted bodice showed off just enough curve around her breasts . . . she refused to torture herself in corsets, yet her billowing skirts made her look stylishly slender, feminine, and fragile. She laughed, and swept her long blond hair into a swirling topknot, wishing for Viry's expert hand at controlling her waves. After rouging her cheeks — McClanahan liked women who wore paint — she put on Mama's pearls for luck. McClanahan didn't stand a chance!

When she went downstairs to the kitchen, Idaho's eyes lit up. "Missy, you're a sight to behold," he murmured. He touched her puffed sleeve wistfully, and then went to the pie safe. "I baked you some gingerbread, because you hardly touched your supper. We can't have you turning all weak-kneed and woozy when McClanahan gets here."

"This is hardly a social call," Emily mumbled. Then she bit hungrily into the warm, spicy cake, reminding herself that Idaho, too, had a stake in her performance.

His eyes were wide with worry as he watched her eat. "Do you really think he killed Mr. Elliott and my Viry? He seemed nice enough when he brought his hat here for me to clean — and I doubt he'd come on such an errand if he murdered our family."

Emily raised her eyebrows at this information. "I guess we'll soon find out," she replied quietly.

The colored man nodded, brushing a crumb from her chin. "You be careful, you hear? Nobody else loves old Idaho the way you do. I'll be saying my prayers for you, Miss Emily."

She hugged him, but let him go before his tender words could weaken her resolve. Straightening her shoulders, Emily stepped into the dining room, where Silas and Clancy were talking at one end of the table. They looked up, appraising her silently through the haze of their cigars. Donahue sucked in his breath, gazing at her as though he were a beggar at a banquet.

Silas stood up, his face expressionless. "You're trying for a confession, young lady. Not a seduction."

"My uniform's hardly appropriate," Emily replied with a lift of her chin. "And I certainly can't wear my overalls from the mine."

"She'll bring McClanahan to his knees, Silas!" the barkeep exclaimed. "He'll forget all about who she is and what she's tryin' to pull when he gets a look at her."

That was Emily's strategy exactly, but she wouldn't admit it to Clancy. She watched Silas walk toward her, desperately wishing for his approval. Would McClanahan bolt before she could expose him as a murderer? Or would he expose *her* before she could explain her deception to Miss Chatterly and the men at the mine?

Her father's partner stopped in front of her, his face softening as he studied her hair and gown. "Elliott would be very proud that his daughter's so beautiful, and so brave," he murmured. Then he glanced at the mantel clock. "You'd better get in there before McClanahan arrives. Do you know what you're going to say?"

"He's not the only one with a smooth tongue." Emily hoped she sounded more confident than she felt as she entered the study.

"We'll be right outside, listening," he called after her.

"Fingers on the trigger," Clancy added with a laugh.

Emily closed the door and leaned on it. The paneled room was cozy, with its rich Persian rug, and shelves full of books, and chunks of mineral ore that gleamed with a familiar warmth. The study at the ranch was decorated much the same way, but this one had paintings that ran more to Silas's taste. Flaming logs crackled in the fireplace beneath Papa's portrait. Emily hoped that even though Elliott Ross Burnham hadn't spent much time in this room, his spirit would guide her tonight.

Her hands were clammy and her shoes were starting to pinch . . . maybe Silas should be in here, in case she twisted her words into a noose around her own neck instead of around McClanahan's. There was a loud knock on the front door — damn, he was punctual! Emily chose a spot behind the heavy walnut desk, so Papa could face his murderer with her and McClanahan's back would be to her bodyguards. She prayed again for the right words, then forgot everything she'd intended to say as Silas spoke on the other side of the study door.

"Right in here, Mr. McClanahan. She's waiting for you."

The door opened and he came inside, wearing a dark suit and glossy black boots. A gold watch fob glistened between his vest button and pocket, and he looked devastatingly handsome.

"Eliza?" Matt glanced around the study, then approached her with a wary smile. "You look wonderful, honey. But didn't your uncle tell you about the meeting? I'm here to see Emily Burnham."

Emily suppressed a grin. He was gazing at her as though he anticipated a rendezvous later, but she was about to change his plans. "And so you are," she said as she stepped from behind the desk.

He frowned. "You don't understand. I'm looking for Elliott Burnham's daughter—she was to come in from Colorado Springs to discuss a supervisor's—"

"Do you have any questions about the position?" Emily asked with a coy smile.

McClanahan glowered at the lovely young woman before him. "Yes, ma'am, I do. Who do you think you *are*, to—"

"You weren't listening?" she interrupted sweetly. "I'm Emily Rose Burnham."

"Elliott's daughter?"

"Yes." His blue eyes were blazing at her, and it was all she could do to keep from laughing at his confused expression.

"And why should I believe that?" Matt approached her, glaring at her graceful dress and hairdo as he realized he'd walked right through the loophole in Silas and Eliza's story. "You told me you were Hughes's niece, staying here because your father abandoned you. And everyone knows Emily Burnham's been wasting away since her father was shot. Now what's going on here?"

Emily smiled primly and decided to keep him off-balance for as long as she could. "I believe we're clarifying who I am, Mr. McClanahan. If you'd like to sit down, we can discuss your new role as—"

"The hell we will! You're the picture of health—quick enough to outrun me, and so damn devious you've

52

passed yourself off as a naive little—"

"A fact I take great pride in." Emily gasped when Mc-Clanahan reached out to shake her by the shoulders, but he stopped, his hands framing her like parentheses. His blue eyes were anything but beautiful now. They pierced right through to her soul, and she was suddenly afraid she'd gotten herself in so deep that Silas and Clancy couldn't rescue her in time.

Then McClanahan stepped back and stuffed his hands in his pockets, disgusted that he hadn't figured her out before. "Let me see if I can piece this together," he said in a strained voice. "Hughes and Donahue are outside, listening. Am I right?"

Emily nodded, her heart pounding beneath her pearls.

He relaxed and let out a long breath. If she was indeed Burnham's daughter—and he believed she was—she'd certainly inherited her old man's grit. Her eyes were as round and golden as harvest moons, unwavering despite the brazen tricks she'd played on him. He cleared his throat, deciding to see what other aces she might have hidden up her dainty sleeves. "You haven't been in Cripple very long—and you obviously haven't been holed up in your room these past four months. So where have you been?"

"At the ranch in Colorado Springs," she insisted quickly. "We were having problems with rustlers. I thought rumors about my failing health would make those outlaws careless enough that we could catch them."

McClanahan raised his eyebrows, yet he wasn't surprised that Miss Burnham was so adept at covering for herself. "A good foreman could handle rustlers," he contended. "E. R. Burnham's heir should've been checking on the mine before now, and overseeing the Golden Rose—certainly the most extravagant investment of its kind in Cripple Creek."

"I prefer working cattle to watching over whores." Emily widened her eyes at him, then rested her hand on the cool, solid desktop. "Papa opened the Rose as a favor to

Victoria Chatterly—and because he thought another high-class house would do well in Cripple—but my interests have always been at the ranch. When Papa died, I kept abreast of all his businesses through Idaho, and I've kept his books for years, so I know exactly how all my investments are doing. I—I made Papa a pretty good partner, actually."

"You'd also make a helluva poker player, Miss Burnham," he said as he stepped toward her again.

Emily frowned uncertainly. "Why's that?"

"Because reliable sources claim that Donahue signed on at the Rose to get away from the foreman at the Flaming B, and that Idaho left because he couldn't stand to live there anymore without his wife. That's a lie, isn't it? Just like Idaho telling me you were in no shape for visitors when I stopped by the ranch a few times."

She was curious about his sources; the rumors about Clancy and Idaho weren't totally untrue, but that didn't really matter now. Maybe Papa's spirit was here, or maybe her blood had turned to ice water, because Emily suddenly felt serenely confident. She opened the desk drawer and pointed the pistol at McClanahan.

Matt stared. "What's *this* all about? I—"

"I've been wanting to ask you about your visits, McClanahan," she said coldly. "And you'd better give me the right answer. Why'd you kill my father?"

"What makes you think I—"

"You were there that night. I saw you from the upstairs landing." Her pistol clicked as she cocked it. "And I swore I'd do whatever it took to make you pay."

McClanahan took a step backward, noting the set of her jaw and the steady barrel of her gun. "Yes, I was there," he said quietly. "Trying to see who *did* shoot him."

"And why should I believe that?" she demanded.

Matt saw a slight tremor go through her arms, and he looked at the stony expression on her face. It was a sure bet Hughes and Donahue would gun him down if Emily didn't, so he put together his most persuasive argument. "Your father and the housekeeper were still alive—

54

barely — after the gunslinger galloped off. And frankly, I'm a better shot than whoever attacked them," he added with what he hoped was a convincing smile. "And if I'd killed them, I certainly wouldn't come calling afterward, or ask Idaho to clean up the hat you ruined."

She grunted, watching his expression for signs of a lie. "Why not?" she demanded. "It would be the perfect smoke screen, wouldn't it?"

McClanahan let out an exasperated sigh, yet he had to respect her quick thinking and unwavering stance as she aimed the pistol at his chest. "Eli — Miss Burnham — I think you're sharp enough to realize that this killer was a desperado of the worst sort. If I'd shot your father and the housekeeper, do you think I would've dismounted to drag them into the house and risk getting caught? I was hoping they'd be tended to instead of being shot again."

Emily blinked. As many times as she'd recalled that awful scene, and the way Papa and Viry had expired in her arms before she could call for help, she'd never considered the intruder's motivations. But she tightened her grip on the pistol. "It looked to me like you were coming in to see who else you could shoot — or what you could steal," she challenged.

"I didn't do a very good job of it, or I would've found you."

"So your *partner* shot him?"

"I don't work with a —"

"Then who *did*?" Her arms were aching, but she held the revolver steady, still aiming it at his chest.

"That's what I came to Cripple Creek to find out." McClanahan sidestepped, then sighed when he saw he was still her target. "I knew your father owned a mine and a parlor house here, and I figured whoever shot him would come to check it out . . . which is the very reason you wanted to keep me at the Angel Claire!" He flashed her a grin, then had to force himself not to laugh or catch her up in his arms. "We're thinking the same way — after the same killer, Emily! But it's not *me!*"

She wanted desperately to believe the dashing, blue-eyed man who stood before her, but he'd sidetracked her with his compliments before. "Who are you?" she asked in a shaky voice.

"Matt McClanahan. Honey, if you'll put that gun—"

"Tell me straight, or this bullet'll bring Silas and Clancy in to finish what I started."

He shrugged and gazed beseechingly into her golden eyes. "Honest to God, my name's Matt McClanahan. I can't tell you any more."

"But I've told *you*—"

He bolted sideways, grabbing for her hands, but Emily stuck the gun behind her and backed toward the wall.

Matt chuckled, shaking his head. "For your own protection, Emily, it's best you don't know any more about me. Outlaws and rustlers come through Cripple Creek every day—any one of them could've shot your father. And if you blow my cover, we may never find out who did it."

"You . . . you don't know?"

"I have an idea," he said with a nod, "but I can't tell you that, either."

Exasperated, Emily pointed her pistol at him again. "That works both ways, you know. If the miners find out I'm really Elliott Burnham's daughter, there'll be hell to pay." She stepped forward, backing him toward the door in case he had any more tricks in mind. "So the way I see it, this gun either makes you a supervisor who'll keep his mouth shut, or it makes you a dead man. What'll it be?"

McClanahan smiled suavely, again pleased by her grit. "Do you really know how to use it, little lady?"

"Do you want to find out?"

He stopped, and Emily halted a few feet in front of him. "It goes against my grain to take orders from a woman, but I never met one quite like you," he said softly. "So I'll take that supervisor's job, and you'll have to keep on being a clerk at the mine, and a housekeeper at the Rose, so no one suspects we're partners. If either of us hears anything, we'll keep each other posted. Deal?"

Emily thought for a moment, and nodded.

"Give me your pistol, before somebody gets hurt."

A surge of relief flowed through her, and she relaxed her grip so Matt could take the gun. He returned it to the desk drawer, smiling at her. Then Emily was very aware of his warm hands holding hers, and of bold blue eyes that followed the curves of her dress.

"Emily Rose," he murmured. "A fitting name for such a lovely young woman. How old are you, honey?"

Her pulse played a duet with his as he lifted her fingers to his lips. "Not quite nineteen," she breathed.

"Old enough to know what you're doing to me . . . but how have you held this escapade together? I have a feeling it was all your idea." Matt stroked a delicate tendril at her temple, lifting her face as he awaited her reply.

"Papa was all I had. I have to find the man who—"

"And we will, rosebud. I promise you." He wrapped his arms around her, nuzzling her delicate ear with a sigh. "Shall we seal that promise with a kiss?"

Emily couldn't have pulled away if she'd tried. She'd nearly killed him! The strain of this encounter, coupled with the knowledge that Matt McClanahan had been working with her all along, left her trembling in his embrace. His lips brushed hers, then pressed into them tenderly. She closed her eyes and leaned against him, holding her breath—then giggling—as his tongue coaxed hers into following its lead. His mouth moved in a seductive rhythm, and when Matt ran a trail of silken kisses down her neck, she let her head fall back in the utter luxury of his touch.

"Emily," he breathed, "honey, please say I can see you someplace besides the mine and the Golden Rose. You're so different—a woman like I've always wanted to find. But we can't be seen together until we've caught your father's—"

The door flew open behind them and Clancy Donahue hollered, "Get your hands off her, you goddamn murderin'—"

57

"Wait! Don't shoot!" Emily shrieked. She pulled away from Matt to see three pistols pointed at them: Silas, Clancy, and Idaho were poised inside the doorway, their faces deadly serious.

Blushing, she brushed nervously at the bodice of her dress. "I—I think you better put your guns down," she said in a quavery voice, "so McClanahan can explain everything."

Chapter Six

Matt was still chuckling Wednesday morning, recalling Emily's spunk as she'd pointed her pistol at him, her eyes ablaze with loyalty for her father. There was no doubt in his mind that she would've shot him, and her scream would've put at least three bullets in his back. As he'd talked with Silas and Idaho about acting as a liaison for the supposedly grief-stricken Miss Burnham, he knew they'd included him in their scheme because they didn't believe he was a killer. But Donahue was another story. The redheaded bartender had glowered at him through the whole conversation — which was no surprise, considering the way he'd caught Emily in the arms of the competition.

McClanahan stuck his head inside the door of the Angel Claire's office, where Emily was intent on her record keeping. He looked around to be sure no one else would hear, and then crooned, "Hey, little tomboy."

Emily glowered from beneath the brim of her dusty hat. "Call me that again and you're asking to be shot," she teased in a low voice. "Now get out of here, before the men notice you hanging around."

McClanahan laughed and walked back toward the mine buildings. Emily Rose Burnham . . . Emily Rose *burned* him, all right. He couldn't recall ever meeting a woman whose spunk and intelligence he respected more. She could never be dismissed as clingy or frivolous, and she didn't use her femininity as a weapon. Or

59

did she? Matt grinned, recalling the swell of her breasts beneath a dress that made her eyes take up her whole face . . . silky-sleek thighs and a rounded, firm bottom. Even if he had no reason to be in Cripple Creek, it would be worth staying just to see more of such a golden-haired minx. A lot more.

But for now he had other concerns. Only yesterday he'd been a common mucker—the lowest of unskilled mine workers—and this morning, dressed in a vested suit, he'd been introduced as Emily Burnham's business manager. He knew damn little about the workings of the Angel Claire, but he didn't have to understand the miners' mutterings to read the mistrust in their eyes. Nigel Grath and his union buddies had been watching him from every corner of the mill, the shaft house, and the other buildings while Hughes introduced him to the various supervisors.

Silas also invited him to the house for noon dinner, and after Idaho set steaming plates of chicken and dumplings in front of them, the gray-haired mine superintendent cleared his throat. "Will this scheme work, or are we fools to fall for Emily's enthusiasm?"

Matt smiled. "It's good that we're calling me a liaison between all of the Burnham investments, because it gives me the freedom to come and go, to follow any leads I get. And it keeps me from causing a lot of tension—especially among your union members."

"Do you think we'll have problems with the Federation?" Hughes asked as he buttered a slice of bread.

"It's too soon to tell." McClanahan chewed a chunk of the tender chicken, chuckling. "Guess I'd grumble too, if the mucker I shoveled beside one day showed up as my superior the next. They probably think I'm spying for you and Emily."

"We can't afford to ignore their rumblings," Silas replied matter-of-factly. "I hear Bill Haywood and Charlie Moyer are trying to increase Federation membership in all the mines. They proved they could shut us down in '94, and they'll do it again if they feel provoked."

Matt nodded, and after finishing the delicious meal, he pushed his plate back with a satisfied sigh. "I'll keep a low profile, and let you know if I hear anything."

"I'm concerned about the reactions of the other mine owners, too. Have you heard of Spencer Penrose and Charles Tutt, from Colorado Springs?"

"Who hasn't?" he replied with a grin. "Wouldn't mind having my name on their bank accounts."

Hughes let out a short laugh. "You're obviously no pauper yourself, McClanahan. But these fellows and some others are trying to form an owners' association, which could get sticky when they ask why Emily hasn't signed on. Elliott was actively involved in all of his businesses — always here at the first sign of trouble."

Matt nodded, thinking he would've been better off searching for Burnham's killer alone. But now that Emily had so cunningly cornered him, he had no choice but to become part of her manhunt — to protect her, if nothing else. "I'll move as quickly as I can, Silas. We've all got a lot at stake."

Hughes rose and brought a box of cigars from the sideboard. "Do you think the man we're looking for is at the mine?"

"I'm not sure yet. But I've got a hunch he's sniffing around *somewhere* among Elliott's businesses, and the gold boom makes Cripple Creek the likeliest place to look for him." Matt lit up and puffed until the end of his cigar glowed red. "What can you tell me about Nigel Grath, besides the fact that he likes to stir up trouble?"

Silas shrugged. "He's a loner — standoffish to the point that even his friends know better than to test his sense of humor. A damn good blaster, though."

Recalling the wiry miner's beady eyes and giggle from when they'd met in the Angel Claire's office, Matt raised an eyebrow. "You trust him down the shaft with dynamite? He impressed me as being a little . . . unstable."

"Ornery as hell. But down the hole, there's nobody more accurate with explosives — the men'll tell you that, and they stake their lives on it every day." Hughes flicked

61

his cigar ash with a wry smile. "They also hint that he hits the pipe."

"Opium?"

"They say he frequents the dens on Myers Avenue. I can't condone his habit, but I can't interfere with it either." Hughes let out a slow stream of smoke, returning a steady, gray-eyed gaze. "My doctor friends tell me that as long as Grath gets all the drug his system requires, he'll behave and perform normally on the job. I can't fire him—or even reprimand him—for a problem I can't see. Not when he might blow us all to kingdom come."

"I see what you mean." Matt considered this information and the way Grath had baited Emily with his blasting caps, and decided to keep the obnoxious little blaster under close observation. "So you try to avoid confrontations, and hope to hell he doesn't get trapped with your other men during a cave-in?"

"Precisely." Silas rubbed out his cigar and smiled as he stood up. "Elliott would've liked you, McClanahan. But I don't understand how you came to be at the ranch the night he was shot—or why you're looking for his killer."

Matt inhaled deeply, letting the rich smoke drift out of his mouth as he considered his reply. "You've given me access to Elliott's ledgers and investments, not to mention entrusting me with the safety of his daughter. You'll just have to trust my motives, too, Mr. Hughes."

That evening, McClanahan spread the wanted posters Barry Thompson had given him across the bed in his hotel room. He crossed his arms against his bare chest, studying the criminals' faces in turn. The first man looked familiar, but the scar was wrong. Another man's picture was so blurry the crook could've walked right in front of him and gone unrecognized. He thought back to the men he'd seen at the Angel Claire, and along the streets the past few days, and he still came up blank.

A knock at the door made Matt shuffle the posters

into a sloppy pile and shove them into the drawer of the mahogany highboy. "Who is it?" he called out.

There was a pause. "A friend."

It wasn't Emily's voice—she had sense enough not to follow him around like an adoring puppy, thank God. He opened his door to a raven-haired woman with a fox-like smile. "Gracie! Not on the warpath tonight?"

She entered his room, teasing his nipple with her fingernail as she passed in front of him. Her hair was tied back at the nape, and in her modest skirt and blouse, she could've been a preacher's wife. "Everybody needs time away from the daily grind," she replied with a wink.

McClanahan thought she looked peaked despite her dark complexion, and as Grace gazed around his richly decorated hotel room, he sensed she needed a friend. "How about dinner? It's the least I can do, after you provided my alibi for Silas on Monday afternoon."

She laughed slyly. "That's true enough. But I ate at the Rose. I tend to lose my appetite when I eat among Cripple's blue-bloods."

Matt chuckled, and as he shrugged into a fresh shirt, he realized her remark disguised her reluctance to appear in a restaurant where her wealthy clients would be dining with their wives. That the passionate savage of the Golden Rose would have such qualms surprised him a little, but every woman had her pride and McClanahan knew better than to make light of it. "How about a walk, then? I could use some air after a day at the mine."

"Are you sure the rising star of E. R. Burnham's empire wants to be seen in public with the likes of me?"

He smiled wryly. "After the way I barged into the parlor dressed only in my birthday suit, maybe it's *your* reputation we should worry about."

Grace's laugh was sudden and raucous, and it took ten years off her face. "Sorry if I'm being a wet blanket," she murmured. "I was trying to congratulate you on your promotion."

"Congratulations accepted." McClanahan took her elbow as they started downstairs. "Did the news travel word-of-mouth, or did Donahue tell you about my new job?"

At the mention of the bartender's name, her face tightened. "Good news travels fast. Let's don't spoil it by talking about that mangy beast, all right?"

She'd never said Clancy was giving her trouble, and now she didn't have to. Donahue apparently had sense enough to keep his mouth shut about his connection to Eliza and to himself, but McClanahan was enraged all the same. "Promise me that if he touches you — or even threatens to — you'll come get me," he said tersely. "If I'm out of town, fetch Barry Thompson. All right?"

Nodding, Grace looked pointedly at the shop window they were passing.

McClanahan caught the glimmer of a tear and wrapped an arm loosely around her shoulders. It was time to drop the subject of Donahue for now, but if Victoria Chatterley learned of his abusive behavior, she'd have no choice but to fire him. Then she'd try to contact Miss Burnham at the ranch and Emily's identity would be exposed, all because of the bartender's greedy lust. Matt put on a smile, for Grace's sake. "What other news have you heard lately?" he asked. "In a a house full of women, tongues must wag night and day."

She brightened as they approached the pillared porch of the Golden Rose. "Eliza was watching for you this afternoon. Any messages?"

"I'll carry my own tales, thanks."

"Maybe you could carry your tail up to my room," she replied in a sultry voice. "Nobody else I'd rather see."

Her expression told him she already knew his answer, and McClanahan's original hunch about befriending this unusual woman was reconfirmed. Grace Putnam, beneath her bedroom eyes and brothel talk, was very insightful — an observer he could trust, as long as she didn't get any more involved with him than she did with her customers. "Maybe another time. Early day tomorrow."

Grace raised an eyebrow and gave him one of her suggestive grins. "How about Saturday, then? It's Miss Victoria's birthday, and the champagne's on the house. Maybe after a few dances you and I could disappear."

Matt smiled and opened the door for her. "I'll keep it in mind. Thanks for stopping by tonight."

"Thank *you*, McClanahan." She stood on tiptoe to brush his cheek with a kiss. "For a man who keeps it in his pants, you're a helluva nice guy. See you Saturday."

Chapter Seven

Festooned in bright pink and gold streamers, the ballroom of the Golden Rose vibrated with anticipation. The ladies were wearing their prettiest dresses, bustling about to put the finishing touches on the decorations. Clancy was preparing the ballrooms bar, looking unusually dapper in a crisp white shirt with an apple-green vest.

Emily smoothed the ruffles of her modest pink gown and surveyed the serving tables. The Waterford bowls were brimming with champagne punch. Crystal cups and trays of sandwiches and sliced meats were waiting on the sideboards. A three-tiered birthday cake decorated with yellow roses stood on a table of its own, surrounded by gleaming plates and forks.

She walked over to the ballroom's upright grand, where Josh LeFevre was practicing a snappy song as two fiddlers tuned up on the dias nearby. His elegant brown hands danced down the bass octaves in a tricky rhythm Emily liked immediately.

"I've never heard anyone play the way you do, Josh," she said when he stopped for a moment.

The pianist grinned. "That's ragtime, Miss Eliza. It's a piece I heard Scott Joplin play at the Columbian Exposition in Chicago. Ooh — would you looky there!"

Josh swept the keyboard with a showy flourish as Victoria Chatterly entered the ballroom. With her snowy hair swirled around a jeweled tiara, a peacock silk gown flowing gracefully over her generous figure, and the glitter of rings and pendants, she would've turned heads even if she hadn't been Cripple Creek's most illustrious madame. With a dainty wave to Clancy, she approached the piano.

"Happy birthday, Miss Victoria," Josh said with a wide smile. "And many happy returns."

"Thank you, dear. And isn't the ballroom lovely?" Her aqua eyes sparkled as she gazed at bouquets of fresh yellow roses accented with lace and gold ribbons — flowers rushed in on Wells Fargo from the coast. "The girls have done themselves proud tonight. Are the musicians ready?"

"Yes, ma'am," he replied. "Got a couple horns and a banjo comin', too. Just like you wanted."

Victoria's face lit up with girlish delight, and she took Emily's elbow. "Let's have one last look at the refreshments," she said as she swayed toward the tables. "Be sure to keep the punch bowls filled, and the sandwich and meat trays fresh — but you know all that. You look very pretty tonight, Eliza."

"Thank you, ma'am. So do you," Emily murmured. She caught a scent of rose perfume as the woman plucked at her sleeves with motherly care, to make them puff more prettily around her shoulders.

"Is your uncle coming?" Miss Chatterly asked with a sly lift of her eyebrows.

"I think so. He asked Idaho to air out his best coat and trousers."

"Good. Silas needs to socialize more — and here come our first guests."

Emily watched Miss Victoria greet two local bankers with open arms. Sam Langston and Conrad Stokes kissed her plump cheeks and complimented her on staging such a lavish birthday celebration. There would be a sea of wealthy, smiling faces here tonight — men she'd heard Papa and Silas speak of, but who certainly wouldn't qualify as the killer she was looking for. The band struck up a graceful song, and it was time to go to work. Emily ladled up cups of the sparkling punch for Darla and Lucy, two of the Rose's more flamboyant residents, and then began to fill more.

When she glanced up from the table, Miss Victoria's arm was linked through Matt McClanahan's. He looked extremely elegant in a dove-gray suit with a cravate of powder blue.

"Congratulations on your promotion, Mr. McClanahan," the madame was saying with a flirtatious smile. "I'm glad Silas decided someone should be hired to look after Elliott's affairs — and I understand you interviewed with Miss Burnham herself. How is the poor dear?"

Considering his reply carefully, Matt wondered whether it was Silas or Clancy who'd informed the curvaceous madame about his meeting with Emily. "She's pale — a mere shadow of herself, as I understand it," he said. When he caught sight of Emily, who looked exquisitely vibrant in her pink satin gown, he had to nip back a grin.

Emily concentrated on ladling punch as Matt and Miss Chatterly came toward the refreshment table. "I really should go to the ranch and offer my condolences," Victoria continued, "but I feel a bit awkward, since her father and I were . . . well, we were very close. When Silas offered to escort me to the funeral, I stayed here in Cripple rather than embarrass Elliott's daughter. He was very protective of her, you know." The madame reached for a cup of punch, her smile brightening. "And I'm sure you remember *this* young lady."

"How could I forget her?" Matt kissed Emily's knuckles, his eyes flirting with hers. "You look absolutely angelic in pink, Miss Eliza."

Emily felt her cheeks redden as Victoria laughed. "Much more of a lady than when she ran through the parlor with your clothes, soaking wet," the madame said in a lilting voice. "That little incident has several of our gentlemen asking for her company —"

"I'm sure they are."

" — but of course Silas would never allow such a thing. And there he is!" Miss Chatterly's gaze traveled up and down the mine manager's imperially-slender figure. "Wouldn't it be nice if Elliott were with him, like old

68

times?" she said with a slight sigh. "Excuse me, Mr. Mc-Clanahan. Please, make yourself at home."

Matt sipped a cup of punch until Miss Victoria was out of earshot, then he leaned toward Emily. "Has she said anything else about E.R.'s daughter?"

"She asked Clancy about me once, when he first came here from the ranch," she replied in a low voice. "But that's the only time, that I know of."

"Was it Donahue who mentioned our interview, or Silas?"

Emily glanced around to be sure no one could hear them. "Silas did. He thought Victoria would be less likely to stumble onto my identity if she knew you were handling the businessess now," she said quietly. "But she thinks you talked to me at the ranch rather than at Silas's house."

Nodding, Matt noticed how the young woman's smile had faded somewhat. "I'm sorry if what she said about your father bothered you, honey. You did a helluva job pretending she wasn't talking about *you*."

Emily rearranged the sandwiches on a tray. "I figured out that she was his mistress long before he hired her away from a bordello in Denver," she said with a tiny smile. "He would never have married her—he was in love with Mama to the end—but I knew all his trips to Denver and Cripple didn't involve real estate and gold mining."

McClanahan smiled when pink spots appeared in her cheeks; Elliott Burnham had probably been so protective that he never realized his daughter had inherited his passionate nature—and *that* was a subject Matt knew he'd better not think about right now. "Does she suspect you and Donahue knew each other before you started working here?"

"No. So far, she's under the impression that Silas was doing us both a favor by recommending us for these jobs. If business weren't good enough to warrant more help, Victoria wouldn't have hired Clancy—and had Hughes not said I was an excellent bookkeeper, I wouldn't have access to her ledgers." Emily flashed him a warning glance, then ladled punch for a handful of guests. When she and Matt were alone again, she lowered her voice. "Most of these men know Papa had a daughter, too, but Silas is the only one who ever saw me before."

"Even so, we'll have to find the murderer before your father's friends start trying to buy you out . . . among other things." McClanahan let his gaze wander over her delicate pink gown. Emily's innocent beauty made her stand out like a dew-kissed bud on a bush full of faded roses, and it was only a matter of time before the locals started asking for her company. "Is there a chance you'll be recognized tonight? You look a bit like Elliott, and in that dress you could certainly be his daughter rather than a chambermaid."

Emily glanced at other guests as they arrived, answering their smiles with Eliza's shy grin. "I doubt they'll notice the resemblance. Papa left me at the ranch when he came here — said a boomtown was no place for a young lady."

"He was right, you know." Matt drained his cup and gave her a quick wink. "I'd better mingle. Your favorite bartender's watching us."

She sighed, noting how suavely McClanahan greeted henna-haired Darla and a few of the other ladies before he slipped his arm around Princess Cherry Blossom. Emily didn't have to look — she could *feel* Clancy's gaze from the bar across the room — so she fetched another pitcher of punch from the kitchen. She'd been eager for Victoria's party all week, yet now she felt as flat as day-old beer. It was going to be a long evening if Matt ignored her for the sake of her identity.

On her way back from the kitchen, Emily paused in the curtained alcove between the back hall and the ballroom. The Golden Rose was alive with light and loveliness, a gaiety she hadn't felt since the last Christmas party at the ranch. The band's spritely music had all the ladies dancing with debonair partners — except for the Indian Princess, who had apparently spirited Matt away. Miss Victoria was smiling up at Silas as he led her deftly around the room in a two-step.

Champagne and whiskey were flowing freely, and Emily found the excitement contagious despite the fact that she was acting as the Rose's serving girl rather than its owner. Papa would've been proud to entertain his friends here — his employees' morals might be questionable, but they provided the best decadence in town — and she found herself smiling in spite of the way her heart still ached every time she thought of him.

As the evening passed, she sliced birthday cake onto plates and made polite conversation with men she'd often seen here. Emily found her foot tapping under the table as she watched Miss Victoria and the ladies flirt and giggle in the arms of wealthy men who adored them for it, and when a large hand gently gripped her ladle, she looked up into a tanned, masculine face.

Marshal Barry Thompson smiled down at her, looking extremely handsome in his frock coat and white shirt. "Your uncle's given me permission for this dance, if you'll give me the pleasure," he said smoothly. "You're too pretty to be a wallflower all night, Eliza."

Emily hesitated. "But Miss Victoria wants me to —"

"She expects her help to enjoy themselves, too, honey. It keeps the customers happy."

She smiled and came around the table as Josh began to play a ragtime waltz. Barry was surprisingly graceful for a tall man, and she had no trouble following his lead as they began to glide in time with the other dancers.

"How's it going at the mine?" he asked. "Do the men tease you about the trick you pulled on McClanahan the other night?"

"They know better, because I'd report them!" she replied with a chuckle. The marshal's question was merely conversational, yet she knew people were beginning to notice Eliza's presence around town. Did they realize that Clancy's arrival, and then McClanahan's, were more than mere coincidence, too? As the waltz ended, she thanked Barry with a curtsy, glad to return to the safety of the refreshment table.

But as the opening chords of a polka rang out, another large hand was grasping hers. Clancy wheeled her toward him, grinning rakishy. "Come on, little girl. I need to stretch my legs."

Emily looked frantically around the ballroom. "But there's Maria — and Lucy — "

"I can dance with them any day of the week. It's you I want."

She despised being bullied, but she was powerless in his burly arms. Donahue clutched her close, and as he took her across the floor at an ungainly gallop, Emily smelled whiskey on his breath. When she tripped over his boots a second time, he gripped her harder.

"Stop it. You're crushing me," she snapped.

"It'll feel better when we're alone." Clancy lifted her from the floor, pressing her against his broad stomach. "I'll give you a ride home, and then — "

"I'm going with Silas," Emily hissed.

The bartender snorted and whirled her around so unevenly she thought they would crash into the wall. "No sense wasting this dress on *him*," the red-bearded Irishman muttered.

Emily shrieked when he raised her above his head as though she were a rag doll. The couples around them chuckled and tried to stay out of Clancy's path, while McClanahan sent her an infuriating little grin. He was standing in the doorway with the Indian Princess, obviously enjoying her embarrassment.

"Clancy, you're drunk," she said with clenched teeth. "Put me down!"

"Not till you say you'll see me tonight."

The song ended and Emily scrambled out of the bartender's arms, toward McClanahan. "Matt, please — help me," she pleaded in a loud whisper.

He glanced at the Goliath behind her and shrugged. "Sorry, sweetheart. I don't dance."

"What a shame," Clancy jeered.

As the band began another waltz, Donahue pulled her toward the center of the room again. The swaying beat

72

seemed to soothe him, but Emily was still petrified as she struggled to avoid his clumsy feet. It was past midnight, and the men around them had also had their share of liquor. None of them — not even Silas — would challenge Clancy Donahue unless he was causing her bodily harm, so all she could do was wish for the end of the song.

Without warning, the huge man scooped her up and kissed her wetly on the mouth.

Emily struggled, kicking and pounding on him until he set her down. "You big—"

He clamped his hand behind her head and kissed her again. His boozy slobber nauseated her, and she jerked away, raising her hand to strike him. Then someone stepped under her uplifted arm and waltzed her toward the center of the ballroom in perfect time to the music.

"Good thing you're left-handed," McClanahan teased as he slipped his arm farther around her waist.

Emily glared up at him. "Why didn't you just wait until he tore my dress off?"

"In a place like this? I didn't want the other ladies feeling inferior." Matt chuckled at the sparks he saw in her amber eyes. "Ignore him, Emily. He's drunk enough to call you by your real name, out of spite."

McClanahan was right. He was also a good dancer, so she relaxed and enjoyed matching her steps to his. "This is getting complicated," she murmured. "I wish I could just be myself. The Princess wouldn't stand a *chance* with you if I weren't playing this charade."

"She's only a friend, honey. I can't pay much attention to you in public . . . but I want to. I was mad as hell when Donahue gave you that sloppy kiss."

Emily leaned back against his arm, wanting this dance to last forever. Matt lowered his lashes seductively, and as he held her closer to guide her through a series of pirouettes, his leathery cologne reminded her how utterly male he was. When her head stopped spinning from their quick turns, she realized they were in the dim, curtained alcove between the ballroom and the hall. The music went on, but Matt stopped dancing. His face was shad-

73

owed and handsome as he leaned her against the wall.

"Who *are* you?" she murmured.

McClanahan chuckled. "I'm the man who rescued you from that bartending baboon. And all I get are questions in return?"

Emily raised her face for the kiss she knew was coming. Matt pressed into her, his lips seeking out her secret desires and revealing a few of his own. His mouth lingered on her cheek and behind her ear, and then returned to her eager lips.

He moaned and eased away from her. "That's how a lady should be kissed," he whispered. "Now go straighten your hair. You look like you've been ravished."

After correcting her appearance in the hallway mirror, Emily returned to the ballroom and saw that the crowd was thinning out. Princess Cherry Blossom was escorting Barry Thompson toward the parlor. Other guests were either pairing off with one of the ladies or giving Miss Victoria a birthday kiss goodnight.

Silas drained his whiskey tumbler and set it on the sideboard. "I've been looking for you," he commented. "Ready to call it a night?"

Emily nodded and walked toward the door ahead of him. "Goodnight, Miss Chatterly," she said quietly.

"Goodnight, dear. And thanks for all your help." The madame leaned closer, surrounding her with the scents of champagne and rose perfume. "Shall I speak to Clancy? The other girls are used to his advances, but—"

"I'll try to stay out of his way." Emily walked past the bar, where Donahue was glowering as he poured McClanahan a whiskey. Matt reached out for her hand and gave it an affectionate squeeze. "Goodnight, Miss . . . Eliza," he murmured. "Sweet dreams."

But Emily's recollections of Clancy's behavior were certainly not sweet. And as she sat at a table in the Rose's pantry the next morning, updating the ledgers, her frown deepened. The house had been packed for the party, yet the receipts were less than an ordinary weeknight's. On a busy evening, Clancy sometimes stashed money here in the pantry to keep his cash drawer from being a temptation. But the safe was empty.

Walking slowly down the hall, she considered her next move carefully. Donahue probably had a hangover on top of the grudge he'd be nursing — and there was a chance that he'd stuck the money someplace else. Emily glanced around the parlor. The Sunday crowd hadn't started arriving yet, and Bob was ready to work his shift at the bar, so now was the best time to straighten this out.

"Clancy, may I see you?" she asked quietly.

The bartender threw her a sour look. He tossed his polishing rag on the back counter and followed her down the hall, his steps heavy behind hers. "About time you apologized," he mumbled. "You had no call to be on such a high horse last night."

Emily slipped behind the pantry table, ignoring his scowl. "Did you forget to give Victoria some of the cash from the bar? We're short — by a couple hundred dollars at least."

Donahue stuffed his hands into his pockets. "I put it in the safe, like always."

"Are you sure? You would've been away from the bar for several minutes, and you're not usually that careless." Emily watched the thoughts play across the former ranch hand's face: she was giving him rope enough to either pull himself out of a lie or tie a noose, and he considered her suggestion before he answered.

"Now that I think about it," he began stiffly, "I recall stashing money in a glass and hiding it behind some bottles on the bottom shelf, there in the ballroom."

"Where is it now?"

"When I was cleaning up, I couldn't find it. Hard to believe one of those millionaires would pocket such a penny-ante amount, but that must be what happened."

"And you didn't report it to Victoria?" Emily crossed her arms, knowing damn well who'd pocketed the cash.

Clancy's green eyes glimmered as he returned her gaze. "Victoria was busy. Sam Langston, I think."

Slamming the ledger shut, Emily glared coldly at the

red-haired bear before her. "From here on out, Mr. Donahue, you're to stay behind the bar and you're to stay sober. Papa wouldn't have tolerated your behavior, and neither will I."

Chapter Eight

"Whoa, boy. I'll see if I can find us some company."
Matt tied his horse to the post in front of Silas's house and
gave the animal an affectionate slap on the rump.

As he walked toward Elliott Burnham's Cripple Creek
residence, he noted its resemblance to the Golden Rose:
both structures were large and cream-colored, with intricate gingerbread trim on the gables. The Rose had
stained-glass panels in a gold floral design around its double doors, and Burnham's house had a geometric pattern
in greens and blues. A few years back, McClanahan
might've had a similar home built for himself, but now he
saw no reason for such a showplace to sit empty.

He knocked, and after a few moments he heard Idaho
shuffling through the vestibule. The colored man's face lit
up when he opened the door. "Mr. Matt! It's a fine afternoon for courting, but Miss Emily's out on her horse."

Matt smiled. "I came for my Stetson."

"Why, sure you did. And it's ready, too." With a knowing grin, the old housekeeper gestured for McClanahan
to follow him.

The parlor and dining room were hushed, except for
the stately ticking of the mantel clock. Once again he was
impressed by Burnham's taste — substantial mahogany
furnishings, with upholstery in greens and golds. A
man's house, without the frivolous clutter that was so
fashionable. "By yourself this afternoon, Idaho?"

"Yessir. Mr. Silas is at the Elks Club. When Miss Emily returned from the Rose in a stormy mood, he found a
quick reason to leave."

Matt smiled to himself, picturing the fiery eyes and

77

flushed cheeks Clancy Donahue had undoubtedly inspired. The aroma of seasoned beef lingered in the kitchen, and the small table was covered with pages of circular charts and scribblings. "Interesting," he said with a glance at a thick, yellowed book. "I didn't realize you were an astrologer."

"I play at it. Used to tell fortunes in the bunkhouse when I was a single man." Idaho let out a long sigh. "But after I married Viry, I found better ways to pass the time."

McClanahan nodded. "I hope we find the man who shot her — and soon."

"Yessir. Too late to do *me* much good, but it'll help Miss Emily settle herself." Looking at the topmost chart, he pointed a gnarled finger. "This lunar progression to Mars indicates ambition and a tendency to take risks. But the way Emily's other planets line up, I'm guessing it'll be a month or two before Mr. Elliott's killer gets snared."

"You think so?" He saw worry lurking in the old man's eyes, and hoped his prediction was overly cautious.

"Astrology's like the Bible — everybody has his own interpretation," Idaho explained. "Miss Emily's chart shows Venus in Scorpio, too, which means she's highly passionate and emotional. Can't argue with that."

"No, I don't guess we can," McClanahan said with a laugh.

"She needs a steadying hand now, Mr. Matt. Don't let her get attached to you unless you mean to make it permanent, or you'll both be sorry. I'll get your hat." Idaho opened a door and started down the cellar stairs with an uneven shuffle and a grunt.

While he waited, McClanahan looked at the elaborate charts, which were crisscrossed with lines and symbols he didn't understand. The tattered old book was written in English, yet meaningless to him. He didn't put much store in horoscopes, but he sensed Pearce had a feel for things that went beyond the average man's perception. Even so, he planned to catch the murderer much sooner than Idaho had predicted.

When the old Negro handed him his hat, he stroked the

felt and sniffed it. "Mmm . . . quite an improvement."

"Yessir. Pine oil corrects a lot of faults." Idaho chuckled, running a finger around the Stetson's rim. "That's a mighty fine hat, Mr. Matt. Suits you better than it does Miss Emily."

"I'm surprised she'd try it on, after the way she threw it around last Saturday night."

"She's been ornery since she was a baby." Idaho shook his head with an indulgent smile as he closed the cellar door. "Miss Emily was born early, and when we lost her mama, Mr. Elliott swore his little girl would be raised tough. He had her on horseback before she could walk — taught her things about ranching and account keeping. But I guess you know she's smart that way, without me bragging."

Matt smiled. "You have a right to be proud. You and Viry get a lot of the credit for raising her."

"Miss Emily was the light of our lives after Miss Claire passed away," the cook said reverently. "Viry couldn't have babies, and she loved that little golden-haired girl like her own. Couldn't usually make her behave like a rich man's daughter should, but we tried."

The old man shuffled over to the coffeepot, questioning Matt with misty eyes. McClanahan nodded and changed the subject. "So if you were a ranch hand at one time, how'd you end up keeping house?"

"I wasn't just a hand — I was the foreman," Idaho answered proudly. "Best horse trainer Mr. Elliott ever had, too. And when you're herding, or branding, or driving a thousand head of cattle to market, your horses have to respond to the slightest touch."

Matt grunted appreciatively. "What happened?"

"Damned if I know for sure, Mr. Matt. One minute I was riding fence to see where some cows were getting out, and the next I was on the ground with my horse raring on top of me." He set two cups of steaming coffee on the table, then eased into a chair. "Broke my leg in three places, and I had to shoot the mare. If Mr. Elliott hadn't come along when he did, I would've been breakfast for the buzzards."

McClanahan scowled. "It's not like a good horse to turn on her trainer. Any diseases or infections passing through the other livestock?"

"No, sir. We thought she got into some locoweed—but damned if we know *where*." His brown eyes clouded, as though he had some theories he didn't want to talk about. "Mr. Elliott moved me to the house so Viry could look after me, but the leg was never the same. I figured he'd put me out when he saw I wouldn't spend another day in the saddle. But Mr. Elliott wasn't that kind of man."

"So you helped your wife?"

Idaho nodded. "Did the gardening, too, and the repairs around the ranch. It's good Viry taught me such things—a man could go crazy without useful work. Miss Emily's the only reason I have to hang on now."

"She needs you, too, Idaho," Matt answered quietly.

"Yessir, she does." His face lit up, and he crossed the kitchen to take a basket from one of the cabinets. "She doesn't always listen, though—like when I told her my charts predicted this would be a fine day for romance? Steamed as she was when she got back from the Rose, she called that pure nonsense."

Matt laughed and watched him slice some roast beef onto a plate. "Do *you* believe it?"

"*You're* here, aren't you?"

He smiled as Idaho wrapped cornbread muffins in a linen napkin, sliced some pumpkin pie, then tucked the food into a basket with a bottle of wine. "I got what I came after, so I guess I'll be going—"

"Take this lunch and her shawl. Miss Emily was too upset to eat, and she'll take a chill when the sun sets."

McClanahan slipped his hat on, fighting a grin. "What makes you think I'm planning to see her?"

"Doesn't take an astrologer to read the stars in those eyes of yours, Mr. Matt."

From her grassy seat on the side of Mount Pisgah, Emily looked out over the vast beauty of the autumn landscape. Golden aspens shimmered in the afternoon sun. Crimson sumac and the deep green shadows of the pine groves soothed her as nothing else could, and in the distance, a dusky haze settled at the base of the Cascades. She was still in her uniform — and still angry at Clancy — but the breeze coaxed a smile to her face. Emily wiggled her bare toes in the grass. Then she swung her braid over her shoulder and began to unwrap it.

Why were her emotions in such a tangle these days? Was it loneliness for Papa that made her temper flare at the least provocation? It was dangerous, this anger: she could reveal her identity while fighting with Donahue as easily as he might betray her out of spite. At the ranch she'd never argued with anyone, yet now she was snapping at Idaho and ordering Silas around as though he were a servant. A surge of misplaced hatred had nearly killed Matt McClanahan — and the next moment she'd been kissing him, her heart pounding for an entirely different reason. It didn't make sense. Not to a girl who'd been taught to bide her time and let her opponents make the foolish, impulsive mistakes.

Emily shook her hair over her shoulder, letting the wind's fingers comb its ridges. She felt like herself now — free, as she did at the Flaming B. Smiling, she recalled how Matt had wanted to unbraid her hair . . . and he seemed able to *do* something about Papa's killer. But who was he?

Her thoughts wandered back over everything she knew about the handsome newcomer. Then she blinked and looked up from the columbine she was holding. There it was again: *bob bob WHITE*.

Sundance was nickering, his bronze ears pointed toward visitors. Then she saw Matt McClanahan leading a spirited bay gelding up the hillside, carrying a basket and her shawl. He grinned and adjusted his hat. "Didn't mean to startle you. You were miles away."

"You do a pretty good quail." Emily smiled, hugging her knees. "I come up here to think, when I need to be

81

alone."

"I'll leave, if you want."

"No, no — I'd hate to spoil Idaho's plans." She patted the grass beside her, and when McClanahan was seated, she pulled the thick packets of food from the basket. "You'd better join me. He didn't send all this just for me."

McClanahan chuckled and coaxed the cork from the green wine bottle. "I've got the distinct impression that Idaho'd do anything in the world for Miss Emily. He did a nice job cleaning my hat, too."

With a giggle, Emily plucked the brown Stetson from his head and placed it on her own. It was much too big, but Matt was enjoying her playfulness, so she left it on. Thinking the afternoon had suddenly become wonderful, she split one of the tender muffins and offered Matt half.

"Hard to believe a horse trainer can bake this way," Matt murmured as he bit into it.

"Viry was a good teacher. They had the happiest marriage I ever saw . . . but Idaho's new job made a few of the hands jealous," she replied in a faraway voice. "They didn't think he deserved a foreman's pay for doing woman's work. Especially since he's colored."

Matt looked into her tawny eyes as he considered this information. "Did Clancy feel that way, too?"

"He was one of the worst," she replied. She tore into a slice of beef to relieve the anger she felt whenever she thought about the Irish bartender. "And he's not much different now — thinks *he* should be living with Silas instead of in the attic at the Rose. I told him he could certainly afford a hotel room, but he didn't see it that way. Couldn't wander into his choice of women's bedrooms whenever he felt like it."

McClanahan chuckled at her barbed tone, and he couldn't resist tucking a stray lock of her warm, golden hair back over her shoulder. "And what did he do this morning to get you so fired up, Miss Burnham?"

"He claims someone stole his extra cash last night."

Matt thought back to the elite crowd who'd celebrated

82

Victoria's birthday, frowning. "It was in plain sight behind the bar when I left."

She snorted and sipped some wine. "The fool thinks I'm too stupid to see through him—thinks I'd actually consider *marrying* him." Emily glanced at the pumpkin pie, but tipped the green bottle to her mouth instead. "Dumbest thing I ever did, letting him work at the Rose. Silas would never have recommended such an uncivilized beast for that job, and Miss Victoria's going to figure that out pretty soon. I should've—"

"You should ease up on that wine. And on yourself." Matt took the bottle, and after recalling Idaho's warning about letting Emily get too attached to him, he draped his arm around her anyway. "You've shouldered a helluva load since your father was shot—anyone in your situation could make a few mistakes. And I can certainly understand why Clancy wants to marry you."

Emily almost made a sarcastic remark, but the warmth of his arm was working its magic on her. She gazed into eyes the color of columbines, hoping McClanahan would understand her doubts and fears. "After tagging along with Papa all my life, doing pretty much what I've wanted to, I'm not sure I'm suited to housewifery," she admitted. "I certainly couldn't resign myself to being a man's slave."

Matt smiled, admiring her innocent independence. "You make marriage sound like a prison sentence, Emily. Not all men are as rough around the edges as Donahue."

"Not many are like Papa, either." She settled against him, sighing. "Mama'd been gone ten years when he bought the mine, yet he named it for her . . . still gazed at her portrait in the parlor when he was alone."

"You're luckier than most women, honey. You can afford to wait for a man you love." McClanahan let his hand drift down her back, knowing suitors would swarm to her door when Elliott Burnham's murder was solved and she came out of mourning. Would she still share her picnics—and her thoughts—with him then?

Emily smiled up at him. "There's no doubt in my mind I can oversee Papa's holdings; he's hired top-notch managers. But what comfort will his money be after we've caught his killer, when I'm alone?"

Matt wanted to vow that he'd be there for her—that she'd never spend another lonely day—but it was too soon. And as though she were reading his thoughts, Emily stood up. She smoothed her uniform, gazing toward lilac streaks of sunset as she walked over to the horses.

"You've got a fine-looking mount, McClanahan," she said as she stroked the animal's glossy black mane.

"Arapaho's got good lines, but I like your palomino's conformation, too." He got up to join her, studying the gold gelding with a trained eye. "Was he a present from your papa?"

"No," she said with a grin, "he was a gift from the most notorious man I ever met. Right, Sundance?"

"Sundance? Harry Longbaugh gave you this horse?" McClanahan stroked the palomino's firm flesh with increasing interest, biting back a smile.

"Papa met him on one of his real estate trips," Emily explained. "He mentioned that I loved to ride, and a few weeks later the Sundance Kid came to our ranch."

"And while Longbaugh was sweet-talking you, the rest of Cassidy's gang were probably rustling your father's stock." He scowled, and then looked over at her. "Do you suppose one of them came back to kill him?"

"I thought of that, but it doesn't make sense," she replied. "He gave me this horse nearly two years ago, and since then he and Butch have been busy holding up banks and trains farther west."

McClanahan chuckled. "So you knew the horse was stolen?"

"We didn't question him about it." Matt was studying her intently, but she couldn't tell if it was her horse or her moral character he was more interested in. "I had a feeling Papa did him some sort of favor, so I couldn't very well refuse his token of appreciation, could I?"

"Not to mention his attentions," Matt replied with raised eyebrows. "Is he as handsome as they say?"

"In a horsey sort of way." She shrugged, a secret smile

84

curving her lips. "Hard to believe such an interesting man could be a hard-boiled outlaw."

"You were too taken in by his looks to think about his livelihood, sweetheart."

Emily laughed and grabbed his hand. "No need to be jealous, McClanahan. His eyes aren't nearly as blue as yours."

Matt fought the urge to kiss her impish grin. Barefoot, with his hat cocked over her mischievous eyes, Emily Burnham was the most playful temptress he'd ever met. He squeezed her hand, ready to tell her so, but a distant, reedy bellowing interrupted him. The buglelike sound echoed around the mountains, followed by loud grunts and clatterings.

"Look—those elk are rutting." Emily stared, wincing each time the two huge bodies collided below them. "You'd think they'd be killed, battering each other so fiercely."

'That's nature's way of making sure only the fittest bulls breed. The winner of this fight'll spend the next few weeks servicing his harem—might even die from all that mating." McClanahan chuckled low in his throat. "What a way to go, huh?"

"Reminds me of Donahue, rutting and strutting," she mumbled. Emily shielded her eyes from the brilliant sunset, thinking how strong McClanahan's hand felt around hers. "I know you can't pay a lot of attention to me in public, Matt . . . but you won't let Clancy force me into anything, will you?"

Her wistful tone left him defenseless. Matt pulled her into his arms, kissing her ravenously until the immediate need for her touch was satisfied. Emily's lips were warm and full, and she was clinging to him as though she'd never let go. When she came up for air, he had to catch her to keep her from staggering backward.

"I—I shouldn't have made such a forward remark," she stammered. "The wine must've gone to my head."

"Is that all that's affecting you?" he teased.

"You know better, McClanahan." When she lowered

his head to kiss him again, his hands followed the curve of her hips up past her waist, and then fitted themselves around her breasts. Other men who'd fondled her had gotten slapped, but Emily leaned into Matt's caress. Her pulse was galloping as his tongue danced around hers.

"Emily . . . honey, this is more than I can stand," he murmured. Idaho's instincts were right, and he couldn't keep Emily's identity a secret if he allowed this to continue. But with her firm young body rubbing his in all the right places, McClanahan was speeding toward the point of no return.

She led him toward the spot where their abandoned picnic lay. Then Emily removed the Stetson and coaxed Matt down into the cool grass beside her, caressing his rugged chest with inquisitive hands. His eyes were shining with a desire that matched her own, and she smiled shyly. "Are you going to make love to me now?"

Her wide-eyed naiveté threatened the last shreds of his resolve. "I . . . I'm not sure I should," he rasped.

"Why? Would you rather be with the Indian princess?"

"Not at all. I *want* you, rosebud, but —"

"You were in her room during the party, weren't you?" Emily searched his urgent face for signs of a lie, wishing she hadn't kissed him so insistently.

Matt sighed. "Grace got tired of me watching you, so we took a walk. She's a friend, Emily. Not a lover."

"Then what's the matter?" she demanded shrilly. "Have Silas and Clancy told you stay the hell away? Took you *forever* to kiss me today, and —"

His finger silenced her. "I've never wanted anyone the way I want you, Emily. But your affections are yours to give, not mine to take. Especially this first time."

Emily gazed into clear blue eyes that made her pulse pound. And as the meaning of his tender words sank in, she realized Matt McClanahan was a special man indeed — perhaps in the same league as Papa. She fumbled with the top button of his shirt. "Touch me the way you did at the Rose that first night, Matt. Only don't stop."

"Are you sure?" he whispered. "Will you want me as

much tomorrow as you do now? The wine's making you—"

"I'll probably want you more."

Matt cradled her against his length and kissed her. As he nuzzled beneath the fragrant cascade of her hair, Emily's breathing tickled his ear. Her hands were ruffling the hair on his chest, making his stomach muscles tighten with desire. "Maybe we should leave some clothes on so we won't get cold," he suggested.

"If *you* won't take them off me, I *will!*" She sat up, tugging at her apron strings.

Matt wanted to stop her—or help her—but the sun's rays playing in Emily's hair as she stepped out of her skirt was a sight he could appreciate more fully while he was flat on his back. Her blouse fell away in the breeze, revealing a lithe body clad in the flimsiest of pale pink underthings. She grinned and grabbed his ankles.

As Emily tugged at his boots, a laugh welled up inside him. She was pure pleasure, this mountain nymph—and now she was suspended over his outstretched leg, her breasts bobbing beneath her frilly camisole.

"Are you laughing at *me*, McClanahan?"

"The last time I did that, my clothes ended up in a trough." He sat up to grasp her hands, smiling at the feminine curves so temptingly displayed before him. "We're not running a race, honey. A woman's first time with a man isn't her best, so let's slow down. You'll enjoy it more."

Emily nipped her lip. "Will it hurt? Some ladies say it's more duty than pleasure."

"I doubt you'll ever have that problem. Come here, rosebud. Let me love you." He coaxed her down on top of him, kissing her eyelids and her pert little nose before claiming her mouth. Her hips were round and full beneath the thin fabric of her pantaloons, and when he slipped his hands under her camisole, the warmth of her velvety skin made him hold his breath. "Now isn't this better?"

Emily smiled, weaving her fingers into his thick black

waves. His face was dim beneath the curtain of her hair; his eyes glimmered with passion, and once again she marveled at the sleek softness of his skin. "Your heart's pumping as fast as mine," she whispered.

"They'll pump faster before we're finished." Gently grasping her sides, Matt slid her up to sample her breasts with his mouth. She tasted warm and clean, and as his tongue slithered under her camisole, Emily squirmed against him.

"Please . . . I want to feel your skin against mine." She sat up, watching Matt lift the undergarment over her head. He molded his hands to her bare breasts, massaging in a circular motion that nearly drove her crazy, yet uncertainty gnawed at her. "Am I built all right, McClanahan?" she asked in a tiny voice. "You took me for a boy when you first came to the mine."

Hearing doubt rather than the desire for a compliment, Matt smiled. "That was the furthest thing from my mind when you were pointing your pistol at me. All I could hope was that after you shot me, you'd hold me in your arms so I could nestle against you before I died."

Emily giggled, then sucked in her breath when his thumbs coaxed her nipples into rigid little buds. He was rock-hard beneath her, rubbing in a rhythm that sent shimmers of heat throughout her body. "Matt. . . ."

"We'd better do something about these pants." He slid her off to the side of him and unbuttoned his fly. Emily turned to pull his trouser legs down, presenting a firm, pantalooned bottom that begged for a playful slap.

When his palm stung her skin, she cried, "Hey! I won't be manhandled like the ladies at—"

"I'd never hurt you, honey. Never." Matt smiled, slipping his fingers under her waistband. "Do you wear these frilly little things under your overalls, too?"

Emily grinned wickedly.

"Oh, Lord. I won't won't be able to see you at the mine without thinking of ruffles and lace . . . oh, rosebud. You *are* lovely, honey," he breathed.

She stood nude before him, pleased at the way his eyes

burned with blue fire. He stood up to remove his underwear and then pulled her close, his hands roaming over her flesh with a gentle firmness that almost made her cry out for wanting him. Matt slid his manhood between her thighs, moving against her until fingers of desire curled in the pit of her stomach. Then he stood still, teasing her neck with feathery kisses. "If you stop, I'll explode," she breathed.

"If I keep on, you'll explode too soon," he said with a chuckle. "Let's lie down, honey."

Emily reclined in the lush grass. As Matt lowered his powerful body, he swept her with a hungry gaze. His weight was warm, his caress laden with anticipation.

"I'll try to go slowly, so it won't hurt so much when I — Emily!"

With one fluid movement she found what her body ached for. Wrapping a leg around him, Emily arched until they were joined. The pain was piercing for a moment, but then she couldn't stop pressing against him, again and again.

"Rosebud, tell me if I'm — "

"You're fussing over me like Idaho does," she whispered. "*Love* me — like Matt McClanahan!"

He leaned into her warmth and forgot his qualms. She was returning thrust for thrust, kissing him with lips as urgent as his own. Emily fit against him perfectly, and McClanahan forced himself to slow down until he felt her body tensing with uncontrollable pleasure.

Emily was suddenly overwhelmed by the mysterious power surging through her, building toward a peak from which she couldn't turn back. She cried out, exploding in a shimmering sunburst as he found his own release.

After a moment, Matt rose up on his elbows to kiss her. She was so still . . . her eyes were closed and her head had lolled to one side. "Emily? Honey, can you hear me?" he asked softly. "My God, she passed out."

She shook with a giggle and then laughed aloud as Matt repeatedly swatted her cheek. "McClanahan," she murmured, "if this was pain, I won't be able to stand the pleasure when we make love again. And again."

Matt laughed and kissed her. Then he held her sweet, sated body against his, wondering how he'd get through the week — even a day — without loving her every time he saw her. "We'd better put our clothes on, before someone comes looking for you."

"Why would Idaho do that?" she asked playfully. "He trusts you, or he wouldn't have told you I was up here."

McClanahan sighed. "It was Silas I had in mind."

Emily reached for her underthings, which were damp with dew as she slipped them on. "He can't fire you. And he can't tell me how to feel about you, either."

As he stepped into his trousers, Matt kept his doubts to himself. Was he strong enough to withhold his emotions until each time they were absolutely alone? One winsome grin, even from under Eliza's dusty mining hat, would have him wanting her no matter where they were.

She watched his expression vacillate between boyish glee and a wise smile that fascinated her, as everything about him did. "How old are you, McClanahan?"

Emily's question came like a shot out of nowhere, a trait he knew he'd better get used to. "Twenty-seven. You think I'm too old and worn out to tame you?"

"No. I was just wondering how many more years of this I have to look forward to."

Matt clutched her, feeling utterly invincible as she hugged him back. "It's too soon to say, honey. But I'd like to find out, too." He kissed her fervently on the mouth, then picked his hat up off the ground. "I'll ride with you to the livery stable, and then — "

"But what if someone sees us together?"

He plucked a blade of grass from her hair. "I'd never forgive myself if some drunk got ahold of you while you were walking home," he insisted. "The streets may be lit, but they're not safe."

Emily nodded and gathered the picnic things into the basket. She tied her shawl around her shoulders, needing its warmth now that Matt wasn't holding her, and swung onto Sundance.

They let the horses set the pace down the dark mountainside. The only sounds were their mounts' breathing and muffled hoofbeats on the hard-packed road, until they trotted onto the pavement in town. Boisterous laughter came from the gambling halls, and men were milling from one establishment to the next, so no one noticed them. After Emily got Sundance settled for the night, she stepped into Matt's stirrup, letting him hoist her onto Arapaho in front of him.

The ride to the house was too short. With her thighs rubbing Matt's and his warm hand resting beneath her breasts, Emily felt another rush of desire as they rocked along. McClanahan tugged on the reins, stopping before they entered the squares of lamp light coming out of Silas's parlor windows.

"Emily, I—"

She kissed him, not wanting to spoil the evening's perfection with mere words. Then she swung a leg over Arapaho's neck. "Goodnight, Matt." She patted his supple boot and hurried toward the house.

"Goodnight, sweetheart," he whispered after her.

When she opened the door, the vestibule mirror confirmed her fears. She was rumpled and flushed, and with her hair falling over her shoulders in wavy disarray, she looked exactly like what she was: a young woman who'd tasted love and swallowed it whole. She jumped when Silas cleared his throat.

He'd been reading his paper, and now he was approaching her with a stern scowl. "You're playing with fire, young lady," he said tersely. "And your carelessness will get us all burned before this is over."

Still intoxicated from the wine and Matt's touch, Emily faced him boldly. "I'm not stupid, Silas," she retorted. "Nobody saw us—"

"It's *quite* obvious how you and McClanahan feel about each other, and that you've both lost control of the situation," her father's partner replied. "I thought I could trust him to—"

"He didn't take anything I didn't offer, Mr. Hughes."

Silas's mouth became a tight line. "That's *precisely* the attitude I'm talking about," he said in a strained whisper. "I've risked my reputation—laid my very livelihood on the line for you, Emily, because I thought you were mature enough to respect that. What will Victoria and the men do when they find out I've *lied* for you? And *I'm* the one who got Donahue his job at the Rose, supposedly because Elliott's distraught daughter sent him here. What happens when this farce blows up in our faces?"

Emily knew better than to make another flippant remark, yet she refused to let his tirade go unanswered. "With McClanahan helping us, we'll find Papa's killer before anyone's the wiser," she insisted. "You worry too much, Silas—and your nerves will give us away as easily as anything McClanahan and I might do."

Hughes shook his head in disgust. "Your father must be rolling over in his grave right now," he muttered, turning toward the stairs. "Good*night,* Miss Burnham."

Chapter Nine

"Good morning, Mr. Matt!" the colored cook's voice rang in the vestibule. "Mr. Silas and Miss Emily just sat down to breakfast. You'll join them, won't you?"

"Thanks, Idaho, but I've eaten."

Emily looked up from the egg she'd been piddling with. She and Silas had little to say to each other, and she hoped Matt's presence would improve the dark mood that was hanging over the table like a storm cloud. But when she saw his jeans, she knew his plans didn't include working at the mine today.

"What's new?" Silas asked as McClanahan crossed the dining room. His scowl relaxed, as though he were separating his personal misgivings about Matt from his need to keep abreast of the manhunt.

McClanahan pulled out a chair and sat facing the mine manager. "Emily told me where she got her horse, so I've decided to check with the lawmen around Colorado Springs," he said. "If they spotted Longbaugh or any of the Wild Bunch around May seventh, when Elliott was killed, we may have something solid to go on."

Silas grunted. "Sounds like a long shot. Longbaugh's specialty is horse thieving, as I recall."

"It's the closest thing to a lead I've got."

Emily looked glumly down at her yolk-smeared plate. They were talking as though she weren't even in the room, and Matt's idea sounded like a convenient excuse to get away from *her*. "How long will you be gone?" she mumbled.

"Probably two or three days. I'll check on some other possibilities . . . maybe go on up to Denver, too."

"That'll fit with your new position, if people ask where

you are," Silas said with a nod. "And I'm more likely to overhear something pertinent if the men don't know when you'll be in and out of the Angel Claire."

"I thought so, too. I'll let you know what I've learned as soon as I get back." Matt glanced at Emily and stood to put his Stetson on. "Try to behave while I'm gone, all right?"

He might as well have been talking to his little sister. As Silas walked McClanahan to the door, Emily tossed her napkin onto the table. She stood before the mirrored étagère to coil her braid underneath the hat she wore at the Angel Claire. In the glass, she saw the mine manager studying her from across the dining room, but she had nothing to say to him.

"It might be best if you varied your schedule, too, so the employees don't suspect anything when you need to be gone," Silas suggested quietly.

"Don't worry—I can't *embarrass* you by mooning over McClanahan today," she replied bitterly.

Hughes walked up behind her, meeting her eyes in the mirror. "I realize how badly you miss your father's affection," he said with a sigh. "Elliott thought it was time to be finding you a husband—and I feel better, having McClanahan to look out for you when I'm not around the office. But we know so little *about* him."

"Papa would've liked Matt," she challenged. "Idaho thinks so, too."

"But he would *not* like his daughter parading around with her hair loose, like some strumpet from Myers Avenue," Silas stated. "McClanahan could've at least—"

"Haven't you ever run your hands through a woman's hair, Mr. Hughes?" Emily turned, mocking him with a grin. "I'll *bet* you've never cavorted on Mount Pisgah in the all-together."

The mine manager grabbed his hat from the shelf beside her. "I don't put my private life on display, Miss Burnham. And you'd be wise to follow suit."

Her life returned to the way it was before Matt Mc-

Clanahan showed up, yet the next three days were unbearably long. Emily called a truce with Silas by apologizing for her unladylike remarks — she didn't really understand her vicious tongue any more than he did. His idea about varying her schedule was valid, so she explained to Miss Victoria that sometimes Idaho needed her help in the kitchen after dinner. Clancy eyed her suspiciously as she told this story, but Emily felt no need to justify her actions to a jealous, thieving bartender.

But what if intensifying her efforts to find Papa's killer didn't help? She heard no tell-tale remarks when the men at the Angel Claire grumbled about low wages and the oppressive heat in the mine shaft, as they aways did. The Golden Rose had settled into its normal routine, now that Miss Victoria's party was a pleasant memory. It was as though Elliott Burnham and his daughter were tending to business as usual: from a distance.

Would Papa approve of Matt McClanahan? Or was she making another impulsive mistake, falling for the man who'd roused her passions so quickly and effortlessly? Even the simple act of dressing, whether in overalls or her uniform, became an ordeal because she couldn't put on her underthings without recalling how Matt's hands had lit fires all over her body when he took them off her. And yet he'd left town without a hint that he'd miss her, or that he felt anything more for her than he did for Silas. He'd stolen her heart, dammit! And for all she knew, he'd disappear with it as suddenly as he came.

Emily was staring blankly at the Angel Claire's ledgers Wednesday afternoon, when she discovered she wasn't the only one who resented the way McClanahan had come in from nowhere and taken over. Nigel Grath swaggered into the office, his belligerence as apparent as the stench of sweat and blasting powder.

"McClanahan around?" he demanded.

Emily shook her head and returned to her bookkeeping.

"Good. Know when he'll be back?"

She shook her head again, sensing trouble as the wiry miner leaned on the front of her desk. Grath giggled, focusing his beady eyes on her until she couldn't ignore him. "Well, he won't be tendin' E.R.'s business much longer," he said in a conspiratorial tone. "One sonuvabitchin' know-it-all's enough at this hellhole."

As he looked purposefully around the little office, Emily dreaded what he'd say next. The blaster seemed higher-strung than usual as he raked his fingers through his stringy hair and replaced his gritty hat. His body odor was overpowering, and she glanced toward the window, hoping to see Silas.

"McClanahan ain't who he says he is," Nigel began in an ominous whine. "The boys think Burnham's daughter sent him here to spy on Federation doin's, but I know for a fact she *didn't*." His laugh was humorless as he looked down at her. Then he blinked, and added, "I mean — McClanahan don't know a mine shaft from the crack in his ass! So he's gonna go sky-high!"

Grath's high-pitched laugh set Emily's teeth on edge, and again she looked outside for Silas.

Then two hands grabbed her overall straps and Nigel's stubbly face was in hers. "But you ain't sayin' nothin' to Hughes about this, Miss Britches, 'cause you're smart. And you ain't givin' McClanahan any clues either. Got it?"

Emily grabbed her hat as he banged her against the back of her chair. How did he *know* Emily Burnham hadn't hired Matt, unless —

"I better see you nod that tomboy head, or you'll be the next one to disappear. Understand me?" Grath demanded.

She swallowed hard, nodding.

"That's better." He released her with a shove and looked at the papers on the desk. "Now where's the payroll sheet? I'm signin' in for my shift tomorrow."

Emily stared. Surely he didn't expect her to —

"Find it, dammit! And you don't know *nothin'* if Hughes comes sniffin' around, wonderin' where I'm at. Right?"

Hands quaking, she hastily wrote the next day's date across the top of a fresh page and handed it to him. As he scrawled his name on line, she wondered how he intended to find Matt. But she knew from experience that the obnoxious little man had a maniac's instinct of how to inflict the worst harm with the least effort.

"You're smarter than you look, Miss Britches. And you'll keep this to yourself—unless you'd like dynamite shoved up your butt, like McClanahan's gonna get."

Emily watched him walk to the building where the men changed their clothes before they left the mine. She wanted to run and find Silas, but the little weasel was probably poised around a corner, waiting for her to do just that. So she gripped the seat of her chair, staring frantically at the filing cabinets. Had Papa's killer been under her nose the whole time she'd been in Cripple Creek? Had Grath been dropping hints about the murder all along, and she'd been too infatuated with McClanahan to notice that he'd figured out who she was?

In a flash of inspiration, Emily pulled the May payroll files from the cabinet. Her finger shook as she ran it down past the names listed for Saturday the seventh, the night Papa was shot in cold blood.

Nigel Grath hadn't reported for work that day. Or the following Monday, either.

That evening Emily fidgeted in her room. She felt numb and dirty, despite the bath she'd taken when she got home. Idaho knew something was desperately wrong, because she'd barely touched her baked ham and yams. And she expected Silas to come upstairs any minute, demanding an explanation for her unsociable behavior.

But what if she didn't tell Hughes about Nigel Grath's plan? There was no doubt in her mind that the ferretlike blaster would find McClanahan and follow through with the threat on his life. She had to warn Matt, yet she sensed Nigel would find that out—and who would know Grath had shot Papa if he killed her, too?

Idaho's clear tenor echoed downstairs in the vestibule. "Why, good evening, Mr. Matt! Good to see you back. Mr. Silas is in the study."

97

He was alive! Emily hopped off her bed and smoothed her pale green dress. She dabbed perfume behind her ears, then pulled her hair back with a green ribbon before hurrying down the stairs.

When she peeked into the study, Silas was seated at the desk and Matt's profile was toward her. They were talking quietly over cigars, but Emily couldn't contain her relief. Grinning, she rushed over to hug McClanahan. "How was your trip? What'd you find out?" she gushed.

Matt looked at her as though she'd interrupted something terribly important. "Not much. As you said, the Sundance Kid spends most of his time rustling farther west. I did clear up one mystery, though."

"What's that?" she asked in a deflated voice.

McClanahan smiled wryly. "Longbaugh stole your horse from my herd. His lines looked awfully familiar, and my records confirm that a palomino yearling came up missing a couple years ago."

Emily stared at him, her heart pounding into her throat. "Well, you can't have him back!"

"I wouldn't think of taking him. You need a good mount, and he's found a devoted mistress."

"And you'll be riding him to Phantom Canyon tomorrow," Silas stated quietly.

Emily looked from one man to the other, wondering what they'd been plotting while she was upstairs. Phantom Canyon was a few miles south, winding from Victor to Florence, and one ride between its high, eerie cliffs had convinced her never to go back.

"I heard a disturbing rumor today," the mine superintendent continued. "Somebody's planning to sabotage the tracks of the Florence and Cripple Creek Railroad, and McClanahan needs your help in spotting any evidence of explosives. It'll get you both away from the Angel Claire while I — what's wrong, Emily?"

The blood was draining from her face, and she thought her knees might buckle at any moment.

"Maybe you'd better sit down," McClanahan suggested. He rose to help her, but she shoved his hands away.

"Grath came into the office today, saying he'd blow you sky-high," she began in a tiny voice. "Somehow he *knows* I didn't really hire you. He—he signed the ledger for tomorrow, but he won't be there. He was absent when Papa was shot, too."

Silas leaned on the desk, frowning at her. "Why didn't you tell me this earlier?"

"Because if word gets out, he promised to come after *me*," she exclaimed. She gazed at McClanahan's virile face, overwhelmed by the thought that Nigel Grath could've blown him to bits and she would never have seen him again. "Matt, I thought he'd kill you before I could warn you! He kept saying—"

McClanahan gripped her hands. His eyes softened somewhat, but he remained exasperatingly cool. "You know how Grath shoots off his mouth, Emily. But we'll approach this very carefully." Glancing at Silas, he added, "We should ride to Victor separately, and meet at the mouth of the canyon."

"This could be a trap, McClanahan," Hughes warned.

"We can't afford not to check the rumors out. Trains run through there several times a day and hundreds of lives are at stake." He turned back to Emily, his eyes as expressionless as a dead man's. "Better go on up to bed now. You'll need to get an early start."

Chapter Ten

As the first rays of dawn peeked through the overcast sky, Emily slowed Sundance to a trot. Her heart was torn in two: as cold as Matt was last night, she didn't relish spending long hours searching Phantom Canyon with him. But with McClanahan's life and countless others on the line, she couldn't refuse to help him. She scanned the winding grades and railroad tracks that led down into the canyon for a familiar bay gelding and his rider.

Bob bob WHITE!

McClanahan waved from a clump of trees. He showed no sign of a smile, and Emily sensed it would be an endless day.

Matt glanced at the gear tied behind her saddle. "Slicker, canteen, bedroll . . . think we'll need all that?"

Emily shrugged, noting his identical equipment. "If we have to search the whole forty miles of track, it'll be dark before we get home. I'd rather camp than have Sundance lose his footing on these rocky ridges."

McClanahan nodded as his horse fell into step with hers. "The Special made it through this morning, so nothing's been blown up yet. What are we looking for, besides signs that the ground has been disturbed?"

"Stray blasting caps, scraps of fuse." Emily gazed along the rocky edge of the narrow-gauge track, but nothing seemed out of place. "We should also watch for little tunnels that hold dynamite—probably in the sides of the hills under the track."

"I don't guess we'll spot anything obvious, like a detonator box or wires."

She snorted. "Grath's a pro. We could patrol this canyon for days and not see a sign of him until he makes us into confetti. He could tie explosives to a trestle five minutes before a train crossed and we'd never catch him."

Matt slowed Arapaho to study his side of the track. "For all we know, he's watching us right now."

"You think I wore Eliza's mine outfit because I *like* it?" Emily glanced around, goosebumps rising on her neck when the wind whistled through a nearby rock formation. "He could be behind any one of those boulders or trees. This place gives me the willies anyway. Feels . . . haunted."

They were descending into a narrow gulch that ran between high, rugged bluffs. Scraggly trees clung to the cliffs, their roots reaching out of the rock like bony fingers. Oddly-shaped boulders were perched atop the canyon walls like sentinels, silent and disapproving. Above them, thunder clouds gathered in ominous clumps. Emily concentrated on the ground around the tracks. Was someone sneaking along behind them, or was she hearing the echo of their own horses' hooves?

"Better move over to the creek. Train's coming," McClanahan said quietly.

They dismounted and allowed the animals to drink from a stream that gurgled through the canyon. Emily felt tremors running up her legs, and a deep rumble filled the gulch several moments before the locomotive came into view. Steam belched out of its smokestack while car after car clacked past them. The passengers seemed blissfully unaware of the potential hazard of being blasted to kingdom come. As the train disappeared around a bend, the man on the caboose waved to them.

"They didn't even thank us for trying to save their lives," Matt commented wryly.

Emily gave him a smile that felt tacked on. McClanahan was acting very polite—which was precisely what bothered her. What had she done to turn him from a passionate lover into a man who behaved as though she *were* the tomboyish Eliza? Perhaps her body hadn't pleased him at all . . . maybe he'd only been interested in claiming her virginity, like a hunter prized an antelope's rack on his wall. As the hours dragged by, Emily became increasingly aware that Sunday afternoon's lovemaking wouldn't be repeated. McClanahan had stolen her heart and her honor, and she hadn't mounted even a token defense.

As the oppressive narrows gave way to more hills, Emily felt compelled to look back. *Was* someone following them, concealed behind those trees, or in that abandoned shack? Or was her imagination working overtime, spurred on by a growling stomach and a tired bottom?

Up ahead, the tracks ran along a narrow ridge between two deep ravines, where jagged rocks warned them not to lose their footing. McClanahan fell in behind her, his eyes scanning the stony ground. Emily was ready to quip about needles in haystacks, just to hear a voice, when she spotted something. "Whoa, Sundance. You stand still, fella, while I take a look at this."

"What'd you find?"

"Loose dirt . . . some holes." As she slid out of the saddle, large raindrops splattered around her. There were barely two feet of earth on either side of the track, so Emily knelt and eased her feet slowly over the edge of the gulch. McClanahan joined her, sending a parade of pebbles down the hill as he looked over her shoulder.

"He must've gotten interrupted. These are the three foundation holes," she said as her finger traced a rough triangle between the openings. "They explode first, and when these two edger holes blow, the dynamite in this top position cuts loose. There's supposed to be another hole below this formation, to give the whole explosion a final boost."

McClanahan gripped a railroad tie and knocked

against the hard ground. "He's a persistent sucker. It took hours to do this much work without a drill."

Emily let out a humorless chuckle. "Grath's a man with a plan. An explosion here would send the train tumbling down into the ravine, and it'd take weeks to reconstruct the track."

"Just what I was thinking."

He scowled and began scrambling up the bank behind her. "Train's coming!" he yelled. "Let's get the hell out of here!"

Startled, Emily lost her footing and fell flat. The metal rail shook as she gripped it to pull herself up. She'd heard the rumble, too — thought it was thunder — but the steady roar belonged to the smoking black engine that was speeding around the bend toward them, only yards away.

When Matt tried to grab her shoulders he was nearly knocked off balance, because the horses were skittering around him, their nostrils flaring.

"Run for it!" Emily hollered as she clambered onto the track. "You've got to go first to get out of my way!"

McClanahan mounted his gelding, trying to coax Sundance to turn around, too, but the ridge was so narrow he couldn't get close enough to reach the palomino's reins. He swore, wheeling Arapaho in a tight circle.

As the train's whistle blasted and its brakes squealed, Emily swung onto Sundance. He balked, but as her hands closed over the reins he pivoted and galloped after Arapaho. She clung to his neck, praying he wouldn't trip over a tie as they raced toward a spot wide enough to stand on. The engine was directly behind them now, making the ground quake and piercing Emily's head with a thundering cacaphony that came straight from hell. They seemed to be traveling in slow motion, as in a nightmare where her pursuer was gaining . . . gaining. . . .

And then she was beside McClanahan. The horses huddled together in the rain, their backsides against the rugged cliff as they shrank away from the screaming locomotive. Boxcar followed boxcar, producing a deafening racket. Sundance was stamping nervously, tossing his head to avoid the flying sparks from the wheels, so she leaned on his wet neck. "Whoa, boy . . . easy now," she murmured as she clutched him. "Settle down, it's almost over."

When the caboose clattered by, it took Emily a moment to adjust to the quiet.

"Honey, are you all right?" Matt's eyes stung as he gripped her arm. Her hat and shirt were soaked, and he wasn't sure if she was shaking with cold or fright.

Emily let out the breath she'd been holding, and suddenly she was laughing so hard her stomach hurt. She wasn't sure *why,* but it was as uncontrollable as the raindrops that drenched her face.

"What's so funny?" McClanahan asked cautiously. Was she hysterical? He thought about slapping her out of it, but he was afraid she'd fall off her horse.

"I—I guess I'm too damn scared to cry!" Emily took a shuddery breath, wiping her face with a soaked sleeve.

McClanahan pulled her as close as their shifting horses would allow. "I was afraid I'd get off the track just in time to see you rolling down the ravine with Sundance on top of you. Jesus—Emily—" He kissed her fiercely, trying to force the near-tragedy out of his mind as the train's whistle faded into the distance.

Emily tasted desperation in the welcome warmth of his lips, yet she pulled away. "What is this?" she challenged. "Last night you acted as though you didn't even know me. And for three days I worried about what I'd done, because you left without even—"

"If I'd allowed myself to touch you, I would've been a lost cause, honey," Matt pleaded. "It's been hard enough to keep my mind on the tracks and rocks today, riding along beside you. And in front of Silas—"

"You're not keeping any big secret. He knows about us." Matt's jaw dropped, and judging from his expression, she could've knocked him off Arapaho with one finger.

"You *told* him? Emily, you—"

"I didn't have to. It announced itself." For a moment there were only Matt's startled blue eyes and the steady patter of rain. Then Emily chuckled. "After you took me home from Pisgah, Silas said I looked like a strumpet parading on Myers Avenue."

"Hughes said that?" He laughed and wrapped his arm around her again. "You *were* pretty free with it, but—"

"*Me?* I was only following—"

"—the happiness you gave me was something money can't buy from the most talented lover," Matt whispered. "And I'm glad you're mine, honey."

The raw emotion in his voice made her head spin. But was McClanahan declaring his love, or claiming her as his whore? "You—you just wanted to be the first to—"

"You know that's not true, Emily. All you had to say was no."

Matt's pained expression pierced her heart, and she looked away. "Sorry. I—I've eaten a lot of my words lately."

McClanahan smiled. She looked so young and vulnerable he had an overwhelming urge to protect her forever, but ideas like that were premature. "We're soaked," he murmured after he kissed her again. "Let's go back to that cabin till it quits raining."

In a few minutes Arapaho and Sundance were scaling a wooded hill toward a dilapidated shack. Emily carried their gear inside while Matt unsaddled the horses.

The door creaked and a small animal scurried out the broken window as she entered the cabin. It had probably been a miner's home at one time, as there was a rough table in front of the fireplace. Rusted springs and a bedstead rested against one wall, and a few wooden kegs stood in the corner.

"How is it?" McClanahan asked as he brought the saddles inside.

"Drier than we are. Cold, though." She hugged herself to keep her teeth from chattering as she looked around the shack's rough, shadowy interior.

105

He dropped his load in the corner, grinning. "Bet *I* can stoke your furnace, young lady."

"But there's no mattress, and the floor's such a mess—"

She was silenced by a lingering kiss as Matt wrapped his arms around her. "When a man needs a woman this badly, he'll improvise," he murmured. "Honey, it tore me up to think I might not hold you again. Can you understand why I want to love you right this minute?"

Emily nodded, unable to look away from eyes that glowed with desire in the gray light from the window. Death had breathed down both their necks: the same fear that had made her laugh uncontrollably was prompting Matt to reaffirm a life force that had flowed between lovers since the beginning of time. Emily held him tightly, stroking his strong, wet back as his kiss made her insides melt. He wanted her . . . had never stopped wanting her.

"We'd better get you out of these soaked overalls," McClanahan teased as he plucked her soggy hat off. When he unfastened her straps, she shivered. "There's wood piled out back, and we can wrap up in our blankets while our clothes dry by the fire," he suggested. "But first, we'll start a few sparks of our own."

Emily felt her feet leave the floor as McClanahan lifted her onto the table. He removed her boots with swift efficiency. As he tugged her pants down over her hips and knees, his face was taut with emotions that matched her own. "Matt . . ."

"Honey, you're all I could think about while I was in the Springs," he murmured as he slipped her pantaloons off. "I don't mean to hurry—don't want to hurt you—"

"You won't." Emily laced her fingers in his dark, warm hair and kissed him firmly on the mouth. Her pulse pounded as she watched him unfasten his gunbelt and fly buttons. Even with his shirt on, McClanahan's virility overwhelmed her in a heady, wondrous way. His lips roved over hers, and as he stepped between her legs his hands massaged her bottom.

"Rosebud, you're so warm . . . Oh, Lord—" Unable to help himself, he plunged into her tight sweetness.

She whimpered and locked her ankles behind him as he leaned her back against the table top. Her head was spinning with pent-up joy while her body abandoned itself to Matt's rapid rocking. Spirals of desire raced through her when he peaked and crushed her to his chest.

Through the euphoric haze inside his head, he heard a kittenlike voice. "Please . . . don't stop yet." McClanahan raised himself on his elbows, watching the pleasure ripple across her lovely face as he rubbed against her with deliberate patience. Emily bit her lip, then shuddered and gave herself up to uncontrollable passion.

She ran her heels down his bare hips, grinning. "Maybe I *am* a strumpet, to let a man love me even when he smells like a wet horse."

Matt kissed her exuberantly. "We'll have our times on scented sheets, but for now it feels awfully damn good to know you want me as badly as I have to have you. That doesn't make you a whore, honey."

A little while later they sat cross-legged before a blazing fire, wrapped in blankets as they shared the food they'd packed. Their pants and shirts were draped over the table's edge, and rain still dripped from chinks in the roof, but Emily felt cozy and content.

"Something tells me you're more comfortable here than you are at the mine." Matt brushed a crumb of biscuit from her chin, smiling.

"I've only been going to the Angel Claire to find my father's killer, and when Grath's behind bars, I'll gladly return to the ranch," she replied. "But I'll miss tending the herd with Papa. It—it won't be the same."

He nodded, noting a tremor in her lower lip. "He'd want you to continue supervising your home place, or he wouldn't have taught you so well. Most women would've fallen apart after the day you've been through, but you handled yourself like a pro. He'd be proud of you."

Emily smiled and snatched a chicken leg from his bundle of food. "It was kind of fun, wasn't it? I mean, after the train got by, and we knew we were safe?"

"Talk like that could age a man pretty fast." McClanahan chuckled and drank from his canteen. "I'm not sure I agree with your theory on Grath, though. The pieces just don't fit."

She frowned. "Matt, the man *knew* I didn't hire you. And how else could he have found that out, unless he's been snooping around at the—"

"But if he's after *my* hide, why would he blow up the Florence and Cripple Creek tracks?" he asked earnestly. "I never ride this train—and if he wanted to damage your father's mining business, he'd sabotage the Midland Terminal line so his ore couldn't get to the mill."

"That would shut the other mines down, too," Emily argued. "The owners would consider it a union ploy and dock wages till the trains were running again. The Federation wouldn't stand for that."

"No, and it's just the sort of ruckus Nigel Grath would glory in. If he did kill your father, why's he threatening *me*, when he could do more damage by killing Silas?" Matt saw a storm brewing in her light brown eyes, so he kept his voice low and serious. "Grath's just lashing out against authority—any authority—because he'll never be anything more than a mine worker."

"But he's a *killer*, McClanahan. Can't you see that?" Emily threw her chicken bone into the fire.

"The days he was absent from the mine coincide perfectly with Papa's death. You saw the blasting pattern— and you practically dropped your saddle on a keg of powder."

He glanced doubtfully toward the corner where he'd deposited their gear. "Would that stuff work in place of dynamite?"

"Sure—they rolled their own cartridges with it before nitroglycerin came in sticks. Powder's not as temperamental as dynamite, and it's more reliable, but nowadays we use dynamite because it's more convenient."

McClanahan didn't doubt her sincerity or her information, but he wasn't convinced. "What makes you think Grath stored it here?"

She heaved an exasperated sigh. "He said he was going to blow you—"

"And with more than four hundred mines in the district, each with a blaster, how do you know someone else couldn't have—"

"McClanahan, you're impossible!" Emily gestured wildly with her arms, flinging her blanket away from her bare shoulders. "If you didn't believe Grath's threat, then why are you here?"

As the firelight illuminated her ivory skin, Matt could think of two tempting reasons he wouldn't want to be anywhere else, but he gave her a straight answer. "I came because Silas asked me to, and because we can't ignore rumors that endanger hundreds of lives. We've proven the rumor true now. But if Grath really wanted to kill me, he could've done it dozens of times today."

He was right about that—hadn't she felt beady eyes following them from behind boulders and underbrush? "Then what're you saying?" Emily snapped.

"I think it's a test," he replied patiently. "Whoever started the story about blasting these tracks wanted to see how Silas would react. And by telling Eliza he was after me, Grath guaranteed I'd put the stories together and come out here."

Emily's pulse pounded weakly. "He . . . used me to set you up?"

"Just a theory. Eliza's too loyal not to tell me such a thing, and Grath knows I'll protect a defenseless young lady. Kind of heartwarming, when you think about it." Her braid brushed across her back as she turned away; the girl who'd outrun a train and laughed about it was getting quivery around the chin when she thought she'd betrayed him. Matt stepped out of his blanket to kneel behind her, gripping her shoulders gently. "It's all in a day's work, Emily. Don't blame yourself for—"

"But what if he *had* killed you? I'd never forgive myself." At the insistence of his warm hand, Emily looked into blue eyes that sparkled with understanding . . . and maybe more.

"I know that, honey," he whispered. "And if I didn't trust your instincts, I would've dismissed the whole story. Right?"

Emily nodded meekly. "Do . . . do you think Grath realizes who I really am?"

"I don't see how he could, if your father's friends haven't figured you out." Matt coaxed her to her knees, his desire rising as her silken skin brushed his own. "But I'm certainly glad *I* know the truth about you."

He was doing it again, arousing her with so little effort that she wondered if she *was* a wanton, to respond without any resistance. "I think our clothes are dry," she mumbled. "And listen — the rain's stopped."

Chuckling, Matt gazed at the pert peaks of flesh pressing against his chest. "You want to leave about as badly as I do, rosebud. We've found the evidence we're looking for, so there's no need to search further — the marshal can do that. Plenty of time to enjoy each other and still be home before dark, don't you think?"

She *couldn't* think. Anticipation smoldered within her as she watched Matt arrange their blankets before the fire. His movements were quick, his arousal apparent as he invited her to the pallet with a searching, blue-eyed gaze. Refusing him was as impossible as stopping an explosion once the wick was lit.

They made love slowly this time, making the sensations last as long as they could without reaching a peak. Matt kissed her in places where no man's lips had ever lingered, delighted by the way she explored him in return. As he coaxed her to straddle him, Emily caressed the enticing dark hair which hid nipples as taut as her own. She rode him with firm deliberation, ignoring the hands that insisted she speed up, until her own thrusting hips refused to slow down. A starburst flared between them, and she collapsed in his embrace.

After a moment Matt nuzzled her ear. "I should be

110

pushing you away, swearing I'll never hold you again. Yet I'm trying to figure out how we can be alone this week."

"With Silas watching my every move?"

"He sent us *here* together." Matt lifted her shoulders, smiling at the concern in her eyes. "Of course, whether he approves or not, it wouldn't do for Eliza and me to disappear at the same time very often."

"You're very perceptive, McClanahan," she replied with a wry grin. Seeing that the fire was now a red bed of embers, she kissed him and reluctantly stood up to dress. "And if you make any moves at the Rose, you'll have Clancy to deal with."

"I'd rather contend with a man I can keep track of than a sneak like Grath." Matt sat up, then rolled their blankets back into their slickers as he recalled something the Indian Princess had mentioned during Miss Chatterly's birthday ball. "What goes on at Victoria's teas? Maybe I can wrangle an invitation for next Thursday."

"I can't see you with your pinkie poised over the handle of a cup," she replied with a chuckle.

"They really drink tea?"

"With crumpets and little cakes and scones. Victoria's a great one for celebrating her English heritage." Emily stepped into her overalls, gazing up at him as he fastened her straps and tucked her shirttail in.

Matt let his hands wander down her back, and then slipped his fingers beneath her pantaloons to fondle her bottom one last time. "Perhaps if I tip the maid enough, she'll find me a bottle of something stronger . . . maybe join me in a tub of hot, bubbly water?"

"Perhaps." She kissed him playfully, until his arms tightened around her and his mouth made her want him all over again. "Matt, we should be . . . what was that?"

"What, rosebud?" He held her tightly, listening.

A strange shriek pierced the silence of the canyon, so close to the cabin Emily hugged McClanahan harder.

"Some sort of a bird. Maybe a hawk or a woodpecker," he whispered with a reassuring pat.

111

But as Emily tucked her braid up under her hat, the eerie noise rang out again — not once, but twice. It made her skin crawl, because it sounded exactly like Nigel Grath's laugh.

Chapter Eleven

McClanahan propped his foot against the front of the desk in Barry Thompson's cluttered office. A few rowdies were snoring off their hangovers in the cells down the hall, but otherwise the jailhouse was quiet. "What can you tell me about Nigel Grath?"

The marshal shrugged, blowing cigarette smoke from his nostrils. "He stays the night here now and then—has a way with words a lot of guys don't like. Most times I think I'm locking him up to protect him from fights, scrawny as he is, yet I know damn well he starts them."

Matt nodded. "Where's he from?"

Thompson stubbed out his smoke with a thoughtful expression. "I think he worked in a few other mining camps on his way to Cripple, but I haven't seen any warrants or posters on him. Why?"

"Silas Hughes asked me to check out some rumors about the Florence and Cripple Creek Railroad being sabotaged. We think Grath's behind it."

The marshal leaned heavily on his desk, his eyes narrowing. "Did you find anything?"

Not wanting to have Emily's name bandied about during an investigation, Matt worded his response carefully. "I spent most of yesterday scanning Phantom Canyon. Found a blasting pattern, and there's some powder and fuse stored in an abandoned cabin nearby."

"Jesus, only a maniac would blow . . . I'll have some of the boys look it over. Oh—got something here that might interest you." Barry shuffled through the papers that littered the top of his desk, and handed a poster to McClanahan. "What do you think of this?"

Matt studied the photograph of a man with close-cropped hair and a face pitted with pockmarks — or maybe low-quality printing was to blame for his blotchy complexion. He read the description at the bottom of the page, smiling slowly. "Keep this under your hat, will you, Barry?"

"Want any help?"

"No more than what you've already given me, for now. Next time we're at the Golden Rose, the bottle's on me." He stood, keeping a triumphant grin to himself. Evidence was lining up like notches on a gun barrel, and if he could tie it all together he'd earn a handsome reward — not to mention Emily Burnham's undying gratitude.

"I understand next Thursday's tea is a coming-out party for a new gal," the marshal said with a sly smile. "Have you gotten an invitation yet?"

Matt raised his eyebrows. "No, but I'd like one."

"Miss Victoria's taken a shine to you, and her Thursday afternoons are reserved for preferred customers." He studied McClanahan with the satisfied air of a man who'd become a member of an elite organization without having to apply. "Watch your box at the hotel."

"I didn't think tea and tarts were your style, Barry," Matt said with a chuckle. He was turning the doorknob when the marshal spoke again.

"This business you're on wouldn't have anything to do with that little yellow-haired housekeeper, would it?"

McClanahan gave the lawman a pointed look. "The less she hears — about me, or what I'm doing — the better."

"Yes, sir. Can't tell her what I don't know, can I?" Thompson flashed him a boyish smile. "Don't turn your back on any cowards this week, Matt."

"Same to you, Barry."

He stepped outside, folding the poster into his pocket.

He was itching to corral Elliott Burnham's killer *now*, while the element of surprise was in his favor. The sooner her father's death was avenged, the sooner Emily would accept another man in her life . . . a man who wanted her love and didn't need her money.

Yet instinct told him to wait. A final piece of evidence was required to connect the criminal in the picture to the man buried at the Flaming B Ranch. Matt smiled to himself and headed down the street. Miss Burnham was set on finding her father's killer herself—and she would, before long—so his best move was to stay a few steps ahead of her and keep trouble out of her way. Remembering Emily sitting cross-legged beside him in the cabin, her eyes aglow as she snatched a chicken leg, still made him grin. Recalling the *other* things she'd done made him quicken his steps to the Imperial. He had to see her soon, alone.

And the opportunity was waiting for him at the front desk: an envelope sealed with an ornate V in red wax. Matt walked up to his room to read it.

Miss Victoria Chatterly and the ladies of the Golden Rose request the pleasure of your presence at tea this Thursday, September 22, at 4 o'clock. We will be presenting Miss Zenia Collins for your entertainment and enjoyment, and we hope you can attend.

Matt inhaled the fragile fragrance of roses, which made him think of arms and legs wrapped tightly around him . . . a face innocent of makeup and pretense, grimacing in ecstasy as she lost control. He chuckled. Zenia Collins was undoubtedly alluring and accomplished, but she'd never be his reason for going to the Rose.

Chapter Twelve

"The table looks lovely, Eliza," the white-haired madame purred. "I'm glad Idaho could spare you this week, because my other girl just isn't as efficient."

Emily smiled and helped Miss Victoria fill the teapots with boiling water. At Silas's suggestion, she was staying away from the Angel Claire until they found proof that Nigel Grath killed her father — proof *she* didn't need. The days were endless, because McClanahan was keeping his eye on Grath rather than on her, so working at the Rose had passed the time. "We've had a lot to do, getting Zenia ready," she commented.

"Yes, we have." Miss Chatterly's voice was low and confidential. "What do you think of her, dear?"

"She looks very pretty in those new gowns."

"She ought to, much as I paid Mrs. Delacroix to make them! She seems so . . . unsullied, to have come from a sporting house in Creede. Or maybe she knows how to use her looks that way." Victoria glanced around the parlor, where the ladies were helping Josh raise the lid of the grand piano. "Josh, dear — play us some of your ragtime. The guests should be arriving any minute now."

"Yes, ma'am," he said with a wide, white grin.

"Have you and Zenia rehearsed her songs?"

"Miss Victoria, that girl sings like an angel. The men'll be so taken by her, these other ladies'll be twiddlin' their thumbs."

Lucy and Darla and the others twittered, and Princess

116

Cherry Blossom rolled her painted eyes. As Josh played a lively piece, the doorbell chimed and the ladies strolled past the bar to answer it. With a glance at Clancy, who seemed terribly pleased with himself for having discovered Zenia Collins, Emily went to the pantry for another tray of pastries.

When she returned, the parlor was humming with quiet conversations. Miss Victoria was pouring tea, her plump fingers glistening with rings as she handed china cups to men who accepted them with quiet smiles. "Here, try one of these little cakes with the strawberry glaze," she said to a portly banker named Conrad Stokes. Then her eyes widened. "Mr. McClanahan! How lovely that you could make it — and don't you look dashing today."

Emily's heart thudded as Matt kissed the madame's cheek. He was wearing the gray suit he'd had on at Victoria's birthday party, and his hair lay in glossy waves. "I was pleased to be asked," he responded suavely. "Thought I'd come early, to see the new lady with the exotic name. Or did *you* think of that?"

Victoria chuckled as she filled his teacup. "No, we shortened her real name, which is Zenobia. I hope we did the right thing, bringing her here. Elliott's daughter hasn't responded to my letter about her."

Matt frowned slightly as he glanced at Emily. "It could be that she hasn't seen it. When I was at the ranch, she was feeling better — getting ready for roundup — which took her away from the house for a few days."

The madame sighed, toying with an opal pendant that rested above her ample bosom. "It's a good thing Silas hired you, since he's too busy to keep track of Elliott's affairs. Clancy claims Zenia is just what our clients have been asking for — and *I* have no objection — but I'm not sure Elliott's daughter would approve."

Matt glanced around and stood so that only Victoria and Emily could hear their conversation. "What seems to be the problem?"

"Zenia's a Negress, Mr. McClanahan. Elliott insisted

on paying his colored help the same wages as the rest of us, but not everyone shares his views." Victoria waved coyly at a group of men who were entering the parlor. "Perhaps I should visit Miss Burnham at the ranch—"

"I think you'd better stay here and keep an eye on Clancy," Matt responded quietly. "His side of the ledger doesn't balance as perfectly as yours does."

As she glanced toward the bar, the madame's aqua eyes narrowed. "You have a point. But when you see Emily, tell her she'd be wise to come visit the Golden Rose. Excuse me—I have to see what's keeping our Zenia."

Emily watched Miss Victoria sway gracefully through the room, greeting guests on her way to the staircase. "Quick thinking, McClanahan," she said in a low voice.

"Part of the job," he replied with a wink. "Has Clancy given you any trouble this week?"

"No. He fetched Zenia on Monday, and he's been congratulating himself ever since." She glanced toward the bar, where the men were gathering after their obligatory cups of tea. "What about Nigel? Has he threatened you, or asked where I was?"

Matt shrugged. "He's kept to himself. Silas is acting as though his absence last week was legitimate, until we can prove he sabotaged the tracks."

Nodding, Emily spotted a buckskin dress and a jaded, dark-eyed smile. "I guess I'll play maid now, since the Princess has spotted you."

She smiled at the woman in the feathers and war paint, and passed among the guests with a heaping tray of crumpets and little cakes. Josh grinned his thanks as she set a lemon tart on the piano. The ladies were making eyes over their china cups, at the same stock brokers, mine owners, and bankers who usually attended these gatherings. Barry Thompson laced his tea with brandy from the crystal decanter on the étagère, and she wagged a teasing finger at him.

Around the piano, several voices rose in a chorus of "There'll Be a Hot Time in the Old Town Tonight"—

until Josh abruptly stopped playing. He gazed toward the stairway as though he'd been bewitched.

Zenia Collins seemed to float down the stairs, wearing a sea green taffeta gown that accentuated her slender yet well-endowed figure. Her doelike eyes widened as she took in the rapt faces of the men below her. She was one of the most beautiful colored ladies Emily had ever seen . . . and one of the youngest.

Behind Zenia, Victoria Chatterly followed like a regal mother hen. "Gentlemen, may I present Miss Zenia Collins, our newest resident here at the Golden Rose. We think she's a very special young lady, and you will, too. Zenia, dear, will you sing something for us?"

Murmurs rose as the guests assessed the girl in green. Smiling shyly at Josh, she steadied herself against the piano as he played a few introductory bars. "Drink to Me Only with Thine Eyes" was a familiar tune, yet when Zenia forgot her nerves and sang it in a soprano that was sweet and clear, the words seemed to take on new meaning. The guests applauded enthusiastically and demanded an encore.

Emily saw no sign of Matt or Princess Cherry Blossom, but she couldn't miss the way the men were eyeing Zenia like randy bulls, or the way Clancy strutted behind the bar, telling his customers how he'd found such an enticing morsel. Disgusted by his cocky grin, she went to the pantry to refill the tea trays. When she returned, Conrad Stokes was smiling broadly as he offered a pudgy arm to Miss Collins, patting her fragile brown hand. No one would be wanting more tea, so Emily returned to her table in the corner of the pantry.

She knew such things went on, yet the sight of the portly white banker and his tender black prey troubled her. She picked up the latest *Rocky Mountain News,* trying to put the realities of the prostitution business out of her mind.

"Well! It's not often you see a woman reading a newspaper in a whorehouse."

Emily looked up to see McClanahan grinning at her.

119

"Habit, I guess. Even though I know who killed Papa, I like to keep track of what other outlaws are in the area."

"Me, for instance?"

"You're the first one I thought of."

Matt lowered himself into the armchair across from her, patting his lap as he set his whiskey bottle on the table. Her tawny gaze was as eager as he'd hoped it would be, and he gave her a rakish once-over.

"Don't get any ideas, McClanahan. The bathing suite's occupied," Emily teased.

"I know. The Princess is entertaining Thompson — cowboys and Indians, they call it."

After a week without his touch, Emily couldn't resist the playful invitation that was written all over his face. She picked up her paper and perched demurely on his lap. "And what would *you* like to play?" she murmured.

Matt chuckled, his desire rising as he caught the heady scent of her perfume. "Don't be silly, rosebud. I came in here to read." He turned her so she was balanced on his lap, facing the doorway. "You hold the paper, and I'll hold you. How's that?"

"Shh! I'm reading."

"Fine. So will I."

Emily opened the *News* wider, creating a screen between them and whoever walked by the open door. It was a struggle not to laugh, because she knew damn well McClanahan wasn't paying any more attention to the pages than she was.

Matt poured a drink, slipping his free hand around her waist. As he sipped, his chin brushed lightly against her temple, and it was all he could do not to loosen her silky hair.

She felt his warm breath falling on her cheek, and a hand closing gently over her breast. "Uh — looks like Pug Ryan's still on the loose," she said in a strained voice. "Guess you heard about him shooting those deputies in Breckenridge, after he helped himself to everybody's valuables in the Denver Hotel game room."

"Yep. They'll catch him one of these days." Matt nuzzled the wispy hairs that had come loose from her braid. Grasping her hips, he shifted her weight more strategically over the bulge in his trousers. "I see your Wild Bunch friends made the paper, too."

"You mean this piece from Steamboat Springs, about Cassidy calling for a meeting of all the outlaws?" Emily chuckled as she pointed to the column. "He thinks they'll get amnesty from the law by enlisting in the Spanish-American War. I'll believe that when I see it."

"The Army'll be too short of horses to fight, if they let *those* fellows enlist."

She turned to grin at him. "Well! It's not often you hear a man making intelligent conversation with a woman in a whorehouse."

"Maybe I should stop. It could ruin my image," he said in a husky voice. His right hand found its way between the buttons of her blouse, and his left was unfastening her skirt. With a low moan, he skimmed the velvety skin beneath her clothes until he felt coarse curls and the moist slickness below them.

Emily sucked in her breath. "Somebody'll see—"

"Two sets of legs and a newspaper," Matt breathed. "Perfectly innocent, unless you keep squirming this way. But don't stop on my account."

His skillful fingertips made waves of warmth swirl up from the pit of her stomach until her head was in a fog. "What if someone walks in?" she murmured. With his rigid manhood prodding her bottom and his hands creating such an intimate torment, she was afraid Clancy or the guests would hear her crying out before long.

McClanahan caressed her until they were both straining for release, and then he stopped. It took all his strength to clasp his hands over the waistband of her apron. "All right, then," he said in a teasing whisper. "What shall we talk about now, Miss Burnham?"

"Uh—Zenia! What'd you think of Zenia?"

He ran his tongue along the edge of her ear. "She's pretty, but I prefer fair-haired virgins myself."

"She's no virgin. Clancy hired her away from a house

in Creede."

Matt's eyebrows went up. "Then why was he selling her innocence to the highest bidder at the bar?"

"What?" Emily jerked around to face him, dropping her newspaper.

He groaned against her shoulder. "You'll end up on the floor if you don't watch where you swivel those hips, sweetheart," he rasped.

"Sorry." She stroked McClanahan's cheek, scowling over what he'd told her. "You're saying Stokes paid to be the first? That bastard Donahue promised Victoria—"

Matt clapped his hand over her mouth. "Shh . . . maybe that's just the game for the day. Whores build their business on fantasy, honey, and they've got a story for every gown in their wardrobe."

Emily recalled Zenia's wide, childlike eyes and her halting entrance into the parlor, and she knew now why the colored girl's situation bothered her. "It's still disgusting," she hissed. "And I'm going out there to—"

"What good would it do?" McClanahan countered. He adored her flushed cheeks and flashing eyes, yet her sense of propriety pleased him more. "Like it or not, this is a whorehouse, Emily. You can't challenge Donahue—not in front of the Rose's most generous customers. Just be glad she's with Conrad instead of with Clancy."

She let out an impatient sigh. "When I see Donahue alone, I'll—"

"Be careful, Miss Crusader. You know he'll retaliate."

Emily blinked. And as she studied the handsome, compassionate face that was only inches from her own, she also knew how lucky she'd been that McClanahan had taught her the first lessons in love. "You're right—I'd better watch myself," she murmured. "Just hold me for a while, Matt. I . . . I've missed you this week."

"I've missed you, too, rosebud."

His arms encircled her and she relaxed against the steady rise and fall of his chest. She felt like a child, cherished and protected, yet free to express her inner feelings as she could with no one else. How would she be surviving the aftermath of Papa's death if it weren't for Matt McClanahan?

He kissed her forehead and felt himself hardening again. His passion for her was growing more dangerous by the day — the consequences of accidentally exposing her identity were dire. Yet he couldn't let her go.

To prolong his state of anticipation, Matt poured another drink. "Want a sip?" he whispered. "They say it makes a lady . . . freer with her lover."

She laughed softly. "I've been too free with you already, McClanahan." Emily returned his gaze as he drained his glass and set it down. He pulled her close for the kiss she'd wanted since the last time their lips had met, his whiskey-flavored tongue slithering between her teeth. He was holding her so tightly she could feel his hard, round pocket watch as well as something else poking her from beneath his clothes.

"I'm going to shut the door," he breathed.

"What if someone comes in here looking for more tarts, or—"

"Too bad," he said with a chuckle. "This tart's taken." McClanahan carried her with him, and when the door was closed he sat in the armchair again, with Emily facing him. He slipped his hands under the hem of her uniform. "The last time I held you this way, I remember finding silk stockings. Mmmm . . . and here they are."

Emily felt a shimmer of goosebumps as he caressed her thighs. "You were naked that night. First man I ever saw in the buff."

"You didn't seem to mind."

She giggled softly, and as Matt grasped her hips beneath her pantaloons, Emily kissed him all over his rugged face. The fire he'd started earlier was rekindled, and she was throbbing with a desire only he could satisfy. "Why do you lead me on this way?" she murmured.

"Because you've got the sweetest little ass I've ever seen," he whispered. "Unfasten my pants. Take them down just far enough to ride me, like you did in the cabin."

His words sent a shiver of anticipation up her spine. Emily kissed him hungrily, moaning as he responded with tongue thrusts that matched her own.

The pantry door opened and shut, and they heard a muffled sob.

Emily yelped, clutching her clothes as she sprang from McClanahan's lap. Zenia Collins was burying her face in the corner, her slender brown body shaking beneath her pink camisole and pantaloons. "Zenia, I thought—"

"I—I'm sorry. I didn't know anybody was in here," she said with a hitch in her voice.

Emily glanced warily at Matt as she struggled to fasten her clothes. "What's wrong? I saw you go upstairs—"

"I couldn't do it, Miss Eliza." Zenia took her hands from her tear-streaked face. "Clancy explained how I was supposed to let the man touch me and. . . ."

Matt walked toward the colored girl, pulling his handkerchief from his pocket. "Did Mr. Stokes hurt you, Zenia?" he asked gently. "Miss Chatterly won't tolerate violence against any of her girls."

"No, he wasn't mean or nothin'," Zenia replied in a shuddery voice. "He's just so *big*, and when he got his clothes off I couldn't *believe* I was supposed to—"

The door opened again, and Victoria Chatterly stepped inside. After glancing at Matt and Emily, she focused sternly on the quaking girl beside them. "Why are you hiding down here?" she demanded in a tight voice. "You knew you weren't signing on as a Sunday School teacher when you came to the Rose."

Zenia's eyes grew huge. "Don't beat me, Miss Victoria—please! I—I'll try again. I—"

The madame's face softened and she grasped the girl's slender shoulders. "Clancy didn't find you at a brothel in Creede, did he?"

She shuddered and looked away.

"Tell me the truth, Zenia. Things'll go much easier for you." Victoria glanced up, her expression tense yet apologetic. "May we borrow your coat, Mr. McClanahan?"

"Certainly." Matt slipped his jacket around the girl's shoulders and then led her to the chair. "We're not going to let Clancy hurt you, Zenia, but we have to know your side of the story. Everything."

The girl looked pitifully small as she clutched Mc-Clanahan's gray frock coat around her. She blew her nose and then, in a high, childlike voice, she began. "My . . . my daddy, he's a miner in Leadville, but he's got no job right now. And my mama, she takes in washin' but it don't nearly feed us six kids. So when Mr. Donahue come along sayin' he had a job for me—and he give Daddy an advance on my pay. . . ."

Emily cringed, wondering how Zenia had blossomed into such a graceful beauty. She'd probably lived in a squalid little shack and thought Donahue was Santa Claus—or the Savior himself—flashing his money at her father.

The madame sighed. "Clancy told me you were eighteen when I let him hire you, Zenia. How old *are* you?"

Zenia looked at the floor. "Fourteen, ma'am."

"You've never been with a man either. Have you?"

Zenia shook her head forlornly. "No, ma'am. Mr. Donahue told me and my folks I'd be doin' honest work. But Mama says it's a sin to whore."

"Yet you understood what sort of business you'd be involved in here, Zenia—"

"Yes, ma'am."

"—and you could've said something before we spent hundreds of dollars at the dressmaker's. The whole point of those pretty gowns and underthings is for men to take them off you, dear."

The girl nodded, her full lips quivering. "I know, Miss Victoria. I—I'll try again, 'cause I don't want to owe you for them dresses. Don't want nobody mad at me, neither." Her eyes filled again, and she pressed Matt's tear-splotched handkerchief to her face.

Emily sensed there was something—or someone—else behind Zenia's nervousness. "What'd Clancy threaten to do if you told anyone about this?" she asked

125

quietly.

Zenia's dark, wet eyes grew round with fright. "He . . . he said he had a big bull whip."

"Well, he's not going to use it," Victoria stated. The planes of her porcelain face hardened and her tiara trembled in its white nest. "I'll see that Mr. Stokes finds other company, and you—"

"She can go home with me, until things have settled down," Emily said.

Miss Victoria considered her response for a moment. "You're sure Silas won't mind? I hate to impose on him."

"You won't be." Emily smiled at Zenia, pleased that the girl was looking less agitated now. "He goes to his club on Thursdays, and Idaho'll be glad for the company."

The madame reached for the doorknob with jeweled fingers. "That'll give me a chance to straighten this out with Clancy—and we *will* come to an understanding. But that doesn't mean I'm letting you out of this, Zenia. I expect you back here tomorrow, ready to work."

"Yes, ma'am. A deal's a deal."

"Eliza can go upstairs and get your things," Miss Chatterly added. "And Mr. McClanahan, I'd be pleased to provide you with complimentary entertainment after you escort these girls to Silas's. I'd appreciate your being here when I talk to Clancy, too."

"Certainly, ma'am," Matt replied with a smile. "It'll be my pleasure."

126

Chapter Thirteen

Victoria Chatterly's boudoir was as plush and elegant as the lady herself, yet as Matt lounged in one of her overstuffed chairs he knew the frilly pinks and ivories around him were chosen by a woman with a spine of steel. The lamps were low, the atmosphere perfect for an evening of splendor in the madame's brass bed. But watching Donahue squirm would be better sport by far, and he lit his cigar with a grin of anticipation.

The door opened, and Clancy glared around the room. "Should've guessed you were behind this, McClanahan. Where's Victoria?"

Matt arched his brow. "Preparing herself. Amazing, how she keeps the Rose open till all hours and still has the energy to entertain two men at once."

"Don't give me that bullshit. You've been sneakin' around like a snake ever since you got to town," the bartender snarled. "You're the biggest phony I've ever—"

"Takes one to know one, they say."

Clancy pointed his finger like a pistol. "When I tell Miss Chatterly how you pulled the wool over Hughes's eyes, you'll be out on your ass, McClanahan. You're no more the manager of the Burnham—"

"Go ahead—*tell* her who Emily is," Matt challenged. "I want to hear you explain how you got *your* job."

The bearlike Irishman stopped in front of him, glowering. "And what do you mean by *that?*"

McClanahan blew a stream of smoke toward his face.

"You must've spun some mighty convincing lies to get Emily to bring you here. You were just a common cowpoke—weren't in charge of any people, didn't handle any money."

"The Rose has hauled in a helluva profit since I've become the manager of—" The door opened, and Clancy turned to see Victoria Chatterly's icy glare.

"We'll discuss your performance later, Mr. Donahue," she said in a low voice. "Right now I want you to explain *this*." The madame held up a whip so long that it hung from her hand in several coils.

"Who gave you permission to go through my—"

"Elliott Burnham put me in charge of this house, and I intend to know what goes on here." Victoria walked slowly toward Donahue, her genteel sway and mannerisms gone. "So tell me why you hired Zenia Collins."

Clancy's face registered self-righteous shock. "Do a damn nigger a favor, and she'll stab you in the back every time. I took her off her pa's hands—"

"Her father doesn't run a brothel in Creede," the madame countered coldly. "This is your second stupid mistake, Mr. Donahue, and another of your lies. I've told you I don't sell virginity here, and now I'm over a barrel because her wardrobe cost me a small fortune."

"Where is that whorin' little—"

"It doesn't matter," McClanahan interrupted pointedly. "You've had your hand in the till, and I've heard complaints about how you're treating the other ladies, too. We're telling you you're on the verge of being unemployed, Mr. Donahue."

The bartender's eyes flashed. "You can't prove *any* of that! And you can't fire me—you're only a—"

"I can and I will," Matt responded coolly. "And Miss Chatterly has the same prerogative."

Clancy smoldered with resentment; his beefy fists clenched and unclenched. "I'll get you for this, McClanahan. You're a goddamn—"

"I'm merely protecting Miss Burnham's business interests, as I was hired to do."

" — fake, and I can prove you lied to Emily and Hughes to get your job."

McClanahan stood up very slowly. Donahue's words rang with the dangerous desperation of a trapped animal, and this was no time to arouse Victoria Chatterly's doubts about his credentials. "I think you'd better apologize to this lady, Mr. Donahue," he said quietly. "Hughes had second thoughts about recommending you — and *I* wouldn't have hired you in the first place — so it's toe the line, or get the hell out."

The madame moved to stand beside Matt, her stance equally firm.

Clancy stalked across the boudoir and yanked the door open. "So tell me where Zenia sneaked off to. A couple gentlemen were askin' for her — and it's my *job* to keep our customers happy," he added sarcastically.

"She'll be back tomorrow." Victoria winced as the door slammed. Then she poured herself some sherry from an etched decanter on her night stand. "I should never have trusted him. Had Zenia gone wailing through the parlor, the afternoon would've been a disaster." She sipped from her tumbler, looking Matt in the eye. "Has Silas expressed doubts about Clancy, or did you say that for the sake of argument?"

Emily had been his inspiration during the entire conversation, so McClanahan continued with her point of view. But he sensed Victoria would soon see through their masquerades. "He's never liked Donahue much, and when Miss Burnham heard about his thievery, she admitted to me that Clancy's size and strength were all he had in his favor. His polish is wearing awfully thin."

She nodded, her pale eyes wide with concern. "I have a feeling he'll hurt Zenia — and maybe Eliza, for sheltering her. I know you're busy, Matt, but you'd be doing me a big favor if you'd keep an eye on him. Marshal Thompson considers the Rose the most respectable house in Cripple Creek, and I'd like it to stay that way."

McClanahan took his Stetson from the madame's marble-top vanity, and then kissed her cheek. "That's what I'm here for, Victoria."

"You'd better have some more chicken and biscuits, Miss Zenia," Idaho insisted. "A girl can't do her growing up on that little bit you ate."

Zenia smiled shyly across the dining room table at the old colored man. "I can't hold another bite," she replied in a meek voice.

Idaho chuckled and chose a crisply-fried chicken thigh. "Bet you'll have room for dessert, though. *Nobody* says no to my gooseberry pie."

All through the meal, Emily had watched a friendship blossom between a bereaved old man and a scared young girl who had nothing in common save the color of their skin. But it was enough. Idaho's wrinkles had turned into smiles, and he was humming when he stood to clear the table.

"Idaho won't think I don't *like* his cooking, will he?" Zenia whispered when he'd shuffled to the kitchen. "I hate to waste anything, but I just couldn't stuff it all in. Never seen that much food all at once."

Emily smiled. "He used to pile food onto my plate, too. It's his way of saying he loves you."

Nodding, the girl looked around the dining room with wide brown eyes. "I'm grateful to you for takin' me in tonight, Miss Eliza — yet here I sit, when I should be helpin'." She hopped up and scraped her scraps onto Emily's plate, but Idaho took the dishes from her.

"You girls go on into the parlor. I'll be out with that pie as soon as I clean up the kitchen."

"But it's only polite to —"

The old man patted Zenia's shoulder, smiling warmly. "Miss . . . Eliza doesn't have company her own age nearly often enough. You'd be doing old Idaho a big favor just talking girl-talk with her. Go on, now."

With a grin that showed her even, white teeth, Zenia followed Emily into the parlor and settled onto the love-seat. She smoothed the skirt of a buttery-yellow dress from Emily's closet, then stroked the arm of the love-seat. "Mr. Silas must be a wealthy man. You sure he don't mind—"

"Relax, Zenia. He and Miss Victoria are good friends . . . and maybe he can convince her to let you leave the Rose." Emily had been trying to think of a way to repay the madame for Zenia's expensive gowns herself, but it would seem very suspicious if Eliza the cleaning girl came up with that much money. If she could make it look like a gift from Silas. . . .

"Oh, no, Miss Eliza. I told Miss Victoria I'd work for her and I'll stick by it." The girl's coffee-colored fingers caressed the folds of her dress with a wistfulness Emily could hardly bear. "I can't go back home now—and I couldn't run off, knowin' how much Miss Victoria paid for them dresses. It's prob'ly more money than I'll make in my lifetime."

Emily had no doubt that an exotic beauty like Zenia Collins could repay her debt in a very short while . . . unless Clancy skimmed her wages. Seeing her in such a nervous state made Emily wish again that she'd never fallen for Donahue's speech about being such a perfect bouncer—a bodyguard and *protector* for the ladies and herself, he'd claimed. "It's Clancy you're really afraid of, isn't it?" she asked quietly.

Zenia focused on the crackling flames in the fireplace. "On the way here from Leadville, he kept sayin' he wanted me for hisself. Nearly stopped the wagon to do it, too, but I told him I had the curse."

"You can't use that excuse very often, or he'll keep track," she said with a sigh. Idaho was carrying a tray full of pie and tea things through the kitchen door, so Emily lowered her voice. "At least Victoria knows he's threatened you, so she'll watch him more closely."

"This talk sounds mighty serious for two pretty young

131

girls," the old man teased as he set the tray on the coffee table. He lowered himself onto the sofa beside Emily and lifted a generous wedge of pie onto a plate.

The reason for Zenia's coming here had distressed Idaho, but there was no avoiding the subject completely. Emily handed the pie to her guest. "We're trying to figure out how we can keep Zenia away from Clancy. If Victoria lets her leave, he'll probably go after her."

The housekeeper scratched his white-sprigged head. "You know, Miss Zenia, I was thinking while I washed the dishes, and I have some—"

Someone pounded on the front door, and Idaho's glance darted between the two of them. "Now who could that be?"

"Maybe it's Matt," Emily replied as she walked to the vestibule. "Maybe he's come to tell us about his talk with Miss Victoria."

Zenia was fighting a grin. "He makes you a handsome beau, Miss Eliza. Sorry I barged in when I did."

Emily felt her face redden, and then she opened the door. "Well, Josh! You're just in time for pie!"

The pianist grinned at her, but when Josh LeFevre's chocolate-brown eyes caressed Zenia, Emily knew dessert was the furthest thing from his mind. He settled on the loveseat beside her, taking her brown hands in his. "Miss Victoria said you were here. I was so worried—"

"It's all right," Zenia murmured. "Miss Eliza and Idaho're takin' good care of me."

"Donahue's been so testy I thought he might take a bite out of that mahogany bar," he continued earnestly. "You won't be safe if you go back there."

Zenia lowered her eyes. "I can't leave now, Josh. Miss Victoria's bought them dresses—"

"She can let some other girl wear 'em! Zenia, honey, you're too good—too *fine* to be a whore."

"I—I've got no money to travel on," she replied in a wobbly whisper.

"Well, I do! We can leave now, before Clancy comes

132

lookin' for us," Josh declared. "There's hundreds of dance halls where we can play and sing."

The idealistic ring in the young man's voice made Emily nip her lip. Idaho had stopped dishing up pie, and he was watching the sudden drama along with her.

Zenia gazed up at Josh with brimming black eyes. "That ain't right, now that I've promised—"

"Whorin's not right!" he whispered hoarsely. "Marry me, Zenia. You stay at the Rose even a week, and you'll lose your soul like the other ladies. I could never look at you again without blamin' myself for lettin' you become that redheaded bastard's slave."

Emily glanced nervously at Idaho, wondering if they should leave the parlor. Zenia was gripping Josh's sleeve, looking torn between his romantic declarations and her own sense of obligation. Her bosom trembled in the snug bodice of the yellow dress, and she was blinking rapidly.

"Honey, those other ladies got nothin' to lose, but you—you're special," Josh pleaded. "That voice of yours could make the hardest-hearted heathen *believe.* But not if you stay here." He turned toward Emily, imploring her with large, dark eyes. "Tell her I'm right, Miss Eliza. Tell her how Clancy'll ruin her and steal from her, just like he does from the others."

Emily took a deep breath, stunned by the young man's fiery eloquence. "She knows all that, Josh. I—I can't make her say yes."

"And I can't sit by and watch you young folks get swallowed up by that whorehouse," Idaho insisted. "Bad enough that Miss Eliza does *honest* work there. I've got some money laid by—"

"Oh, Idaho, you've already done too much," Zenia insisted. "What if Clancy—"

"Hear me out, child." The old man's eyes misted over, and in a voice that sounded world-weary and defeated, he continued. "Worked most of my life on a ranch where they paid me and my wife good money. They were like

133

family, and my Viry and I set by as much as we could so that when we got too old to work for them, we wouldn't be a burden. We were planning to get a little place of our own and. . . ."

Emily's mouth dropped open. She took Idaho's hand, appalled at how withery his skin felt and how weak his grip had become.

"I want you to have that money," he stated, "but only if you promise to *make* something of yourselves."

Josh's lips pursed in a frown. "But you might need it, sir. You've still got some years left."

Idaho waved him off. "Now that Viry's gone to her reward, that money's worthless to me. You think on it while I fetch my flour sack."

Watching him shuffle toward the kitchen, Emily's heart ached for her lifelong friend while it sang for Josh and Zenia. They were so young — a decent, comfortable living would be hard to come by, but she sensed their innate goodness and faith would carry them over the rough spots. Zenia was gazing at the gracefully-built man who pulled her into his arms, and his eyes held a longing that had been smoldering since the day she'd arrived. Emily sensed a kiss was coming, so she stood to excuse herself.

Someone else started pounding on the front door then, more forcefully than Josh had.

Emily smiled, hoping it was Matt. McClanahan would think of a solution that was fair to Miss Victoria yet would also keep Clancy at bay. And who could tell? Maybe the romance between Josh and Zenia would rub off, and Matt would admit that he loved her — words she longed to hear.

But when she opened the door, Clancy Donahue brushed her aside. "Came to fetch those niggers."

"I don't recall asking you in," Emily said brusquely.

"And I don't recall ever takin' orders from you," the bouncer snapped. "Now where are they?"

Emily stepped in front of him. "Zenia is *not* your

134

property, Clancy," she whispered tersely, "and this business of selling her to the highest—" Her words were pinched off by the Irishman's grip on her shoulders.

"I could've broken her in myself, you know." He looked down at her, his beard splitting in a derisive grin. "I'm tryin' to take you away from all this sordid business, little girl, but you keep remindin' me that I'm beneath you. I know damn well you're sneakin' around with McClanahan. And maybe he's exactly what you deserve."

She had to catch herself as Clancy shoved her out of his way. Emily followed him into the parlor, knowing how the bartender would react to the scene before them. Zenia was still in Josh's arms, and Idaho had just returned, clutching a cloth bag.

"What's in the sack, old man? You playin' Santy Claus?" Donahue demanded with a mocking grin. He snatched the bag, his sarcastic expression hardening when he saw its contents. "You plannin' to send these lovebirds on a honeymoon? The only place they're goin' is out to my wagon. Now get on out there."

Josh pulled Zenia closer, his eyes defiant.

"They're staying here until tomorrow," Emily stated firmly.

"The hell they are." Clancy pivoted, jabbing the air with his finger. "I've taken all I'm goin' to from McClanahan and Chatterly, and I *don't* intend to listen to *you.*"

"Fine. We'll let Silas order you out," she replied boldly. She stalked through the dining room, her steps clattering angrily across the hardwood floor.

"He's playin' poker at the Elks Club," the bartender jeered. "This is none of his business anyway."

Emily entered the study undaunted and pulled the pistol from the top desk drawer. If she could point a gun at McClanahan, she figured shooting holes in Donahue would be no problem, if it came to that.

She returned to the parlor with the pistol in plain

135

sight, cocking it. "I don't want trouble, Clancy. So leave. *Now.*"

Donahue backed away to position himself behind Zenia and Josh. "You could no more shoot me than—"

"I'd take her at her word, Donahue," a voice came from the kitchen. "Because if she misses, I won't."

They all stared at Matt McClanahan, who was approaching them with a revolver in his hand.

Clancy bared his teeth in a vicious grin as he headed toward the vestibule. "One of these days you won't get here in time, McClanahan," he sneered. Then he glared at Josh and Zenia. "And if you two turn up missin', I'll put a price on your heads."

Matt followed the bartender to the front door and shut it firmly behind him. Then he looked from Idaho to the couple huddling on the loveseat. "You'd better figure on returning to the Rose, at least until you've talked to Miss Victoria about it," he told them quietly. Then he looked at Emily. "And now I need to see you, young lady."

As he ushered her toward the study, Emily tried to clear the muddled emotions from her mind. She was relieved and grateful he was here, yet still angry and trembling from her confrontation with Clancy. She let Matt put her pistol back in the desk. "I—thanks for showing up when you did."

"Figured he'd pull something like this," McClanahan muttered. As he studied her, the glow in her amber eyes told him what he had to do. "I'm staying here tonight."

Emily grinned impishly.

"Sleeping in the vestibule," he added.

"Oh. Of course."

Matt chuckled, cupping her jaw. "I still want you from this afternoon, rosebud," he murmured, "but it'll have to wait. Zenia and Josh aren't really running off, are they?"

"I'm not sure," Emily mumbled. "It came as a total surprise when Idaho offered them his life savings. And now that Clancy knows about it, he'll make things worse for them."

McClanahan nodded. "He certainly won't forgive and forget, now that Zenia's made a liar of him."

Emily sighed, wishing she could hold the man who was keeping himself a few infuriating inches away from her. "Tomorrow's Friday. Miss Victoria usually shops first thing in the morning, to prepare for the weekend."

"And most of the girls will be sleeping then. We should be at the Rose bright and early."

"We?" She looked up into his handsome face, unable to read it.

"You bring Zenia, and then keep Donahue distracted while I slip in the back way. I'm guessing he won't give her much time before he goes after her, and I'll be ready for him."

Emily frowned. "Sounds like an ambush."

"Just a precaution." Matt grinned boyishly. "Lucky for us Zenia's room adjoins Gracie's."

"Who?"

"Grace Putnam—Princess Cherry Blossom," he explained. "She's been trying to get me up there for weeks, and now she'll have her way with me."

The sparkle in his clear blue eyes told Emily not to jump to any jealous conclusions. She ran a finger along the virile shadow of his jawline. "Why're you getting involved in this, McClanahan? I mean, besides the fact that you and the Princess are such, uh, good friends."

He brushed her lips with his and forced himself to let her go. "You'll have to trust me on that one, rosebud. Leave the front door unlocked. I'll be in after Silas is home and everyone's in bed."

Chapter Fourteen

Emily's head felt as thick as the fingers of autumn fog curling around her feet while she and Zenia walked toward the Golden Rose. The girl beside her was silent and apprehensive, which gave Emily a chance to plan how she'd sidetrack Clancy Donahue.

A familiar bay gelding stood at a hitching post on Fourth Street, so Emily sped up. "Come on, Zenia. Better not keep McClanahan waiting."

The girl clutched Emily's shawl closer, sighing as she walked faster.

"It'll work out, I promise," she said softly. "What're you going to tell Victoria?"

Zenia took several more steps before she answered. "I ain't sure. Prayed on it all night, but seein's how the Lord let me live to face it, I guess Miz Chatterly'll just hear whatever comes out."

"She'll probably be there. It's awfully early to do her shopping."

"Yeah."

The Rose stood proudly ahead of them, its ivory sides glistening with dew as the first rays of the sunrise lit the sky. Unlike its neighbors, the house was centered on a grassy lot, which gave the brothel an air of grandeur Emily wasn't sure it deserved. The ladies were expensively dressed and they catered to a wealthy clientele, yet it was the same business girls conducted in the dingy cribs along Poverty Gulch. Sordid, Clancy had called it, and for once Emily thought he was right.

The parlor was hushed and dim when they entered, and no one was behind the bar. Emily gave Zenia a quick hug. "Go on up to your room now. I'll tell Miss Victoria you're here."

The young girl nodded and hurried quietly up the stairway. The aromas of bacon and coffee drifted in from the kitchen, and the cook was humming, but otherwise the place was steeped in a rare, peaceful sleepiness. Emily went down the hall and knocked quietly on Miss Victoria's door.

"She's gone to the hairdresser's."

She turned to see Clancy balancing a wooden crate on one shoulder as he came up from the cellar. He looked shaggy and uncombed, like a bison that hadn't slept well.

"Did you bring Zenia?" he asked gruffly.

"She's as good as her word."

Donahue grunted. "What about LeFevre?"

"Josh went home. He'll show up when he's supposed to." She followed him toward the bar, and when he crouched behind it to pry the nails from the whiskey crate, Emily glanced down the long hallway. There was no sign of McClanahan.

What should she do? After threatening the bartender with a gun last night, she couldn't just stand here watching him. Emily emptied the ashtrays and brushed pastry crumbs from the tables with efficient hands, and then she crossed the parlor to pour the debris into the fireplace. McClanahan still wasn't at the back door.

After tidying the bathing suite, Emily was getting nervous. The ladies would be waking up soon, and if she were cleaning upstairs — as Clancy would expect her to be — she couldn't watch for Matt. She stood beside the bar, where she had a view of the door if she leaned back slightly. What she was about to do was no more a lie than pretending she was Eliza — and that role was surprisingly easy for her now — yet the words

139

dragged in her throat.

"I . . . I got a little carried away last night," she mumbled. "Ladies don't solve their problems by pointing a gun at people."

Clancy gave her a guarded glance from under the bar, where he was positioning new bottles of whiskey, but he didn't say anything.

Emily shifted her weight. "I guess you were only doing your job," she continued. "We wouldn't have much of a business if our girls just stayed long enough to latch on to a new wardrobe."

A hint of a gruff smile showed beneath his rust-colored beard. He studied her with pale green eyes that were as sly as a cat's. "You sayin' you're sorry?"

She refused to apologize, and had to clench her jaw not to tell him so. "I—I was too busy taking Zenia's side to understand yours," Emily replied quickly. "Things have happened awfully fast lately, and I can't seem to control my temper." *And you're not helping matters, McClanahan. Where ARE you?*

When Clancy looked into his crate again, she peeked down the hallway. At last! Matt was cautiously stepping inside the back door, questioning her with raised eyebrows. Emily flashed him a thumbs-up, and walked behind the bar. She let her skirts brush Clancy's backside, and pretended to be extremely interested in a set of decanters on the opposite end of the counter.

"Pretty early to be drinkin', little girl." The bartender placed the last bottle of whiskey on the shelf, eyeing her warily.

"Oh, I'm not! Just looking at these decanters. We— we have such pretty things here at the Rose." Emily swallowed. Could he see how her hands were shaking as she fingered the etched crystal?

Donahue straightened to his full height, hitching his trousers up. "You're either up to somethin', or you're tryin' to make amends, Emily. Which is it?"

When he stepped toward her, she forced her gaze to remain locked into his. "Well, I—I could've *shot* somebody. Papa would've been appalled at my behavior last night." As she widened her eyes at the barkeep, Emily caught a glimpse of Matt tiptoeing by, carrying his boots. He winked at her, and he was fighting a laugh.

Clancy leaned against the counter, letting his eyes linger on her bosom. "Your daddy raised you to be a lady, darlin'. And ladies shouldn't concern themselves with anythin' but marryin' a good man and bearin' his children. You thought any more about that?"

She felt the edge of the bar against her back, and her head was pounding. And there was McClanahan pausing on the stairs to watch her humiliate herself!

"A girl thinks about those things every day," Emily hedged. Clancy was getting closer, enjoying her agony, judging from the glitter in his eyes.

"Then you'd be smart to forget about McClanahan," he replied. "He comes on like a big hero, but he'll run like a rabbit when people start suspecting he's a fraud."

"Wh—what do you mean?"

Clancy rested his huge hands on her shoulders, his gaze roving over her face and neck. "I think he's the killer you're lookin' for. You made a big mistake hirin' him, darlin'—gave him too much access to your daddy's records and properties. If you want me to show him up for the crook he is, you just let me know."

Fiendish pleasure was glowing in the bouncer's eyes, and Emily tried to look away without being too obvious. McClanahan was gone. It was time to change the subject, without arousing Clancy's suspicions. "Would—would you explain something else?" she asked quickly.

He blinked, then continued kneading her shoulders. "Like what?"

Emily gave him her shyest smile, ducking out from under his arms. "Well, yesterday when Zenia came down the stairs, all the men looked at her like she was . . . special."

"Honey, she's a nigger," he said with a snort. "Even if she was ugly as sin, most men would pay extra because

141

they don't get her exotic kind of nectar on a regular basis. That's *not* the sort of thing ladies speculate about, Emily."

"I just wanted to know." She was facing the stairs now, wondering how to get up them without the bartender following her. "I mean, you claim you want to marry me, yet you look at Zenia as though you want to . . ." Too late Emily realized she may have put her colored friend into more danger. When Clancy pressed himself against her, a stiff ridge prodded at the small of her back.

"That's the way it is with a man, darlin'," he murmured against her ear. "Just thinkin' about a woman . . . what she'll do to him with her private parts, is all it takes to make him want her. And right now, I'm thinkin' about *you*, little girl."

Sickened, Emily pulled away. "Clancy, please—some of the ladies might see—"

"Why would they care? They all get their turn." He chuckled, reaching around her to squeeze her breasts. "Why, some of 'em might even want to help. This isn't a place where innocence can survive for very long, darlin'."

"Stop it! Let me go!" she demanded. She heard the sleeve of her uniform tear as she jerked out of his grasp.

Clancy laughed, a wicked chuckle that made her insides shrivel. "So you've kept it away from McClanahan—or maybe he's not man enough to take it. He never seems interested in the women here, who all but throw themselves at him. That's odd, Emily. Real odd, you know?"

Emily glared at him and backed out from behind the bar. Reeling with revulsion, she hurried down the hall and slammed the pantry door behind her. She couldn't stay here long—Clancy would either find her, or head upstairs to vent his passions on Zenia—but she had to have time to think, time to put a plan together before all her efforts to protect the young girl fell apart.

* * *

McClanahan knocked quietly on Grace Putnam's door. "You awake, Princess? Open up—it's Matt."

"Forget it. I'm busy," came the brusque reply.

McClanahan scowled; he hadn't thought about her having an overnight customer. "It's important. I need a favor, and I'm in a hurry."

Grace's laugh was humorless. "Do it yourself, then. I don't like rush jobs."

Chuckling, he gripped the doorknob. "Come on, sweetheart. I'll pay the other guy for the rest of his time. Or if he isn't ready to go yet—"

"That's not the problem. Come back in half an hour."

He didn't dare wait that long, and the last thing he wanted was to attract attention here in the hallway. Matt opened the door just wide enough to slip into her room.

Grace gasped, then glared at him. "Dammit, Mc-Clanahan, is nothing sacred?" With a pointed glance at his fly she added, "You don't look desperate to me."

"What in the hell are you. . . ." She was nude, sitting on the floor beside her bed, holding a bottle and a wet, red-brown rag. One of her legs was noticably darker than the other.

"So much for Cherry Blossom's Indian secrets," Grace muttered. "How do you think I keep myself from looking like those other palefaces?"

Matt set his boots down. He crouched beside her, shaking his head as he read the label on her bottle. "Mahogany stain? I suppose you dye your hair, too."

"So? We weren't all blessed with Little Yellow Hair's natural beauty, McClanahan."

Her tone was tough, but he realized he'd found another of Grace Putnam's vulnerable spots. Gently, Matt lifted her long raven hair so she could see to rub the stain on her other leg. "You're one of the best-looking women I know, Grace. I didn't mean to hurt your feelings—I enjoy a little mystique as much as the next

143

man."

"Right. That's why you keep me so busy I don't have time to see anyone else. So make yourself useful—do my backside." Without waiting for a reply, Grace shoved the bottle and rag into his hands and then twisted her hair into a coil, which she held against her head.

Her back curved gracefully down to a slender waist, and Matt realized he'd gotten himself into a hell of a spot. Grace's skin was soft and warm, and she relaxed as he began to stroke the liquid over her spine and shoulder blades. "Who usually does this for you?" he murmured.

"Darla. I give her a new tattoo now and then."

He chuckled, then sat flat on the floor with his legs on either side of her. As he rubbed the stain in slow, even strokes, Grace leaned forward and let go of her hair. Her bottom was long and rather flatter than he liked, but as she brushed her shapely legs against his he found himself overlooking that minor flaw. "I, uh, came up here for a different sort of a favor, Grace."

She sighed. "Why did I know you were going to say that?"

"It concerns Zenia Collins. Victoria asked me to watch out for her, because it seems Clancy misrepresented her age and experience."

"She ran out on Stokes, didn't she? I wondered why Donahue was nastier than usual last night." Grace turned to look at him, her dark eyes serious.

"She went home with Eliza. Then Clancy showed up—found her there with Josh—and his mood didn't improve any when Eliza ordered him to leave," Matt replied. "Pick up your hair, so I can do your neck."

"Zenia has no business being here. Though I suppose Clancy fed *her* a few lines too." She arched her back with a throaty giggle, pointing her elbows toward the ceiling as he daubed the stain behind her ears. "For a celibate, you've got damn fine hands, McClanahan."

"Who said I was celibate?"

"Aha. It's Eliza, isn't it?" Grace rose onto her knees and turned to face him, a sly smile shining in her eyes. "Do my arms now, and then my front."

"But you can reach—"

"If you're going to use my room, you'll have to follow my rules." Grace shook her hair over her shoulders with a low laugh, and extended one arm until her hand rested on his shoulder. "After all, what're friends for?"

Matt sucked in his breath. Her ebony hair and brown skin gave her a savage aura which appealed to his sense of adventure, and he had the feeling Grace did indeed know a few tricks that weren't in the average woman's repertoire. "If something happens next door, we'll hear it, won't we?" he asked in a strained voice.

"The walls are like paper, dear. Adds to the atmosphere when you hear springs creaking on both sides of you." She cast a seductive glance down the front of him and reached for his top button. "Maybe we shouldn't get stain on this nice shirt."

"I don't think you ought to—"

"Wait in Zenia's room, then. If Clancy comes up, I'm sure he'll be pleased to see *you* in there."

McClanahan turned his attention to the slender arm in front of him. It was firm without being muscled, and by the time he'd covered it with mahogany stain, Grace was ruffling the hair on his chest with her other hand. He held his breath—was that Zenia's door that just opened and shut? "Other arm now," he rasped.

Muffled voices came through the wall, and Grace was listening, too. "Can't tell who it is . . . could be Victoria checking on her," she murmured. Her eyes were a piercing ebony and her nostrils quivered. "Put this stuff down, McClanahan. You're driving me crazy."

Before he could protest, she rocked him backward and landed between his legs. Matt set the stain an arm's length away, then gently gripped her shoulders. "Gracie, I may have to leave very suddenly."

"Come on, McClanahan. I'd give up a day's pay to

145

spend just an hour making love to you," she whispered hoarsely. She placed feverish kisses on his mouth and eyelids before running the tip of her tongue inside his ear. "You want it, too. You're hard as a rock."

"Damn you—" She was writhing against him like an impassioned snake, her breasts warm and loose against his bare chest.

"I knew you wanted me, Matt," she said in a husky, triumphant voice. "You won't regret it—I've forgotten more about pleasing a man than Eliza will ever know."

Emily's face flashed before him and McClanahan came to his senses. Then he realized that the noise he heard wasn't Grace's knees bumping the floor—it was coming from the next room. "Let me up," he groaned.

"McClanahan, you—"

"Listen! Something just hit the wall in there."

When Grace rose up, he rolled onto his side and gave her a gentle shove. "Those footsteps are too heavy to be a woman's. Put a robe on—see if Victoria's back."

She scowled and swore at him, but she went to her door and took a scarlet satin wrapper off the peg. Matt pressed his ear to the wall and listened intently.

Nothing. Then he heard plaintive whimpers followed by a *smack* and a string of mumbled curses. The voice was low and threatening, unmistakably Donahue's. Something bumped against the other wall . . . had he propped a chair under the doorknob?

McClanahan pulled his boots on and shooed Grace into the hall ahead of him. "Hurry," he whispered. "I may need somebody to keep Zenia out of his reach."

He waited until she was downstairs, then took a running jump from across the hall. His feet landed squarely against Zenia's door, splintering it and shoving Clancy's barricade aside. The redheaded bartender was stripped to the waist, his hairy belly hanging low as he leaned over the bed. When Donahue whirled around, Matt saw that he'd tied the young girl's wrists to the spindles of the brass headboard. Zenia wasn't moving.

"You goddamn—" Donahue lunged toward him, but McClanahan sidestepped.

"I'd say *you're* the one who's damned," Matt snarled. "Couldn't take a warning. Had to go from bad to worse."

Clancy recovered his balance and came at him again. "You should keep your nose out of my business, McClanahan," he snapped. "I might just make you into mincemeat."

Dodging a flying fist, Matt ducked and grabbed the Irishman's knees. He had to fight dirty and well, because he was outsized by several inches and at least a hundred pounds. Donahue landed on the floor with a heavy thud, swearing violently, but he was quicker than he looked and Matt felt his foot being yanked out from under him.

"You little—"

A thick fist punched McClanahan in the stomach, but as he fell to the floor, he aimed the toe of his boot at Clancy's crotch.

The bouncer squealed like a wounded pig, then he caught McClanahan's arms in a death grip that nearly snapped the bones. "Give it up and I won't kill you—this time," Clancy grunted.

Matt put his legs together and kicked with both feet, landing them in the bouncer's fleshy thighs. "You don't stand a chance. Thompson's on his way over here."

"You expect me to believe that?"

Matt jerked away from him and rolled to his feet. From the corner of his eye, he saw frightened faces and robes in the doorway, but he couldn't spare them any attention. Donahue was lumbering toward him again, and he suddenly wished he'd brought his gun: his opponent was lifting a bullwhip from the post of Zenia's bed. In a room this small, he'd have to jump out the window to escape its rawhide lash.

Clancy laughed, then the air quivered with the force of the whip.

Matt ducked.

147

The lash whickered again and again as Donahue drove him toward the corner of the tiny room.

There was a commotion outside the door then a shrill voice hollered, "Dammit, get out of my way! Are you going to watch McClanahan get killed?"

"Emily, no!" Matt realized immediately that he'd called her the wrong name, but there was no time to cover his mistake. When the whip grazed his cheek, McClanahan bolted over Zenia's motionless body, hoping to get Donahue's timing off.

But the bartender had already been distracted. When Clancy turned to confront the intruder, Matt saw that Emily had whacked him with a fireplace poker. The blow barely fazed him, but it gave McClanahan the break he needed. He leaped, landing on the brute's back. "You touch one hair on her head and I'll—"

Donahue gasped and swore as the poker handle gouged his middle. He shook McClanahan off and turned, but Matt was ready for him. A roundhouse to his jaw snapped Clancy's head back, and as the bartender staggered, Matt landed one more solid punch. "That's for treating every woman you know like a whore," he muttered.

Footsteps were hurrying down the hall, and Victoria Chatterly bustled between the women in the doorway, followed by Barry Thompson. "Oh my God, I knew he'd—somebody see to Zenia!" She turned to McClanahan, grasping his arm. "Are you all right? Thank goodness you were here."

Matt was gasping for breath, but he managed a grin. "I don't guess he'll be bothering anybody for a while."

"No, he won't," the madame agreed. "Barry, lock him up until I know what to do with him. I simply *must* talk to Emily Bur—"

"I'll be seeing her this weekend. I have business at the ranch," McClanahan said quickly. He glanced at the worried, sleepy faces in the doorway and added,

"Why don't you ladies go on back to bed now? Give the marshal some room to maneuver."

They nodded and left, except for Grace, who was helping Emily untie the cords around Zenia's wrists. Miss Victoria walked to the bedside, gazing at the colored girl's inert form. "He didn't . . . kill her, did he?"

Emily held up a small bottle. "Laudanum. As tiny as she is, a small dose would pack quite a wallop."

The madame shook her head and looked back at Matt. "When did you say you're leaving for Elliott's ranch?"

"Tomorrow morning." Matt watched the marshal pour a pitcherful of water over Clancy's swelling face. Then he saw something fall to the floor as the bartender shook his head. He picked it up—a gold tooth. "Put this with his other stuff," he murmured to the lawman. "And while he's in jail, round up all his guns for me, will you?"

"You bet," Barry replied with a nod. "Get up, Donahue. I sure as hell can't *carry* you out of here."

When he saw that Victoria and Grace were sponging Zenia's forehead, Matt walked over to Emily and rested his arms on her shoulders. When he smiled, his cheek stung.

"He got you," Emily murmured as she gingerly touched his face.

"Just a chafe. It'll heal." Her eyes were liquid, limpid gold, and as he gazed down at her, Matt realized his heart was pumping faster now than it was when Clancy had cornered him. "You're a helluva fighter, honey— and in the nick of time, too," he whispered. "Why don't you go tell Silas I'll be leaving first thing tomorrow? It'll save me a trip."

Emily nodded, trying to mask her disappointment.

McClanahan chuckled and grabbed her up in a bearhug. "I owe you for this, rosebud, and for a whole lot more," he murmured against her ear. "Pack a bag. You're going with me."

Chapter Fifteen

Emily hiked up the hill to the Angel Claire so fast her legs ached, still agitated about the scene at the Golden Rose. Zenia was moaning and coming to when she left, and Clancy had scowled blackly at her as he preceded Marshal Thompson out the double doors. But she knew what was really making her short of breath: *Pack a bag. You're coming with me.*

She hadn't been to the ranch since she and Idaho came to Cripple a few weeks ago. Often, when she'd been out on Sundance, she'd been tempted to turn him toward Colorado Springs and just keep on riding until she reached the Flaming B. But she wasn't sure she could face Papa's spirit again until she'd caught his murderer. Maybe McClanahan sensed she *needed* to go home, and she hoped he had a plan to bring this whole ordeal to an end. Spotting Silas's tall, dark figure outside the ore house, Emily trotted toward him.

"Good Lord, what's happened?" Hughes glanced around the grounds of the Angel Claire and ushered her into the office. "The men aren't used to seeing Eliza dressed —"

"Clancy just got thrown in jail!"

The mine manager froze, staring at her. "Because of that colored girl?"

Emily nodded rapidly. "Matt figured Donahue couldn't leave her alone, so he was waiting in the room next to Zenia's. He — he tied her to the bedposts and knocked her out with laudanum. When I got upstairs, he was going at Matt with a whip, and—"

"Whoa . . . slow down, Emily." Silas held her by the shoulders, his expression grave. "Victoria won't want him around, after all that. I suppose McClanahan's filling in until she can hire another bouncer?"

"No, Bob'll handle things. Miss Victoria insisted that Emily should know about this, so Matt's going to the ranch," she said in a rapid jumble. "And I'm going with him."

Silas studied her closely. "Are you sure you want to? It won't be easy, and the hands are bound to speculate about you and Matt—"

"I know. But I need to see how things are going—talk to the foreman about roundup, and check the mail."

He nodded, raising an eyebrow. "I suppose Mc-Clanahan plans to follow another lead about the murder. He wouldn't make the trip just to appease Victoria."

Hearing the suspicious, knowing edge in the mine manager's voice, Emily frowned. "Don't *you* trust him either, Silas?"

"We've only known him a few weeks," he replied with a shrug. "Matt seems reliable enough, but he may just be another fortune hunter in a handsome disguise. Don't you let him talk you into anything, or sign any papers while you're there."

"Silas, I certainly know better than that!" she protested. "Anything official would have to be handled by Papa's attorney anyway."

Her father's partner removed his hat to smooth the white streak in his peppery hair. "All right, I'm jumping to unfair conclusions," he said gently. "But be careful, Emily. You're quite capable of taking care of yourself, but you might not be at your best when you set foot in a house full of memories again."

Emily nodded; she'd thought of that.

"Is Idaho going?"

"Not that I know of."

Doubts about McClanahan's intentions were written all over his face, but Silas was tactful enough not to voice them. "Catch your breath before you start home, and then relax in a hot bath. You've been burning the candle at both ends lately and I want to see you looking completely rested when we sit down to dinner." He gave her shoulder a quick squeeze, then frowned. "What happened to your sleeve?"

"Clancy tore it."

Silas scowled. "I'll see if I can be of assistance to Victoria while you and McClanahan are gone. If she asks my opinion, I'll tell her to let Donahue rot behind bars and hire someone dependable. That's what your father would've said at this point."

Emily nodded and watched him walk toward the mine buildings. She felt too jittery to rest, so she updated the ledgers, realizing that Silas had handled the Angel Claire's many duties quite well before she'd done his bookkeeping, and that he'd continue to do so after Eliza disappeared. But when would that be? She closed the book, rubbing her forehead. Her lack of sleep was catching up with her.

As she shut her eyes to refresh them, Emily had the eerie feeling she was being watched. She looked up to find Nigel Grath leering over the desk at her.

"Whatsa matter, Goldilocks? Like this place so much you're gonna play maid?" he asked in his reedy voice.

"Go home, Grath. Silas'll be coming around any minute to check—"

The blaster let out a giggle, and suddenly he was hauling her up out of her chair with a grip like two steel bands around her arms. "Hughes just left, Blondie. And I warned you about what I'd do if you told Mc-Clanahan—"

"I didn't! Silas already knew," she gasped as he clutched her tighter.

"Did he, now?" Grath laughed, sounding like a howling hyena. "Got wound up pretty tight when I saw Mc-Clanahan kissin' you, after that train nearly ran you

152

down. But that wasn't no tomboy he was humpin' in the cabin, 'cause I got a good look, sister. You were givin' it right back to him."

Emily felt the blood draining from her face. "I'm not your sister," she countered weakly. "You filthy—"

The wiry little man set her down hard on the edge of the desk. "And you're not too smart either—played right into my hands. But I know why you're in Cripple, you and McClanahan. You're spyin' on me, tryin' to catch me at what I done, but you can't prove nothin'."

"Let me go!"

"Why? I ain't held a pretty little Goldilocks like you for a long time." He was standing so close she could see a small scar beneath the center of his single eyebrow. " 'Fess up, Blondie. What's your real name?"

"Eliza," she spat. "Now let me go, or I'll—"

"Holy mother of Christ! Why didn't I see it before?" Nigel looked at the wall beside them for a moment, and then focused his wild little eyes on her. "That's your dear departed ma—Claire—in that picture, ain't it? And E. R. Burnham was your old man!"

"You crazy son of a—"

"Crazy? Hell, *anybody* could see the likeness—which is why you always cram that hat down over your eyes! Jesus, this is *perfect!*" His cackle trailed off and he shook her gleefully. "You're checkin' us out, ain'tcha? Some of the boys been wonderin' when you'll give up the ghost, so wait'll they find out that Miss Britches is really Burnham's grievin' little girl! And that she's bein' held for ransom!"

Emily was ready to protest, but Grath shoved her down against the desktop and reached into his boot. The wicked gleam of his knife only inches in front of her face convinced her to keep quiet.

"Yeah, I'll just put you in a safe place till you tell Hughes to gimme a bag of cash," her captor crowed. "And if you don't, I figure Hughes'll cough up anyway, as a deposit against seein' the Angel Claire blown sky-high! Them blastin' holes you seen below the train

153

tracks was only a decoy, Blondie. I done my *real* work here—been plannin' a takeover—and I ain't givin' up till I get my fair share of the profits."

His threats about blasting the mine and then claiming the profits didn't make a lot of sense, but Grath's logic was the least of Emily's concerns. When she tried to gasp that Silas and Matt would find her themselves before they paid off a kidnapper, her words were cut off by a hand around her throat.

"You ain't gonna scream, are ya? That'd be real stupid, sister," Nigel said in a menacing voice. His gaze raked over her flattened body, and a sickening shine lit his little eyes. "Or maybe you're thinkin' 'bout how Mc-Clanahan put it to you when you was layin' on that table in the cabin, just like you are now. You screamed then, didn'tcha? Pantin' for it. . . ."

Emily clenched her eyes shut when a stealthy hand slid up under her skirt. Every muscle in her body cried out to strike or kick at him, but he was tickling her neck with the tip of the knife blade. Where was Silas? Surely someone was passing by outside and could see she was being held hostage by a lunatic!

Nigel suddenly straightened himself and pulled her up with him. "Too many people around here. We'll go where it's dark and safe—and if you don't want to bloody up this office, you'll keep your mouth shut. Got it?"

She nodded frantically, her heart pounding.

"The men're down the main shafts now. But I know one that's real private." He shoved her toward the door, chuckling when she stumbled. "Long as you don't move 'cept when I tell you to, you and me'll get along fine. Real fine, sister."

Powerless to do anything else, Emily struggled to keep up with Nigel's quick steps. He was clutching her against his side, still holding his knife to her while they climbed the rocky hillside. They ducked between the Angel Claire's buildings and followed the shadows to a shaft that was no longer in use.

Where *was* everyone? Surely someone inside the ore house had spotted them—yet with the noise from the hoists in the shaft house, and the steam and clatter of a trainload of ore leaving the mine, Emily realized that Grath could stab her right then and there and no one would notice. Her heart sank when they got to the weathered shed that shielded the abandoned mine shaft. From this angle, no one could possibly see them.

"Ever been down in your daddy's mine?" Nigel asked as he pulled on a long rope above them.

"Only once," she mumbled. She winced at the shrill racket the squealing pulleys made as he brought a man-size bucket up to ground level.

"No place for little girls who're 'fraid of the dark, is it?" He crushed her to his side, baring his yellowed teeth in a grin. "Get in, Goldilocks. I seen how you handled your horse when that train was comin' at you, so don't turn sissy on me."

With a futile glance backward, Emily lifted her skirt so she could swing her leg over the top of the makeshift elevator car.

Nigel gave her an impatient shove. "Move that ass! You think I'm gonna take all day with this?"

He swung into the bucket beside her and began lowering them with quick hand-over-hand tugs on the ropes. Darkness swallowed them in one sudden gulp. The air was dank and heavy, colder as they plummeted along the passageway. Emily felt for her shawl and realized it must've slipped off. Or had she left it in the office? She was too scared to remember.

The wiry man beside her shuttled them swiftly along the ropes with wide arcs of his hands. He'd worked a full shift and he smelled like it; down among the drills and lights of a busy shaft, the temperature usually topped one hundred degrees, but Emily was shuddering with cold and apprehension. The thought of his monkeylike body rutting against hers was enough to make her sick to her stomach.

The bucket thudded to the ground. Emily fought to

155

keep her balance, and then the air rang with stillness. It was so dark she couldn't see Nigel, or anything else. She heard him breathing — and smelled him, of course — but the silent suspense was driving her crazy. "Aren't you going to light a lantern?" she asked hoarsely.

Her words echoed in the shaft, along with Grath's shrill laughter. "This hole's like home to me, sister. No sense lettin' you see the rat tails. Let's get out of this thing — I ain't much on doin' it standin' up."

Rat tails . . . Emily stifled a whimper and tried to control her runaway fears. What would Matt do in a tight spot like this? What had Papa taught her that could possibly be of help right now?

As Nigel clambered out of the bucket, she took a deep breath, hoping the right answers came to her in time. She stiffened as she felt herself being lifted out so effortlessly by a man hardly an inch taller than she was. "Wh-why are you doing this?" she asked in the strongest voice she could find. "Do you hate me so much, when you don't even know me?"

"Hell, I hate everybody," he replied cheerfully. "It don't do much good to hate suckers poor as me, but men like Hughes and your daddy — *they* can make it worth my while."

Grath had just handed her the key she needed, and Emily could hear Papa's voice whispering, *In order to outsmart somebody, you have to think the way he does.* "So it's the ransom money you're after, rather than me?"

"I ain't picky. I'll take it all."

He pulled her against his hard, skinny body, and Emily was thankful she couldn't see Grath's evil face. When his stubble scraped her cheeks as he sought her lips, she pushed against his chest. "Please! I — I could see that you got however much you wanted, if you leave me alone."

"Who'd care? You sure ain't no virgin," he said with a cruel laugh.

"Hughes cares, and so does McClanahan — he's got

156

money, too," she pleaded. "If I told him you didn't mistreat me, you could collect from *him,* as well."

Grath grunted. "How much you figure you're worth to him—assumin' I don't do nothin'?"

"How much do you want?" she asked boldly.

The wiry man walked her backward until she was against a damp dirt wall, and for a moment there was only the sound of his breathing. "I ain't buyin' it. Once I collect from Hughes, McClanahan'll hold out—"

"He doesn't have to know!" Emily insisted. "You can set your price with Silas—he's a millionaire in his own right—and wrangle a wad from McClanahan, and make enough that you'll never have to work another day in your life. By the time they figure out how you double-dipped, you could be anywhere you want to be! Free and clear!"

Nigel shifted his weight against her. "Sounds too easy. Must be a catch."

"Everything's easy for people with money and power," she said slyly. "Easy for those men to cough up, and the easiest money you'll ever make in your life. Think about it, Grath."

He was still for a moment, but then his laugh came out like a whine. "Ain't never had me a rich bitch. And the way you was takin' it from McClanahan, it might be worth a little less cash to have my way with you, Goldilocks."

The bottom fell out of Emily's stomach. Grath began pinching her breasts and rubbing against her with the ardor of an excited dog. Had he seen through her scheme? Or did he doubt Silas and Matt's willingness to cooperate? She tried pushing him away but he didn't seem to notice—he was tearing at her uniform, and then he fumbled under her pantaloons. "Stop it!" she gasped. "I inherited everything Elliott Burnham owned, and I'll give you whatever you want, if you'll take your hands off me."

Grath pulled away slightly. "Along with the money, I gotta have your guarantee of silence—plus the cash from McClanahan and Hughes. And you cain't never breath a word about this, to the law or nobody else, or I'll kill you."

If she agreed to those terms, he could blackmail her for the rest of her life. *But he won't live that long,* she reasoned. *He's admitted to sabotaging the mine, and all but confessed to killing Papa . . . and Matt and Silas probably realize I'm missing by now. They must be on their way . . .* "All right," Emily murmured. "Get me out of here and I'll—"

"Are you *crazy?*"

Crazy . . . crazy . . . crazy came the echo.

Grath shoved her back against the rough shaft wall. "You're my ace, and you're stayin' in the hole till I get a couple notes sent. Hope Loverboy and Hughes are as anxious to see you again as you say, or it'll get mighty damn cold down here. Now gimme your underwear."

"*What?*"

"Your skivvies," he insisted. "They'll need proof I got you, and that purty perfume'll have 'em scramblin' to the bank, thinkin' how your ass is exposed."

Emily hesitated, her throat tight with humiliation.

"Do I hafta take 'em off you myself?" Nigel jeered. "Let me have 'em—a stockin' for Hughes and the pantaloons for Studs McClanahan."

Holding her breath so he wouldn't hear her whimper, she removed the garments and held them out. Grath snatched them in the darkness, and then she heard him climbing into the metal bucket. "Please— can't you leave me a light?"

"Ain't got one, Goldilocks. I'll tell 'em you've got no food, neither—maybe they'll pay up first thing, insteada wastin' time tryin' to find you themselves." There was a noisy creaking of pulleys. "And don't forget," Grath added, "the day I fetch you outta here, you're gonna hand over your share of the money. And if I don't get it, *you'll* have no use for it either."

When the elevator's squeals faded, there was only the thick, damp blackness. Emily put her shoes back on and buttoned her uniform, wondering if she'd made the right deal. She'd appealed to Grath's deep-seated greed and saved herself from rape, but what would she suffer while she waited for someone to find her? She hadn't had the stomach for breakfast, what with Clancy to face, and it was way past time for dinner. She was cold, and the sound of water dripping somewhere back in the cavern didn't help. The darkness was so intense she had to touch her nose to know her hand was in front of her face. If she'd given him what he was after, maybe she'd be on her way up the tunnel. . . .

"Don't be ridiculous," she muttered.

. . . *uss* . . . *uss* . . . *uss* . . . echoed around her like the flutter of bats' wings.

Talking was a bad idea, so she admitted to herself that Grath probably would've stranded her down here even if she had given in to him. She was, after all, his ace in the hole. Emily winced at his words, and felt her way down the gritty wall until she was sitting on the damp dirt floor. To pass the time and stay warmer, she slowly unbraided her hair and combed her fingers through it.

Rat tails. Emily held her breath, listening. Was that the grinding of her own teeth, or were there rodents scratching in this abandoned pit? Too bad she hadn't paid closer attention to the miners' talk these past weeks; perhaps she would've learned how to get out of a mine shaft without any help.

Had she been here hours now, or only minutes? Her watch was useless in the inky blackness, its ticking a reminder of how deadly quiet it was at the bottom of a hole. Surely they were looking for her—Silas and Idaho had been expecting her long before this.

Her muscles were cramped from hugging her knees, so Emily stood and reached tentatively above her. If she could find the right rope, maybe her weight would be enough to bring the bucket back down here. She'd exhaust herself jumping up to grab for it over and over, but it was better than doing nothing. Even just sitting in the bucket would be more comforting than being surrounded by borderless black oblivion . . . but two or three horrifying steps away from the wall sent those thoughts flying from her mind. She could fall over something and hit her head . . . she might stumble into another pit and *never* be rescued . . . rat tails. . . .

Emotionally drained, Emily found the rough wall again and sat down. She wanted to sleep, but she was afraid to. She was desperately thirsty, but she wouldn't drink the water she heard dripping even if she had the guts to go groping for it. Shivering, she pulled her knees up against her body, wondering if Papa and Viry were this cold and lonely in their graves at the ranch. Emily waited . . . for what, she wasn't sure.

Rat tails.

Chapter Sixteen

Was she half asleep, or half crazy? Emily held her breath as the little squeaks got louder and louder, echoing around her in the dank, still air. Rat tails! She squeezed her eyes shut despite the darkness, tucking her skirts tightly beneath her legs. "Go away!" she whimpered. "Leave me alone, dammit!"

"Emily, are you down there? Can you hear me, honey?"

"McClanahan? Matt, hurry!" She looked up to see a pale light bobbing down the shaft, and then she stood so quickly her legs nearly collapsed beneath her. As the bucket landed with a loud thump and McClanahan scrambled toward her, Emily began to sob hysterically.

He set the lantern down and clutched her, his desperation replaced by an overwhelming urge to kiss away her fears. But Emily needed release; she was small and cold and shaking in his arms, and as her wails filled the cavern he stroked her loose hair and murmured reassuring nothings against her temple. When she was down to hitches and sniffles, he studied her tear-streaked face. "Honey, did he hurt you? If Grath so much as touched you, I'll—"

"N-no, nothing like that." Emily wiped her cheeks with her sleeve. "I told him you and Silas would pay more if he didn't do anything. Lord, I thought you'd never get here!"

Matt removed his jacket and wrapped it around her

161

shoulders. "Bad enough the bastard didn't leave you a blanket," he said angrily. "But to take your underwear's about the lowest —"

"H-how much did he ask for?"

Smiling patiently, he stroked the damp hair away from her face. "I came to the mine to tell Silas that Victoria might appreciate his help for a few days. Grath was just leaving, and there were ruffles peeking out of his dinner pail. That's how I knew something was wrong."

Emily sneezed loudly. "So he won't be demanding any money?"

"Nope. When he refused to tell us where you were, Silas escorted him to jail while I kept looking for you. He can't hurt you anymore, rosebud."

McClanahan's endearment was suddenly sweeter, after endless hours of wondering if she'd ever hear it again. She wrapped her arms tightly around his neck. "He knows who I am, Matt. If he shoots off his mouth —"

"Shhh . . . we'll get you home now, and let Silas and the marshal worry about that. You've had a helluva day, Emily." He kissed her softly, tasting salt as his lips wandered to her damp eyelids, smiling as her mouth sought his. The same hellcat who'd attacked Donahue with a poker to save his life was now clinging like a kitten, and he suddenly realized that he loved her. He helped her gently into the bucket, hesitant to say anything about his feelings just yet.

As they rose through the shaft with the lantern's light throwing shadows around them, Emily pulled Matt's coat tighter around her shoulders. It smelled like him — a piney, leathery pungence so different from Nigel or Clancy. "What time is it?" she asked.

"Nearly eight. It took us awhile to quiz Grath about where he'd stashed you. Your shawl was in the office, but . . ." In the flickering light, Matt saw how she was nipping nervously at her lip, so he stopped hauling on the rope. "What's wrong, honey?"

Emily looked away. "I feel so stupid. Only down there ten hours and I thought it was *days*," she mumbled. "Please—don't tell Silas I was blubbering like a fool."

"Sweetheart, even experienced miners go crazy in total darkness. During cave-ins, when they don't know how long—"

"But he'll think I'm not strong enough to handle Papa's estate, or—"

With a final heave on the ropes, Matt pulled them onto the shaft's platform and the bucket thumped to a halt. "Nobody will ever doubt your strength, Emily," he whispered as he massaged her shoulders. "You'll feel better after we get you home to dry clothes and a hot meal. All right?"

She nodded meekly. And as Arapaho carried them slowly through the twilit town, she let McClanahan cradle her sideways in his lap. Not used to being babied, Emily relaxed against his solid chest and savored each tender nuzzling along her forehead and brow. It *had* been a hell of a day, and with Grath behind bars, she could only wonder . . . would she lose Matt now that Papa's killer was caught? Once she paid him for his time and help, she had no hold on him.

McClanahan escorted her into the house, where Idaho was waiting with a worried scowl. The soup he was simmering filled the downstairs with the tempting aroma of beef broth and vegetables, but Emily insisted on a hot bath first. She scrubbed her skin and scalp until she smarted all over, removing the real and imagined filth of the mine. Then she put on a long flannelette gown and a robe, and went downstairs to dry her hair in front of the oven.

Matt took the brush from her hands, his strokes firm yet tender as he lifted and shaped her long blond mane around her shoulders. He inhaled its clean sweetness and kissed the nape of her neck. "Will you be up to leaving tomorrow, or should we wait?"

"We'll go," she whispered. She longed to kiss him,

163

but Idaho was shooing them to the table for soup and slices of fresh, hot bread.

"Eat some dinner now, Miss Emily," the old black man teased. "And we'll keep Mr. Matt busy with a *big* bowl, so he won't get caught making over you when Silas comes home."

The three of them talked quietly about the day's events as they ate, until the mine manager strode into the dining room, studying Emily as he approached the table. "Are you sure Grath didn't hurt you? He didn't. . . ."

She shook her head, blinking back tears when she saw the deep concern etched on Silas's face.

"I'd never forgive myself if he'd laid a hand on you," the steely-haired man continued in a hushed voice. "Damn bastard weaseled out of answering all my—"

"He knows who I am, Silas. And he all but confessed to killing Papa," Emily said quietly.

Silas sat down hard on his chair. "Really? Why do you think—"

"He was too interested in cashing in with you and Matt to say so, but he knows too much not to have shot him." Emily spooned up the last of her soup, feeling a luxurious sense of fullness and sleep stealing over her.

The mine manager looked cautiously at McClanahan, and then back to her. "Well, he can't tell anyone else about you while he's locked away. More rumors are floating around now, about how he's sabotaged the Angel Claire. If the men think you've been spying on them, we'll have a helluva time getting them to come to work, much less search for Grath's explosives. The ranch is the best place for both of you, at least for a few days."

"My thoughts exactly," Matt said with a careful smile. He squeezed Emily's slender hand under the table, hoping she'd understand why he wanted to reveal the feelings in his heart before she figured out the truth about the two men they'd put in jail today.

* * *

"What took you so long? I thought you'd stood me up," Emily teased the next morning.

Matt smiled as he watched her tighten Sundance's saddle girth. In the fragile light that filtered through the livery stable window, she looked rested and playful. "I figured you'd sleep in, after the day you had yesterday."

"I'll do my sleeping at the ranch, where the air's clear and there's peace and quiet." She swung into the saddle, grinning down at him. "Then again, maybe sleep'll be the furthest thing from my mind."

As he mounted Arapaho, McClanahan felt a familiar tightening in his stomach. Even in overalls and a shirt, with a broad-brimmed hat similar to his own, she was every inch an Emily Rose. Being alone with her at the Flaming B was a dream come true—the perfect time to tell her how much he loved her. "You sure you wouldn't rather take a wagon? Idaho was hinting that he'd like a few things from the ranch's root cellar."

"It won't be much longer before he can go to the cellar anytime he wants." She smiled, refusing to remind herself that these next few days might be her last with McClanahan. "Besides, it's a perfect day to be in the saddle."

Seeing the light in her tawny eyes, Matt realized that Emily loved the freedom of the open range as much as he did. They rode south to Victor and turned onto the Gold Camp Road that led to Colorado Springs before they slowed their pace. Trees and hills were dressed in their fall finery, and a hint of winter bit the brisk air. Traveling at an easy canter, they exchanged smiles often as the horses carried them along the well-worn trail. Was it happiness and love making her so radiant today, or was he merely seeing what he hoped to see?

They passed beside pastures where cattle grazed, on the vast Love Ranch, and then continued through the tiny town of Clyde. When they came to Beaver Creek, they dismounted to let the horses drink. Matt

165

stretched, and then draped his arm around her shoulders. "Do you have any plans for while you're home?"

"Besides pestering you?" she replied with an arched brow. "I need to talk to Richard, the ranch foreman, and read the mail—which won't be much fun, since the letters from a distance are still addressed to Papa."

Noting the slight catch in her voice, McClanahan stroked her back. "Emily, I'll need to check with the sheriff about something pertaining to the murder while we're there. You might not want to go with me."

She looked up at him with questioning eyes.

He sighed. "I have to get the bullets that were in your father's body, so we can identify the gun that shot him. If there was any other way—"

"I understand. You have to have evidence," she murmured as she gazed toward the horizon. "Maybe I'll visit with Richard then. Catch up on what's been happening."

Matt nodded and placed his hands on her shoulders as they looked out over the lush green grassland. "What does Richard know about your papa's murder, honey?"

"Everything. He heard the shots—came to the house right after you left. It was a Saturday night, so all the hands were in town," Emily explained. "The men were shocked when they came home, because Papa always took a personal interest in them. They were very protective during the investigation—swore they'd shoot any suspicious character who set foot on the ranch. When I left to search Cripple Creek, they decided to act as though the rumors about me still being in mourning were true, figuring the gunslinger might try to bilk me out of my inheritance. I—I couldn't ask for more loyal employees."

She was doing her damndest to sound strong, and because McClanahan knew the agonizing emptiness she was feeling, he admired her more than any woman he'd ever met. He wrapped his arms around her and leaned her back against himself. "So how'd Donahue become involved?"

Emily rolled her eyes. "I wish he never *had*, but he dug Papa and Viry's graves, and spent weeks in the mountains with the sheriff, tracking the killer. When I decided to go to Cripple, it looked like a good time to get Clancy away from the Flaming B, too. He claimed he should've been foreman instead of Richard Crabtree, and Richard and I thought the promotion to the Golden Rose would settle his resentment. Boy, were *we* wrong."

"But the idea wasn't yours alone," Matt reminded her with a hug, "so neither is the blame. And Donahue's locked away now, and we've got several days together, so let's just forget him — shall we?"

The tenderness in his voice touched Emily's heart and she turned to meet his blue-eyed gaze, wishing his romantic notions were all she had to think about. "We'll still have to be careful," she warned him. "Richard and the men will be watching you, Matt. They'll be suspicious of an outsider who's suddenly in on our plot."

"You must inspire a great deal of loyalty, Miss Burnham."

Emily smiled up at him. "It was in Richard's best interest to keep my whereabouts a secret — I promised him a new house as payment for his help . . . and with Grath in jail, it won't be long now before he can build it. We should order the lumber while we're here, and we should be prepared for the hands to start asking questions, too. They'll want to know how things have gone in Cripple. And they'll probably ask you point-blank about your involvement with the investigation — and me."

Matt chuckled. "It's incredible that your men know the truth, yet they're keeping so quiet."

"Why do you sound so sure of that?" She turned, gazing up at him from under her hat.

Emily's trusting expression almost made him spill a few secrets of his own, but they'd have plenty of time for the whole truth this week, after he revealed his feelings and intentions. "Let's just say Crabtree's story was

167

as closely woven as yours," he replied with a careful grin. "The last time I was in Colorado Springs I visited the Flaming B—pretended to be buying cattle. When I wanted to discuss the deal with you personally, Richard doubted you'd ever be able to conduct business again. Got downright misty-eyed about it."

"You've *met* my foreman, and you didn't tell me?" Emily demanded as she turned to face him.

He caught her playfully by the shoulders, pleased to see her usual spunk had returned. "It's part of my job to keep abreast of what's going on."

"And you didn't let on about who you were, or that you were working for me?" She stared up at him, not sure whether to be pleased or enraged by McClanahan's devious tactics.

"When we get there, we'll explain that I was testing to see how tight his mouth was. Helluva nice guy, from what I can tell." McClanahan hugged her, vowing to share his love and his dreams—and the whole truth—as he let his hands wander to the tempting swell in the back of her overalls. "Shall we ride? The sooner we check in with Crabtree, the sooner we'll have the evening to ourselves."

Emily held herself away from his kiss. "What *else* should I know about? It's not fair for you to be privy to my private life without telling me—"

He tilted her head back to claim her mouth with his, a move he'd been wanting to make for days. "All in due time, Emily. Let your hair down . . . it looks glorious when it catches the sunlight." Lifting her hat, he watched the golden waves uncoil and tumble over her shoulders.

She realized Matt had suavely avoided her questions again, but she couldn't be angry with him. He wove his fingers through her hair, his blue eyes ablaze as he leaned down for a kiss that held the promise of shimmering days and blissful nights to come. "Let's go," she breathed. "We have better than an hour's ride yet."

"Maybe I can't wait that long," he replied with a teasing smile. "Maybe I'll take you right here in the grass."

Laughing, Emily ran for Sundance. She felt as light and free as a child—not the least bit guilty about leaving him to stare after her, because she knew it would only increase his desire.

Matt mounted and caught up with her, barely aware of the tricky spots in the trail or the rolling foothills around them. All he could see was Emily, how her body moved at one with Sundance, how her hair floated in golden splendor behind her . . . how her face shone brighter as they approached Colorado Springs. They cut north of town, and when they stopped on a ridge for their first glimpse of the boundless Burnham ranch, Matt recognized the fierce love and joy in Emily's eyes. He was feeling the same way as he looked at her.

Chapter Seventeen

As they passed through the gateway of the Flaming B, greeting the cowboy on guard, the main house came into view. It was a majestic structure of dark, rough-cut timbers reminiscent of a fine old lodge, built to accommodate a large family and withstand the bitter winters of the open range. A monument both to Elliott Burnham's financial genius and to his love of the land, it exuded a masculine strength while extending a homey welcome to them. McClanahan saw Emily's mouth tighten as they approached the veranda, and their gait had slowed considerably. "Why don't I tend to the horses and talk to Crabtree?" he suggested gently. "It'll give you some time alone — unless you don't want to be."

Emily glanced at Papa's favorite wicker porch chair, where he'd taken two bullets instead of the nightcap Viry had been bringing him, and then she looked at Matt. "That's a good idea. I'll see you in a little while."

"Take your time, rosebud." McClanahan watched her swing gracefully down from her palomino, and he took her reins before pointing Arapaho toward the corrals.

"Matt?"

He turned, smiling kindly at the girl who looked so fragile and small on the porch.

"Thanks for bringing me along. I feel better already."

"My pleasure, Miss Burnham." With a wink and a tip of his hat, McClanahan started toward the stable.

Emily paused with her hand on the doorknob, then stepped into the parlor. Everything looked the same as she'd left it. The comfortable old room was hushed — too quiet, she realized, because the Tiffany mantel clock had stopped. She turned its key with a sense of reverence . . . Papa had insisted the works were too delicate for a child's impatient hands, and the weekly winding had remained his special duty until he died.

Mama smiled down at her from above the stone fireplace, wearing the wedding dress that Papa'd stored away for *her* to marry in someday. Emily smiled. Why did Matt come to mind now, when for all these years the dress hadn't evoked any particular image or sentiment?

Letting her fingers trail across the green velvet loveseat, Emily continued through the dining room and kitchen. She could still see Viry peeling potatoes by the sink, or placing clean china dishes along the plate rail of the walnut hutch. These rooms seemed to glow with a tenderness she didn't feel in Silas's house, even though they'd been furnished in the same colors by the same man.

Saving Papa's study for last, Emily climbed the stairs. She hadn't realized how worn the carpet runner looked, or how much she'd missed this familiar creaking beneath her feet. From the landing, she'd had her last look at Papa while he was barely alive, and her first look at Matt McClanahan. So much had happened since that night, she could hardly comprehend it all.

Papa's room felt chilly — but then, he'd preferred the northernmost bedroom for that reason. The cherry rocking chair and bedposts gleamed in the afternoon light; the comforter and dresser scarves were threadbare in spots, but he'd kept them because Mama chose them when he brought her to this house as a bride. When she opened the massive armoire, Papa's suits and shirts waited in a neat row. Back in the shadows, draped with a sheet and tangy cedar sachets to keep the moths away, hung Mama's elegant ivory wedding gown. Emily ran her fingers over the intricate beadwork on its bodice, unable to keep a smile from her face. *Someday soon,* she thought.

She passed a room with a vanity and a porcelain tub, then a water closet they'd added a few years ago, at her insistence. Then came the largest bedroom, its pale pink walls and white furnishings so inviting . . . yet childish, somehow. Had she outgrown the four-poster bed with its ruffled canopy and counterpane these past few weeks? Her dolls and trinkets lined the shelves; well-worn books nearly ran off the end of her mantel, but these things could easily have belonged to someone else. Feeling strangely detached, Emily peered into the two guest bedrooms and went downstairs. No need to invade the third-floor dormer room Idaho and Viry had shared—not when the study seemed to be beckoning her to its door.

Emily entered Papa's sanctum slowly, not sure what she was apprehensive about. If there *were* such things as ghosts, Papa's would never intentionally scare her, and yet she was hesitant to touch the Indian pottery and the chunks of pyrite, pink gypsum, and shiny black agate he'd collected, or the books she'd read as she sat in his chair on a rainy day. She straightened a painting on the wall—a Charles Craig buffalo hunt, Papa's favorite picture. Richard had stacked the mail on one corner of his massive desk. Shuffling through the pile, she saw Victoria Chatterly's red wax seal on one envelope, and other more official-looking pieces she wasn't ready to open yet.

For several minutes she gazed at Papa's armchair. The cushion was crushed, as though he were sitting in it, and its odor and the little burn holes on the arms attested to the hundreds of cigars he'd smoked over the years. It had always been Emily's favorite chair when Papa was away on business—a comfort during the lonely months since his death. Yet now . . . maybe she didn't really feel like sitting down after all. She turned, her eyes smarting as she studied the familiar titles in his bookcase.

"Dammit, it's the only chair I ever liked," she muttered, and with two quick steps she was rushing into its arms. She stroked the mulberry velvet, blotting her tears against the wing that always cradled her head when she was reading. "Papa . . . Papa, I came to be near you for a while," she whispered. "Are you still here? Did we catch the right man?"

There was only stillness as Emily held her breath, waiting. Then, as she rested her head and inhaled the chair's smoky aroma, its arms seemed to wrap around her as they had when she'd been a lonely little girl waiting for him to come home. She smiled, and for a few precious moments her heart soared up to be with Papa's.

As far as Matt could see in any direction, the range looked fresh and green — not overgrazed, as some ranches did this late in the season. The buildings were in good repair and recently painted, which meant Crabtree had kept the men busy between the spring and fall cattle work. He led the horses into a large corner stall in the stable, and was reaching for a bale of hay when he heard a rustling up in the loft.

"How's it going, McClanahan? Saw you ride in."

Matt smiled up at the stocky, curly-haired man who was descending the ladder. "So far so good."

"Make up your mind about those cattle?"

McClanahan held Richard Crabtree's gaze as long as he could before they both began to chuckle about their little deception. "Well, I'm back, aren't I?"

The foreman stepped into the stall beside him, slapping Sundance's rump with a smile that sent slender tunnels down his weathered cheeks. Crabtree was rather short, with a face that exuded honesty and a genuine pride in managing the Flaming B Ranch as efficiently as he did when E. R. Burnham was alive. "How's Emily?"

"Considering what she's been through the past couple days, she's extremely chipper. Thought I'd give her a little time to look the house over."

Richard nodded. "She's one of a kind. A fine little lady." He lifted the palomino's saddle and set it in the corner with a grunt. "How goes the manhunt?"

"I've got him locked up," Matt replied as he removed Arapaho's damp blanket. "Just a matter of gathering the final proof."

Crabtree grinned, looking cautiously optimistic.

"Anybody we know? Or is it some renegade miner with a grudge against Elliott?"

For a moment McClanahan was tempted to reveal the irony of those questions, but he decided Emily should have the priviledge of discovering the truth for herself, rather than hearing the hands talk about it. "All in good time, Richard. Till I get a bullet or a confession — or both — I can't leave anything to chance." He smiled apologetically, but he could tell the foreman wasn't satisfied with his reply.

"Have you told Emily how you came to be involved in this whole business?"

McClanahan looked directly into Richard's hazel eyes. "No — but not because she hasn't *asked* a dozen times."

"Feisty little thing, isn't she?" he said with a chuckle.

Matt smiled slowly, and decided Crabtree could be trusted with a confidence of a more personal nature. "I'm going to ask her to marry me when this investigation's wrapped up. Till I do, though, I'd appreciate you holding your tongue."

Richard raised his bushy eyebrows. "Don't keep her in the dark too long, McClanahan. She might backfire on you."

"True. Emily's got a mind as quick as wildfire and a temper to go with it." He forced his thoughts away from her soft golden hair and delightful smile, clapping the foreman's shoulder as they walked toward the sunlit door. "Come visit with her, if you've got a minute. After all that's happened in Cripple Creek, she'll be glad to see a friendly face."

"She and Idaho don't get along with Hughes?"

"Oh, that's worked out — I think Silas is more attached to her than he'd ever admit," he replied with a grin. "But Donahue's caused some problems at the Golden Rose, and then yesterday one of the miners left her down in an abandoned shaft after he figured out who she was."

"Jesus. You better close this case pretty fast," Crabtree said in a low voice.

174

"Yeah." As they walked toward the main house, Matt looked for Emily on the second-story widow's walk and along the spacious front porch. "But what if she just hands me my check and goes on her way? Plenty of Elliott's friends would do a fancier job of courting her than I can."

Richard chortled. "Surely a good-looking chap like yourself isn't having trouble with *Emily*. She's so ripe she's ready to fall off the tree."

Stepping up to the porch, Matt eyed him cautiously. "I'm not going to rush her while she's still mourning her father. Emily's in no danger, now that our killer's under lock and key, and I want to be damn sure I do things right this time around."

He opened the door and walked into the parlor, followed closely by the foreman. Once again McClanahan was impressed by the tasteful masculine lines and colors of the Burnham residence, and his eye lingered on a large portrait above the fireplace, of a woman with red-blond hair and a faraway smile. "Emily certainly favors her mother. She'll be every bit as beautiful when she gets older, too."

"I beg your pardon. I'm accustomed to being told I'm beautiful *now*."

When he saw Emily grinning impishly in the doorway of her father's study, he knew she'd come to terms with whatever doubts she'd had about returning to an empty house. "That's because Idaho's half blind and Silas isn't tired of you yet," he teased. "Personally, I prefer a woman who's all ribbons and lace, and who keeps her pinkie pointed over a teacup."

Crabtree laughed as he looked at Emily's overalls. "If this is what ladies wear in Cripple Creek, I'm not sure you should go back."

"Just a gold miner's daughter," she quipped. She crossed the parlor and hugged the foreman fondly, then stepped back to smile at him. "Has McClanahan told you we've locked Papa's killer away?"

"He mentioned it, yes," Richard replied in a careful

tone. "Says it's only a matter of presenting some evidence."

Emily nodded. Matt had obviously revealed his identity and told Richard his real reason for his previous trip to the ranch, too, because the men appeared quite comfortable in each other's company. "Any problems with the roundup while I've been away? I've missed riding the range with you and the men . . . and Papa."

"I've heard a few questions, but nothing pressing." The stocky foreman smoothed his sandy curls as he looked from her to Matt. "We've found no evidence of any rustling lately either. The men're wondering how long you're planning to stay in Cripple, because guard duty gets a bit tiresome when there aren't any suspects coming around."

"Maybe a bonus will keep them interested. The profitable year we've had certainly merits one, and I appreciate their extra efforts." Emily smiled, then took hold of Crabtree's leathery hand. "I couldn't have done this without your help, Richard. I'll order the lumber for your new house while I'm here. Once the hands finish the fall herd work, building it will keep them occupied until we can wrap this murder up. It shouldn't be long now."

He squeezed her hand hard before letting it go. "How's Idaho?"

"Some days are better than others. He's a sad old man, Richard."

They were silent for a moment, until the foreman brightened. "Well—I've got chores, and you folks probably want to get, uh, settled after your ride. I think you'll find everything's in good order, Miss Burnham."

As they watched the curly-headed foreman step off the porch and head for the stable, McClanahan slipped his arm around Emily's shoulders. "Are you as contented as you seem, or was it an act for Crabtree's sake?"

"As much faking as I do in Cripple, I refuse to play a role here," she replied in a low voice. "I'm fine, now that I've been through all the rooms. It's still home, Matt. Even without him."

Noting the dried tear-streaks on her dusty cheek, he smiled and tweaked her nose. "May I give you a bath, Miss Burnham?"

Emily studied his virile face, a grin playing at the corners of her lips. "Only if I can return the favor. You smell like a horse, McClanahan."

"Is that so terrible?" He pulled her close, letting his hands wander to the curve of her waist and beyond. She was gazing up at him, tousling his hair, wearing a smile that threatened to turn him inside out.

"Not terrible at all," she murmured. "I'm very fond of horses. But I'd never sleep with one."

"Will you sleep with me?"

Emily nodded, her pulse quickening.

Matt kissed her willing mouth, tasting dust and salt and the sweetness that could only be Emily's. "Honey, the only thing I've been able to think of lately is making love to you," he murmured. "And I've finally got you all to myself."

Emily sucked in her breath when his hand slipped beneath her overalls. "Who said anything about making love? I thought we were taking a bath."

"You ornery little—" He kissed her hard on the mouth, and her eager response made him wonder if they'd make it up the stairs. "Why don't you pick out a dress to wear tonight, while I get the water ready? It'll be nice to see you in pretty clothes, even if I don't leave them on you for long."

Emily went to her room and chose a dress the color of Matt's eyes, with more ruffles and lace than she cared for—until he'd said he wanted to see her in them. She stripped down to her underwear, then stood before her mirror to pin her hair on top of her head.

When she returned to the bathroom, steam was rising from the tub and Matt was shaving—naked, as he'd been the first evening they met at the Rose. But rather than frightening her, his powerful body fascinated her this time. She perched on a stool to watch him scrape the last of the lather from his neck. "You'd look good in a beard,

McClanahan."

"You think so?" He grinned and rinsed his face. "I've grown one a few times, in the winter. But I didn't want to give you whisker burn tonight."

As he approached her with sparkling eyes, Emily's heart thumped in her chest. His hands were warm on her neck, but his gaze made her temperature rise even higher. She reached for him, murmuring his name.

It was all he could do not to rip her underthings off. "Don't you think you're a little overdressed?" he breathed.

"What do you plan to do about it?"

Her sultry challenge whetted his appetite even more. Matt lifted her silky camisole, marveling again at the softly rounded peaks it concealed. When his hand slipped down the back of her pantaloons she stood, rubbing against him with a chuckle that told him she knew damn well what she was doing to him. "First things first," he said in a husky voice. "Step into the tub, young lady."

Emily smiled demurely, and when she was seated in the warm water, Matt leaned toward her with a cake of rose-scented soap. He took an agonizingly long time working up a lather between his hands, smiling at her.

"Close your eyes, rosebud. We'll save the best for last."

His soapy fingers massaged her forehead and temples so tenderly she let her head loll back against the tub. How could a man who'd battled a bartender half again his size coax the dust from her face with such a delicate touch? Matt made swirling circles down her neck and continued in the hollows of her collarbone.

"Close 'em tighter," he whispered. "I'll rinse you before I go on."

As the water trickled down her cheeks, Emily thought she'd passed into another world. But it was nothing compared to the sensation of his wet, slippery palms caressing the underside of one breast, then the other.

"Scoot forward, sweetheart. Let me in behind you."

Emily felt the water rise, and then two darker legs were surrounding her. Matt's hands became more insistent as they rubbed her back in slow, soapy spirals. She rested her head on her knees, inhaling the steamy scent of roses while the problems of the past week slipped away. How did he sense exactly what she needed? It was a little scary when a man she barely knew was so attuned to her innermost feelings, yet she was beginning to feel like herself again for the first time since she'd left home.

When he'd rinsed her back, Matt leaned her against his chest. His hands found the soft roundness of her breasts while he kissed damp tendrils of hair behind her ear. "You're awfully quiet," he said. "Is there something else I should be doing to please you?"

Closing her eyes, Emily turned to seek his lips with hers. His cheeks were satiny smooth, and as his tongue parted her teeth, she moaned low in her throat. One broad hand continued to make her breasts ache until she thought they'd burst, while the other was trailing in a leisurely path up and down her thigh. When a single finger found its way between her legs, she arched against him. He stroked her, increasing the pressure until the spasms inside her were traveling so fast she was ready to explode.

Then he stopped. "My turn to be washed, Emily."

"Dammit, McClanahan—finish what you started!" she gasped.

"You'll just have to hold it. Like I am," he replied with a chuckle. "Here's the soap."

Emily turned, wishing she knew more about a man's body so she could wreak the most potent revenge possible. She grinned wickedly. "Lean back and put your feet up. You're going to suffer for what you just did, Matt."

"I never doubted it for a moment." He slid down to rest his head against the edge of the tub, watching her through half-shut eyes. She was soaping his toes, working her way toward his sensitive arch, and he held his breath hard to keep from laughing. Emily's eyes glowed amber in her ivory face, and he relished her playful punishment.

"Ticklish? Good!" Emily raised his foot, then leaned back against her end of the tub, gripping his ankle. She slyly slid her leg toward him. "Gonna give you some of your own medicine, Mr. McClanahan."

When her instep met his manhood, Matt's eyes widened and he gripped the edges of the tub. Jesus! The little innocent was nibbling at the sole of his foot, making him squirm against her heel as he laughed uncontrollably. "Emily, stop!" he pleaded between howls. "You'll have me exploding before—"

"Just *hold* it," she teased. "If you can't take the heat, get out of the bathtub."

"It doesn't work that way with a man, honey."

"What makes you think it worked with *me?*" She kneaded him with her heel, then tickled the tip of him with her big toe.

"Truce!" he cried. "We'll compromise—we can make love *before* you wash me."

"No we can't." Chuckling, she withdrew her foot. Matt's eyes were huge and blue, his cheeks flushed as he flashed her a devilish grin. Emily realized she was no more able to prolong their play then he was—she had to feel his sleek skin rubbing hers, had to satisfy the need gnawing inside her.

She quickly soaped his legs and then submerged them. Avoiding his swollen shaft, Emily leaned forward to rub his stomach and chest, lathering the dark swirls of hair with brisk, eager hands. Then she was kneeling, and Matt steadied her as she placed her knees on either side of his hips. "Lean into me. I'll do your back," she murmured. "You're going to end up smelling as flowery as I do."

"At this point, I'm beyond caring." He hugged her, his breath coming in short gasps as her hands worked their way down his spine. She was warm and wet and wonderfully soft against him, except for two hard buds that teased his collarbone. Spanning her ribcage with careful hands, Matt raised her out of the water so he could suckle.

The soap hit the floor and Emily whimpered, clutching him. She slid down his thighs, and instinctively impaled herself on him with a quick thrust.

"Whoa . . . this is too good to rush, honey," Matt whispered hoarsely. "Kiss me now. Make me wait, and I guarantee you it'll be worth it."

Still straddling him, Emily slipped an arm beneath his neck and kissed him hungrily. She tasted the silk of his inner lips and nibbled gently all the way along his neck. His pulse was throbbing with her own, and she could feel the forces within him growing hot and urgent as he grasped the halves of her bottom.

Guiding her hips, McClanahan realized it was useless to try to control Emily Burnham. She was giving her passions free reign as few women knew how, driving him insane with her unstudied lust. The moans near his ear were sounding more desperate every second, and then she was straining against him, crying out his name again and again.

Emily was aware of water sloshing around her, and Matt's tightening arms, and an ecstatic frenzy that passed from his body into the deepest parts of hers. She collapsed against him, unable to speak.

He let out a long, satisfied sigh. "I don't know how this can get any better, rosebud," he whispered. "Yet I have a feeling it will."

Chapter Eighteen

"You drive a hard bargain, Miss Burnham," Matt said as he helped Emily up onto the carriage seat. "Had I bought Crabtree's lumber myself, I would've paid half again as much."

The frosty morning air was making her cheeks tingle, and she felt them warm with McClanahan's compliment. "Papa did a lot of business with Homer Kline over the years," she explained. "What with the rumors about my health, I probably *surprised* him into giving me a better price . . . but we'll have to be careful, Matt. I can't have family friends suspecting I've deliberately lied to them these past few weeks."

"That's exactly what I was thinking." Matt clapped the reins over the horse's back and headed them toward the main business district of Colorado Springs. It pleased him that Emily conducted her business so competently, when only hours ago she'd again abandoned herself to his passionate whims in her four-poster bed. Was it possible to have such an irresistible young woman as both a lover and a friend? Members of the weaker sex were usually so dependent, yet she made *him* feel as though his life would be incomplete unless she was forever a part of it.

When he pulled the wagon to a halt in front of a familiar row of shops, Emily glanced at him. "Do you have some errands to tend to? I could look at —"

"You're going to have a new gown or two made, rosebud," he said as he went around to help her down. "The heir to the Burnham empire should dress accordingly, even if she's been in mourning, so—"

"But I have plenty of suitable—"

"—the men she'll be dealing with won't think they can take advantage of her bereavement," he finished. Matt held on to her for a moment after he lowered her to the street, adoring her rosy, upturned face. "Of course, *I* intend to take every advantage I can, before anyone else has the chance."

Emily saw the sparkle in his blue eyes and smiled. "And what did you have in mind, Mr. McClanahan?"

Kissing her, showing her off, making her his wife . . . he had other ideas, too, and McClanahan realized he didn't deserve an answer to his proposal until he cleared up the unknowns in his past to Emily's satisfaction. He escorted her toward a dressmaker's shop, hoping the tightness he was feeling inside didn't show on his face. "If I told you what I was thinking, would you promise to hear me out before you made your reply?"

Her heart began to pound so loudly she didn't notice the shop door opening. Could he possibly be considering—

"Emily, dear, how wonderful to see you! The rumors about your condition had me wondering if I'd ever sew. . . ." The tiny, elegant seamstress finished her sentence by studying Emily with concerned eyes, and then she focused on Matt with obvious interest. "Well, let's just say I'm pleased to see you recovering so *nicely.*"

Emily chose her next words with care. "Mrs. Andersen, this is Matt McClanahan, a liaison between Papa's holdings. He's pointed up the need for some suitable dresses to wear to meetings and—"

"Actually, I was hoping you'd outfit her for some upcoming parties," McClanahan interrupted suavely. "Social events are every bit as important to Miss Burnham's image as her business appointments—and a more appropriate way for a young woman to come out of mourning, don't you think?"

Mrs. Andersen's eyebrow went up, yet her smile showed her approval. "I have just the thing—and some new patterns from Paris we can look at. If you'll have a seat, sir, I'll take good care of her."

Emily saw the triumphant, mischievous flicker of Matt's grin and kept her mouth shut; it wouldn't be proper to argue with him in front of the genteel seamstress, who already had suspicions about their relationship. She followed Mrs. Andersen into a dressing room, her eyes widening when the woman gestured toward a flowing crimson gown on a dressmaker's form.

"Try this on before we look at patterns, dear," she said. "It's a lovely thing, but the customer I made it for decided not to take it. Unless my eye's not what it used to be, it's nearly a perfect fit."

Running a finger along a glistening sleeve, Emily hesitated. "I'd hate to see such a pretty dress go to waste, but—"

"You don't have to buy it," Mrs. Andersen insisted, "and I know you're not accustomed to so much lace, but you *do* need to consider your age and social status, Emily. Your father would expect me to see to that, now that he can't."

Emily suddenly felt as though Papa and Matt and Mrs. Andersen were conspiring against her conservative taste, yet she liked the dress. And a few minutes later she was turning before the dressing room mirror, unable to hide a smile as the red satin skirt rustled around her shoetops. "You're sure this dress won't be claimed, Mrs. Andersen? It's hard to believe someone would order it and then refuse it."

The petite seamstress knelt to turn up the gown's hem. "They say this customer's mistress up and left him for a man who was more the marrying kind," she mumbled around her pins. "And that was well over a month ago. I'm just pleased the dress becomes you, dear. Perhaps Mr. McClanahan would like a look."

"Tell him I'll be out in a minute." When the little woman left the dressing room, Emily stepped back and made a final appraisal. The garnet fabric added a glow to her cheeks. The rounded yoke was trimmed with narrow white lace and tiny mother-of-pearl buttons, as were the leg-of-mutton sleeves, and the skirt fell gracefully over her hips. She straightened her collar, and then stepped into the main room of the shop.

One spark from McClanahan's eyes told her what she wanted to know. "What do you think?" she asked as she turned in front of him. "It's awfully dressy, but I suppose I could wear it—"

"How soon can you finish the alterations?" Matt asked the dressmaker.

"In about an hour. All I have to adjust is the hem."

"Fine. We'll take it." He focused his full attention on Emily, gripping his lapel to keep from pulling her into his arms. She'd turned heads at the Golden Rose in a simple pink gown, but in deep red, Emily Rose Burnham *glimmered*. "It'd be perfect for a ball or a Christmas party, but I hope you'll wear it sooner. You can't forgo your social obligations forever, Miss Burnham—and your father wouldn't expect you to stay in seclusion all winter," he added for the dressmaker's benefit.

Emily nodded, glancing toward the woman at the counter. Mrs. Andersen had made most of her clothing for years, but showed no sign of disapproval because she'd agreed to such a bright color after supposedly being in mourning for so long. "I'll go change then."

She hummed as she removed the lustrous dress, oddly pleased at how dainty she looked in it. Plainer clothes had always seemed more appropriate at the ranch, and her frilly underthings were a secret she enjoyed keeping from the men she dealt with each day—until McClanahan came along. But the way Matt's lashes had lowered when he first caught sight of her convinced Emily that a change was in order. She was, as he'd said, a wealthy young woman of influence, even if society seldom saw her. Perhaps her more tomboyish attire was suitable only at the Flaming B, now that she was almost nineteen. Emily stopped humming to listen to the conversation in the shop.

". . . has always looked lovely in browns," Mrs. Andersen was saying. "And this cocoa with the fawn stripe has been quite popular this fall."

"How would it look made up like the one she had on?"

"Very flattering, sir. Perfect for daytime functions or —"

"Leave the lace off that one. She'll be more likely to wear it."

"Yes, Mr. McClanahan."

"For this blue dress, though, I'd like lots of ruffles," Matt continued. "And instead of a collar, give it a neckline with some scoop to it."

There was a pause. Emily tugged her blouse on, trying to think of a way to give McClanahan a piece of her mind without offending the seamstress. Of all the nerve, assuming he could —

"Emily *does* have flawless skin, sir. But no proper young lady would be seen wearing . . . I — I'm certain Mr. Burnham would send the dress back, if he were —"

"How much do I owe you for the three gowns?" Matt said in a low voice. "I'll pay you for them right now."

What must Mrs. Andersen think? Emily fumbled with the buttons on her skirt then bustled into the shop. "Put the dress on my account, as usual," she said in the calmest voice she could muster.

The seamstress scowled in confusion, looking from Emily to Matt. McClanahan smiled indulgently as he glanced at her bodice. "I think you need to check the mirror, Miss Burnham."

Emily glanced down and then stalked back to the dressing room, flushing furiously. Her blouse was gaping open between the top button and her waistband, and it was all she could do to get it fastened, she was so flustered. Meanwhile, McClanahan was covering his tracks with a honeyed voice that made her blood boil.

"The blue one's for a costume party. Won't Emily

186

make a stunning Southern belle?" he said in a conspiratorial tone.

"Well, now that you mention it—"

"I'd appreciate it if you didn't. It's to be a surprise for her birthday."

Stray tendrils of hair dragged on her collar, but Emily left them hanging. Recalling Viry's teachings on etiquette—and who she was—she walked sedately out to the front counter again. She smiled at Mrs. Andersen, ignoring Matt. "I appreciate your understanding about this matter, and I'll look for your bill at the end of the month."

The dressmaker nodded demurely. "Certainly, Miss Burnham. The garnet satin should be ready in about an hour, and the others—"

"The red one's all I ordered," Emily said with pointed innocence.

"And whenever you need anything else, perhaps for the upcoming holidays or a special occasion, you just let me know."

"We certainly will, ma'am," McClanahan said with a boyish grin. He opened the door and let Emily precede him out to the sidewalk, chuckling as he read the storm warning in her fiery amber eyes. "You look terribly fetching in red, rosebud. Instead of just picking the dress up, why don't you change into it before we go to dinner at—"

"I ought to *cancel* the damn thing, but someone's already stuck her with it once."

McClanahan glanced at the shoppers strolling around them, and back to the young woman striding angrily at his side. "Don't you think you're overreacting to—"

"And *you're* overstepping yourself, Mr. McClanahan. I can certainly afford to buy nice clothes, without—"

"I don't think all of Colorado Springs needs to hear this," he said as he steered her toward a deserted alley. When only the backs of the buildings surrounded them, he let her shrug out of his grasp. "Emily, I never implied that you were short of money. You were eaves-dropping, weren't you?"

Emily glared. "You certainly weren't *whispering* to Mrs. Andersen. I've known her most of my life, and now she probably thinks I've taken up with some decadent—*Romeo*—who's been hanging around at the ranch while I've been too weak to leave my bed. A Southern belle? A neckline with some scoop to it? *Really,* McClanahan."

Matt leaned against a building and crossed his arms, smiling patiently. "I can just see you sittin' on the lawn, sippin' a julep," he drawled. "All that luscious skin just a-temptin' the young lads who—"

"Oh, stop it! The point is, you didn't *ask* me before you ordered those dresses. I won't be a kept woman, Matt."

He wanted to laugh and catch her up in his arms, but he knew better. Emily's fists were on her hips and her golden-eyed gaze was boring straight into his heart. "It's only natural for a man to give you pretty things. Your father certainly did."

"But that's what fathers *do.* You're a—a—"

"I'm a what, rosebud?" He reached out to stroke her crimson cheek, but she jerked her face away.

"I . . . I don't know. I'm not sure I like having you buy things for me." Emily looked down the alley, wishing her expression and her jumbled thoughts would stop betraying her. "I already owe you so much for rounding up Papa's killer, and those dresses must've cost you plenty. Mrs. Andersen doesn't work cheap."

"And I'm certain she won't gossip about our transaction or discolor your reputation, either. Is that what you're worried about?"

"Well, no . . . she said somebody's mistress left that red dress behind, but she wouldn't say whose." She glanced at the shiny toes of his boots. What *was* she worried about? The seamstress wouldn't make her a dress that didn't become her any more than she'd spread rumors about "that Burnham girl's" escort. It wasn't good business.

Matt took her hand and rubbed it between his own. "The gowns are gifts, Emily. Maybe they're of a more personal nature than some people consider proper, but you're not the type who gushes over little trinkets or stuffs herself on sweets. Are you?"

"Well . . . no." His hands were warm and gentle, and she was beginning to think her tantrum had been not only childish, but out of place as well.

"So accept your dresses in the spirit in which I'm giving them," he said quietly. "You've made me happier than I've been for a long time, and I'd like to return some of that happiness. You certainly deserve it, after all you've been through."

Her pulse quickened, and Emily studied him through lowered lashes. "I thought you were merely helping me solve Papa's murder. Now you sound like a man who's come courting."

"Maybe I'm clever enough to do both."

"Maybe you chase after damsels in distress wherever you go," she quipped. "I should check your past for a string of broken hearts."

"Do you think I seduce every female I meet?" he asked as he clutched her other hand. "How many women do you think I've loved in a bathtub — or a miner's shack — after they pointed a gun at me?"

Emily chuckled, adoring the way his blue eyes captured her in their gaze. "I don't know, Mr. McClanahan. Perhaps *I* should be asking those questions."

"Well, the answer's *none*," he murmured as he pulled her against him. "And if you're not careful, we're going to be adding this alley to our list of locations. Now kiss me — just a short one — and then behave yourself, dammit. A young lady of your ilk should never allow herself to be led into such . . . questionable situations."

His lips teased at hers until she whimpered for more, and then he released her. With a devilish smile, Matt escorted her out of the alley as though he'd arranged such rendezvous hundreds of times. Perhaps he had

—Emily wondered again if she should be taking Mc-Clanahan for granted so quickly. Should she believe in the implicit faith Richard Crabtree seemed to have in him, or was it Silas's warning she should heed? As they stepped back into the flow of people along the busy street, it really didn't matter. She was too much in love with him to even *think* of letting him go.

And later, when he stepped out of the tailor's back room in a black suit he'd ordered on his earlier trip to town, Emily realized anew what a dashing companion Matt McClanahan made. The dark coat matched his hair, and its cut emphasized his broad shoulders. A fresh white shirt made his face look ruddy and masculine. His vest front was royal blue brocade, and Emily couldn't decide which was more dazzling—the elegant fabric, or the way his eyes outshone it as he smiled at her.

"No comment? That's not like you, Miss Burnham."

She tried to get rid of the sappy grin she felt on her face. "I almost hate to admit it, but you do have excellent taste, McClanahan. I can only wonder where you plan to *wear* such a handsome outfit."

Chuckling, he turned to the tailor. "I'll keep this on. I think the lady would prefer it if you boxed the clothes I was wearing."

When they'd stashed his parcels in the carriage and strolled into some of the other shops, they returned to Mrs. Andersen's. She was reconciling her accounts, and her sewing tools were put away for the day. "You've come for the red dress," she said with a smile. "Let me find you a box."

Emily glanced up at Matt, who nodded. "I'd rather put it on, and let you wrap this outfit instead."

Noticing Matt's elegant clothes, the seamstress smiled coyly. "You're going somewhere tonight? A party, perhaps?"

"Yes, ma'am," McClanahan answered. He glanced

190

around the shop, then walked toward a chair near the window. "I'll make myself comfortable. Take as long as you need, Emily."

Her heart thudded as she handed her skirt and blouse to Mrs. Andersen from the dressing room. Where would he be taking her, that they'd wear such finery? She'd assumed they'd eat and go dancing, as he'd suggested yesterday, and she'd dressed for that sort of outing this morning. Emily slipped the garnet gown over her head, lost in thought until the diminutive dressmaker returned.

"I've just the thing for your hair, dear," she said with a knowing smile.

Emily took the stool she offered and watched in the mirror as the woman fussed over her. She brushed the long blond tresses lovingly, gathering them into a becoming topnot which she pinned securely at the crown. "We'll turn these little stray pieces into ringlets," she said as she wielded a curling iron. "And to finish it, I made some roses of this same red satin, trimmed with lace and streamers. I had a feeling Mr. McClanahan was taking you somewhere tonight!"

"Thank you, I . . . didn't realize you had such a way with hair, Mrs. Andersen. It's never looked prettier." Emily turned to the right and left, admiring the ornaments tucked into both sides of her crown. The seamstress dusted her cheeks with pink powder and stood back with a girlish grin.

"You've grown into a beautiful young lady, Emily," she whispered. "And it's good to know you're in circulation again. I only wish your father could see you right now."

A pang went through her heart, because Papa would never know his efforts to feminize her had finally succeeded. Emily smoothed her skirt as she blinked away the mist in her eyes. "Thank you again," she murmured. "I think Mr. McClanahan will be quite pleased."

When she emerged from the dressing room, Matt

sucked in his breath and stood to gaze at her. How could such a transformation have taken place in the time it took for his thoughts to wander only as far as their next destination? Emily Rose looked radiant and regal, and it was for damn sure he wouldn't give any other man a chance to so much as grasp her hand. "You've done it again, rosebud," he murmured as she turned before him. "You've caught me by surprise, and I don't know what to say."

Emily smiled as she felt the color flooding her cheeks. "You could start by thanking Mrs. Andersen for styling my hair."

The petite woman came from behind the counter with an ornate perfume bottle. "A finishing touch — just a dab behind your ears," she said as she lightly applied the stopper to Emily's skin. After inhaling the ethereal sweetness of lilac that wafted around them, she chuckled. "You two have a wonderful evening!"

Matt flashed the little woman a grateful grin as he ushered Emily to the door. He could hardly watch where they were walking to looking at her, and it was an effort not to embrace her right there on the sidewalk. "Is it my imagination?" he said as he helped her up onto the front seat of the carriage. "Or did every person we pass turn to gaze after you?"

"How would I know?" she asked demurely. "I was too busy looking at you to notice." His eyes burned with a fire that made her so warm she wondered if steam would drift out of her ears. Even at his most passionate, intimate moments, Matt McClanahan had never looked as though he'd fall over with the slightest tap of her finger. It gave her a heady sense of power, this newfound femininity. "Where are we going now?"

He blinked, as though bringing himself out of a trance. "I'd had a restaurant in mind — a private little place — but now I've decided to accept an invitation I received awhile back. A birthday ball, with a buffet supper. Is that all right?"

"Well, I suppose. But —"

4 BESTSELLING HISTORICAL ROMANCES BY YOUR FAVORITE AUTHORS CAN BE YOURS, FREE!

Kensington Choice, our newest book club now brings you historical romances by your favorite bestselling authors including Janelle Taylor, Shannon Drake, Rosanne Bittner, Jo Beverley, and Georgina Gentry, just to name a few! Each book is filled with passion, adventure and the excitement of bygone times!

To introduce you to this great new club which is part of Zebra Home Subscription Service, we'd like to send you your first 4 bestselling historical romances, absolutely free! And once you get these 4 free books to savor at home, we'll rush you the next 4 brand-new books at the lowest prices available, as soon as they are published.

The way the club works is that after your initial FREE shipment, you will get our 4 newest bestselling historical romances delivered to your doorstep each month at the preferred subscriber's rate of only $4.20 per book, a savings of up to $7.16 per month (since these titles sell in bookstores for $4.99-$5.99)! All books are sent on a 10-day free examination basis and there is no minimum number of books to buy. (And no charge for shipping.) Plus as a regular subscriber, you'll receive our FREE monthly newsletter, *Zebra/Pinnacle Romance News*, which features author profiles, contests, subscriber benefits, book previews and more!

So start today by returning the FREE BOOK CERTIFICATE provided. We'll send you 4 FREE BOOKS with no further obligation: A FREE gift offering you hours of reading pleasure with no obligation...how can you lose?

We have 4 FREE BOOKS for you
as your introduction to
KENSINGTON CHOICE!
To get your FREE BOOKS, worth
up to $23.96, mail the card below.

FREE BOOK CERTIFICATE

Yes! Please send me 4 Kensington Choice (the best of Zebra and Pinnacle Books) Historical Romances without cost or obligation (worth up to $23.96). As a Kensington Choice subscriber, I will then receive 4 brand-new romances to preview each month for 10 days FREE. I can return any books I decide not to keep and owe nothing. The publisher's prices for Kensington Choice romances range from $4.99-$5.99, but as a preferred subscriber I will get these books for only $4.20 per book or $16.80 for all four titles. There is no minimum number of books to buy and I may cancel my subscription at any time, plus there is no additional charge for postage and handling. No matter what I decide to do, my first 4 books are mine to keep, absolutely FREE!

DF03K7

Name

Address _____ Apt.

City _____ State _____ Zip

Telephone ( )

Signature

(If under 18, parent or guardian must sign)

Subscription subject to acceptance. Terms and prices subject to change.

4 FREE
Historical
Romances
are waiting
for you to
claim them!

(worth up to
$23.96)

See details
inside....

KENSINGTON CHOICE
Zebra Home Subscription Service, Inc.
120 Brighton Road
P.O.Box 5214
Clifton, NJ 07015-5214

"Much more elegant than a dance hall. And I'm certain your father would've approved, because the host is a good friend of his, and he sent you an invitation, too." Matt picked up the reins and started the horses toward the edge of town. "It's time you were attending these events, sweetheart, and I'm pleased to be escorting you."

Emily was too intrigued to remark about the possessive tone of McClanahan's comment. As they passed the dry goods store and the blacksmith's, she tried in vain to remember whose mail sat on Papa's desk. They left the business and residential districts behind and were heading toward the foothills before she guessed their destination. When Matt pulled the wagon into a driveway bounded by Douglas firs, leading back to a mansion that was invisible from the road, Emily's eyes widened. The owner of this magnificent estate was known all over Colorado Springs for sparing no expense when it came to indulging his wife or throwing lavish parties. "You know Taylor West?" she murmured as he halted the horses.

McClanahan smiled mysteriously. "Well enough to help celebrate Olga's birthday. Why the frown?"

"I—I didn't send an acceptance, or bring a gift, or—"

"I had one delivered this afternoon. A crystal candy dish from you, and imported liqueur candies from me. Not that she needed either of them."

Emily tried to smile as the uniformed attendant helped her to the ground. When Matt offered his elbow, she tugged him to a halt beside the veranda. "But Matt, Papa's friends will know the minute they see me that I haven't been wasting away all these months. If they think I've lied about my health, they won't trust me to conduct Papa's affairs—"

"So we'll let the truth speak for itself. None of these men would be crass enough to challenge you about it in public." He gazed down at her with a fondness that made his heart swell. "When they see you, Emily,

193

they'll be so enthralled they'll forget all about the rumors—which are exactly what they've heard. If it becomes uncomfortable for you, we'll leave early, but I thought an evening like this would do you good."

She hadn't been to a party since the ball Papa had hosted last spring. And as another couple was welcomed inside and strains of music and laughter drifted through the ornately-carved doors, Emily couldn't help smiling. She stood on tiptoe to peck Matt's cheek, then took his elbow again, vowing to set her concerns about appearances aside.

"Any more of that brazen behavior's liable to land you on your backside behind this shrubbery," he murmured as he gave her a roguish wink.

A doorman in a red frock coat let them in, and Emily immediately felt overwhelmed by a luxury that was almost ludicrous. A few years ago when she'd visited the West home for a Christmas reception, she'd noticed the sheer mass of *things:* bric-a-brac on every spare inch of the marble-topped tables, clusters of photographs amid the sterling pieces on the ponderous buffets, cut-glass paperweights, ruby glass souvenir cups, curios, and lace doilies *everywhere*—and they seemed to have multiplied. As they followed an aproned maid up the grand staircase to the ballroom, she relaxed.

Matt gave her a questioning look.

"I was afraid to breathe, for fear I'd knock something over," Emily whispered.

He chuckled and covered her slender hand with his. "Same here. West probably travels to his brokerage houses just to escape Olga's clutter."

A chamber orchestra was playing as guests gathered at small tables on one side of the room or helped themselves to the buffet, which ran the entire length of the opposite wall. Emily recognized several of the men and their wives, and for a moment she wondered how much information about the murder she should reveal to these bankers and real estate tycoons. Some of them had caught sight of her and were already watching her with open curiosity. McClanahan's arm tightened around her waist.

"Olga, you've outdone yourself again," he said as he bowed over their plump hostess's hand. "And yet you never appear to age. How do you do it?"

Mrs. West's smile was as wide as her magnificent diamond necklace. "You *are* the flirt, Mr. McClanahan — and those little candies are *wonderful!*" She eyed Emily, smoothing her lavender taffeta dress with gemstone-studded fingers. "And you, dear! Why, Taylor, I thought you told me Elliott's daughter was confined to the ranch because of her declining health. She looks perfectly sleek and sassy to me."

Her husband's gaze made a quick, appreciative trip along Emily's profile. "She's still rather thin, darling, but she's certainly done a splendid job of recovering. Perhaps we owe the roses in her cheeks to McClanahan."

Emily laughed, trying to word her response carefully. "Mr. McClanahan is my business manager now. And when I received your invitation, I thought it was high time to come out of seclusion, since moping at the Flaming B won't bring Papa back," she explained.

"An admirable attitude — one Elliott would expect of you," Mr. West replied with a wide smile. Then he focused his attention on Matt, his expression more businesslike. "First chance you get to come by my office, I've got an investment opportunity you'll undoubtedly be interested in for the Burnham portfolio." The portly little man glanced toward the door, buttoning his coat over his straining vest buttons. "Shall we greet the Harveys, dear?"

"Yes, of course." Mrs. West patted Emily's sleeve and smiled up at Matt. "And thank you both for your remembrances. Help yourselves to the buffet and have a lovely time."

"I'm sure we will." McClanahan nodded, and when their hosts were on the way to the door, he leaned toward Emily. "You should inquire about that invest-

195

ment sometime tonight. Taylor isn't generous with his business tips."

"After the way he so pointedly addressed that remark to *you*, do you really think he'll indulge me with such information?" she asked archly.

Matt shrugged. "You've been involved in Elliott's affairs for years—probably know as much about your father's investments as Taylor does."

Emily sighed and glanced toward the buffet. "To these men, I'm still Elliott Burnham's little girl. A blonde bit of fluff who can't be taken seriously or invited into their board rooms."

"And you're just the woman to prove how wrong those assumptions are." He gazed at her upswept hair and gossamer skin, pitying the fools who fell prey to her beauty without acknowledging her business acumen. "You'll have to appear in his place from here on out, rosebud. Might as well let his friends know you mean business."

The responsibility of managing the Burnham estate was nothing new, yet here among her father's peers, who were assessing her with covert glances, it seemed much more a reality . . . almost frightening. "Maybe for tonight I'd like to be the coddled daughter," she murmured. "Since I'm dressed for the part, I might as well play it."

Matt chuckled and guided her toward tables covered with silver trays of attractively arranged food. "I won't treat you like *my* daughter, rosebud," he replied with a low laugh, "but I'll see that you have a good time. The other guests are noticing the exquisite young woman by my side, and I intend to enjoy every one of their envious looks."

As she chose slices of succulent turkey breast and spoonfuls of tender vegetables, Emily realized McClanahan was only half right. Most of the women in the room were eyeing *him,* as though they didn't know him but wished they did. He was following her so closely that his arm brushed hers, and a thrill of happy pride went through her for the first time in her life. In a room full of middle-aged financiers and stout entrepreneurs, Matt McClanahan cut a bold, intriguing figure in his black suit. And he was hers—if only until Nigel Grath was brought to justice.

But who was he? Once again Emily reviewed what she knew about the swarthy man who'd come to the Angel Claire from out of nowhere. He'd done some ranching—worked with horses, she recalled—and seemed to have a passing acquaintance with everyone she knew, whether it was the Sundance Kid or Taylor West. If McClanahan ran in the same circles as she and her father, why hadn't she seen or even heard of him before Papa was shot?

"Why so somber? I was looking forward to idle chatter with Elliott Burnham's coddled daughter." Matt seated her at a table in the most secluded corner of the ballroom.

"I haven't had much practice at idle chitchat," Emily admitted. "But I bet *you* can tell me what proper ladies talk about."

He laughed as he sat down across from her. "Topics so scintillating I can scarcely recall them, such as what they heard at the hairdresser's, or who's hostessing the Ladies' Aid meeting next week. Nothing so mundane as the quarterly profit percentage on their cattle or what their stock broker recommends for the coming year."

She swallowed a bite of baked pheasant, grinning. "I can tell you how each of Papa's businesses has done—"

"I'm certain of it."

"—and I'll bet you," she continued as she glanced at their host, "that West'll recommend utilities or transportation for the portfolio. His last tips on electricity stocks and a streetcar company made a bundle of money."

Matt reached across the table, smiling as he took her hand. "No bet. I'd rather discuss something much more suitable, considering the candlelight, and the music, and the excellent food."

Emily's heart fluttered. "Such as?"

He leaned closer, enjoying the way her golden eyes widened. "Shall we slip away for a while after we've eaten? Find a spot to make love before we dance?"

"You can't be serious!" Her fork clattered to her plate and she stifled a giggle. "What if someone walks in on us? Or what if our clothes get rumpled? People would know damn well what we'd been doing."

Matt laughed and sat back, still holding her hand. "I'll bet you at least one man here couples with a woman tonight. Maybe not the woman he came with, but—"

"And how would you know about these things?"

McClanahan shrugged. "Men talk about their conquests, Emily. I've never seduced anyone at a party myself, but only because none of the women interested me. Which certainly isn't the case tonight."

The intense sparkle in his eyes told her just how badly he wanted her, and Emily's heart went hammering up into her throat. But what an outrageous idea! A proper lady would never consider. . . .

"How about tasting one of these oysters?" Matt asked as he tapped his fork on his plate. "They're supposed to be an aphrodisiac. Not that either of us needs one."

Emily flushed and tried to finish her meal. The meats were fork-tender, and the fresh carrots and pickled beets were much more flavorful than the ones from Cripple Creek stores, yet she ate without tasting any of them. When Clancy Donahue made such forward suggestions she dismissed him as lewd, but there was no ignoring the attractive man across from her. Matt knew her too well.

McClanahan pushed his plate back and gave her a subtle grin. "Dance with me? You like to waltz, as I recall."

Nodding, Emily let him guide her to the center of the ballroom. Elegantly-dressed couples dipped and swirled around them, yet all she could see was the gleam in Matt's eyes as he held her close. His step was perfect; his hand was warm against the small of her back, and his lips were parted slightly, as though he were only a heartbeat away from ravishing her right here on the dance floor. As the orchestra played another refrain of "The Blue Danube," she let the graceful tune carry her into a blissful state she'd only dreamed of before tonight. Perfect music . . . perfect partner who so obviously wanted her. . . .

"Come on, honey, let's find a hideaway," he whispered as the dancers applauded. He guided her between the other couples, nodding with a tight smile when he recognized someone. Emily was inflamed, and one look at her *would* tell everyone what they were up to, if he didn't escort her out of the ballroom fast enough.

"Must we run?" she asked nervously.

"Rosebud, you've got the face of a lamb being led to the slaughter. Relax," he murmured back. He nodded to Charles Tutt and Clayton Avery, and tightened his grip on Emily's back.

"But I don't want to come sneaking back as though— and your new suit'll get wrinkled, and so will my dress," she pleaded as they broke out of the crowd.

"You think I don't know ways around that?" he said with a sly chuckle. "And I can certainly buy you another gown if I get carried away and spoil this one."

Emily whirled around and slapped McClanahan's face as hard as she could. The *smack* caught everyone's attention, and the ballroom fell into an expectant hush.

Matt looked stunned. Then his eyes narrowed and he grasped her offending hand. "What in the hell was *that* for?" he muttered.

"I refuse to be bought, or treated like a whore." Hundreds of eyes were watching them and a low murmur slithered through the crowd, but Emily kept glaring at the man whose grip stung her wrist. "Maybe I act a little wild at times, but I'm enough of a lady not to—"

"A *lady* wouldn't be causing a scene right now," he interrupted tersely. "A simple *no* would've sufficed, Miss Burnham."

Her cheeks flared and her palm was smarting from the blow she'd delivered. Thank God the music started up and the onlookers began to dance again. Matt's gaze remained stony, riveted on hers, as a distinct red handprint appeared on his cheek. Emily bit her lip. "I—I didn't realize I hit you so hard."

"Damn near broke my jaw, girl."

She blinked and looked away. "If you'd hit *me* that way, I'd be pretty hot about it. It's just that—"

"I'm hot, all right."

"—I don't like being pushed into things. If you'd—"

"If *I* hadn't pushed so insistently, we wouldn't be squabbling. No need to apologize, Emily."

Emily challenged him with her eyes. "I'm not apologizing, McClanahan."

"I'm not either. Not my fault you're so easily embarrassed."

A full minute passed before the flicker of a grin gave him away. She laughed softly, reaching up to touch his cheek. "Does it hurt?"

"Not as badly as something else I could mention."

Emily gave him a coy smile. "Your ego, I assume?"

"What else would I be discussing with such a lady?" As he looked down into her lovely, playful face, Matt fought the urge to kiss Emily full on the mouth, regardless of the onlookers and her protests.

She glanced toward the couples on the dance floor, clearing her throat. "We could two-step, I suppose. My skirt would disguise your predicament."

"It was dancing with you that caused the problem."

Emily widened her eyes to tease him. "What'll you do, then—pout? Or leave without me?"

"And let some other fool fall prey to you? Not a chance." McClanahan took her elbow, trying not to laugh as he guided her between the other dancers. He admired her all the more now: Emily Rose Burnham wouldn't be cowed into any compromising positions, and wouldn't snivel in self-pity or bemoan whatever fate she shared with him. Because it was a fate she would fashion herself.

Emily closed her eyes and danced as closely to him as she could without stumbling over his feet. Were all men as confusing and hair-triggered as McClanahan? She was no prude — she knew that — yet the West's party hardly seemed the place to let her passions show. If the other men later recalled her dalliance with Matt, they wouldn't be as likely to forgive an impulsive slap . . . and they'd never negotiate Papa's business seriously if they knew she could be wheedled into quick, secret trysts.

It wasn't over, of course. McClanahan would have his way eventually, and the thought of how he'd seek his revenge made her heart beat faster. As the song ended, another man's teasing voice made her realize what a silly grin she must be wearing.

"Emily Burnham? My Lord, who'd ever believe you came here with *this* rake?"

Her eyes flew open and she backed awkwardly out of Matt's embrace. "Mr. Penrose — I — goodness, it's been so long since —"

"Too long. Glad to see you out and about, because I for one never believed Elliott's daughter would knuckle under." Spencer Penrose gave her a jovial smile and extended his hand toward Matt. "So you got lucky, McClanahan. Took a pretty young lass like this to bring you out of hibernation, did it?"

Matt chuckled. "I'm only here to protect the other guests from her —"

"Feisty little gal, isn't she?" He raised his dark eyebrows as he glanced briefly at the handprint on Matt's cheek. "But undoubtedly worth the trouble."

As he raised a glass of champagne to his lips, Emily's thoughts raced. Spencer Penrose was one of the wealthiest, most influential citizens in Colorado Springs — the man who'd suggested Papa get in on the ground floor of the Cripple Creek mining boom — and she had to talk carefully and intelligently in his presence. He was known for his jokes, but no one would be laughing if he caught her toying with the truth. "How are things at your mine?" she asked with a polite smile.

"The C.O.D.'s the place to be," Penrose quipped. He smoothed his short, dark waves and gave her a penetrating brown-eyed gaze. "I hear you've got a maverick blaster causing problems at the Angel Claire. But I guess Silas doesn't worry you with such things."

"I, uh, see the balance sheets, but I let Mr. Hughes handle the personnel," she replied cautiously.

Penrose chortled and took another sip of champagne. "Guess you just know about the paper figures on your father's newest establishment, too—but I hear McClanahan's more personally involved. The Rose is quite a place isn't, it?" His mustache, which was waxed into a tiny tip at each end, quivered as he laughed.

"Cripple Creek's finest," Matt replied smoothly. "And I'm pleased Emily's asked me to help her look after her father's concerns. She's quite a lady."

"Yes, she is. And you're doing a fine job for her, too." With a knowing smile and a wink, Mr. Penrose took a step back. "I won't interrupt any longer, because I can see you take your managerial duties seriously, Mr. McClanahan. Try to have her home before sunrise, all right?"

As he walked back toward the buffet, Emily let out a long breath. It was all she could do to stand still, her knees were knocking so badly.

"What's wrong?" Matt draped an arm around her shoulders with a concerned scowl. "He's obviously pleased that your father's death hasn't kept you from—"

"He certainly knows about *us*."

McClanahan chuckled, hugging her. "Even before you left your mark on me, I'm sure people surmised—"

"But Penrose'll have everyone talking even more. He *loves* to tease, and—"

"Let him talk. We can handle it." He turned to face her, smiling at the heightened color of her cheeks. "And if he's gossiping about us, people won't be as likely to speculate about the state of the Burnham empire."

Emily let out an exasperated sigh. "But Matt, they'll think—"

"That we're lovers? We are, rosebud."

"But these people know Papa would never have allowed such flagrant carryings-on," she protested. "Men like West and Penrose may joke about it to our faces, but they'll assume you've taken the reins, where Papa's businesses are concerned. They may lose faith in—"

"I'd never presume to control either you or your estate, Emily—even if I really were your business manager. And socially, I'm not doing anything that *any* man wouldn't try." McClanahan wasn't sure if this sudden fit of jitters was caused by her conscience or by the glances they'd gotten all evening. He massaged her shoulders, deciding he loved her all the more for her unpredictability. "One more dance and then I'll take you home. Tomorrow we'll ride out and check your herds—get some fresh air and do anything we please, where only the cattle can talk about us. All right?"

Nodding sheepishly, Emily reached for the handsome man in black and savored a final waltz. When would they dance this way again? Maybe not until Papa's murderer was convicted, and maybe never. The answer depended entirely on Matt McClanahan, and knowing what *he* would do was next to impossible.

Chapter Nineteen

Matt stopped on the stairs, ready to tease her about taking so long to bathe and dress, but when he caught sight of her, the words didn't come out. Emily was in her father's room, wearing a lace gown he recognized from Claire Burnham's portrait in the parlor. She was barefoot, holding her hair up in an untidy topknot, yet as she turned in front of the mirror with an expression that was both critical and pleased, her unstudied beauty stole his breath away.

It was time to declare himself. Emily knew his intentions—just as he now realized she was waiting for him to announce them—but the idea of proposing marriage unsettled him. He loved her without question, and his wealth and background made him as qualified as any man to claim Emily Burnham's affections . . . yet he felt hesitant. Depending on her whim, the woman modeling her mother's wedding gown was as likely to laugh at him as she was to admit she loved him. McClanahan had been derided and slapped before, and had put those women in their places, but Emily wouldn't tolerate such domineering behavior from him. Nor did she deserve it.

Matt slipped down the stairs, shaking his head. When had he started bowing to a woman's wishes? Utter nonsense, to consider a naive little blonde his equal. Yet he knew damn well Emily could outsmart him if she chose to, and she could certainly live without him. As he checked the horses and the saddlebags a final time, he hoped the right words would come when he needed them, because he wasn't so sure that spending the rest of his days and nights without her would be much of a life.

When she heard him come in from the stables, Emily bounded down the stairs with a smile full of sunshine. "Sorry I took so long. Are the horses ready?"

"Hours ago." Matt caught her up in an exuberant kiss, and then couldn't turn her loose.

Emily giggled, straightening her hat when they came up for air. "What was that all about?"

McClanahan shrugged. "Even in pants and a shirt, you look very kissable, young lady."

"And *you* look sleepy. If you fall off your horse today, I'll leave you at the mercy of the cattle."

"If someone hadn't wakened me — *twice* — I'd have the energy to turn her over my knee for making such a threat."

"You loved it, McClanahan."

Recalling her eager, willowy body as she'd coaxed him into one bout of frenzied lovemaking and then another, Matt smiled. Emily's tawny eyes were teasing at him again, and a kiss on the tip of her nose was all he dared give her. "We'd better get started, Miss Burnham. It's a long ride over your vast estate."

"Yes, sir. Lead on."

They rode out beyond the corrals and stables, over rolling pastureland that was green and uninterrupted for as far as the eye could see. Occasional clumps of trees were turning cinnamon and orange, and the autumn air was invigorating while being unseasonably warm. As he watched Emily's graceful form fall into the rhythm of Sundance's canter, Matt searched for the words that would win her. He considered himself reasonably articulate, yet he couldn't think of a damn thing that didn't sound silly or gushy when he practiced it. But he had to say something; he couldn't expect her to read his mind.

When they stopped midmorning to water the horses at a stream, McClanahan plucked a pale blue columbine and stroked her cheek with it. "What do you think about when you're riding, Emily?"

Her smile was wistful as she gazed across the limitless sun-drenched acres around them. "How good it is to be home. How . . . complete I feel, now that I'm back on the land Papa and I shared."

Matt nodded, though he'd hoped for a better opening. "I'm not much for cities either. Rather go for months just seeing a good friend or two than spend another day in town."

"Me, too." Emily took the flower from his hand, gently fingering its delicate, pointed petals. "Is that all?"

"All what?"

She tossed him a teasing glance. "All that you've been thinking about? You've been awfully quiet this morning."

He wanted to blurt out how much he loved her and crush her in an embrace as she whispered the same to him, but instead he cleared his throat. "Did I tell you we're doing double duty? I sold Crabtree a few cutting horses from my herd, and I told him we'd bring them back with us."

Did her smile falter, or was he only imagining she'd expected more intimate conversation? Emily ran her toe across a dusty spot in the grass. "Your spread's within a day's ride of the Flaming B?" she asked doubtfully. Then, as though she felt as awkward as he did, she grinned and adjusted her hat. "Well, if these horses are anything like Sundance, I'm sure we'll get our money's worth out of them."

"Yep. My trainer's the best — and I've got a pretty good eye for horseflesh, you know." Why couldn't he speak his mind? His hand wandered to the golden

206

cascade of hair flowing down her back, and it occurred to him she'd worn it loose to please him. "Emily, you're so pretty that sometimes I can't . . . can't even think straight."

She looked confused; maybe a little nervous. "I . . . thanks, McClanahan. Uh, looks like the horses are rested."

"Yeah." He reached for Arapaho's reins and handed Emily her own. "Let's head north, to where those cattle are grazing."

Emily nodded, and once they were mounted he was alone with his thoughts again. He grimaced and jammed his Stetson down tighter. Any sane man would've swept her into his arms — would've kissed her until the words came tumbling out of their own accord. But he'd lost the moment.

It was no different when they stopped to eat. They sat in the shade, their hats off as they devoured ham and biscuits, and McClanahan could easily have tried again — could've made *love* to her, the way she was lolling on the blanket, pretending she was interested in cracking a leaf into tiny, dry flakes. But he was tongue-tied; frozen by the prospect of being refused after stumbling through a proposal.

By the time they stopped to make camp, Matt wondered if he'd ever be able to converse intelligently with her again. His thoughts were constipated, and Emily was obviously as confused by his silence as he was. After days of teasing and coaxing and complimenting her — having her body and mind all to himself most of the time — he strained to make the commonest of talk about the condition of the grass and how the streams might not hold out through the winter without a good rain or two.

Not even the sunset inspired him. After they'd cleaned up their dishes and built the fire up for the night, McClanahan thought surely he could string a few appropriate words together. Emily sat cross-legged on her blanket beside him, watching periwin-

207

kle clouds drift across the glowing pink sky. He couldn't have asked for a more willing listener, or a more perfect setting as the hush of dusk settled around them. The only sounds were the crackling of the logs and the callings of a few night birds roosting in the nearby trees. The flames bathed her in an inviting light, and the aroma from the coffee grounds they'd discarded lingered around them.

Emily sighed. "Guess I'll turn in. It's been a long day in the saddle."

He cleared his throat. "Rosebud, I—"

"What'd I do, McClanahan? Don't you love me anymore?"

The agony in her plaintive voice made him want to laugh and cry at the same time. He grabbed for her, rolling her onto the blankets as he kissed her neck, her forehead, her damp cheeks. "I do love you, Emily Rose," he murmured hoarsely. "Jesus, I've been trying to get it out all day and I've done such a damn poor job of it you must think I—"

Her mouth closed over his, and loving her became a simple, basic celebration again. She'd saved him from his own fumblings, and Matt was humble enough to realize that it probably wouldn't be the last time Emily came to his rescue. He rested on his elbows, lying between her legs as he gazed at a golden face dappled with firelight. "How long have you known?"

"Oh, ever since you came to the mine," she answered softly. Relief pounded through her, and she reached up to stroke the shadowy stubble on his face.

"You sound awfully sure of yourself. And as I recall, you were dressed in overalls and—"

"You saw through my story about being Silas's niece that night at the Rose, didn't you?"

Matt thought back to the skittish girl in the maid's uniform who'd nearly unmanned him with her innocence. "I suspected something wasn't quite right about Eliza, but I wasn't sure *what,* till you were pointing that pistol at me a few nights later. That's when I realized you were different, Emily. You might be the death of me, but you'll never, never bore me."

Emily laughed and shifted beneath his warm weight. "Pretty brash, wasn't I?"

"No. Just being your own inimitable self." McClanahan stroked her cheek as a droplet dribbled toward her ear. "Why the tears? Aren't you glad we've finally figured out how we feel about each other?"

Nodding, she looked toward the fire. "I . . . I didn't know I could love anybody so much. Especially after Papa . . ."

"Oh, rosebud." He gathered her into his arms and kissed her tenderly before brushing his lips against the damp streaks on her face. Following in E.R.'s footsteps would be a formidable challenge and responsibility, yet he was certain now that he was up to it.

"Sorry I'm such a crybaby lately. It's not like me to—"

"Don't be sorry, sweetheart," he whispered. "Riding with a dolt like me couldn't have been as much fun as you'd hoped for. You *were* hoping we'd have fun today, weren't you?"

Emily nodded, grinning despite her tears.

"And *I* wanted to be the first to confess how much I loved you." Matt tweaked her nose, chuckling. "You're supposed to let the man take the lead, Miss Burnham."

She shrugged and felt terribly mischievous, now that she was sure her handsome lover's heart was hers for the taking. "Sometimes I jump the gun," she replied coyly.

"I should know that by now. But I love you anyway." Still holding her, he turned them onto their sides so he could caress her more freely. When Emily's lips sought his, McClanahan was secretly pleased that she was more aggressive than was fashionable. She moved provocatively in his arms, moaning softly as their kiss deepened.

"You claim we think alike," she murmured against his ear, "so what's going through my mind right now?"

Matt chuckled. "Thoughts so improper I shouldn't discuss them in mixed company."

"Will you marry me anyway?"

He gaped and caught his breath. "Don't you listen? I just said you should let me—"

"Sometimes I like you better when you don't talk, McClanahan." Emily kissed him again, deftly unbuttoning his shirt to comb the coarse curls on his chest with her fingers. His body fascinated her, and as she ran her hand over the curved muscles and flatness of his stomach, her desire burned hotter than the campfire behind them.

"Maybe we should leave our shirts on," he breathed. "Even though it's warm for this time of—"

"No."

Her throaty command sent him over the edge. Matt could barely restrain himself as he unfastened her clothes, pressing his mouth to hers with an abandon fueled by her eager response. How many times had he made love in his life? How many times with Emily? Yet he felt his customary control slipping into the starry night, along with his reservations about reviving his past sorrows and memories. She was his—*wanted* to be his—and all that mattered was trying to please this woman so she'd love him forever.

McClanahan's urgency didn't go unnoticed. Emily rolled and raised herself as he removed her underthings, amazed at the wonder she saw in his crystal blue eyes. Had declaring their love made such a difference? His hands refused to let her go as she struggled with his pants. He kept pulling her close, rubbing against her, with skin and hair and denim until she whimpered with frustration. "If you won't let me undress you, then do it yourself, dammit."

"Do what? To whom?" He gave her a teasing grin as he sat up to yank his boots off.

"Everything—to yourself, unless you start playing fair."

"You couldn't keep your hands off me. You'd go crazy just watching, Emily."

"You think so?" With a snort, she rolled away from him. But the the sudden coldness of grass beneath her back made her shiver, and when Matt stood to remove his pants, she realized how right he was. The flames highlighted his rugged body, giving his dark hair and skin a glow she couldn't resist. He stood a few feet away, magnificent and masculine against the indigo sky as he gazed at her.

When McClanahan drew his hands slowly up his thighs, she sucked in her breath. His thumbs grazed his stiffening manhood and then continued up until they were circling his nipples . . . they'd be as rigid as her own, and her fingers itched to touch them . . . her tongue longed to seek out their tiny indentations. The moment he went into a crouch, Emily scrambled back onto the blanket.

"Cold?" he teased as he stretched out beside her.

"Hot as hell. What do you plan to do about it?"

With a moan he rolled onto her, his lips wandering across her chest until they left each of the little pink buds harder than when he'd found them. She was already aroused and squirming, but Matt was determined to wait until neither of them could stand it before he gave in to his need. He kissed every velvety inch of her stomach, tickling her navel and then laughing with her. When his tongue slid into her warm, sweet cleft she nearly suffocated him with her thrusting.

"Matt, please," she breathed. Fire was racing through her veins, rushing along tiny fuses to the core of her womanhood, and she couldn't lie still. Emily kneaded his shoulders, then coaxed him away from making her explode just yet. "Kiss me," she

211

whispered. "Take me now. I want to—"

"Don't move."

Her eyes flew open and Matt was suspended above her, his lips parted as he gazed hungrily at her.

"I want you to lie absolutely still. No response— not a wiggle. Understand?"

"But I—"

"Just try it."

McClanahan braced his muscled arms on either side of her shoulders and entered her so slowly she thought she'd die. His face was tight with concentration. He moved in a hypnotic rhythm, his inner caress so controlled it was all Emily could do not to writhe up to meet him each time. Her hands tightened on his forearms, but otherwise she strained to match his challenge. Primal fingers coiled and uncoiled within her, tighter and tighter, until she realized she wasn't even breathing. Just when she thought she'd lose consciousness, a low moan welled up from the depths of her and came out as a scream that shattered the night silence.

Matt let go, flooding her with his love until he had nothing left of himself to give. Then he fell into her arms, thrusting and rolling with her until he knew that Emily, too, was drained of desire and strength.

As she lay in his embrace, she was certain her instincts hadn't failed her. Even though he was the only man who'd ever touched her, physically or emotionally, Matt McClanahan was also the only man who could possess her. Emily snuggled against him, smiling as he drew the blankets around their sated bodies.

With a deep sigh he cradled her head on his elbow, weaving his fingers through the silky, golden strands that spilled over her shoulders. "You were beautiful last night in your lace and finery," he murmured, "but you were never meant to be any man's parlor decoration, Emily. Promise me you'll stay a little bit wild, like the golden roses that only grow on

212

the prairie, and I'll love you forever."

Emily hugged him hard, speechless at his eloquence. When his lips met hers, she tasted the sweetness of a surrender she never realized was possible. "I love you, too, Matt."

He smiled, puzzled yet oddly content about the sense of domesticity that overtook him. "The answer's yes."

"Hmm?"

"I'll marry you, rosebud," he said as he saw his smile reflected in her tawny eyes. "And I don't care whether you dress in gowns or overalls or just frilly little underthings, but I intend to wear the pants in this family."

Emily nipped her lip playfully, and before he could catch her, she was rolling away and grabbing his trousers from the pile of clothing beside them. "Fine. But you'll have to take them away from me first."

"What the—" As he sat up, she was already scurrying toward the tethered horses, and Matt knew all too well that she'd delight in dumping his only pair of pants miles from the campfire. He bolted from the blankets, ignoring the sudden chill to chase after her.

Her laughter ringing out, Emily grabbed Sundance's reins and swung onto his bare back. The full moon shone so brightly she could see the despair on McClanahan's face. Draping his trousers in front of her, she circled him, staying just beyond his reach. "Who's got the pants now, McClanahan?" she teased. "Gonna let your woman show you up this way?"

"Nope." Gauging the palomino's gentle trot, Matt leaped, planted his hands on the horse's rump, and carefully cushioned his landing against Emily's back. He reached around her for the reins, chuckling at her amazed expression.

"Where'd you pick *that* trick up?" she gasped between laughs.

"Ever heard of Arizona Charley, the stunt rider?" He settled against her, easing Sundance into a gentle

213

canter as they made a wide arc around the camp area.

"Sure, he rides in all the rodeos around here."

"And he buys his horses from me. Gives me a few pointers when he comes to pick them up."

Emily smiled wryly over her shoulder. "I suppose you've sold some to Buffalo Bill Cody, too?"

"Yep. Offered me a fringed jacket and a spot in his Wild West show, but I turned him down." He nuzzled her hair and tightened his hold around her waist. "I couldn't see going from town to town, unable to honor all the requests from the adoring women in the audience."

She suspected he was bluffing—about Buffalo Bill's offer, anyway—but it really didn't matter. The night was drenched in gold. Open pasture glowed in the moonlight for miles around them, and she was intensely aware of so many new sensations . . . the flowing warmth of Sundance's hide beneath her bare thighs, the night air caressing her body, and a sense of freedom she'd never known. Matt was molded against her backside, his legs hard beneath hers as they gripped the palomino's ribs. The gentle canter caused a delicious friction between their bodies, which was every bit as suggestive as the sound of Sundance's breathing.

Emily chuckled and leaned back. "If you're such a hotshot horseman, Mr. McClanahan, why don't you make love to me?"

"*What?* Honey, you don't—"

"Come on," she teased softly. "We're both good riders, and Sundance'll do most of the work."

Matt stifled a groan, yet he couldn't help smiling at her adventurous naiveté. "It's not a matter of horsemanship, sweetheart. A man can't just do it again and again, even if he *wants* to."

Feeling a distinct ridge growing against her back, Emily smiled. "You're fibbing. You want to try it as badly as I do."

With an exasperated laugh, McClanahan clutched her to keep his balance. Her suggestion was outrageous, and yet . . . the palomino's steady gait and the breasts bobbing gently against his arm made him reconsider. A familiar lightning streaked through his loins, and as he thought fleetingly about the possible dangers of her idea, the novelty became a necessity. "Hold on tight and take it slowly. If we fall off, it'll be the last time we'll ever make love."

Emily nodded, her pulse racing ahead of the horse's hoofbeats.

"Lean forward . . . balance against his neck."

She grasped Sundance's pale mane with one hand and steadied herself against his powerful, flowing shoulders. Matt loosened his grip on her, hardly daring to look at her as he wondered how she'd talked him into such a stunt. "All right," he murmured, "point your bottom at me. Hold on with your knees, like you were jumping a creek."

Emily focused on the fistful of coarse ivory hair she was gripping. She raised up, creating a draft between herself and McClanahan until the broad hand spanning her stomach guided her slowly down. At the first moment of contact, she sucked in and forced herself to stay poised above him. The ground below them was going by at an alarming rate, and she couldn't let herself imagine the consequences of the slightest loss of concentration.

"Ready?" he breathed. Thank God she nodded, because his pulse was pounding so loudly in his ears he wouldn't have heard her response. Matt tugged lightly on the reins, and when the horse slowed to a gentler lope he lowered Emily onto his lap. "Relax with it . . . tell me if I'm hurting you."

Emily could no more speak than she could let go of Sundance's neck. The earthy smell of her warm horse, coupled with the new sensations as she slid up and down Matt's swollen shaft, had her reeling in a world of intense pleasure. She arched, instinctively finding the best angle for both of them. The giddiness of accomplishment overtook her, followed by the gradual spiraling of fire in the pit of her stomach.

McClanahan leaned his head lightly on Emily's back, allowing her rhythm to seduce him into a frenzy beyond words. He couldn't move — couldn't let his legs slip for fear he'd be singing soprano for the rest of his life — so he clutched the horse and his lover and the reins until he strained against the need for release. "Whoa, boy," he rasped. "Whoa, Sundance. Hang on, sweetheart."

As the horse slowed to a halt, Emily lowered herself onto his firm, tawny neck and clenched her teeth. Matt was rocking furiously, battering against her with little animal cries that carried her over a mind-shattering threshhold of delight. She yelped, and then steadied Sundance as McClanahan shuddered against her with a final groan.

For several moments there was only the whisper of a breeze and the horse's shifting steps. As Matt regained his senses, he was aware of Emily's sweet-smelling hair and her heavenly warmth — and a triumphant, heady sense of power he thought he'd left behind with a cockier youth. "We didn't really do that, did we?" he said with a chuckle.

Emily let go of the breath she was holding and relaxed against Sundance. "We did, and something tells me we'll feel muscles we forgot we had, come morning."

Patting her bare thigh, Matt gave his heart a chance to stop hammering and then sat up. He eased away from Emily's damp bottom, still feeling rubbery and weak from their heart-stopping embrace. "Makes you wonder what we'll try next. But give me a night's sleep first, all right?"

Her body shook with a giggle. She rose from her horse's neck, surprised she could notice the silkiness of Matt's arms against her stomach, after all she'd experienced these past few minutes. Turning to meet his mouth, Emily kissed him with all the passion she had left, certain the well of her affection for him would never run dry.

Chapter Twenty

Everything's so perfect, Emily thought as she slowed Sundance from a gallop to a walk. A hundred head or so of Herefords bearing the Flaming B brand grazed along the stream that cut through the bottom of the foothills. The rich grassland rolled and quivered in the morning breeze for miles around, and only the sound of her horse's heavy breathing broke the pastoral stillness. She patted the palomino's damp neck, grinning. "Good boy, Sundance. You miss these runs when we're in Cripple Creek, don't you? And you could've beaten Arapaho hands down if I'd given you your head."

Matt trotted his bay up beside her, adjusting his windblown hat. "Just remember where that mount came from, young lady. I could've made a nice profit on him, had your buddy Longbaugh not procured him for you."

"Still perturbed about that?"

"Nope. I got him back, in a manner of speaking—not to mention the little filly who rides him." He leaned toward her for another coffee-flavored kiss, wondering how she could look so fresh and vibrant. He tried to tell himself it was because he wasn't used to sleeping on the ground, but the lithe little body in his arms was what kept him awake long after she was breathing deeply. "You're wearing me out," he murmured when her lips became more insistent.

"Maybe I spoke too soon," Emily teased. "Should I put you out to pasture, or sell you to the slaughterhouse with my other worn-out bulls?"

He chortled. "You'll learn fast enough how hard it is to sleep alone again. I bet we won't be back in Cripple a day before you're slipping into my hotel room."

"We'll see about that, Mr. McClanahan."

She clucked at Sundance, and as they headed north, she tried not to think about returning to the guest room at Silas's. In a few days she'd be dealing with Nigel Grath again, doing all she could to wrap up Papa's murder and see that justice was done. Now that she knew the handsome man beside her wouldn't ride into the sunset once he collected his pay, Emily was confident she could start a new chapter in her life. Matt had kissed away her doubts about being a wife, and she anticipated a marriage that would be anything but ordinary.

As they approached a distant barbed-wire fence, Emily scanned the horizon. "We should stay alert along this boundary. Wickersham's men tend to be trigger-happy."

Matt gave her a mischievous smile. "I don't anticipate any problems. They know better than to aim at *me*."

Scowling, she urged Sundance into a canter behind Arapaho. Surely McClanahan wasn't planning to cross the Wickersham ranch to reach his own spread—wherever it was. Bert Wickersham had died in the blizzard of '86, but his foreman, Gus Veatch, still lived by the surly cattle baron's motto of "shoot first and ask questions later." Anyone familiar with the ranches around Colorado Springs—which Matt apparently was—would know that. When he dismounted beside the fence and took wire cutters from his saddlebag, her mouth dropped open. "Matt, that's trespassing! People have been hung for less than that!"

"No law against a man cutting his own fence."

Emily blinked as the strands of wire *pinged* into wild spirals, and he held them aside so she could ride through. "But this place never went up for sale! When Lorna Wickersham died—"

"I inherited it."

"What?" Her mind fumbled with pieces of a puzzle that just didn't fit. "But the two sons—Steve and Bill—"

"Got smallpox five years ago, which removed the final barrier to claiming a ranch that was rightfully mine." With a broad smile, McClanahan led his horse through the hole in the fence. "Surprised you, didn't I? I'd better fix this gap before your cattle find it."

Stunned and confused, Emily watched him mend the barbed wire with deft, practiced hands. While it was true she'd led an isolated life on Papa's ranch, she knew all the neighbors and had played with their children. The Wickershams were blond with fair complexions—nothing at all like Matt—and no one had ever spoken of another son or brother. For the three years since Lorna's death, Papa had acted as overseer for the ranch's new absentee owner . . . a man she'd assumed was an English relative of Bert Wickersham's, because Papa never told her any differently. Why hadn't he mentioned Matt McClanahan?

When he was beside her on Arapaho again, Matt kissed her nose, still grinning. "I bet you're wondering why we didn't just ride through my front gate, instead of sneaking across the back forty like rustlers."

Emily smiled weakly. "The discrepancy *had* crossed my mind."

McClanahan's laugh rang out as he hugged her shoulders. "Haven't you ever heard of taking the long way home when you're with your favorite lady? We'd have arrived in time for supper if we'd used that entrance—and I for one wouldn't have missed last night's moonlight ride for anything."

How could this dashing man have been her neighbor, and yet she'd never seen him until the night Papa died? Emily gazed into his handsome face, trying desperately to read the secrets in the sparkle of his beautiful blue eyes. They walked the horses across lush pastureland that was a continuation of her own, and Matt reached over to take her hand.

"I love you, rosebud," he began in a reverent voice. "And one of the things we share is our deep feeling for the land. Not many women understand that sort of thing—and I almost missed out on it myself. Your papa must not've told you what happened on this ranch before you were born."

Emily listened, her eyes fastened on a horizon of green grass and crystal blue sky she wasn't really seeing.

"Well, back then this place belonged to Michael and Lorna McClanahan, my parents. I was about four when my dad was struck by lightning out on the range, and when Mama refused the foreman's advances, he quit. Left her with me to raise, and a handful of unorganized cowboys, right before roundup." McClanahan's expression was thoughtful as he squeezed her hand. "I guess you can understand how desperation and this prime pastureland made her a target for any fortune hunter who came along."

She smiled. "I can't imagine Bert Wickersham spent much time romancing her either. Sour old cuss, from what little I remember."

"And he wasn't keen on raising any competition for land rights," Matt continued. "So after the wedding, he announced that I'd be living with my dad's brother Owen, north of Denver a ways, and that I'd have no claim whatsoever to the McClanahan ranch. Mama didn't have any choice but to go along with him. And after Steve and Bill Wickersham were born, the inheritance question was pretty well settled."

As they rode slowly over the grassland, their hands locked between them, Emily's brow puckered with thought. "But Bert died a long time ago—"

"During the blizzard in 1886, which left Mama like a sitting duck again—a *poor* sitting duck, because Bert lost a lot of money in the market crash of '85, and the blizzard wiped out most of the herd that was left. Steve and Bill were eleven and ten. Not old enough to do much ranch work, but they had to eat, all the same."

"I remember Viry boxing up vegetables and canned goods to send over," she replied quietly. "I was six . . . which made you what? About fourteen?"

"Fifteen. Mama sent word to Uncle Owen that Bert was dead and that she wanted me to come home, but by then I was apprenticed in Owen's blacksmith shop. Told her I didn't want to be another mouth to feed," he said with a sad laugh, "but I was still bitter about being cast out. I didn't understand that Bert had forbidden her to write or visit me all those years."

"And you were too independent to accept two younger half-brothers?" Emily asked slyly.

"You know me pretty well," Matt said with a chuckle. "And it wasn't until smallpox got them five years ago that I learned Mama had reinstated me as the heir to the ranch. I was as surprised as you are to find out about it."

Emily scanned her memory for the details that would complete the puzzle. "I don't understand," she said with a shake of her head. "Your mother was broke, with two little boys, when Bert died. But she never remarried or sold any land, and yet the herd got built up again."

"I have your father to thank for that."

Emily pulled her hand out of his and tugged on her reins, staring at McClanahan. "But Papa was running *our* place—traveling to Denver, and later to Cripple Creek—"

"And his generosity kept the Wickersham ranch in the black till it was self-supporting again." His eyes glimmered as he stopped Arapaho beside her. "Mama didn't want another husband taking her life over, so your papa paid Gus Veatch to stay on as foreman and provided more cattle for him to manage. He also advised her to raise some horses, because they're less work and the market for them's steadier. So by the time my half-brothers died, the debt was retired—but even if they'd outlived Mama, they wouldn't have inherited the ranch, because she'd made me her heir right after Bert passed on."

"But when Lorna died in the fire three years ago . . ." Emily's voice trailed off when she saw McClanahan's face fall. He suddenly looked older, and his eyes hinted at an unspeakable sorrow.

"That's another story entirely, rosebud," he said with a sigh. Matt reached for her hand again, brightening somewhat. "Someday I'll tell you about it, but for now I'm just damn glad to have you. Surely you knew your father was overseeing this ranch for its absentee owner?"

She nodded, wondering what in the world he'd reveal about *that*.

"Well, Elliott obviously never told you *who* the owner was—just as he never told *me* about his beautiful daughter. I guess he thought that information could wait for happier circumstances." Matt gave her an exuberant kiss on the cheek, his grin returning. "But here we are, together. I never expected to have a spread of my own, much less marry the girl next door!"

She had trouble fathoming such a turn of events herself. And as they rode on, Emily ran his story through her mind, realizing that the dates and circumstances did indeed mesh with her memory—as far as those details went. But was it too . . . *convenient*

223

that she was hearing them now, after she'd confessed her love for McClanahan? Too many gaps had opened up in the past few minutes for her to accept Matt's story without questioning it.

"Takes a while for all this news to soak in, doesn't it?" Matt asked cheerfully. "I was going to tell you about myself before I asked for your hand, so you wouldn't think I was taking advantage of you—the way Wickersham did with my mother. But you beat me to the punch."

Had she? Emily bit her lip and tried to ignore the knot that was tightening in her stomach. McClanahan always claimed they thought alike, yet all this time he'd had the benefit of facts she'd never heard. . . .

"Here, rosebud—look out over this ridge, and then toward your place, and think of it!" he said as he opened his arms wide. "With our cattle, and our combined acreage, and the horse business I've built up, this'll be the biggest, richest spread between Denver and Colorado Springs. We were neither one paupers before, but *now!* Can't you just see it?"

Emily looked toward distant barns, stables, and corrals of horses that were as tiny as toys. Set slightly apart from the other buildings was the charred foundation of the main house, where Lorna Wickersham had suffered a fiery death. Only the stone fireplace remained, its chimney pointing like a blackened finger—a warning, perhaps? "I . . . I think I've seen enough," she mumbled.

McClanahan reached for her hand with an apologetic smile. "I understand why you'd want to know more about me, honey, so now I can tell you—"

"Don't insult my intelligence!" she blurted as she backed Sundance away from him. "You've got this big ranch and a thriving livestock business—or you *say* it's yours—but no house to live in, and no woman to keep one for you. So you've cozied up to *me!*"

Matt's mouth dropped open. "How can you say

that? If you'll let me—"

"I've let you talk too much already!" Emily saw the hurt in his eyes and wanted to trust him, but something told her he'd been acting all along. "Why should I believe Papa made any sort of deal with your mother? Or believe that Lorna Wickersham *was* your mother? Papa would've *told* me about these things."

"You were only six when he loaned her that money," McClanahan reasoned.

"He would've told me Lorna had another son! He would've recorded the loan amounts and her repayments in his ledgers." She studied his face, which was becoming ruddier. Was he indeed a victim of coincidence, or had she caught Matt McClanahan in one hell of a lie?

"Emily, you're sharp," he said with strained patience, "but you weren't keeping your father's books back then. You were only twelve! Those ledgers would've been filed away years ago. I can explain—"

"It was only three years ago when Lorna died in that fire—a fire that started when the furnace blew up." Her pulse pounded as awful questions whirled in her head. "How do I know you didn't cause it, McClanahan? You saw what you stood to inherit when she was gone. And for that matter, you probably figured the Burnham ranch would be easy pickings if *Papa* was gone, so how—"

"You're talking nonsense, Emily. Your father and I—"

"—do I know you didn't shoot him?" Her eyes stung with tears as she realized how her naive stupidity had colored her feelings for Matt these past few weeks. "You're friendly with everybody in these parts. You could've found out enough about Papa's business—not to mention his daughter—so you could dupe me while I was in mourning. You figured me for an easy mark; the frosting on the cake, once you married your way into the Burnham estate."

Matt glowered atop his shifting horse. "*You're* the one who proposed."

"And it was the biggest mistake of my life!" she shouted. "I should've followed my original instincts about you, McClanahan. Ever since I accused you of shooting Papa, you've covered your tracks with pretty lies and kisses. You knew all about me, but wouldn't tell me who *you* were till you thought you had me trapped!"

"If you'll stop hollering and listen—"

"I've heard enough. The wedding's off." Emily wheeled her horse in a tight circle and started home. Sundance eased into a full gallop but through her hot, angry tears she could see McClanahan beside her. She scowled, wiping her face with her shirt sleeve. "I'll tell Richard about your tricks, too. And the next time you set foot on Burnham property, he and the men will shoot to kill. Same goes for Silas and Victoria. I'm riding back to Cripple Creek—"

"Rosebud, you're jumping to—"

"I'm not your rosebud, dammit. Not anymore." She clenched her knees harder around Sundance, hoping he would dodge any gopher holes or obstacles she couldn't see clearly. Arapaho was doggedly keeping pace, and she gave McClanahan a final glower before she let her palomino have his head. "Next time you so much as show your face, I'll shoot you myself," she yelled. "And don't think I can't."

McClanahan apparently took her words to heart. He reined in his horse, letting her thunder on across the pastureland toward the boundary . . . and the barbed wire fence. "We've jumped hurdles before," she whispered as she leaned against Sundance's neck. "Please, boy—don't make me unwrap the fence patch and give him a chance to catch up. And please don't fall. I don't have a gun to put you out of your misery, let alone to use on McClanahan if he tries anything else."

When she spotted the evenly-spaced wooden posts

up ahead, Emily held her breath and prayed. "All right, boy . . . it's up and over," she murmured as she raised herself from the saddle. "You can do this. Up . . . up. . . ."

For a few moments she felt suspended in the air, and then she landed with a grunt and a wide grin. McClanahan might be underhanded, but he was right about the quality of the horses he raised. She let the palomino catch his breath, and then urged him into the fastest canter he could maintain. They were making breakneck time over miles they'd ambled across with Matt and Arapaho . . . she tried not to think about the hours she'd spent wondering why McClanahan was so quiet yesterday. He hadn't been wording his proposal at all. He'd been concocting the lie of a lifetime.

As Emily crossed the rolling pastureland, she tried to ignore the beauty of the autumn day. The wind in her hair reminded her of McClanahan's caress, and the sky was the exact color of his eyes when he was laughing. Sundance's hoofbeats pounded steadily, like her lover's heart, and the warm morning air held the fresh scent of sunshine . . . the smell of Matt's clean shirts when he hugged her close. Was there no escaping his hold on her even as she rode away from him? She urged her horse on, not allowing him to walk until she saw her own ranch house and the barns in the distance.

Richard Crabtree came rushing from the stable when she approached, his face furrowed with concern. "Where's Matt? If he's hurt, I'll send—"

"If he comes around here again, you and the men are to shoot on sight." She dismounted and tossed the reins to the sandy-haired foreman. "Take Sundance around the corral a few times to cool him down, and then feed and water him. I'll be leaving for Cripple Creek within the hour."

"But Emily, he's winded—"

"I'll walk him most of the way. We'll have to stop

for the night, and he can rest then." She turned toward the house, her thoughts racing through the preparations for the trip. If she took a quick bath and changed clothes, all she'd need was enough food to—

Richard's hand closed around her elbow. "Care to tell me what this is all about? It must be mighty serious, for you to make your horse suffer, too."

"It's none of your concern," she mumbled as she struggled to free herself from his grasp.

"McClanahan finally talked about the Wickersham place, didn't he?" Crabtree challenged. "I warned him not to surprise you with that information—told him he was inviting a showdown—"

"And *you* wouldn't be angry if—oh, forget it! You wouldn't understand!" Emily rubbed her arm where he'd grabbed her, glaring at hazel eyes and the kind face she'd known for half her life.

"I do understand. A lot more than you do," Richard said in a quieter voice. "A man's entitled to a mistake now and then, but you're making a bigger one if you take off half-cocked before McClanahan can explain everything. He loves you, Emily. And come time to go public with the name of your father's murderer, you'll need a man like Matt standing by you."

She stared at him, still trying to catch her breath from the grueling ride. Or was her pulse pounding because she so badly wanted to believe what the foreman was telling her? Emily shook her head tiredly. "I see he's suckered you into his story, too. But it just doesn't figure, Richard. Papa would've told me about the Wickershams—would've at least mentioned Matt's name and said something about him."

"Elliott had his reasons for keeping quiet. Had he not gotten shot, he probably would've introduced the two of you by now."

She gave a short laugh. "Well, he *did* get shot. And I'm not so sure McClanahan wasn't involved."

"Emily, that's sheer craziness. Matt—"

"I can't take any chances," she said brusquely. "Please—do as I've asked. You're like family to me, but I won't tolerate a foreman who's loyal to Papa's killer. Is that clear?"

Richard raised himself to his full height, his leathery face hardening. "Quite clear, Miss Burnham."

"Fine. Have Sundance ready within the hour."

McClanahan waited until Emily's dust drifted back between the gates before he walked Arapaho around the side of the Burnham barn. Her hair had hung heavily down her back, as dark as Sundance's, which meant she'd taken a bath. He fought the sudden urge to gallop after her—to tell her exactly what he thought of her—but he let his horse rest instead.

"I've got orders to shoot on sight," Crabtree said with a morose chuckle.

"Don't bother. I've already been shot down today." Matt swung to the ground and flexed his aching legs. "Damn. I knew that palomino had some power, but I've been hard put to keep him in sight. Remind me not to breed such strong stock in the future."

"I assume I'll have to wait a day or so for my cutting horses?" The foreman patted his bay's heaving sides, giving him a tight smile. "I got quite an earful from Miss Burnham. Hate to say I told you so, pal, but—"

"So don't. I've got no use for a yellow-haired bitch who won't listen to reason. She thinks I killed Elliott, for Chrissakes!"

Richard let out a long sigh. "She's been through hell these past few months, Matt. Give her a chance to—"

"Nothing doing. Let her sink her claws into some other poor sucker." He led Arapaho toward the barn, avoiding Crabtree's earnest gaze as they walked beside each other.

"So what'll you do now?" the foreman asked quietly. "I thought you and Emily made the perfect pair, and that you'd—"

"Well, we both thought wrong. I intend to finish the job I was originally hired to do, and then get the hell out of anything that involves a Burnham."

Crabtree opened the door to the barn and held it while he and Arapaho passed between the dim stalls. As Matt uncinched the saddle, Richard tossed a fresh bale of hay into the manger. "You don't impress me as a man who lets his woman run off," he commented with a wry smile.

Matt snorted. "She hasn't seen the last of me, Crabtree. I'm going after the evidence we need to prove who killed her father—and after I deliver it, I intend to watch every stroke of her pen as she writes out my paycheck. Wasn't going to charge her, when I thought she was somebody I could care about, but now . . ." He let out a short laugh. "Miss Burnham's going to pay dearly for my services."

He scowled as he piled the saddle and damp blankets in the corner of the stall. The old Matt McClanahan wouldn't have let a woman weasel her way into his heart, let alone threaten his life. Yet earlier today he'd wanted to ride after Emily to explain about the fire—to *make* her understand that he'd known her father, and had liked and respected him a great deal. The little vixen probably wouldn't have listened, set as she was on jumping to conclusions about him being Elliott's killer. . . .

"You'd better walk that horse around a bit before he stiffens up."

Richard's voice broke through his bitter, confused thoughts, and McClanahan let out a long breath. "I suppose I'll be on my way as soon as Arapaho's caught his breath. Got to see if Sheriff Fredricks still has the bullets the coroner dug out of Elliott, and then convict his killer. After that, I probably won't be around these parts too often. Nothing here to come

230

back for."

Crabtree paled slightly, but he nodded. "Let me know if there's anything I can do."

Chapter Twenty-one

As the first streaks of light broke through the cloud cover, Emily awoke. She was shivering and stiff, and her arm muscles ached from hugging herself throughout the cold, lonesome night. Had her feelings for McClanahan altered even the autumn weather when they'd ridden nude in the moonlight? Now, as she rolled up her blankets and took hard biscuits from her saddlebag, the past week with Matt seemed like a dream-turned-nightmare.

"Good thing I woke up from it in time, too," she muttered to Sundance. "That conniving cowboy almost had me roped and tied. What would Papa think if he knew I nearly married the man who killed him?"

The palomino nickered, and Emily swung into the saddle, clucking at him. He, too, seemed drained of his usual energy, so she let him amble along the Gold Camp Road toward Cripple Creek. Before they arrived, she had several puzzles to solve, most of which pertained to Papa's killing. She'd been so sure Nigel Grath had shot him, yet the blaster's motive had never been clear. *McClanahan* certainly stood to gain from her father's death if he married her . . . had he and Grath plotted the episodes in Phantom Canyon and the abandoned mine shaft, to make the miner look guilty while Matt sidetracked her by playing the handsome hero?

Emily recalled the rush of relief she'd felt when she saw McClanahan's lantern-lit face as he descended into the shaft. What an idiot she'd been, babbling about the darkness and how cold she was—and rats' tails! Matt must've known then that she was desperate enough to fall for the most improbable ploy, and if Papa hadn't kept her informed about every detail concerning the ranch, she would've become the dark-haired scoundrel's *wife*. Rat tails, indeed. The only rodent in that inky-black pit was Matt, and he . . .

She stopped nibbling her biscuit, scowling. If Grath had intended to frighten her by mentioning rats, why had he talked about their tails instead of their glistening, beady eyes or their vicious teeth? She'd been so afraid he'd rape her, she hadn't considered how illogical the allusion was. Just as she hadn't recalled that rat tails were the pieces of fuse hanging down from sticks of dynamite before they were lit.

Emily urged Sundance into a trot, her stomach tightening. What had Grath actually said when he told her why he didn't have a lantern? Something like . . . there was no need for her to see the rat tails. What if the rumors Silas had heard about the Angel Claire being sabotaged were true, and she'd been surrounded by the evidence the whole time she was down there? That particular shaft wasn't in use anymore, but it did connect to the rest of the mine, and—

"Oh Lord, Sundance, what if it's already been blown up?" she whispered as she nudged the horse into a canter. "Hundreds of men could've been killed, and here I've been letting Matt sweet-talk me into—giddyap, boy. We've got to get to Cripple Creek!"

Her poor horse tried to obey, but after a few miles he was blowing and wheezing. Emily realized he hadn't rested any better than she had, and as they continued at a walk, her mind raced in frightened circles. What if Silas had been killed in the explosion? The miners would be looking for Matt, and trying to send word to her at the ranch. If anyone thought to question Nigel Grath, he'd probably let out one of his insane cackles and tell the world that he'd shot Elliott

233

Burnham — and that E.R.'s daughter was letting everyone think the heir to the Angel Claire was following him to the grave, when she'd been spying on them for nearly a month. What would her employees do to her when she showed up? What if she couldn't convince them to clean up the rubble, bury the dead, and go back to work?

Emily bit her lip until she tasted the coppery tang of blood. This nervous speculation was getting her nowhere, and as the hours and miles went by, she tried to think rationally about how she should act and what to expect when she arrived. Sundance followed the winding stagecoach road at a steady yet frustratingly slow pace, and just beyond Victor she caught her first sight of Cripple Creek.

From the ridge where she sat to let the palomino rest for a moment, the mining town looked normal, but Emily reasoned that if the Angel Claire had exploded a few days ago, the smoke would've cleared by now. She urged Sundance into a trot, her eyes riveted to the horizon.

Moments later she heard a long, ominous rumble in the distance, and then the earth belched a brilliant ball of flame — on the side of town where the Angel Claire was. Emily's heart thudded weakly. Unable to take her gaze from the horrible column of fire and smoke, Emily was sickened to think that even if she'd been able to gallop Sundance into Cripple Creek, she would've been too late to prevent the disaster. As they plodded along, she imagined the miners' faces . . . how many would've been down in the mine, never to see the sunlight again? How many widows would she have to console? And what if Silas was lost in the rubble, already dead?

Clenching her eyes shut, Emily tried to control her panicky thoughts. Maybe it wasn't the Angel Claire at all — furnaces in homes and businesses exploded now and then, just as the one at the Wickersham ranch had. Or maybe the warehouse that supplied dynamite to all the mines had blown up. They were grisly thoughts, but they kept her from giving in to tears of utter desperation. Had Grath and McClanahan killed Papa and now wiped out part of his legacy, and his partner as well?

Emily grimaced as Sundance entered Cripple Creek. Fire bells were clanging, and scores of people, horses, and wagons were rushing toward the far edge of town. Black smoke was billowing into the sky, and as she turned her horse down one of the less-crowded side streets, her nose protested at the smell of blasting powder and something she couldn't identify. She tugged at the reins, her heart stopping. The Angel Claire's shaft house was engulfed in angry orange flames that threatened the other buildings as well.

Firemen were battling the blaze as more horse-drawn engines and pumps arrived, and a massive crowd was gathering despite the efforts of Barry Thompson and his deputies to keep them a safe distance from the disaster. Her eyes stinging from smoke and tears, Emily tied Sundance to a post a few blocks down the street and pushed nervously between the murmuring onlookers. If Silas Hughes was hurt—and even if he wasn't—it was her responsibility to take charge of the rescue efforts.

Coughing men with scorched, blackened skin were leading or carrying victims toward the street, where wagons from the hospital were pulling up. Emily searched their faces anxiously as she dodged frenzied firemen. There was Tom Bledsoe, his lifeless form draped over Zach Short's bullish frame. Two bodies lying in a tangle near the office were missing some limbs; Emily looked away to keep from retching, realizing that the indescribable, inescapable stench around her came from charred flesh.

At the sight of a slender man in black pants and a torn, bloodied shirt, Emily broke into a run. "Silas! Silas, you're all right!"

The mine manager turned, his smudged face lighting up with recognition. "Emily" he rasped as he drew her out of a fireman's path. "I was just thinking how glad I was that you weren't here to see—"

"I was riding in from Victor when it exploded. How many men were down there?"

"Not the full shift, thank God. Ever since you left for the ranch, we've been trying to find where Grath did his dirty work—I was almost convinced he started those rumors just to be sadistic—and now this." Silas squinted toward the bright flames, sighing heavily. "He must've rigged a trip wire somewhere, or else he has an accomplice. The explosion seemed to start in the abandoned shaft where—"

"It did. When Grath dragged me down there, I thought he was talking about rats' tails instead of fuses." Emily winced and wrapped her arms around him as the ore house roof collapsed. "I should've known—should've been able to warn you about—"

"You were scared for your life when that maniac kidnapped you." His arms tightened around her for a moment before he released her, and he scanned the crowd. "Where's McClanahan? God knows we'll need him, come time to sort out the bodies and arrange the funerals."

Emily's throat constricted. "He's not coming back."

"What?" Silas stooped, as though the roar of the fire and the shouting around them had kept him from hearing her.

"I said he's not coming back. We'll handle the details ourselves."

The gray-haired mine manager scowled. "But we've *got* to have McClanahan—"

"If you knew what he tried to pull, you wouldn't say that," Emily replied bitterly. "We'll talk about it later. These men need our help."

Silas straightened to his full height again, his expression still dark as he studied her. "Put your hair under your hat. Earlier this morning I was asked if Elliott's daughter was finally taking over his affairs. It seems someone saw you at a party in the Springs this week."

She gasped as she wound her hair into a clumsy coil. Surely the men at Taylor West's hadn't had time to spread the word about her here in Cripple, and yet . . . she chided herself once again for becoming so entranced by McClanahan that she hadn't considered the consequences of being seen with him. "What'd you say?"

"I denied any knowledge of it, of course. Oh Lord, here come more stretchers."

As he hurried toward the men who carried inert, mangled bodies between them, Emily had the overwhelming urge to walk away from the heart-wrenching devastation around her. The flames, which had gutted the Angel Claire's shaft house, were being contained by the firemen now, but only in the aftermath would they know the toll Nigel Grath's evil handiwork had taken. She slipped through the crowd to where hospital workers were treating injured miners, and asked where she could be of help.

All afternoon she bandaged blistered flesh and wiped feverish foreheads. She recognized most of the victims, so her ministrations were all the more difficult to perform. The men who were conscious smiled feebly and called her Eliza—some asked where she'd been the past several days—and Emily realized her deception would have to end soon. Miners who'd given their best years, not to mention life and limb, deserved the truth about the young woman who now employed them.

As she saw women slump and dissolve into tears when they found their men among the disfigured corpses, she nearly suffocated from guilt. Her story hadn't *caused* the explosion of the Angel Claire, but perhaps if she'd announced her intentions to search out Elliott Burnham's murderer, he would've been caught before he could kill so many other good men. It was a heavy burden, and Emily realized she'd be carrying these deaths on her conscience for the rest of her life.

It was nearly dusk when the fire above ground had been quenched and the firemen were pulling their hoses and ladders out of the main shaft of the mine. Most of the blackened buildings had walls standing, but the report from the rescuers who'd surveyed the underground wreckage was grim. It would take weeks to clear out the debris and rebuild the mine's network of support timbers, conveyers, and elevators. The crews would be under constant risk of cave-in, knowing that each scoop of dirt could cause an avalanche, or might unearth more victims of today's infernal blast.

Women from several churches were setting up tables of food, and ladies from the Golden Rose and other houses on Myers Avenue were passing out cups of hot coffee and sandwiches. The aromas of beef stew and fried chicken made Emily realize how hungry and exhausted she was, but before she could pick up a plate, Silas grasped her shoulder.

"Let's go to the house," he murmured tiredly. "We'll eat, and I'll have Idaho tend these burns on my arms. And then you'll tell me about this business with McClanahan. People are already asking where he is."

Emily nodded, dreading the discussion as she shuffled toward the post where she'd tied Sundance. She let the horse plod through the thinning crowd, her hat slung low over her face as she tried to piece together a rational argument Silas would accept. When she approached the house, Idaho rushed out, his expression showing both worry and joy.

"Miss Emily, these old eyes are mighty damn glad to see you!" he gushed as he took her reins. "I was working on my charts when your papa's mine went up, and I knew—"

"Please, Idaho, I'm exhausted," she mumbled.

"Why of course you are, child," he replied with a clutching hug. "Mr. Silas should be out of the tub by now. Let's make sure none of this blood's yours, and after your bath you'll have some of Idaho's chicken and dumplings."

Emily eased out of his arms and looked at her smeared, smelly clothing. She climbed the stairs slowly, relieved to hear Silas moving behind his closed bedroom door. But even as she soaked the grime of the fire away and took her time dressing, she knew she was only postponing the mine superintendent's heated lecture — a lecture she certainly deserved.

When she sat down at the table, Silas was finishing his dinner. He set his silverware across his plate with a purposeful air that told her he, too, had been planning what he'd say. His gaze was intent as he pushed his chair back slightly from the table.

"H — how many men did we lose?" Emily asked quietly.

Silas cleared his throat. "Eight are dead and seven in the hospital aren't expected to survive the night. We'll see how many are unaccounted for when we check the rolls tomorrow morning. Had Grath not let those rumors out, *everyone* could've been killed."

She took a tiny bite of chicken, then set her fork down. "We'll cover the funeral expenses, and the hospital bills. And we need to find out if the families prefer their pensions in installments or lump sums. Papa would've wanted it that way."

"I'm making those condolence calls tonight," the man across from her stated. He looked directly into her eyes, letting out a sigh that hinted at strained patience. "My job would be a helluva lot simpler if McClanahan were here, Emily."

His quiet, challenging tone made her stiffen. "Well, he's not."

"Was that your choice or his?"

"What does it matter?" she blurted. "You and I would've handled these details had he never shown up at the mine, and we'll —"

"But he *did,* and everyone in town will be expecting

239

him to carry out his managerial responsibilities." Silas glared, his face growing ruddy. "And how do *you* expect to be any help? You've set yourself up as a cleaning girl and a payroll clerk—or did you forget those roles while Matt was sweeping you off your—"

"McClanahan's nothing but a conniving fortune hunter who—"

"I'd have an easier time believing that if he weren't a wealthy man in his own right."

Emily scowled, her temper rising with her voice. "And all he cares about is adding more to his coffers—annexing the Burnham estate to his, so he'll own the biggest spread between Denver and Colorado Springs."

"If he wants your father's ranch, he can certainly afford to buy it," Silas replied sharply. "He has numerous accounts in Colorado Springs banks, and happens to be a silent partner in Taylor West's brokerage. I have a feeling Mr. McClanahan made you a different sort of offer—"

"How'd you know all that?" she snapped.

He brushed his silvery hair back from his brow, rolling his eyes. "I'm not blind, Emily. You both made feeble excuses about seeing to Burnham business when you left, but—"

"No, I mean the part about the brokerage." Emily caught a catlike smile, which lasted only a fraction of a second before Silas's face turned stern again.

"I did some checking around—something any intelligent manager would do," he added pointedly. "McClanahan's business reputation is above reproach. Which means this parting of ways is a personal vendetta, and I'd bet my shares in the Angel Claire that *you* brought it on."

Emily stood up so fast her chair fell over backward. "Are you forgetting who signs your checks now?"

"How can I?" he retorted. "She's the naive, immature young woman who got me *into* this mess! Surely whatever quarrel you had with McClanahan could've waited until your father's murder was cleared up."

"What if *he* killed Papa? He was trying to wrangle—"

"Emily, that's preposterous. Everything I've learned about Matt McClanahan has overridden my initial doubts about him." Silas stood, pointing, as if to reestablish superiority over her. "If your father were alive, I'm certain he'd hire Matt as a manager. What I can't figure out is why a man of McClanahan's wealth wanted the job of stalking Elliott's killer . . . and why the young woman who'd so obviously fallen for him is now acting like a lovelorn ninny."

She wanted to slap him, but exhaustion suddenly overwhelmed her. Emily gripped the edge of the table, shutting her eyes. "It's none of your business, Mr. Hughes."

"But it *is* my business, Miss Burnham," he said in a low, biting voice. "And it's the concern of every man employed at the mine, and every woman who's suddenly found herself a widow. You were a fool not to keep your personal feelings for McClanahan separate from your business dealings with him. But I was a bigger fool for letting it happen—and for allowing you to deceive people about your identity in the first place. And now I have to visit the dead miners' families. God knows what I'll think of to say to them."

Emily watched him stride toward the vestibule, her pulse still pounding angrily. Of all the nerve, to call her a lovelorn *ninny*, after the grueling day she'd spent patching up her employees and watching her father's mine go up in flames! Yet as she tossed fitfully in her bed that night, she realized that Silas was right, and that he was paying a high price for going along with her fantasies about avenging Papa's death. There was only one decent thing to do now. And as Emily mumbled her prayers before dropping off to sleep, she hoped her decision wouldn't make things even worse.

Chapter Twenty-two

Emily sat down at the table, smoothing the folds of her plainest brown dress. After a night of soul-searching she still wasn't sure how to state her plan to Silas, whose egg-smeared plate and silverware were pushed toward the center of the table. He was engrossed in the *Cripple Creek Times,* his head encircled with cigar smoke as he read the account of the explosion—or else he was doing a fine job of ignoring her.

"Thanks, Idaho," she murmured as the old cook set a plate of biscuits, bacon, and eggs before her. She poured a cup of tea, hesitant to interrupt the mine manager's concentration. It was embarrassing—downright infuriating—to know that Silas Hughes had seen through her feelings for Matt before they'd gone to the ranch. He seemed so certain that McClanahan was above reproach, innocent of Papa's murder. Emily had expected her father's partner to be angry about McClanahan not coming back, but she was appalled that he'd taken Matt's side and not her own.

Maybe she *had* fallen prey to her imagination. Papa had often chided her about jumping to conclusions before all the evidence was presented. She glanced up as Silas turned a page; she owed him an apology for behaving so badly last night, but she refused to discuss her grudge against Matt. "Looks like the *Times* ran a big spread on the explosion," she began quietly.

Silas was silent for several seconds, as though still ignoring her. "Biggest tragedy this town's seen for a few years. I'm not looking forward to being hounded by reporters as the cleanup progresses, either."

Emily nodded and broke a biscuit in half. "I don't suppose I ought to volunteer any information, if they happen to ask me about it."

The mine superintendent's expression was guarded as Idaho shuffled through the dining room to answer a knock at the front door. "That's the most sensible statement you've made lately, young lady."

"Silas, I — I was upset and tired last night, and I said some things I didn't — "

"Excuse me, Mr. Hughes," the colored housekeeper murmured as he approached the table. "Marshal Thompson wants a word with you. Says it's urgent."

Silas scowled. "Show him in. I hope there hasn't been more trouble at the mine."

The tall marshal strode into the room, smiling politely as he refused the plate of breakfast Idaho offered him. He sat down beside Silas and nodded at Emily as he removed his hat. "Sorry to interrupt your meal, but Grath's been flitting around his cell like a crazed squirrel since the Angel Claire blew up. He says he'll talk, but only if you and the girl are there to listen."

Emily's heart rattled against her ribcage as Silas gave her a wary glance. How much did Thompson know about who she really was?

"He's admitting he planted the dynamite?" her father's partner asked cautiously.

"That's my guess. But he's so damn jittery, I wouldn't be surprised if he forgets why I've asked you to come."

"Probably opium withdrawal." The mine manager laid his newspaper aside, letting out a long breath. "What happens if he admits his guilt?"

"He gets shipped to the state pen in Canon City to

await trial," Thompson replied. "Can't happen too soon, far as I'm concerned. He's driving me crazy with that hyena laugh."

Emily pretended to be eating so her nervousness wouldn't show. Why did Grath want *her* there, unless he intended to expose her deception? This was the worst possible day for Cripple Creek to learn about how she'd established herself here under false pretenses.

"We'll be there as soon as we finish breakfast, Barry," Silas stated.

"I'd appreciate it." The marshal rose from his chair and positioned his hat on his thick thatch of hair. "Grath was asking for McClanahan, too, but they tell me he's checked out of the Imperial. You wouldn't know where I could find him, would you?"

"He's still in Colorado Springs, going over cattle accounts at the Flaming B," Silas replied coolly. "We've sent word to Miss Burnham about her mine, but it always takes a while to receive her reply."

Thompson shook his head. "This isn't news she'll want to hear. Sorry you lost so many good men, Hughes. Let me know if I can send some deputies to keep the curiosity seekers away once you start digging through the rubble."

"Thanks, Barry, I might have to take you up on that."

"Miss Eliza," the marshal said with a nod.

She smiled feebly, watching him walk toward the vestibule with long, confident strides. "Is Clancy Donahue still in jail, Mr. Thompson?"

"Yes, ma'am, he is. I hear Miss Chatterly might pay his bail, though." Thompson turned, giving her a cautious smile. "Since Zenia Collins took off with that piano player, the tension's eased a bit at the Golden Rose, but nobody Victoria's tried as a bouncer can keep order the way Donahue did. I'd think twice about getting him riled. Well — see you folks in a bit."

When the door closed, Emily frowned. "Zenia and Josh ran off? I never dreamed she'd leave until she worked off her debt to—"

"Victoria told me the dresses were paid in full," Silas replied with a shrug. "Didn't say who the girl's benefactor was, though."

She looked pointedly at Idaho, who was clearing Silas's place.

"Wasn't *my* money she used," the old man insisted, "but I'd certainly have given it to her. Sweet child like that's meant for a higher purpose than whoring."

Emily nodded absently and let him take her plate. How could so much have happened in the few short days she'd spent at the ranch? When she felt Silas gazing at her, she looked up from her musings.

"Shall we put aside our differences for now and see what Grath has to say?" he asked quietly. "I'm not sure I'll believe all I hear, but it's better for everyone if we can point a finger at the culprit in the Angel Claire disaster."

During the buggy ride across town, Emily tried to keep her thoughts under control. The idea of confronting Papa's killer and her kidnapper frightened her. If those wicked little eyes had seen through her deception, what might the maniacal blaster say about her now that he'd been deprived of his drug for several days?

"Are you all right?" Hughes asked as he halted the horses in front of the marshal's office.

Emily glanced toward the window, where Barry was looking out. "Grath knows who I am, Silas. What if he only asked me here to expose my story? If the miners find out—"

"I doubt anything he says will get past the jail walls unless Thompson wants it to, but you've got a point." Silas secured the reins and came around to help her down. "Maybe it's time the marshal learned the truth anyway. He'll be more help come time to tell the men, if he's had a chance to mull the whole thing

245

over. We'll just have to see what Grath says."

Emily nodded, and decided her best strategy was to remain silent unless she was spoken to. The last thing Silas needed was a write-up in the local papers about shouted accusations and denials between the Angel Claire's saboteur and a young woman who turned out to be Elliott Burnham's daughter.

The marshal's office was small and cluttered, smelling of stale coffee and unwashed bodies. From Thompson's desk she could see down the short hallway to where Clancy Donahue lounged on his bunk, looking like a bear who'd digested a large meal and was ready to hibernate. There was the clatter of a tin cup being raked across cell bars, and a familiar voice rasped, "Bring 'em in here, Thompson. Let's get this show over with."

"Shut up. You'll get your say in due time." The marshal looked at them with an apologetic smile. "Obnoxious little weasel refuses to eat, and tries to bribe me into bringing him a pipe. You might hear things that'll burn your ears, Eliza."

Emily nodded, looking away from his curious gaze. She'd seen Barry Thompson dozens of times at the Golden Rose, yet she'd never felt so scrutinized, as though *she* were under suspicion for blowing up the mine. When the marshal led the way to a small room at the end of the hall, she followed him, focusing on his broad back so she wouldn't see Nigel Grath leering at her from his cell. She took the chair Thompson offered, scooting it closer to Silas as he sat down. The dark, unadorned walls seemed to close in on them . . . how would they protect themselves if Grath went beserk in here?

Yet when Thompson led him in, the prisoner seemed unusually subdued. Grath sat down at the opposite end of the wooden table, resting his shackled hands on its scarred surface. He'd lost weight—what kept him from slipping those skinny wrists out of his handcuffs? Emily felt him watching her, but she avoided the temptation to glare back at him. The marshal leaned against the closed door behind them, silent.

After an uncomfortable pause, Silas spoke first. "Well? Say your piece, dammit. Plenty of worthier men deserve my attention right now."

Grath cleared his throat, and in a slow, gravelly whine, he began. "I said I'd send the Angel Claire sky-high, and I did."

"What the hell for?" The mine manager nearly sprang from his chair, but he caught himself. He clenched his fists, glaring across the little table.

" 'Twas my way of callin' attention to intolerable conditions," Nigel replied, his words accented with hatred. "You men who bank the profits offa that gold—wearin' your fancy suits and drinkin' your fancy whiskey—don't understand about slavin' in that damn hellhole."

Silas crossed his arms stiffly. "That's why the Federation exists—to hear grievances and present them to the management. You could've—"

"I didn't ask ya here for a lecture, Hughes," Grath snarled. He banged his handcuffs against the table, then let out a long breath and sat back. "I've confessed to my crime now. I didn't have to, ya know."

"You sniveling little bastard! You'll roast in hell for killing all those men," Silas said in a menacing whisper. "And I intend to see that you *rot* in that penitentiary—solitary confinement in an unlighted cell until' they put you to death."

Emily shifted; she'd never heard Silas Hughes sound so set on retribution. She fixed her gaze on the taut, white hands that gripped the edge of his chair seat, not daring to look at Nigel Grath.

"Did you dig that blasting pattern in Phantom Canyon a few weeks back?" the marshal asked from his post at the door. "Hundreds of lives could've been lost there, too."

Grath's laugh was disjointed and it echoed in the

247

tiny room. "Your men never found no dynamite, did they, Thompson? I know, 'cause I watched 'em search. Them holes was just a warnin'—a warnin' Hughes shoulda took seriously. Gave me a chance to do my real work at the mine."

So McClanahan had guessed correctly: Nigel Grath was pulling their strings during the whole episode at Phantom Canyon. Emily was glad Matt wasn't here to gloat, yet his presence would've had a stabilizing effect—one more man to subdue Grath as he began to act like the crazed addict the marshal claimed he was. Thompson showed no sign of leading the blaster back to his cell, but surely the prisoner wouldn't confess to anything else. All he could do now was point the finger at *her* and talk about—

"Whatcha so nervous about, girlie? I'd think you'd be dancin' a jig on this table, seein' me gettin' my comeuppance."

Emily didn't respond. She glanced briefly at Silas, whose steady gaze confirmed the wisdom of her silence.

"Lookit me, you lyin' little bitch." Grath said in a loud rasp. "I coulda had you for dessert down in that abandoned shaft, but no—I listened to your damn ransom idea."

"Which proves she's a lot smarter than you are," Silas cut in smugly.

"I wanna hear *her* say that," the blaster taunted. "I'm not the only one who's told a few tales, am I, Blondie?"

Emily eyed him coldly, despising the ferretlike face beneath his scraggly, dark hair. "What decent person *wouldn't* try to get away from you?" she said in a shaky voice. "You're the filthiest, greediest little—"

"Murderer," Grath finished with a nasty laugh. His shiny eyes narrowed as he leaned toward her. "It don't make no difference if I admit to it now, since I'm bein' locked up for blastin' the mine. I *did* kill your daddy, Blondie. Just wanted to be sure you knew

248

that, before they put me away." He stood, letting out a high, loonish laugh as he swayed toward the door. "Show's over, Thompson. Now get me the hell outta here."

Emily's knees knocked, and she could not catch her breath as the lawman grabbed Grath by the shoulder.

"What's this about her father?" Thompson demanded as he pressed the scrawny convict against the wall. "Eliza is Hughes's niece, and her father abandoned her when—"

An ear-piercing cackle rang around the walls of the little room. "Which means Hughes and Blondie are bigger liars than me. That's Elliott Burnham's daughter, Thompson. Been pullin' the wool over our eyes for more than a month."

The marshal shot them a confused glance and then shoved Nigel Grath out the door ahead of him. "I've had all I can take of your crazy yammering. Now get in this cell and shut your. . . ."

As Barry's voice faded down the hall, Emily began to pace. *"Now* what do we do? That damn—"

"We stay calm and answer Thompson's questions," Silas replied firmly. He stepped in front of her, placing his hands on her shoulders. "You heard him—he thinks Grath's out of his head. But if we tell him the truth, Barry'll understand why we kept your name a secret. And now that the murderer's confessed, it's time to set things straight anyway."

"That's an interesting theory, Silas. Maybe you'd better explain it."

Emily gasped when she saw that Marshal Thompson was watching them. He shut the door, and then came over to study her carefully. "Silas was only protecting me from men who might try to take over Papa's estate," she said weakly. "The whole scheme was my idea, and it . . . sort of backfired."

Barry lifted her chin with a broad, calloused hand, a dimple flickering in his cheek. "You really are E. R. Burnham's daughter?"

She nodded, wishing McClanahan were here to help smooth out her tangled stories. Matt might be underhanded, but having the marshal for a friend was a point in his favor at times like these.

"Now why didn't I see that? I've looked you over a dozen times—and I knew Burnham had a girl about your age." He shook his head, releasing her. "How'd it happen, sweetheart? As I recall, you showed up in Cripple Creek several weeks ago."

"Right after Sheriff Fredricks called off his search for Elliott's killer," Silas added quietly. "Emily didn't see the man who shot him, but she thought he might reappear at one of the Burnham businesses—and she was right. Out of respect for Elliott, I went along with her plan to ferret out his murderer, pretending to be her uncle. It's not the most honorable thing I've ever done, but I felt the end justified the means."

The marshal was still shaking his head, looking amused yet bewildered because he'd fallen for her ruse. "Nobody can fault you for helping her, Silas. But if the miners get word that you and Miss Burnham have lied to them—especially now—you might have an uprising on your hands to equal the one a few years back." Thompson focused wide, gentle eyes on Emily, studying her with an intensity that seemed as personal as it was professionl. "Who else knows?"

"Idaho, and Clancy Donahue, and the men at the ranch," Emily mumbled.

"And Matt McClanahan," the mine manager added. "For a while, we thought *he* killed Elliott, but since we've taken him into our confidence we've discovered he's a good man to have on our side."

"I've known Matt a long time, and I've never seen him draw his gun," Barry said. Then he glanced in the direction of the cells. "You'd better find a way to tell your men about this as soon as possible, because folks'll get suspicious if Miss Burnham doesn't come to Cripple, now that her mine's in a shambles. I'll ship Grath to Canon City tomorrow, so he won't cause you any more trouble than you've already got." He paused, stroking his chin. "You think Donahue'll stay quiet about this? Victoria's decided to hire him back, and he and Grath have gotten pretty thick since they've been in here."

"It's in his own best interest to let me do the talking," Silas replied. "Miss Chatterly only tolerates him because he's big, and because she thinks Emily transferred him to the Golden Rose."

"The ranch foreman's not keen on taking him back either," Emily chimed in. "So if he shoots off his mouth, he'll be out of a job completely."

Barry Thompson raised his eyebrows as though he knew something he wasn't telling. "Well — better see to getting Grath out of here. I'm real sorry about the way things've happened, Emily. You and Silas let me know how I can help, all right?"

She'd come this far without giving in to her grief, yet the lawman's sympathetic voice made her eyes sting. Emily preceded Silas out the front door, blinking rapidly as he helped her into the buggy. A tear finally slithered down each cheek, but she made no effort to wipe her face.

". . . drop you by the house before I go to the mine," the man beside her was saying. "And until we figure out how to tell Victoria about this, maybe you'd better stay away from the . . . Emily? You're pale as death. Do you feel all right?"

She let out a shuddery breath and looked away.

"What a stupid thing to say. Of course you're not all right — your whole damn world's caved in." After a moment, Silas's hand closed around hers and he held it tightly. "Emily, we've had our spats but through it all you've amazed me, young lady. You're welcome to stay —"

"Please, **Silas**, don't turn into a marshmallow."

"What?" **He** halted the horses in front of his house, still grasping her hand.

Emily blinked and smiled ruefully at him. "I've made some decisions, Mr. Hughes, and if you act *too* understanding I'll get too weepy to tell you about them."

His gray eyes widened in confusion. "Oh . . . yes, of course. Shall we talk inside?"

With a demure smile, she accepted his help down from the buggy. They went into the study, and while Emily gazed at Papa's portrait, silently summoning his support, Silas instructed Idaho to bring them in a pot of tea. The housekeeper seemed to sense their conversation wouldn't include him, so he excused himself after he filled their china cups.

Silas slipped into the chair behind the massive desk, wearing a pensive expression.

Emily picked up her teacup, and then set it down. "I'm going to see Papa's attorney, Mr. VanAntwerp, and have the Angel Claire deeded over to you," she said quietly. "I feel badly doing it now, after it's been nearly destroyed, but—"

"Don't be ridiculous, Emily." Silas frowned, making his eyebrows meet. "The mine was named for your mother—it's part of your father's legacy, which he intended to pass on to you."

"Please don't argue," she said with a sigh. "The mine would be nothing without your years of supervision and effort. Papa always said so, and I think after all you've done for me, he'd want you to have it. I certainly don't need the income."

The gray-haired manager took a long sip of tea. "Neither do I," he admitted. "I'm flattered by your generosity, but—"

"Then take it. I'm not doing you that much of a favor, when you consider the average life expectancy of a gold mine. I'm signing the Rose over to Miss Victoria, too. Papa built it for her, and it's really not the sort of business I'm cut out for."

Silas smiled, then he actually chuckled. "I have to agree with you on that point. And in all fairness to

Miss Chatterly, we should tell her who you are in person, before she hears it from one of her customers. If you'd like me to call on her—"

"I'll do it. The deception was my idea, so it's my responsibility to explain it." Emily drank deeply of the hot, soothing tea, dreading the moment she had to face Victoria Chatterly. She'd been Papa's lover and confidante, the woman who'd encouraged him to enjoy investing his money again, and the English madame's rare but formidable temper would probably flare up no matter how diplomatically Emily explained her presence in Cripple Creek.

"Perhaps Mr. McClanahan could be persuaded to accompany you," the man behind the desk said softly.

"No," Emily insisted. "He tried to trick me, and I won't tolerate his cavalier attitude any longer."

Silas cleared his throat as he set his teacup back on the tray. "Is it true that you were out shopping with him, and that you socialized with some of your father's associates?"

Emily nodded, again disgusted that she hadn't foreseen the consequences of letting Matt show her off.

"Then let me suggest that you make these arrangements during the next few days, while people are preoccupied with the miners' funerals. By the end of the week, we'll have to announce that you've been here—"

"I'll do it."

Her father's partner gazed intently into her eyes, inclining his lean frame toward her. "You're dealing yourself some awfully heavy penance, Emily. Your father always encouraged your independence, but even he would refuse to let you bear this burden alone. I insist on helping you, dear, because Elliott was my closest friend. And because no matter how able you are to manage his estate, you'll need some . . . impartial advice and support when eligible men find out you're back in circulation."

Emily didn't lower her gaze—that would be conceding to the earnest gentleman across the desk—but she didn't protest either.

"It's settled, then. Was there anything else you wanted to discuss?"

She gave him a wry smile. "I think we've covered enough business for one day. And I know you're wanting to get back to the mine."

Silas rose with a nod. Was that a trace of wistfulness in his pale gray eyes as he looked at her? If so, it disappeared as he slipped his hat on, and his angular face resumed its usual businesslike expression. "I'm sorry McClanahan's disappointed you, Emily," he said. "You two were well suited. Even your father would've thought so."

When his footsteps echoed through the parlor, Emily allowed her grief to well up inside her and pour out. She cried silently, huddled in her chair, feeling utterly, hopelessly alone. After weeks of pitting herself against the wiles of her father's killer, the hardest task still loomed before her. Now that she could tell Papa's friends and associates who shot him, she had no crusade to occupy her time. A cold, bleak winter stretched ahead of her, when there would be nothing to do except ponder not one but two holes in her heart.

"There now, Miss Emily, you blow your nose into Idaho's hanky and tell him what's happened," the old Negro whispered lovingly. He stood behind her chair, leaning over it to wrap an arm around her as he held the square of crisply-creased linen before her. "Is it true? Did Nigel Grath shoot your papa and my Viry, and then blow up the Angel Claire?"

"He says he did. The marshal's shipping him off to Canon City tomorrow," she replied with a hitch in her voice.

Idaho's hug tightened around her shoulders. "So you did it—you snared the killer. And once the details are ironed out, we can go home again. Get on with our lives."

Home again . . . as Emily envisioned the high-ceilinged rooms at the ranch, furnished with their friendly, familiar charm, she knew Idaho was only pretending their days could still have meaning and purpose there — just as she was. Nigel Grath's confession should have filled her with a victorious thrill: despite a few treacherous twists of fate, the loyal daughter had avenged her father's death and thereby proven herself worthy to assume command of his empire.

But why did she feel so empty? And why did the blaster's confession have such a hollow ring to it?

Chapter Twenty-three

Matt McClanahan tied Arapaho to the post in front of the marshal's office, gazing intently into the little building through the early-morning fog. All the lamps were lit, but when he stepped inside, Thompson didn't seem to be around. McClanahan scowled as he walked quickly through the main room and past the empty jail cells. When he opened the door that led to the back alley, two flashes in quick succession made him blink. A pair of photographers adjusted their tripods for another shot, and when Matt saw their subject—an unkempt, skeletal man they'd propped against a hay wagon—he looked again to be sure who it was.

Seeing the glowing tip of the marshal's cigarette in the deep blue of the dawn, Matt crossed the alley. "What the hell happened?"

Barry let his smoke out in a slow stream. "Grath braided his bedsheet and hung himself last night." The marshal studied McClanahan's face, and then he grinned slowly. "They say a man's beard grows fastest when his woman's holding out on him. Or did you lose your razor?"

"Neither," Matt grunted. "It's almost winter, you know. Or maybe I'm growing it to prove a point."

"Uh-huh." They watched the photographers decide who would shoot first before Thompson spoke again. "Guess you heard about the mine, and that Grath confessed to blowing it up?"

"Who hasn't? It's in all the papers—which was one reason I came into Cripple." Had Emily's true identity come out in the aftermath of the Angel Claire disaster? Matt decided to steer away from that subject and get right to the reason for his visit. "Where's Donahue?"

"Victoria bailed him out last night. Seems that for all his faults, he's the best bouncer she can come up with, so—"

"Thompson, didn't I tell you to keep him locked up till I got back? He's a wanted man, dammit!"

The marshal frowned and walked farther away from the photographers, who were eyeing them curiously. "But he's wanted for crimes he committed before he came to Cripple," Barry reminded him in an impatient whisper. "If those other states are so hot for him, they can come and get him! My deputies are too busy keeping order around the Angel Claire to be breaking up fights at the Rose, so I put him back to work."

"What about *my* work?" McClanahan demanded. "I was gathering evidence that would—"

"Far as *I* could tell, you were galavanting around Colorado Springs with a lady friend." Thompson leaned down slightly, his face hardening with anger. "If Donahue was so vital to your case, why didn't you have me lock him up a long time ago? And why didn't you tell me your little blonde was E. R. Burnham's daughter?"

Matt stiffened and then swore at himself for not catching Donahue on his own—and for getting mixed up in Emily's harebrained scheme in the first place. "It was for her own protection, Barry. How'd you find out?"

"Grath dropped that bomb when he confessed to shooting Elliott. Silas and Emily were here—asked me not to let that part of the story out to the papers, so they can square things away with Angel Claire

257

employees after the miners' funeral."

Matt eyed him intently. "Sort of risking your badge, going along with their lies, aren't you?"

The marshal glanced toward the photographers, who were folding their tripods, and tossed his cigarette aside. "This all started out as a favor to you, McClanahan. We're both in too deep to jump out now . . . and I figure with Grath dead, things'll smooth out of their own accord."

He was probably right, and it was pointless to let his frustrations with Emily spoil a friendship that had seen him through some tighter spots than this one over the years. Giving Thompson a friendly slap on the back, Matt felt his anger retreating. "Did they believe his story about killing Elliott?"

"Seemed to. Why?"

He glanced at the departing photographers, a grim smile spreading across his face. "Nigel Grath didn't shoot him."

"And just what makes you so sure—"

"Remember a few weeks back, in front of Delmonico's, when we watched Emily flat-out refuse to marry Clancy Donahue?"

Barry frowned again. "Sure. But that was before I realized she was heir to the Burnham fortune."

"And now that you know—and you've seen how Donahue operates—what do you suppose he's after?"

The marshal cleared his throat, his scowl deepening. "Then why the hell'd Grath confess to killing Elliott Burnham?"

"Maybe he and Clancy made a deal—we'll probably never know," Matt replied with a shrug. "If you rounded up Donahue's guns, like I asked, we'll see if these slugs in my pocket fit any of them."

The marshal's rugged face paled slightly and he started toward his office. "I've got them. When're you going to tell Emily about this?"

"I'm not."

Barry's expression was pointedly grave as he shut

the jailhouse door behind them. "Now that Clancy's out, her life's in danger, McClanahan. You can't just—"

"No more than it's been for the past month," he said quietly. "Don't you see? Donahue's proposals have been a smokescreen, and Grath's confession's the perfect cover for him now. He figures that if he marries Emily, he'll have the Burnham fortune—not to mention *her*—without having to kill her and attract attention from the law. But she's too sharp to fall for his cow eyes, Barry. And while she's stalling him, he's bound to get mad and tip his hand. So she'll catch her father's killer, just as she intended to all along."

Sliding into the chair behind his desk, Thompson gave him a catlike smile. "If Emily's so smart, and if she was so fascinated by your company last week, why'd she come back to town alone?"

"Bullheadedness."

The marshal chuckled softly. "Care to explain that?"

"Nope." He reached into his jacket pocket for the bullets, avoiding his friend's teasing gaze. "I was hired to do a job, and I'll finish it—so Miss Burnham will have the honor of signing my paycheck before I leave her to fend for herself. She had her chance, and she blew it."

"Uh-huh. That's how I had it figured." Barry laid three pistols on his desk: a pearl-handled .38, and two .45 caliber revolvers. "I told Donahue these would stay here for safekeeping, in case he got any ideas about following Zenia and that colored piano player. Think they're what you're looking for?"

McClanahan picked up the nearest .45, studying its hammer closely as he cocked it. "Not this one. The bullets I got from Fredricks were nicked, as though the hammer that fired them was bent or . . . aha—here we go."

Thompson leaned over his desk to gaze at the second revolver, which Matt had cocked and was now grinning at. "Poorest job of welding I've ever seen," the marshal commented. "I could've repaired that hammer better myself."

"Yep. Too bad he didn't have a smith—like me—do the work for him." With a chuckle that made him feel better than he had for days, McClanahan held one of the notched bullets against the faulty hammer. "What do you think, Marshal?"

Thompson cleared his throat. "Out of respect for what Miss Burnham's been through these past couple days, you and I'll keep a close eye on Donahue till she and Hughes settle up with their miners. Then Clancy's *mine*, whether Emily's figured him out or not."

Chapter Twenty-four

As Emily entered the Golden Rose on Tuesday morning, the parlor reminded her more of a hospital lobby than a bawdy house. Darla and Maria were talking quietly on the sofa while Lucy dealt a hand of solitaire onto a marble-topped table. Their faces were rouged, yet their expressions still held memories of the missing limbs and charred bodies they'd seen after the explosion at the Angel Claire. Clancy gave her a smug smile from behind the bar, letting his gaze linger on her deep blue cape and dress. Except for the sparkle of his catlike green eyes, the house seemed dreary and somber — a grim reminder that the mines gave life to Cripple Creek, and occasionally took it away.

Princess Cherry Blossom looked up from lighting her cigarette. "Eliza! After the way McClanahan waltzed you out of town, I thought we'd never see you again." She approached Emily with a sly smile. "Did he give you anything to show for your time? Like a ring?"

"No, I'm here to —"

"And he didn't come with you? I saw him on Bennett yesterday." The raven-haired woman glanced up and down the street before shutting the door. "I suppose he's tending to mine business for Silas?"

"No, he's not." Emily took a deep breath to settle her nerves. Had everyone in town heard about her and Matt leaving together? And why had he come back to

Cripple? "I—I need to talk to Miss Victoria."

The stripes of red and yellow warpaint on Cherry Blossom's check rose with her eyebrows. "She's in her suite. She'll be glad to see you—mighty quiet around here since the Angel Claire blew up."

As she crossed the parlor, Emily could feel Clancy's gaze probing her backside. Her footsteps echoed on the gleaming parquet floor of the ballroom and then she paused in front of the madame's door, praying Victoria Chatterly would respond to this confession with her usual gentility. She knocked quietly. After a moment, the silken rustle of skirts approached her from inside the room.

Miss Victoria's aqua eyes lit up when she peeked out. "Eliza, dear! Come in!" she exclaimed as she swung the door wide. "I was wondering if you and Mr. McClanahan went on a honeymoon instead of seeing Miss Burnham for me. Silas told me you were helping Matt with some business—but you know how Silas has such a modest way of putting things."

Emily managed a halfhearted smile as she entered the sumptuous pink and ivory boudoir. She had the feeling Victoria wanted to hear every little detail about her week with McClanahan, so she had no idea how to begin her story about the search for Papa's killer instead.

"Well, you've certainly shown up on the tail end of all the excitement," Miss Chatterly continued. She ushered Emily toward two pink chairs by the fireplace. "It was all I could do to maintain decorum while Clancy was locked up, much as I hate to admit it. Even with Marshal Thompson and Silas stopping in, the customers seemed so *unruly*. Can you imagine bankers brandishing their fists over a poker game? And then the explosion! I imagine Matt's help has been invaluable to Silas these past few days."

"Well actually, he hasn't been—"

"And isn't it horrid about Nigel Grath? Blowing up the Angel Claire and then *hanging* himself! I bet it's all

Mr. McClanahan can do to keep the papers from spicing that story up with some nasty rumors." The plump madame perched on the chair across from Emily, fingering her lustrous opal pendant. "And I suppose you realized when you came in that Josh and Zenia are gone. Did Matt tell you *he* paid for her dresses? I couldn't bear to make the poor girl stay, anyway. I think they were heading to San Francisco."

Emily's stomach churned as the news of McClanahan's generosity sank in. The madame went on to extol Matt's numerous virtues, oblivious to her awkward silence. Miss Chatterly's white hair was swept up with glistening opal combs, and her fuschia gown put roses in her cheeks. She obviously needed a friendly ear, so Emily nodded during slight pauses in the conversation. She let her gaze wander between the vases of fresh flowers and the intricately-carved ivory figurines that decorated the mantel. How could she interrupt such gossipy chatter to admit she'd been lying to one of Papa's dearest friends?

Then Victoria sighed. "It's probably best that Elliott wasn't alive to witness this madness. His heart would've broken had he seen the disorder here at the Rose—not to mention the devastation of his mine. Did his daughter say when she's planning to arrive, dear?"

Unable to ignore the madame's question, or the poignant tone that so clearly expressed her love for Papa, Emily felt her eyes mist over.

Victoria frowned. "What's wrong, Eliza? I've been prattling on and you've gotten paler by the minute. Is Emily too ill to leave home, as they say? Has she already . . . oh my God."

Emily felt her throat tighten, and her mouth got cottony-dry. When she'd first told Silas about her father's death, she'd relied on the mine manager's stoic strength to get her through the difficult conversation; Richard Crabtree and Clancy had been too occupied with the sheriff's investigation to show their emotions, and Idaho had spared the added weight of his own sorrow by doing most of his grieving for Viry in private. But Victoria Chatterly was the epitome of the feminine graces. Despite her profession, she was a kind, caring woman—upset about Papa's death, as well as the possibility that his daughter was gone, too—and Emily was overcome by the sudden urge to cry. The devious trick she'd played made these the hardest words she'd ever had to say. "She—Emily isn't at the ranch, Miss Chatterly."

The madame looked confused. "I don't understand."

With a shuddery sigh, Emily focused on the marble mantel and tried to put her words in a logical order. "I—I'm telling you this now, before Silas and I announce it to the men at the Angel Claire. McClanahan and I were actually looking for the murderer, and we put him behind bars before we left for the Flaming B."

Victoria's jaw dropped. Then she scowled and dabbed her eyes with a lace handkerchief. "You're not making a bit of sense, Eliza. The investigation was called off weeks ago, and—who did it? Was it one of those Denver cattle barons who wanted to take over his ranch?"

"No. Nigel Grath shot him."

"*What? That awful* man!" The madame sprang up to pace before the fire, her porcelain cheeks streaming with tears. "To think that Elliott lost his life to that mangy little . . . but I still don't see how you and Mr. McClanahan are involved in this. He and Silas told me—in good faith, I thought—that Matt was Emily Burnham's business manager. Why would they lie?"

Emily's swallow clicked in her throat. "This sounds awfully selfish, but I wanted to lock Papa's killer away while his friends and employees thought I was too weak to take action. When word gets out—"

"*You?*" the madame demanded. "Why would Elliott's death matter to Silas Hughes's *niece,* when—"

"That was only a story. Silas's way of protecting me."

Emily stood up, knowing she deserved every lash of Victoria Chatterly's tongue. "I'm really Emily Burnham. Elliott's daughter."

The madame stared, her eyes huge and glistening. "That's the most preposterous tale I've ever heard. Elliott raised her to be a lady—didn't expose her to places like the Rose, and taught her how to run the ranch so she could marry someone worthy of her. She's polite, and respectful, and . . . and. . . ."

"And I can see Papa didn't tell you what a stubborn, impulsive daughter I can be. An heiress who listened only when she wanted to." At a loss for a way to explain her predicament, she reached for Victoria's hand. "I'm sorry I hurt you, Miss Chatterly, because I know how much my father cared for you. But I had to find Papa's killer—figured whoever shot him would come to Cripple to extort money from his mine or the Golden Rose after the sheriff stopped hunting for him. And I had to watch out for myself, too. I'll be getting all sorts of propositions when word of my recovery becomes public . . . I couldn't risk being duped by the man who murdered Papa. Please try to understand."

"I . . . I think I do." Victoria, who had been scrutinizing Emily's features, took a final look at her profile. "Why didn't I see it? You look very much like your mother, except for Elliott's defiant chin. And you certainly have his temperament," she continued in a thoughtful tone. "And frankly, from what I've seen of you these past few weeks, I like the real Emily much better than the sheltered little girl Elliott described. Come here, dear. I think you need a hug as badly as I do."

Emily stepped into the madame's arms, sharing an embrace that nearly smothered her. Miss Chatterly's pillowy breasts radiated the delicate scent of roses as her body shook with a mixture of laughter and tears. It felt good to release her own pent-up feelings—so different from dealing with men, who kept their emotions in check—and as the last of her tears soaked into

Victoria's pink silk shoulder, she wondered if she was crying only for Papa, or if she was missing the other man she'd lost, too. It was no time to be thinking of McClanahan, but dammit, she could certainly use a dose of his uniquely masculine comfort about now.

Victoria blew loudly into her lace hanky and then dabbed her eyes. "Well. Goodness," she said with her usual sense of purpose. "What am I to tell the girls? And what about Clancy? The only leverage I had was threatening to report his inexcusable conduct to Miss Burnham, and now. . . ."

"It was his idea to become one of the Rose's bartenders—he thought he might see the killer, or hear talk of his whereabouts," she added. Then she smiled ruefully. "I'm sorry I went along with him. It wasn't my best decision, and you've suffered because of it, too."

The madame gave a short, sniffly laugh. "We both know there's no crossing Donahue once he's set on doing something. What shall I say, then? The girls will sense that my feelings toward you have changed—and I couldn't *think* of keeping you on as a maid."

Emily nodded. "The miners' mass funeral is tomorrow, and I'll have to reveal my true identity. The men might walk off the job, unless I can convince them that Eliza was as concerned about their safety as she was her own."

"You've gotten yourself into a sticky situation, haven't you?" Miss Chatterly asked quietly.

"It would've been easier had Grath not blown the mine up. We were on the verge of proving he shot Papa, when. . . ."

Victoria grasped her gently by the shoulders. "What's wrong, dear?"

Disgusted with herself for weakening, Emily sighed and looked away. "McClanahan was helping me tie up the loose ends, and he—well, I dismissed him. Even accused *him* of killing my father, which I'm sure now isn't true. Yet I . . . I don't know that I trust him completely, either."

"Your father taught you well, Emily," the madame said with a wise chuckle. "As I recall, Matt couldn't keep those blue eyes off you for long, and I'm sure he'll come around again after this business about the murder's cleared up. Now what was that about the funeral?"

"It's tomorrow morning at ten. Then Thursday, when the men return to work, I'll be talking to Papa's friends and investors, trying to convince them the Burnham enterprises are as sound as ever, despite my method of keeping them that way."

Miss Chatterly nodded, sighing. "We'll close the Rose tomorrow, too, out of respect for your father. I'll want to go to the funeral—so will the girls—and we won't feel much like entertaining."

Emily smiled gratefully. Then she noticed the worry lurking in Victoria's eyes, and sensed the genteel Englishwoman was concerned about her future. "Miss Victoria, I'm deeding the Golden Rose over to you. It's what Papa intended when he built it."

The madame's smile was shadowed by a scowl. "That's very thoughtful, dear, but I'd feel I was cutting you out of income you may need—"

"Not really. I've got the ranch, and his properties in Denver and Colorado Springs." She laughed softly, looking around the opulent pink bourdoir. "And you have a lot more flair for this sort of business than I do."

The skin around Victoria's reddened eyes creased with a grin. "As long as I live, I'll never forget the night you ran out with Mr. McClanahan's clothes!" She stroked the flyaway hairs around Emily's face. "Whatever you do, dear, I wish you the best. You certainly inherited your father's pluck, but if there's ever any way I can help. . . ."

Emily smiled. "The best favor you can do is to keep a close eye on Clancy, and keep my identity to yourself for a day or so."

267

"You don't ask for much, do you?" The madame smoothed the bodice of her gown and straightened the delicate gold chain of her pendant, her expression thoughtful. "How do you plan to reveal who you are to the miners, and to your father's friends? They'll be a tough audience to play to."

"I really don't know," Emily replied with a pensive sigh. "I'm hoping my luck—and my friends—won't run out on me when I need them most."

With eight condolence letters finished and seven more to write, Emily shook her cramped left hand. She and Silas had agreed that her personal notes to the deceased miners' families, along with their settlement checks, might stem some of the resentment after the men learned who Eliza really was. Would anyone dare denounce her or call her bluff when she, too, had suffered a great loss at the hand of Nigel Grath? Silas planned to explain that she'd disguised herself to monitor her father's businesses—a task she couldn't have performed properly had the men known who she was—and she'd managed to flush out his killer after lawmen had given up. Once the miners knew they'd still be working for Silas, at increased wages while they were rebuilding the Angel Claire, they wouldn't question her motives. Would they?

And what about Papa's friends and business associates here in Cripple? They'd witnessed or heard about her capers with Matt McClanahan—would they trust Elliott Burnham's daughter, after she'd posed as a chambermaid in his whorehouse? And once they realized she was taking the reins of his many businesses, would they regard her as his rightful stand-in, or plan to bilk her of her father's fortune? She took another sheet of mourning stationery from its box, thinking its black border suited her mood perfectly. If she'd followed her instincts and left McClanahan out of her scheme, this web of untruths would be a lot easier to untangle. And yet. . . .

Someone banged loudly on the front door. Silas was at the mine and Idaho was running errands, so Emily rose from the desk to see who the visitor was. Through the stained glass in the foyer she made out a large, hulking form and scowled. "Is something wrong at the Rose, Clancy?" she asked when she'd opened the door. "I have a hundred things to finish before the funeral tomorrow."

The Irish barkeep smiled craftily. "I came to offer you my help."

Emily frowned, wondering if Victoria Chatterly had told him she was in on their secret. "Why now? We've been here for more than a month."

"But you're ready to let the cat out of the bag," Donahue replied smoothly. "And when the men around Cripple hear who you are, it'll be open season on E. R. Burnham's daughter. Thought you might want be wanting my protection."

She leaned on the door, noting the deterioration of Clancy's appearance. His beard was shaggy and his hair curled untidily over his collar. There was a gap where McClanahan had knocked out his gold tooth. He'd dropped his feigned humility, as well as the brogue that sometimes sweetened his speech, and as he returned her scrutiny with pale green eyes, Emily thought he now looked more like a desperado than a cowpoke in city clothes.

"Aren't you gonna let me in?" he asked pointedly.

She sensed that he had an ulterior motive, and that he knew she was alone. And since Donahue would read any hesitation on her part as fear, she stepped aside. "I'm due at the dressmaker's soon, so don't get too comfortable."

He preceded her into the parlor, looking about with a proprietary air as he sat down on the loveseat. When Emily chose a chair across from him, he barely hid a smirk. "So you and McClanahan parted ways? It doesn't surprise me that he dropped you, hot as he's been for the Indian Princess."

Emily bit back a retort. "*I* broke off the relationship, Clancy—not that it's any of your business. Now what did you want to tell me?"

The bearlike bartender settled lower onto the loveseat, chuckling under his breath. "To the men around town, it won't *matter* who ended it. You want bachelors your daddy's age—men who've seen you at the Rose—sizin' you up? When they learn you're E.R.'s daughter, the fact that you're young and pretty'll just be honey on their biscuits, darlin'."

"That's ridiculous. Papa's friends will be too busy watching how I handle his financial affairs to pursue any romantic—"

"And what about the men at the mine? Before tomorrow night, you'll have fellas every bit as cantankerous as Nigel Grath thinkin' you just might be their ticket on the gravy train," Donahue said with obvious glee. "They'll figure you owe them the pleasure of your company, for disguisin' who you really were all this time."

Recalling the insidious little blaster's leer and his groping embrace in the abandoned shaft, Emily straightened her shoulders to keep from shuddering. "They won't have that chance, because I'm returning to the ranch the day after the funeral," she stated firmly. "And it's because of who I am that I'll *choose* who I see."

"Just like you did with McClanahan?" Clancy's mocking tone hinted that he knew all about her and Matt, and he studied her with a predatory gaze. "He's one of the few men who realize how . . . willful you can be, little girl."

"I can be very accommodating when the situation calls for it," she replied in a cool voice. Tiring of his game, she looked directly into his glittering eyes. "But I've run out of patience with you, Clancy. Especially after the way you treated Zenia."

"Accommodatin' . . ." he mused aloud. "I bet I

know *exactly* how accommodatin' you were when McClanahan was sweet-talkin' you these past few weeks. Some men don't cotton to a woman with a mind of her own, but some of us find the challenge terribly . . . excitin'."

Emily suddenly realized that there was no hope for rational conversation here—Clancy Donahue had his own agenda, and he would ignore her words whenever he chose to. Threatening to fire him wouldn't bother him either, because he'd be free to harass her any time he wanted to. Changing her strategy, Emily folded her hands in her lap. "I . . . hardly think this is the proper time to discuss such matters, Clancy," she said as she widened her eyes with a coy smile. "I appreciate your concern, but I'd rather wait until my business here is finished—"

"Nope. By tomorrow night, too many other men'll be tryin' to stake their claims." The beefy Irishman scooted to the end of the loveseat closest to her, grinning possessively. "You may not love me the way I love you, Emily, but you *need* me. There's not a man in this town who'll bother you if I'm your bodyguard. Your close, personal companion."

"Don't be ridiculous! No one's going to threaten my life at the funeral or—"

"Don't be so sure. Grath was about the craziest little bastard we've ever met up with, but he's not the only man with a grudge against your daddy." Donahue's mustache twitched with his grin. "And these men may not take kindly to learnin' they've been tricked by a woman—a *girl*, yet."

"I don't intend to tell them," she said, rising to emphasize her point. "I suppose you do?"

"No, ma'am," he answered with a foxlike smile. "But when they, or your daddy's banker friends, realize how sneaky you can be, they'll watch you real close, little lady. Probably never trust you again."

"I'm giving them no cause for alarm," Emily informed him. "The Angel Claire will be in Silas's name before the week's end. They'll never feel they've been taken over by a woman, because they won't be."

Clancy scowled. "Your daddy intended to pass the mine on to you—in your mama's memory—just as he considers the Golden Rose your namesake. You're not signin' *that* over, are you?"

"It's my property. I'll do as I see fit."

"But it's bringin' in—"

"Mr. Donahue, you're my employee, the same as Silas and Victoria," she said tersely. "But they have the common sense and the courtesy not to tell me how to conduct my affairs."

The red-haired Irishman rose to the full, Goliath height that made him a respected man in Cripple Creek. His smile barely disguised his contempt for her. "And which one of them can protect you the way I can? Which would be the husband your daddy would've picked?"

Matt McClanahan, Emily thought weakly. She watched Clancy approach, wishing Matt would rush in from the kitchen as he'd done before—wishing she hadn't given Donahue the advantage by losing control of her tongue.

"Your daddy talked to me about that very subject, you know," the bartender said in a snakelike voice. "He may be dead, but I don't intend to ignore his final wishes."

"Neither do I," she mumbled. She could never give her affections to the bestial man advancing on her, but she knew her objections wouldn't matter. Clancy would take what he wanted, as his due for having kept her secret. Emily took a step backward, and then another. "What's the point in this? We both know you could overpower me with one hand tied behind you."

Clancy laughed, and didn't answer until he'd backed her against the parlor wall. "Not so brave without McClanahan around, are you, little girl? I saw the woman he brought out in you, Emily, and I want her. Every soft, delicious inch of her."

She caught the scent of whiskey, and his perfumed pommade didn't mask the odor of his unwashed hair. His hands kneaded her shoulders briefly before fumbling with her breasts, and it was all she could do not to kick him. "Clancy, please don't—"

His mouth slid wetly over hers. He pressed her to the wall with his undulating hips—an awkward move for a man his size—and she thought she'd smother beneath his overbearing bulk. Emily pushed her palms against his chest, trying desperately to free her lips from his sour, cowlike kisses. Were those footsteps she heard, or just the rapid hammerings of her heart?

"Darlin', take me upstairs," her captor said with a moan. "It's been so long since I had a woman. I thought of you the whole time I was in that damn jail, and—"

The front door flew open and someone rushed into the parlor. "What the hell's going on here? Donahue, get out of my house."

The bartender sneered. "I was invited—"

"I doubt that," Silas snapped. His gray eyes flickered briefly to Emily before he reached for Clancy's thick forearm. "Let her go. She's not some loose woman at the Rose you can paw at whenever you feel like it. Get back to work, Donahue."

"And what if I don't?" The Irishman grinned with leisurely contempt. "You gonna strong-arm me, Silas? Gonna risk hurting Emily just to prove what a man you are?"

The mine manager stepped back to pull a pistol from inside his coat, cocked it, and took aim. "I could blow your brains out without the least threat to Miss Burnham, tall as you are. Now move."

With his hands raised in a mocking gesture of submission, Donahue took a few steps away from Emily. "What brought this on, Hughes? We've gotten to be pretty good friends since—"

"I've tolerated your insolence because I had to, but no longer," Silas replied stiffly. "And I suggest you make plans to leave Cripple Creek after the funeral, Mr. Donahue. Go on—get moving."

Clancy let out a derisive chuckle and lumbered toward the vestibule, with Silas following him. "I'll be seeing you, Emily. Just like we planned," he called out as he opened the door.

Emily moved away from the wall, taking quick, uneven breaths as she smoothed her crumpled blouse. She could still smell Clancy's hot foulness; still tasted stale whiskey when she wiped her mouth with the back of her hand.

Silas came back into the parlor, studying her as he laid his revolver on the mantel. "Are you all right?" he asked in a low voice. "I had no idea that ape would come here, or I'd have told you to go with Idaho. From here on out, I don't think you should be alone." He hesitated, then straightened her collar with tentative fingers. "What did he want?"

"He thinks I need a bodyguard," she said with a wry laugh. "And of course, he thinks he's the man for the job."

Holding her gaze with eyes that were a surprisingly pretty pearl gray, the mine manager shook his head. "I didn't mean to overstep by telling him—"

"You said exactly what I wanted to, but didn't dare. We've had our differences, Silas, but I've never been so damn glad to see anybody as when—well. . . ." Emily's voice trailed off as her father's partner continued to gaze at her. "I suppose I should tidy up before we go see Mrs. Delacroix."

He glanced at the loosened hair around her face, and then he resumed his normal distance from her. "I thought perhaps, since Idaho's been out all afternoon, we might eat dinner in town. If that's acceptable to you."

Emily was at a loss for a moment. "I—certainly. I'll change into a better dress and be back as fast as I can."

"Fine. I'll wait in the study."

What was Silas up to? Emily thought back over their brief conversation as she hurried upstairs to her room. She'd accepted his escort to the dressmaker's without a second thought, because she needed an appropriate outfit for the funeral. But that was business — they were partners who had to support each other's roles and stories. Yet she couldn't translate the rare glimmer she'd seen in Silas Hughes's eyes just now. Was it fatherly concern, or something stronger? As muddled as her emotions were these days, it was safer not to speculate about him.

Chapter Twenty-five

Casting a critical eye on her reflection, Emily turned before the triple mirror in the dressing room. The black gown was simple yet elegant, its unbustled skirt and fitted bodice more confining than she was used to — or had Mrs. Delacroix unintentionally sewn it on the snug side, because she'd never made clothing for her before?

"If you're presentable, Mr. Hughes would like to see you, *chérie*," the dressmaker's lightly accented voice came through the door. "And we should choose a hat now, so I can stitch on the veil."

"All right . . . coming." With a slight scowl, Emily tugged at her waistband. She stepped into the main salon, where colorful bolts of fabric were stacked on the shelves, and the seamstress's assistant was making the sewing machine whir on a mourning ensemble for someone else. Prudence Spickle, the dour hostess of the Delmonico restaurant, was fingering cloth near the rear of the shop. Mrs. Delacroix was listening to Silas, her russet bun quivering slightly as she took in the details of the explosion's aftermath.

"Who could imagine such sordid goings-on? *Quelle horreur*," she clucked softly. Then she gave Emily an appraising smile. "The dress suits you, yes?" she asked as she smoothed the folds of its black skirt. In a whisper she added, "Perhaps a light corset —"

"No thank you," Emily replied with a polite smile. As she turned before Silas, the bell on the door tinkled and someone entered the shop behind them. She studied the mine superintendent's reaction to her dress, which was hard to gauge. "It makes me look anemic, doesn't it?"

"A little," Silas said as he walked around her. "But it's no wonder you're pale, after the fright you had this afternoon."

"Takes more than Donahue's bullying to scare me," she answered with a snort. "Black just isn't my color. Too severe."

"I agree completely," someone said from the corner of the salon. "Scarlet sets off your complexion. Suits your temperament better, too."

Emily's heart pounded as she turned to stare at Matt McClanahan. He was wearing a brown suit that accentuated his dark features, and the beard that framed his face was just long enough to curl. He held her gaze sternly for a moment, until a slow, sensuous smile lit his eyes. "My condolences for your tragic loss, ma'am," he said suavely. "If I may be of service. . . ."

Emily whirled around and walked quickly to the back of the shop, her thoughts in a jumble. Was it McClanahan's brash insinuation that irked her, or was it his dark beard that reminded her of the Devil himself? She picked up one pair of black gloves after another, trying to catch her breath. They'd been apart only a few days, yet it was as though the hours they'd spent making love had never existed — or at least she *wanted* to deny the havoc Matt was wreaking upon her mind and body. Vaguely aware that Miss Spickle was only a few feet away, Emily set the gloves down with deliberate firmness and turned her attention to a bolt of black lace.

The spinster held up a length of gray flannel, and then laid it down to run a scarecrowish hand over some dun-colored wool. "What do you think?" she asked in a thin whisper. "I need a new dress and I just can't decide on a color."

Emily glanced quickly at Miss Spickle's choices, regaining her composure as her answer came to mind. "Why not ask Mr. McClanahan?" she said lightly. "He's always impeccably groomed, and he certainly has an eye for ladies' clothing."

Prudence blinked, and then her face brightened with a tremulous grin. "You're right. And he's gentleman enough to be honest without being blunt."

Watching the woman approach Matt, Emily couldn't help smiling. And when McClanahan listened to Miss Spickle's stammered request for his opinion, his expression made her choke on a laugh. He scowled pointedly at Emily, but she ignored him by selecting a small black hat and handing the lace to Mrs. Delacroix before disappearing into the dressing room.

When she returned to the main salon, Prudence was giving a detailed description of how she wanted her new dress designed — from the gray flannel McClanahan preferred — and Matt had no graceful way of escaping the spinster's spirited discussion. Emily caught a flicker of promised revenge in his eyes as she and Silas carried her new clothes to the door. She smiled sweetly at Matt, feeling better than she had since she'd returned to Cripple.

"That was a nasty thing to do, Emily," Silas commented as they placed the dress inside his carriage. "Once that outfit's made, Prudence will parade it in front of him until he's forced to compliment her on it. And what can you say about a woman who's built like a sack with most of the potatoes missing?"

"Why, Silas," she replied with a giggle, "I never realized you noticed such things."

The man beside her grunted as he steered her down the sidewalk. "I'm not the dried-up old bachelor you take me for. I merely keep my conquests to myself."

Emily didn't comment — she was too busy wondering why her father's partner was revealing more of himself these days. His hand rested lightly on her elbow as he ushered her into the New Yorker, a restaurant frequented by the elite of Cripple Creek. He seated her with practiced ease, at a table set with elegant Irish linens and glistening crystal, before giving her a smile that rivaled McClanahan's handsomest ones.

"What would you like tonight, Emily?" he asked as he sat down across from her. "It's a rare treat to escort such a lovely young woman, and I hope you'll take full advantage of the situation."

Emily looked into his gray eyes for a moment before lowering her gaze to the menu to hide her astonishment. Silas Hughes—the stern, pepper-haired mine manager—was flirting! "I—why don't you order for me? You're probably familiar with the chef's specialties."

With a pleased smile, he asked the waiter to bring them a roasted pheasant with new potatoes, and a bottle of a French wine Emily had never heard of. Silas was acting extremely jaunty—buoyant, considering the funeral speech he would have to orchestrate very carefully tomorrow. When he'd approved the wine, he filled their goblets. "Mr. McClanahan was asking about you this morning when I saw him at the bank," he commented.

Emily coughed as she took her first swallow of the pale, dry vintage. "He probably wants his paycheck."

"Money wasn't mentioned, actually. He wondered how you were standing up under the strain of the past several days. When I told him how we plan to reveal your identity, he offered to speak in your behalf at the—"

"Absolutely not. I'm doing it."

Silas set down his glass, his face somber. "Emily, you have to consider the miners' perspective on this. They're laborers; they'll accept Matt's explanation more readily because he's—"

"This charade has to end, remember?" she said firmly. When she noticed a few of the nearby diners eyeing her, Emily lowered her voice and leaned closer to the superintendent. "We can't act as though McClanahan's going to keep overseeing Papa's businesses.

279

I've had enough of this lying—and I'm perfectly capable of talking about my father's murder and the way I dealt with it."

His expression said that he, too, had heard the quaver in her voice, but instead of rebuking her, Silas covered her hand with his. "I'm not denying your ability to carry through, dear," he replied softly. "You've amazed me a hundred times since your father died, but I wish you'd reconsider—allow *me* to say a few personal words, if you won't let McClanahan speak."

Emily sat quietly, surprised at the tenderness she saw on Silas's face.

"It must've been hell to lose your only parent and then stalk his killer after others had failed," he continued in a whisper. "Personally, I thought McClanahan was just the man to help you bring your ordeal to an end. What has he done that's so unforgivable?"

Realizing that the manager of the Angel Claire never let a question pass unanswered, Emily sighed and looked away. "He tried to tell me he owns the ranch that adjoins the Flaming B. Says it would be mutually advantageous to combine our properties—when what he *really* wants is to have Papa's holdings handed to him."

Silas sat back, his expression intent. "So he proposed marriage. And you saw it as a trap."

A sour taste welled up into her throat until she thought she'd strangle on it. It was one thing for Victoria and the Indian Princess to speculate about her romantic involvements, but to have Papa's exacting, solitary partner read her so accurately was the ultimate embarrassment. "I—I—"

"I'm sorry. It was impolite of me to intrude in such a personal matter, but I *am* concerned about you, Emily. Perhaps more than I have a right to be." He smiled gratefully at the waiter who was placing their plates in front of them, his jubilant mood returning. "Well! We shouldn't let past mistakes ruin our meal. Things will work out."

Had it been a mistake, running away from Matt?

Emily cut into her pheasant, hardly noticing how it fell away from her knife. So much depended on her now: she had to keep her story straight; had to win the confidence of the miners and Papa's peers, so that Silas could continue to rebuild the Angel Claire and Victoria could get on with her business at the Golden Rose. The burden was suddenly very heavy, and she laid her utensils down. Maybe she *should* have Silas . . . or even McClanahan . . . do all the talking at the service. If the men thought she was behaving improperly — if they detected the least hint of hesitation when she was telling how Nigel Grath had. . . .

Silas gently lifted her chin. His smile was boyish, and his eyes actually twinkled. "Don't give up, dear — it was just lunatic luck that Grath figured out who you are. Some of Elliott's closest friends have watched you at the Rose, and they haven't the faintest notion you're his daughter. Most girls would've cowered in their mourning clothes and resigned themselves to marrying for their own protection, so quit your worrying and work on that speech. I expect nothing short of perfection."

The hushed tones of "Abide with Me" filled the auditorium of the Grand Opera House while hundreds of mourners found seats. The balconies were crowded, and ushers were setting extra chairs in the aisles of the main floor. Silas had a reassuring hand on her shoulder as he walked Emily toward the coffin-lined stage, yet she was anything but confident. The heavy sweetness of chrysanthemums and roses, shipped in at her own expense, became unbearable as the temperature rose with the Grand's population. Her stomach rumbled loudly, and her mouth was dry with apprehension as occasional wails broke out around her. Would she be safely anonymous in this crowd until Silas introduced her? Or would she burst out with a distraught confession that would ruin any chance for him, Victoria, and herself to continue operating the Burnham businesses profitably?

281

The mine manager lowered a wooden seat in the front row and coaxed her into it. "You'll be fine," he whispered as he sat down beside her. "By this time tomorrow, we'll be finished with pretending and we can get on with our lives."

Emily nodded, but his calm wisdom didn't soothe her. For the first time in her life she felt fat, because the waistband of the black dress was cutting her in two. She could also feel curious stares coming her way — from widows and bereaved mothers, who wondered what right Silas's niece had to join them in the row closest to the podium. When four clergymen took chairs facing the crowd, the talking stopped. The silence was sudden and complete, without even the creaking of the theater seats to interrupt it.

A pale, cadaverous preacher, Brother Tremont of the Baptist Church, walked to the lectern with his Bible. "Friends and families of our beloved brethren, we're here to commend the souls of these Christians to their Maker, and to pray for those who weren't saved when they were called from this Earth."

Letting her attention drift with the rise and fall of the minister's dramatic voice, Emily heard his words without really listening to them. He spoke of a fiery fate hotter than the mine's explosion for those who hadn't met the Master, and tears streamed down his cheeks as he told of the glories awaiting the souls who'd been called to their heavenly home. Sniffles were muffled around her, and Emily was glad her veil hid the fright that tightened her own face. Was the oppressive heat she felt a warning — a premonition of the hellfire she'd earned with every white lie and blatant deception of her weeks in Cripple?

She patted her brow with her lace hanky, joining the sigh that echoed around the opera house as the Presbyterian minister took Brother Tremont's place. Reverend Bailey was soft-spoken, preferring to recount the virtues of the miners who'd belonged to his flock, and Father Flaherty's Latin intonations had her thoughts flitting between how she'd answer these people's questions, to how badly she wished she were at the Flaming B right now. Had the Methodist minister spoken? He must have, because suddenly Silas was approaching the podium and her stomach was lurching once again.

"As I look at these caskets, and reflect upon the unspeakable loss they represent, mere words can't express my admiration and respect," he began quietly. "These fifteen miners risked their lives every day they reported for work, and spent their final hours searching for the explosives that could've killed every employee of the Angel Claire Mining Company. It was the ultimate sacrifice: greater love hath no man than to lay down his life for a friend."

His eloquence made Emily's eyes prickle. The audience leaned forward to catch every word, holding its collective breath as he spoke to the deepest, most elemental core of their humanity. Never had she imagined Silas Hughes as a skilled orator, yet he tugged at their heartstrings as masterfully as any angel ever stroked a harp. His turn of phrase was powerful in its simplicity and he quoted familiar passages of Scripture that pertained to life in the present rather than the uncertainties of the hereafter. People were crying silently, too moved to mop their faces.

"And while we pray for the souls of our sons and brothers, husbands and friends, it's only fitting to plead in behalf of the three men who remain buried somewhere in the wreckage. It's my first concern to find them now, and I'll expect my crew to work as quickly as is prudent to recover their bodies."

Silas paused, gazing solemnly at the crowd. "I ask you to also say a word for Elliott Ross Burnham, founder of the Angel Claire, who was shot in cold blood five months ago. He never saw his assailant, or had a chance to defend himself, and the finest lawmen in the area failed to track down his murderer. The devastation of the Angel Claire has been yet another tragedy for those of us who knew Elliott, but the cloud has a silver lining: when Nigel Grath confessed to blowing up the mine, he also admitted that he shot E. R. Burnham."

A gasp reverberated through the theater, followed by the hiss of people whispering in disbelief, but Emily barely noticed. Could she maintain the aura Silas had created? Her lips were as dry as parchment and she didn't realize she had a death grip on the arms of her seat until she saw that her knuckles were blue-white.

"Mr. Burnham's daughter was instrumental in catching the criminal, mainly because she refused to let her grief stand in the way of justice," the mine superintendent continued. "Emily Burnham has been here in Cripple Creek this past month, learning her father's businesses from the ground up, now that she has taken the reins of one of the most prestigious business empires in the West. None of us ever imagined she'd have to assume such responsibility so soon, or that she'd be placing herself in such grave danger, but we are greatly indebted to her for avenging her father's death and ridding the Angel Claire of a dangerous employee."

A fond smile lit Hughes's face as he glanced in her direction. "Please don't find fault with the *way* Emily has moved among us, because I felt she would learn more if she were disguised. She's proven herself a competent partner — never too proud to perform the most menial tasks, or too pampered to work as long and hard as any Burnham employee. Hers was the last loving face some of these miners saw, because Emily was laboring alongside the hospital crews after the Angel Claire exploded, binding their wounds and easing their grievous pain."

People were shifting in their seats, straining to see this paragon of virtue — and Emily wanted to disappear between the floorboards. Silas had spun a gossamer web, wrapping a blatant lie in the shining illusion of truth so skillfully that even she had been taken in for a moment. But how could she follow his magician's act? One false word would shatter the fantasy, and all that her father and Silas had worked for would be lost. The deception she herself had started might well bring an end to the legacy she was trying to preserve.

Silas cleared his throat and looked at her again. "I've had the pleasure of providing lodging for Miss Burnham and her chaperone, and I'm pleased now to introduce this lovely young woman for who she really is. I beg your indulgence and respect for her feelings, as she's been under considerable strain since the explosion and Grath's confession. Many of you will recognize her . . . as the payroll clerk at the Angel Claire, and as the chambermaid at the Golden Rose. Emily?"

His arm was extended toward her and his smile overflowed with gentle concern, but it was all Emily could do to stand up. Her knees wobbled as she walked, and with each step she had the horrible feeling that she was about to throw up or collapse or cry—or all three. Grasping the wooden lectern for support, she looked through her black lace veil at the sea of faces. Her vision blurred for a moment. Where was the courage and pluck Silas had spoken of, now that she needed it most?

Emily cleared her throat, wondering if she had a voice. There was Clancy Donahue, wearing a catlike smile as he sat beside Darla and the unpainted Indian Princess. Marshal Thompson was studying her intently from his seat on the aisle. When she found McClanahan, his defiant grin seemed like a challenge from Papa himself. She stood straighter, forcing her thoughts into rational phrases. But when she opened her mouth, all she could get out was, "Please . . . pray for these miners and their families. And pray for my papa, and for me. Lord have mercy—on us all!"

She was vaguely aware of a hush, and of Silas announcing a stockholders' meeting tomorrow morning, and of his hand on her back as he escorted her past the curious gazes of people who waited for them to pass. Her father's partner was silent as he drove them to the house, evidently as ashamed as she was for such a brief, self-centered utterance. Emily hugged her cloak closer around her, shivering with disgrace even after she stepped into the warmth of the kitchen.

A pot of soup simmered on the stove — chicken with Idaho's thick, chewy noodles — yet its tempting aroma only made her cry. She didn't deserve the old cook's devotion; didn't belong on the pedestal Silas had placed her on. Guilt squeezed at her heart, and had demons from Hell come up through the floor to claim her, she would've surrendered to them.

Idaho looked up from the clutter of astrological charts spread before him on the table. He stood quickly, wrapping his arms around her. "Missy, don't fret now. Must've been a fierce lot of grievers, to have it at the Grand, and all that crying can be contagious. That's why old Idaho stayed home."

Emily sucked in a shuddery breath and clung to him. "Oh, Idaho," she mumbled. "Silas gave me such a build-up — had the crowd eating out of his hand, and I — I made a complete ass of myself."

"How can you say that? You were brilliant, Emily. Absolutely brilliant." Silas slid the pins from her hat and carefully lifted it off, so he could look her in the eye. "Your plea had all the fervor of a convert's — Idaho, she moved that crowd as Brother Tremont *wishes* he could. They'll talk of nothing but Emily Burnham's piety for the rest of the day. And tomorrow, when you address your father's associates with your usual sense of purpose, they'll have nothing but respect for the heir to the Burnham throne."

Emily blinked, looking from the mine manager to the colored man who held her. "But Silas, we've *lied*. If Nigel Grath told anyone that this was all my idea while he was in jail —"

"I doubt they'd believe it. He was a known addict — a braggart who murdered more than fifteen miners." Silas's eyes clouded as he sighed. "I don't feel any nobler about this deception than you do, Emily. But your father *was* shot, and we were only trying to protect you while we searched for his killer. Our tales haven't harmed anyone else . . . and I daresay you *are* more

286

capable of carrying on for Elliott, now that you've been closely involved in two of his businesses."

Emily loosened herself from Idaho's hug. "And I guess there's no backing out. I knew that when I started this whole mess."

"It's almost over, dear. And we'll see each other through to the end." With an affectionate squeeze of her shoulder, he looked at Idaho. "I could use a big bowl of that soup, and then I'll tend to some things in town."

"It'll be on the table in just one minute, Mr. Silas," the cook replied. He went to the stove to stir the steaming pot, and when he saw that Silas had left the kitchen, he nodded toward the cluttered little table. "I've been studying our charts, Miss Emily," he said in a low voice, "and they say you've got big secrets and major changes coming your way soon. After you eat some soup I want you to rest, all right? Old Idaho's counting on you to finish this business in short order, so you and I can go home to the ranch again."

The overcast October sky hinted at snow as Silas halted the horses near Sam Langston's bank. Word of Emily Burnham's heroic efforts had spread quickly through Cripple Creek, and Papa's investors and business associates were arriving early to get the best seats. The board room would be crowded . . . Emily breathed deeply, hoping the frosty air would sustain her through the meeting. Once the Angel Claire and the Golden Rose were signed over tomorrow, she'd have no ties here and would close this chapter of her life forever.

But for now, she had to prove herself a competent and trustworthy heir; she had to be alert to false flattery and immune to any praise for catching her father's killer. And while she refused to apologize for her deception, she couldn't appear cocky about it either. In short, Emily had to convince Papa's peers that she was as genteel and ladylike as Victoria Chatterly while being as steel-spined and shrewd as E. R. Burnham himself.

Silas steadied her as he helped her from the carriage. "Ready for this?" he murmured.

"Yes. It's time to put the rumors to rest." She watched the cloaked gentlemen entering the bank, and then straightened her shoulders when a few of them tipped their hats.

"Just do the best you can without upsetting yourself," her companion said in a low voice. "You look pale today."

"I feel fine," she replied with a shrug. "Papa's friends would be appalled if I *didn't* appear to be upset—although it's certainly not a facade."

"All the same, we'll keep the meeting as brief as possible. And the moment I sense you're faltering, I'm sitting you down. Understand?"

Emily nodded, and then was taken completely by surprise when Silas held her in a tight, silent hug before ushering her toward the door. As they entered the bank's board room, she saw several men she knew from the Golden Rose and two rows of financiers and mine owners were seated around three sides of the huge mahogany table. They studied her expectantly; some of them wore curious smiles and a few scowled in disapproval. Matt McClanahan sat near the front, talking quietly to Spencer Penrose and his partner, Charles Tutt.

Silas helped her remove her cloak and then sat down beside her at the head of the table. Those who were just now arriving had to settle for folding chairs in the rear of the room, and Emily wished the onlookers would stop filing in so they could get this ordeal started.

McClanahan gave her a tight smile and then nodded at Silas. Did he plan to rescue her by speaking in her behalf? Or was he here to point out the discrepancies in Silas's glowing funeral speech? Emily clenched her jaw to keep from glowering at the dark, bearded man who regarded her so coolly. His black pinstripe suit was extremely flattering; his all-too-familiar scent of pine and leather drifted her way as the room's temperature rose.

And to make matters worse, his blue eyes seemed to become frostier with each passing moment.

When Silas stepped to the lectern, Emily knew she had to concentrate on him rather than on the distracting desperado in front of her. Once again the mine superintendent's voice soothed her; Papa's associates were listening attentively as Hughes recounted his days of partnership and friendship with E. R. Burnham.

"It behooves us all to follow the example Elliott set," the mine manager was saying. "The Burnham empire was built on a foundation of fairness, mortared with respect for his colleagues and employees alike. Who among us knows when we'll be called to the hereafter? Will our affairs be in order, ready for the next generation to resume command, as Elliott's were? I consider it a privilege to carry this proud tradition into the future with his daughter, Emily."

Emily stood as Silas approached his chair. She clasped his hand, because the burdens he'd borne this past week were now etched plainly on his face. With a calm smile — she'd planned her speech carefully, to include only truth — she looked out over the crowded board room. She felt serenely in control, which was just how Papa would expect her to be at such a time.

"First of all, please accept my thanks for your help when the Angel Claire blew up," Emily began quietly. "I consider it a blessing that my father didn't witness the devastation of his mine — the venture he undertook in my mother's name, to ease his loneliness after her loss."

She paused, breathing deeply to prevent any quavering in her voice. It was disconcerting to see these men eyeing her so intently . . . as though she were a prime cut of beef. Emily pushed the thought from her mind and continued.

"My father wasn't a man who made a big fuss over who his friends were, but he often reminded me that without the faithful interest of his stockholders and investors, none of the Burnham concerns would have gotten off the ground. I appreciated that wisdom while I was working with Mr. Hughes and Miss Chatterly this month, and I'm grateful for your support. Silas will be assuming my shares in the mine—as payment for his loyal service, and so the men at the Angel Claire won't suffer the indignity of working for a woman. Especially one who wears overalls."

As polite chuckles rose from the audience, Emily felt her confidence bubbling up. Only a few more sentences and she'd be finished—free from the burden of her elaborate lie, and far from the predatory gazes Papa's associates were giving her. "And on a more personal note, I want to thank you for making my father's life a full and productive one. While I realize my method for cornering his killer wasn't entirely honorable, I hope you won't—"

She blinked as a prickly wave of heat washed away the rest of her sentence. Sweat popped out on her forehead, and she struggled to ignore it. ". . . think I'm not fit to. . . ."

The last thing Emily saw before she passed out was Silas's startled expression as he sprang up out of his chair.

Chapter Twenty-six

McClanahan came up out of his seat immediately, wincing as Emily's head struck the corner of the table. He caught her before she wilted to the floor, but her pallor scared the hell out of him. Cradling her against his chest, he fumbled with the tiny buttons at her throat and then ripped two or three of them off in his frustration. "Damn dress is too tight. We've got to get her home!"

"Please, let my driver take you," Sam Langston offered anxiously.

"What in God's name — ? She said she felt fine, just before we came in here," Silas whispered. He slapped her cheek lightly, and then with more force. "Emily, can you hear me? Open your eyes, sweetheart."

"She's out cold," Matt replied. "Or probably out from the heat — must be a hundred degrees in here. She'll never forgive us if she comes around to find all these men staring at her, after she's lost control of herself."

"You're right. Get her to the house, and I'll be there as soon as I can," Hughes replied.

Matt lifted Emily's inert form and carried her out of the board room as quickly as the curious crowd would allow. Langston's young driver was holding the carriage door open, gaping at the waxen-faced woman in McClanahan's arms.

"She's not going to die, like the rumors. . . ."

"Emily? Healthy as a horse," Matt responded as he stepped inside. "Nothing a dousing of cold water — or maybe a dose of whiskey — won't take care of."

The slender colored boy nodded doubtfully and shut the door. A few moments later the carriage lurched and they were crossing town at breakneck speed. Matt loosened his hold on her, slipping her body onto the seat and resting her head in his lap. Emily's breathing was shallow and irregular, and she didn't respond when he called her name. He unbuttoned the rest of her snug bodice, and had to close his eyes to keep a tide of longing in check. Even pale and unconscious, she was the most alluring woman he'd ever held. And as his hand came to rest below her waistband, McClanahan suspected that Emily Burnham's condition had nothing at all to do with death.

When they arrived at Silas's, he whisked her upstairs and laid her gently on her bed. Emily's lips were moving now, and she was moaning softly. "Get her shoes off. Find her a nightgown, will you?" he asked the worried cook beside him.

Idaho's eyes widened when he saw that McClanahan was peeling Emily's dress down. "Mr. Matt, I wonder if—"

"Do you want her to be squeezed senseless?" he demanded as he yanked at the stiff fabric. "Look at this! Since when does Emily wear a corset?" He turned her on her stomach to untie the offensive laces, smiling apologetically at Idaho. "Maybe you should brew her some tea. It'll help settle her temper when she discovers what I've done to her."

With the slightest smile, the old Negro nodded and pulled a pink nightgown from the dresser drawer for him.

When Idaho left, McClanahan finished removing Emily's dress with one strong tug. Beneath her corset and camisole, angry red stripes marred her delicate skin, cruel reminders of the stays she'd been imprisoned in. "How the hell did you lace yourself up so tight?" he muttered as he massaged her back and sides. She was murmuring incoherently now, so he quickly slipped the nightgown over her head and got her between the sheets.

Idaho appeared with a teapot and a cup on a tray. "I suppose you two've got plenty to catch up on," he said as he set the dishes on the night stand. He gazed at Emily, who was regaining her color and was nearly awake. "Call me if you need anything."

"Thanks. I think she'll be fine now."

As the colored man limped to the door, McClanahan thought he seemed older, wearier today. He focused on the young woman lying beside him, and decided she'd be more comfortable with her hair loose . . . or maybe he was just indulging himself for one last time. Her waves spilled over the pillow in a lustrous golden avalanche as he removed her hairpins, and he longed to bury his face in their sweet, clean fragrance. Why was he still a slave to her beauty, after her ruthless rejection at the ranch?

Emily jerked, and her eyelids flew up. For several moments she stared at the man who was seated beside her. Her head was spinning like a lazy top, except for her right temple, which throbbed painfully. She rubbed it, trying to remember . . . she was in bed, between crisp, cool sheets, yet she recalled faces . . . men dressed in suits and . . . she blinked. "McClanahan. Took me a while to recognize you with that beard."

He smiled wryly. "I grew it to prove a point about—"

"What happened? I remember being at the bank, talking about Papa, when I got so hot I—"

"Take it easy, rosebud. You gave a . . . memorable speech." He poured her tea, perturbed for letting such an endearment slip out. Barely conscious, and already she was running at the mouth. She didn't deserve any mercy—not after the accusations she'd slung at him—so he would simply see that she was all right and then leave, before he became impossibly entangled with her again.

"I feel pretty stupid," Emily said with a sigh. She took the teacup and saucer, but her hands were shaking so badly she rested the china on her thigh. "Good thing I'd already told those men Silas would be taking over the mine, because by now, they've certainly lost confidence in *me*."

"Far as I could tell, you had them in the palm of your hand." McClanahan lifted the steaming cup to her lips, barely able to conceal his anger. "What *I* want to know is why you were strung up like a damn rolled roast."

293

Emily flushed and looked away. "My dress was a little too snug, so I bought—"

"And why didn't you tell me you were carrying my child?"

Her face stung as though he'd slapped her. "What are you talking about? I—"

"Is that why you ran away from me?" he demanded as he leaned closer. "I have a right to know, Emily. I thought you were a decent enough woman to tell me about such a thing."

"And what makes you think I *knew?*" She could hardly breathe, she was so shocked, yet her eyes were awash with tears. "Nobody told me all the details about being a woman, but I haven't known you long enough to be sick from—"

"Yes you have—if you count back to our first time, up on Mount Pisgah," Matt mumbled. "I figured and refigured on the way back from the bank."

The air rushed from Emily's lungs. How could it be? They'd only been together . . . dozens of times. She'd be naive to deny the signs—tighter clothes, tears that sprang up for no reason—yet she'd been so preoccupied since she'd returned to Cripple, with the Angel Claire's explosion and hearing Papa's killer confess, that the possibility of pregnancy simply hadn't occurred to her.

Emily's expression told him she was as surprised as he was, and as Matt realized how confused she must feel, the last of his resentment melted away. With her hair tumbling over her shoulders, and her butterscotch eyes nearly popping out of her pale face, she looked so fragile and childlike . . . so precious he held his breath, loving her intensely once again. Her brow furrowed and she looked toward the opposite wall. "Honey, what's wrong?" he asked softly.

"What's *wrong?* Really, McClanahan I—I . . ." Emily felt her face pucker up despite her efforts to control it. Without warning, she burst into blubbering sobs that would've sent tea flying all over the bed had McClanahan not snatched up the cup in time.

Matt pulled her close, wishing he had the words to re-assure her and win her forever. He'd always admired Emily's spirit, yet now that she was as soft and helpless as a kitten, all woman, he could forgive her tendency to speak first and think later. "Let it out," he murmured as he nuzzled her damp cheek. "No sense trying to reason this thing through till you're ready."

With final, sputtery cough, Emily rested her head on his shoulder. His shirt was stiff with starch, yet his warmth and the gentle rumbling of his voice soothed her. It felt good to be in his arms, to have him weaving his fingers through her hair . . . too good. She pulled away to wipe her face on her flannelette sleeve. "Sorry. I hate being such a crybaby."

"Goes with the territory, rosebud. I know as well as anyone else that you're not usually this—"

"You don't know the half of it!" she blurted. "What if Silas figures out—and Donahue'll hear I fainted, too! If he guesses there's a . . . baby. . . ."

The roses in her cheeks died suddenly, and Matt set aside his romantic thoughts and desires. "What about Donahue?" he asked in a low voice. "If he's been bother-ing you, or—"

"He's offered to be my bodyguard, of all things," Emily said with a roll of her eyes. "Still has fantasies that he's the perfect husband for me, especially now that everyone knows who I am. Can you believe it?"

McClanahan didn't doubt the burly bartender's inten-tions for a moment, just as he saw through Emily's at-tempt to make light of them. Her words rang with typical Burnham sarcasm, but the tea she was trying to pour came from the pot in a wobbly stream. "Honey, I haven't told you this because I knew you'd figure it out for your-self," he said cautiously. "Thompson and I have been keeping close track of Donahue—watching out for *you*— because we've got proof he shot your father."

Her blood ran cold, and she could only stare at him for a moment. "That's not true," she replied firmly. "Nigel Grath confessed. He tried to blackmail me when he

295

dragged me down the mine shaft—was absent from work. . . ."

"What was his motive?" Matt asked as he watched her chin rise with her obstinance. "Donahue's been casing your assets ever since he signed on at the Flaming B. Before that, he was wanted in Wyoming for rustling."

"Where'd you hear that? You think Papa would've hired a known criminal?" She felt her insides churning, just as she had during her last conversation with Matt at the ranch. "Every time we talk about something besides—*sex*—I get the feeling you're spinning a yarn, Mc-Clanahan. You've told me about everything except *yourself,* and—"

"I've tried, but it seems I get cut off before—"

"What are you, a bounty hunter?" Emily demanded. Her cup and saucer clattered loudly as she set them on the night stand. "You came back to Cripple for Clancy, and to claim your reward, didn't you? Maybe I should have Idaho bring me the checkbook so I can pay you for—"

"You think I care about the *money?*" In utter frustration, Matt grabbed her by the shoulders. "I love you, dammit. And I'm telling you Donahue's a dangerous man. Can't you see he's trying to hide from the law—wants to marry into your fortune so he can take it from you, legally?"

"Sounds a lot like what *you* tried, doesn't it?" Emily fixed a cold glare on him, wishing her head and stomach would stop spinning so she could analyze this information about Clancy. Did McClanahan really love her, or was this another of his convenient fairy tales? "It's no secret that Donahue's a crude, possessive bully. But most men are, in one way or another. So why should I believe you're any better than he is?"

"I'm the father of your child," Matt rasped. "And I *want* to be. Can't you get that through your head?"

Emily felt another crying jag coming on; she was torn between being disgusted with herself and wanting to believe the man whose desperate face was only inches from her own. His mouth was taut and his blue eyes burned with a crystal fire that awed and frightened her. "But . . . but Papa would've told me about the rustling — and about you inheriting the Wickersham ranch."

"Maybe he ran out of time. Maybe he was trying to protect you from one of the realities of the ranching business. If I knew the reason, I'd tell you, honey." Matt could see her wavering; saw the doubts seesawing in her huge amber eyes. It wasn't fair to take advantage of her when she wasn't strong enough to fight back, but being fair might well cost him the love he'd wanted all his life. So he did the only thing he could think of.

McClanahan's kiss came as a shock, and her first reaction was to shove him away. He tightened his hold on her, so Emily tried to bite him — damn him for shutting her up, instead of answering her questions! But he eluded her teeth by opening his mouth wider and forcing hers open with it. Matt's lips were bold, controlling her as he leaned her back against the pillows. When his tongue teased at hers, she gave up all pretense of resistance. The new sensation of his mustache tickling her nose made her giggle deep in her throat.

Matt pulled away with a reluctant sigh. "Emily, we need to talk."

"Oh." She tried to hide an impish grin — was this sudden change of emotions part of being pregnant? Or had she missed his affection more than she cared to admit?

He brushed a silky lock of hair away from her face, choosing words he hoped wouldn't set her temper off again. "I want to take care of you, rosebud," he said softly. "Not just because of the baby, but — and not just because it's the honorable thing to do. . . ." When she laughed again, Matt let out an exasperated sigh. "What's so funny? I'm talking about our future together, Emily."

She saw the utter seriousness in his eyes, yet she couldn't hold in another giggle. "Honorable — us? What sort of parents would we make, McClanahan? A mother who tells colossal lies — and dresses in overalls, and works in a whorehouse. A roguishly handsome father who's a

297

mysterious, wealthy man about town. He comes on as hearts and flowers when the time's right, yet I can't see him letting a woman tie him down."

McClanahan winced inwardly at her impression of him, but he set his pride aside. It was time to show his hand, before Emily Rose Burnham wrote him off as unworthy of becoming a husband and father. "I . . . was engaged once. Her name was Fallon."

Emily stared, certain the pain in Matt's eyes was something that couldn't be faked. She relaxed against the pillows, sensing she'd better hear him out this time. "Wh-what happened? I had no idea. . . ."

"I met her in Denver. She was from a prominent family, and once my smithy was in the black, we were to get married."

His voice was toneless, as though he no longer had any feelings for his former fiancée, yet Emily could tell his memories were difficult to discuss. She laid a hand on his arm, listening intently.

"Fallon and I had high hopes," Matt continued quietly. "My business was picking up. She loved the bustle of Denver, and spent her days planning a big wedding with the help of her friends and sisters. She wasn't anything like you, rosebud. She was tall, with chestnut hair. Chattered a lot."

"Was she pretty?"

McClanahan smiled, squeezing her hand. "I thought she was, but she tried every trick in the beauty books to get rid of her freckles." He cleared his throat, studying the golden rosiness which had returned to Emily's face. "But that's about the time I got a letter from my mother, saying she was alone on the Wickersham ranch and was deeding it over to me. Wanted me to run it while she lived the rest of her life out."

Emily heard a tug-of-war in his voice and tried to recall what he'd told her when they were gazing across the spread that adjoined her own. "I can understand why you'd be bitter about not hearing from Lorna all those years. But your mother was only—"

"My mother wasn't the problem — not then, anyway," Matt replied. "I liked Denver well enough, yet I didn't particularly want to raise my children there. Fallon refused to leave town, though. She'd never been away from her family and friends, and the isolation of ranch life wasn't her cup of tea."

"But if she truly loved you —"

"I'm not sure love was the issue," McClanahan said in a strained whisper. "Some women just aren't cut out for harsh winters and keeping their own company. When I told her I intended to claim my inheritance — which meant I was finally wealthy enough to support her — Fallon threw her engagement ring in my face. Then her father drove my customers away, in retaliation for disgracing his little girl."

Emily's mouth fell open. "Matt, that — that's awful. What'd you do?"

"Spent most of my time and money in the taverns, drowning my sorrows," he replied with a morose chuckle. "I was trying to figure out why my mother chose that particular time to contact me, after years of refusing to *be* my mother, and why Fallon didn't have guts enough to stand by me."

Bitterness hardened his handsome face, yet his voice betrayed the rejection he still felt after all this time. "I didn't think self pity was your style, McClanahan," she said softly.

"Thank you, rosebud." Matt took her hands between his, hoping her understanding would carry him through the rest of his story, and the rest of his life. "Needless to say, I was in no mood for a reunion with my mother, so I put off answering her letter. A couple weeks later I was awakened by a bucket of cold water in my face — Gus Veatch had come looking for me, to tell me I'd better take the reins of the Wickersham ranch before I lost all my employees. He said the furnace had exploded one night, and my mother died of smoke inhalation before the men could save her."

Matt paused when he saw fresh tears in Emily's eyes,

because the last thing he wanted was to manipulate her with his pain. "So after twenty years, I returned home to find that Hell had opened up and swallowed the house. They'd already buried my mother, so I never saw her again."

Her stomach tightened, because the hands at the Flaming B had related pretty much the same story about the disaster. "Matt, I'm so sorry. . . ."

"So was I, honey," he mumbled. "All I could think was that if I'd gone home when Mama first asked me — after Bert died — or if I'd set aside my wounded pride after Fallon jilted me, I would've been there to maintain the house for her. Lord only knows how long it'd been since the furnace was cleaned."

Guilt wasn't something most men felt comfortable admitting, and Emily could certainly understand the sense of loss that still haunted him. "So I never met you because you stayed away from your ranch?"

"What did I have to stick around for?" he asked. "I stopped in often enough to see that Gus and the men were training top-notch horses, and took on a few investments in the Springs. My friends were good about finding other jobs for me now and then. . . ."

Matt's voice trailed off when he saw that the fragile young woman beside him was cogitating about what he'd just told her. He cupped her jaw, hoping she'd listen attentively to what he said next. "Emily, I've been alone for too long," he murmured. "I thought roaming the Rockies and taking jobs I didn't really want was the fate I deserved, but it was just a way to pass the days till I figured out what else to do with myself."

She returned his gaze, her heart hammering weakly as she anticipated his next words. His touch was tender, and everything within her cried out that Matt McClanahan was as compassionate and wonderful as he'd been during their happiest times together . . . every bit as decent a man as Papa.

"I love you, rosebud. I'm not good at saying what's on my mind — especially when those eyes of yours are turn-

300

ing my insides to mush, like they are now — and I haven't always told you everything I knew," Matt admitted softly. "But ever since I've met you, all I can think of is making a home with you. Having a whole life again."

Emily managed a grin. "You've been known to think of a few other things, too, McClanahan. Like that time in the tub, or at Taylor West's party, or —"

"You little . . ." He pulled her into an exuberant embrace, chuckling as he kissed her soft, eager lips. When she wrapped her arms around his neck, it was all he could do not to crawl between the sheets and reacquaint himself with her beautiful body . . . the body that would bear his child and give him a life he thought he could never hope for.

"Marry me, Emily," he murmured against her ear. "You know it's *you* I want — not your money or your ranch. We can live wherever you'd like, and spend our days seeing to our affairs. Please say you want me, too."

She wasn't sure if it was the weight of his body against hers or the impact of his words, but Emily felt her stomach lurch dangerously. She swallowed hard and pressed her palms against his chest. "I — I need some time," she stammered. "Maybe you'd better leave now."

McClanahan frowned, yet he wasn't totally surprised at her request. "Are you all right? Just a moment ago you were laughing and —"

"Please, Matt," Emily said with all the strength she could muster. "I want to be sure of my answer. A lot's happened since I accused you of killing Papa, you know."

He forced a smile and brushed her cheek with a kiss. "How long do I have to wait? When will I know if I should just —"

"Have I ever been one to keep my opinion to myself?"

Matt chuckled in spite of the anxiety she was causing him. "Not that I can remember."

"Then just *go.* Please," she added in a desperate whisper.

As he closed her bedroom door behind him, Matt thought about heading right back to her side to demand an answer, though he knew he'd be courting a refusal. But when Silas entered the vestibule, looking anxiously up the stairs at him, McClanahan decided he'd better leave her alone. Then, as he started to descend, he heard quick footsteps and a violent retching, followed by a mournful gurgle. So Emily hadn't been turning him down — she was just too damn proud to be sick in front of him!

"What in God's name — ?" Silas said as he scowled up at the awful noise. "Is she going to be all right?"

McClanahan fought the urge to laugh out loud and buy Hughes a drink to celebrate. "Emily? Healthy as a horse," he said lightly. "She'll be pestering us again in no time."

Chapter Twenty-seven

"Do you think Mr. VanAntwerp approves of what I've done?" Emily asked as she and Silas left the attorney's office the following morning. "He didn't question turning the Angel Claire over to you, or giving the Rose to Miss Chatterly, yet I had a feeling he wanted to."

"Why should he? You made the decision of your own free will, rather than from financial necessity," Hughes replied with a slight shrug. "Your father undoubtedly mentioned such possibilities to him when he established both businesses, in case something happened to him before you were old enough to assume responsibility for them."

Emily sighed. "I'm not sure I'll ever be old enough, Silas."

The mine manager stopped on the sidewalk, steering her away from the passersby. "You have a face men want to believe in, Emily. A manner that belies strength of character and good sense — not to mention the admiration of everyone in town for the favors you've done them this past week. Don't sell yourself short."

"You're calling me a good liar, aren't you?" she replied with a rueful laugh. "What would Papa think if he knew I pretended to be —"

"Elliott's probably beaming, watching his little girl work the same sort of magic he did. You don't think every transaction of your father's was notarized, or every business ambition entirely aboveboard — do you?" he asked gently.

"Of course not. Strength survives, and money talks."

"Good girl." Silas smiled again and rested his arm

lightly along her shoulders as they started down the sidewalk. "So stop your worrying. It's not like you to fret over such trivialities, Emily."

He was right, and if the observant Mr. Hughes was aware of her emotional turmoil, he'd certainly pick up on the physical reason behind it if she weren't careful. Emily focused on the graceful ivory house ahead of them. The Golden Rose glimmered in the morning light, its butter-yellow cornices and gold molding glowing with the rich warmth of the sun. Despite the tawdry trade it housed, the Rose was still the most beautiful building in Cripple Creek—a fitting memorial to her father.

She gripped Silas's arm when he started up the front stairs. "Let's walk around back. It might be months before I see this place again."

"And you can probably reach Victoria's suite without passing Clancy," he said with a knowing grin.

"Why give him the slightest chance to think I came to see *him?* That's how his mind works, you know."

The mine manager was silent as they strolled across the narrow yard, past rose bushes that were mulched and pruned, and the large, lace-curtained bay windows of the ballroom. A stiff breeze made her shiver as they rounded the corner, a reminder that winter drifts would soon confine her to the ranch. Would she be alone, nurturing the life that grew within her . . . or would McClanahan be there to stoke the fire and coddle her, as he'd promised?

When she and Silas stepped inside the Rose's back door, all thoughts of romance—and even of saying good-bye to Victoria Chatterly—vanished. An overpowering odor of scorched cabbage made her gag and cover her nose. Emily tried to breathe through her mouth, but it was too late.

"What the hell's the cook—Emily!" Silas grabbed her shoulders, just as she doubled over and aimed her breakfast toward the edge of the back steps. "Victoria?" he called into the house. "Can anyone help us here?"

Leaning on the door frame, panting to prevent another upheaval, Emily heard footsteps and voices coming down the hallway. Her head was reeling and she felt sweat on her upper lip, despite the frosty air coming in around her.

"Poor dear, what's wrong?"

"Are you all right? Can you come inside now?"

Emily recognized the voices of Victoria and the Indian Princess, and nodded weakly.

"She was fine when we left this morning," Silas murmured. "I thought she'd recovered from yesterday's —"

"Not everyone has your iron constitution, Mr. Hughes," the madame said. She gently guided Emily toward the nearest room, which was the bathing suite. "And who could tolerate this awful *stench?* I'm afraid the new cook isn't working out."

Emily let the Princess steady her as she collapsed in the chair beside the ornate brass bed. "I . . . I'll be fine now. Thank you," she breathed.

Silas and Miss Chatterly were watching her with concerned faces, as the Princess went to the sink to wet a washcloth. The door opened behind them, and Emily's stomach jumped again—Clancy walked in, peering around to see who'd caused the commotion. His smile repulsed her as he looked her up and down. "Our new perfume doesn't agree with you?" he asked in a cloying voice.

She didn't answer, for fear she'd be sick again.

"Go to the kitchen, Clancy. Brew her some tea," Victoria said briskly. "She doesn't need everyone *staring* at her, poor thing."

"Would you like to rest here while I take care of our business?" Silas asked gently. "I didn't realize —"

Emily nodded, forcing a smile. "By the time you're finished, I'll be fine. I promise."

His gaze lingered on her for a moment. Then he turned and gestured for the others to precede him out of the room, leaving Emily to the Indian Princess's care. The woman's touch was surprisingly gentle as she pressed the soothing cloth to Emily's forehead and cheeks. "Let's slip your cloak off," she murmured.

"Maybe you'd like to lie down for a while."

Emily stood slowly, grateful for Miss Putnam's help and understanding. When she was free of the heavy cloak she eased onto the bed, allowing the Princess to remove her shoes as though she were entirely helpless. "Thank you, Grace. That's your real name, isn't it?"

The Princess's stripes of war paint creased into a grin. "McClanahan told you that, did he?"

"I—I hope you don't mind."

"Nah. Guess I should be pleased he even mentioned me when he was with you." Her turquoise pendant scraped against the beadwork on her bodice as she sat on the edge of the bed. "This little episode wasn't really caused by nerves, or by that nasty smell in the hall, was it?"

Emily's cheeks tingled, but it was no use trying to lie to a lady in Grace's profession. She shook her head, glancing toward the tub to ease her embarrassment.

"Does McClanahan know?"

She nodded, any happiness she might've felt suddenly overpowered by the urge to vomit again. "You'd better bring that basin. . . ."

Grace held the large bowl at the edge of the bed while she rolled Emily toward it with a practiced hand. After a few heaves produced nothing more than a feeble belch, she set the basin aside and fluffed the pillow beneath Emily's head. "I don't mind telling you I wish it were *me* having his child," the Princess said quietly. "But that's just foolishness, at my age. I gave up the right to that sort of life a long time ago."

Emily gazed at Grace's ebony hair and mahogany skin, realizing they were props for a role the slender woman had cast herself in. She no longer felt jealous, or particularly victorious after hearing the Princess's confession; if anything, she pitied Grace Putnam for having to put on such an elaborate performance to support herself. "He—McClanahan—thinks a lot of you," she mumbled. "And I appreciate the way you looked after Zenia when Clancy was causing her so much trouble, too."

Grace raised an eyebrow. "Are you saying that as my employer, or as—"

"I'm saying it as Zenia's friend. And yours, I hope."

The Princess's smile spread across her face, but it turned wary when they heard the door open. It was Clancy with the tea tray, and Grace rose to take it before he could enter the room. "Thanks. She's feeling much better now," she said pointedly.

The red-haired bartender looked toward Emily as though he intended to confirm the diagnosis for himself, until the woman in buckskin began to close the door on him. "Go tell the cook to open the kitchen windows!" Grace ordered. "Do something about this *smell,* before the customers complain."

When Donahue's mutterings had faded down the hall, she returned to the bedside with the tea. "I'm not telling you how to run things, Miss Burnham, but if I were you, that bartender would be doing his business someplace else. He's skimming our pay again, for what he claims is protection from unruly guests. Huh!" Grace glanced sourly toward the door as she handed Emily the teacup. "The only unruly one around here is Donahue himself."

"That's probably the first thing Miss Chatterly will do," Emily replied before sipping the steamy brew. "As of today, the Rose belongs to her."

"You're out of it completely? But your father—"

"Built it as a favor to Victoria anyway." Emily smiled, feeling the strength seep back into her rubbery muscles as the tea warmed her. "And it's not much of a place for a new mother and her baby."

Grace's smile held a wistfulness shared by a lot of sporting ladies Emily had met. "So you and McClanahan are going to build a love nest?"

"I—I don't know yet."

"You'd be crazy not to. He's one of the few men I've ever met whose heart's as good as his looks." Her dark eyes narrowed slightly and she went over to pull a small flask from the dresser drawer. "Here—roll a few drops of this stuff around your mouth. To keep your little illness a

307

secret when you leave."

Emily hesitated, then sipped and gasped as peppermint fire singed her tongue and gums. She looked at Grace questioningly as the woman splashed a liberal dose of the clear liquid into her teacup.

"Schnapps," the Princess replied with a chuckle. "It's a great breath freshener, and the mint helps settle your stomach. How're you feeling?"

As the warmth of the liquor radiated slowly through her insides, Emily waited, testing her reaction. A rosy relaxation made her smile after a moment. "You serve a fine cup of tea, Miss Putnam."

"Remember that, next time you and McClanahan are in Cripple. I'll brew us up another pot." Grace winked, and then picked Emily's shoes up off the floor. "Don't be a stranger, all right?"

As she told Victoria about her plans to return to the ranch, and bid the ladies good-bye, Emily doubted she could stay away from the Golden Rose for too long. It was where she'd grown from a wide-eyed innocent into a woman wise to the pleasures that money could buy, without becoming a victim of the depressing lifestyle the parlor house's opulent decor camouflaged. She spent the rest of the day with Idaho, planning their trip home and packing . . . and wanting to find Matt and invite him to come along. Yet she wished *he'd* stop by to see how she was feeling.

When Emily settled into bed for the night, her thoughts turned toward the future. She envisioned herself in Mama's ivory wedding gown, descending the stairs while Idaho and Silas and the hands — and a bright-eyed Matt McClanahan — watched her happily. Her hand rested on her abdomen, and she wondered how long it would be before everyone knew she and Matt had been tending to another sort of business even before their visit to the Flaming B. Smiling, Emily snuggled deeper into the pillows.

Idaho walked by her room on his way to bed, his tread slow and uneven. Then she heard the house settling, along with an occasional gust of wind. When the parlor clock chimed eleven, Silas's footsteps ascended the stairs as usual — except they stopped in front of her door.

The knob clicked. Emily certainly wasn't *afraid* of Silas, yet she pretended to be asleep. After they'd returned from the Rose he went to the Angel Claire, and then he ate dinner with more reticence then usual. Was he actually sorry to see her and Idaho go? Emily took slow, steady breaths, because her father's partner was standing beside her bed now, silent except for the whisper of his breathing, and it was all she could do to lie still.

The chair beside her bed creaked with his weight. Then he let out a long sigh. "Emily, I hope you don't wake up," he mumbled, "because I couldn't face you again if you knew what this old heart of mine's going through."

Emily closed her eyes tighter, hoping the room's darkness hid any sign that she was awake.

"You're so lovely, sweetheart . . . I can already imagine your radiance as you swell with the child inside you," Hughes continued reverently. "McClanahan was too much a gentleman to say anything, but the joy on his face said what words couldn't. I'd give anything in this world to be twenty years younger . . . to be the one who'd undone your hair and put the flush in your cheeks that day you cavorted on the mountainside in the altogether."

Her heart constricted until she thought it would burst. This explained Silas's recent attentions — the man she'd considered aloof and unfeeling for the past several weeks was baring his soul, and had she been expected to respond, Emily would've been at a total loss for words. She forced herself to lie still, and to take deep, even breaths.

"And knowing how a certain wildness pulses through your veins," Silas added softly, "I'd bet my next ore shipment that you'll put McClanahan off until you're ready to settle down, no matter how long that takes or how much scandal you might cause by doing it."

He chuckled quietly, shifting in the chair. "Back when your father used to come in late to meetings, he muttered about the feisty little minx he was married to. You inherited that passionate nature from your mother, I suppose, but McClanahan's patient enough — and smart enough — to wait you out. And that's as it should be. Lord knows I'd be proud to marry you and raise the child as my own . . . but it'd be a sin for an old goat like me to harness your spirit, Emily Rose. Hell, if I were any sort of a *man*, I'd be saying these things to your face. But I was a lonely old fool when you burst into my life, and I'll stay that way after you leave. It'll be harder, though, now that I realize what I've missed."

He rose hurriedly and had to fumble for the doorknob. And long after his footsteps had faded down the hall, Emily lay awake puzzling over the enigma of Silas Hughes.

As Sundance loped up the path to Mount Pisgah the next morning, the wind whipped at Emily's cloak. The palomino's breath came out in white trails of vapor as he rounded the final curve. Heavy gray clouds warned of snow — snow that could start without a moment's notice and not stop until a dozen or more inches lay on the ground, because of Cripple Creek's elevation. She couldn't stay up here long, or Idaho would never get the wagon through the narrow passes to Colorado Springs. But she had to have one last look.

She dismounted, smiling in awe-filled delight. The Cascade Mountains lacked their usual palette of colors, yet the spectacular panorama held a stark, majestic beauty in the eerie light of the impending storm. Emily clutched her billowing cloak, letting her eyes follow the lines of dark pines swaying in the wind to the irregular rock formations of an eon gone by, to the town that seemed so insignificant and temporary by comparison. It was on this spot that she'd committed herself to avenging Papa's death, and then had fulfilled what seemed to be her undeniable destiny by giving herself to Matt McClanahan. The memories nearly overwhelmed her, they were so strong. Nowhere else had she felt so alive . . . so much a woman.

Others had seen the change in her, too: Silas, whose fleeting glances at breakfast had tugged at her heart; Idaho, who'd probably sensed her pregnancy the moment she and McClanahan had become one. And of course Matt, whose passion for life had made her complete, yet had driven her away from him with a virile strength that still scared her a little. But she loved him . . . always had, and always would. Emily smiled, and with a final glance at the blustery mountainsides, she remounted Sundance to find her mysterious, handsome lover and tell him she was accepting his marriage proposal.

Only a few yards down the path, the palomino's ears pricked up and he nickered expectantly. When they got past the next clump of trees, Emily jerked on the reins. Clancy Donahue blocked her path, sitting astride his horse with a cocky grin that chilled her to the core. She was utterly defenseless, a mile from town. And as she caught the maniacal gleam in his green eyes — the look Silas had associated with Nigel Grath's lunatic luck — she realized with sickening certainty that Clancy had watched her come up here, and that he'd been waiting for just such an opportunity to trap her.

Chapter Twenty-eight

Emily cleared her throat, forcing herself to return the beastlike bartender's gaze. "What're you doing up here, Donahue?"

His nasty laugh got caught in the wind and seemed to come at her from all sides. "Didn't I tell you I'd be watchin' out for you, Miss Burnham? Makin' sure nobody takes advantage of you, or relieves you of the wealth your daddy said should be mine someday?"

"I'm perfectly capable of protecting myself."

"Is that so?" He laughed again, flashing the gap where his gold tooth had been. "Then how do you explain the faintin' spell in the board room, and the way you puked out the back door of the Rose yesterday?"

Glaring, Emily patted Sundance's neck to settle the horse's impatient shifting. "I've been under a lot of—"

"You're pregnant, bitch! Carryin' McClanahan's child, when you knew damn well you were promised to me. I've half a mind to horsewhip you, little girl."

Her heart hammered as Clancy lifted the coiled snake of rawhide from his saddle horn. Recalling the whistle and *snap* of his weapon when he'd attacked Matt in Zenia's room, she tugged slightly on the reins to get Sundance to back up. "You touch me with that thing and every man in town will tear your hide off, Donahue. You wouldn't stand a chance if—"

"You back that horse another step, and this lash will be chokin' you. Pullin' you to the ground." The bearlike man dismounted with surprising agility and grabbed Sundance's bridle. "Get off. You're ridin' with me."

Fighting panic, she looked down at him with all the beli-

312

gerence she could muster. "You're going to send my horse back to town without his rider? That's not too smart, Donahue."

"Where you're goin', it won't matter," he replied with a smug laugh. "Now are you gettin' down on your own, or do I throw you to the ground?"

Emily knew better than to hope the burly outlaw was bluffing—and any escape she'd try would only make him angrier. He'd think nothing of maiming her so badly she couldn't crawl away for help . . . probably kick her in the stomach . . . so she reluctantly swung down from Sundance. She gritted her teeth to keep from crying as the red-bearded Irishman smacked the horse's haunch and swore at him to make him gallop down the hill.

The Goliath beside her was armed with a whip, a pistol, and his own brute strength, while she had only her instincts. "Idaho's waiting for me—he knows I've come up here," she said pointedly. "He and Silas will fetch McClanahan. They'll have Marshal Thompson and all his deputies out looking for us."

"By the time they realize you're not comin' back, you'll be mine, little girl," he said with a nasty laugh.

She inhaled deeply, hoping the frosty air would keep her from getting sick. "And you honestly think I'll marry you? Why in God's name would I—"

"Because I said so. Because you *will.*" With a quickness that caught her off guard, Clancy grabbed the collar of her cloak. Its hood slipped down, and as her hair spilled out into the wind, he gazed at her with a lust he didn't bother to hide. "You really believed that fairy tale Hughes told at the funeral? Believed that all those miners and bankers would fall for it, without questionin' the way you came sneakin' around here?"

Emily held her tongue, her eyes riveted on the pale green ones several inches above hers. She decided to listen carefully, because whatever ploy Donahue devised would be dangerous to everyone involved if he was provoked into using it. "Silas is highly respected," she began in the strongest voice she could muster. "The people of Cripple would certainly believe his word over—"

"Silas is a lovesick old jackass," Clancy jeered. "He'd say anything to cover for you—tellin' how you were so loyal and brave when the mine blew up! If you're such a model daughter, why'd you lie about who you were and what you and McClanahan were up to?" he demanded. "Your story leaks like a sieve! And now Silas is in as deep as you are, because it looks to me like you gave him that mine so he'd keep coverin' for you!"

She'd considered that angle, yet Papa's friends had expressed nothing but admiration for the way she corralled Grath, and approval when she signed the Angel Claire over to Silas. Clancy had obviously missed that point: he thought Hughes should lose all his credibility, as the new owner of the Angel Claire who'd profited from Emily Burnham's deception—which meant Donahue's jealousy was overruling his logic. The thought that he'd retaliate against Silas after he was through torturing her made Emily's stomach churn. "None of that really matters," she said quietly. "Marshal Thompson and McClanahan know there's a price on your head—"

"You've got an irritatin' way of shootin' your mouth off," Donahue muttered. He yanked her up until she was quivering on her tiptoes; he reeked of whiskey, and the grip on her collar threatened to choke off her breathing. "You better do less talkin' and more thinkin', little girl. Because when McClanahan comes to rescue you this time, I'll tell the lawmen with him how he faked his way onto your payroll and then knocked you up, so nobody else could claim you. He'll try to play the hero, sayin' he's protectin' you and the child, but I may just have to shoot him—along with Silas and the nigger—for bein' such nuisances to society. What do you think about that?"

Clancy was angry because she knew about his past—which verified McClanahan's story—and he was nearly as deranged as Nigel Grath, if he planned to ensure his escape by eliminating everyone around him. It was pointless to reason with him, but talk was the only weapon she had. "What good will all this killing do?" she challenged. "Do you think anyone will believe your word over Silas's, or Matt's? Or give you the chance to gun them down?"

"They won't know I was responsible," he said with a short laugh. "I'm mighty good at lurin' my prey into a trap and then coverin' my tracks."

Emily gasped as his grip tightened. "Do you think Papa's friends and attorneys would allow the Burnham estate to fall into *your* hands, if they knew I was forced to —"

"They'll never find out. I'm takin' you —"

"I'll *tell* them!" she said in a frantic shriek. "Why on God's earth would I want to marry such a vile —" The force of Donahue's slap snapped her head back, and she tasted blood.

"No more talk, you hear me?" he demanded as he shook her like a rag doll. "You'll marry me, because it's the only way I'll keep quiet about your lies — because you don't want to see Hughes shamed right out of business. And you'll marry me because from here on out you'll need me to stay alive."

Forgetting all strategy and reason, Emily kicked at his bullish body and was immediately pinned against the nearest tree trunk with a slam that made her head spin.

"You ought to be damn glad I'll still have you, Miss Burnham," he said with a menacing leer. "Don't get attached to that baby, because you're not keepin' it. And you'd better start actin' like the perfect wife — obedient to your husband. Because first thing tomorrow we're seein' the preacher."

When Emily realized he was leaning down to kiss her, everything within her revolted. She tried to protest — tried to warn him she was sick — but Clancy was too enamored to listen. His lips crushed hers and then he jerked away, swearing violently as her breakfast splattered all over his shirt.

"You goddamn — I should whip the livin' daylights out of you!"

But he didn't have to. Emily was already slumping, sliding down the tree trunk unconscious.

* * *

315

She felt a gnawing hunger . . . felt so cold her whole body was shaking . . . but as Emily became aware of a light she couldn't yet identify, the only thing she knew for sure was that her head was throbbing. Instinct warned her to pause on the brink of consciousness, to listen. There was a crackling . . . a smoky warmth that didn't quite reach her. Cautiously she opened her eyes and focused on the dark, irregular walls of a cave. Six feet in front of her, a small fire popped and hissed. Upon seeing that she was alone, she immediately tried to flee but her hands and feet were bound.

Fighting desperation and a numbing, all-over pain, Emily struggled into a sitting position. Her mouth tasted like blood and vomit, and her lower lip was split. Had Donahue tied her up and left her to die?

He wouldn't be that kind, she thought woefully. *Without me, he couldn't lay claim to Papa's money.*

There was a rustling at the cave entrance, and Clancy came in with his shirt in his hands. He draped it over a rock and then gave her a malicious grin. "Cold?"

Emily nodded hesitantly.

"Put your cloak on. It's right there beside you."

As his laughter filled the cave, she realized he had no intention of draping the garment over her. Too uncomfortable to be proud, Emily scooted closer to the fire. Her hair was hanging in her face, but by the flickering light she saw that her pants and shirt were intact, if smeared with dirt. At least he hadn't raped her while she was unconscious, but a whiff of whiskey and the gleam in his eye as he approached her told her he wasn't finished with her.

"We could've been checked into a hotel by now, gettin' to know each other," Donahue grumbled as he crouched beside her. "But what respectable place would take a man who smelled like puke? I had to wash it out of my shirt with snow — should've made *you* do that, but I couldn't stand the smell any longer."

Emily knew he was baiting her, so she kept her retort to herself. It hurt to open her mouth, but she had too many questions to remain silent. "Where are we?" she asked in a voice that was raspy and weak.

"Out in the hills . . . nowhere in particular," he replied vaguely. "But don't you worry, little girl. I've already made the arrangements with the preacher—told him we didn't want any delay or fuss, because you were in the family way. And when I laid a bag of gold coins in his skinny fingers, he agreed pretty quick that there was no need to tell anybody about this weddin'. Just you, me, and the Lord as our witness, darlin'. You hungry?"

Emily nodded forlornly.

Clancy smirked, pushing her hair from her face with a roughness that nearly knocked her off balance. "That's too damn bad!" he mocked. "We could've been eatin' a fine dinner right now, at the hotel, if you'd kept your breakfast to yourself."

She stifled a smart remark because she knew he was lying: he wouldn't have let her eat *anything* in public, for fear she'd cause a commotion. But that didn't make her any less hungry or cold. Emily shivered, wishing McClanahan were here—wishing she'd accepted his proposal when he'd taken her home from the stockholders' meeting, so none of this nightmare would have happened. A tear dribbled down her cheek. Her nose was dripping, and with her hands tied behind her back, she couldn't even reach her shoulder to wipe it dry.

"Quit your cryin', dammit. It's your own fault we're here," Donahue growled as he put another chunk of wood on the fire.

Her snuffling would only make him angry, but Emily couldn't control herself. She pulled her knees up to her chest, muffling her sobs in her dirt-smeared pant legs.

"By God, if you're still blubberin' when I get back, I'll put a gag on you. Whether you're sick to your stomach or not." The burly outlaw hunkered awkwardly in the low-ceilinged cave, glowering at her. "You think about that while I'm out tryin' to scare up our dinner."

When his mutterings died out and she was alone, Emily wriggled closer to the fire. It was stupid to waste her energy

317

feeling sorry for herself—she *knew* that. Yet planning an escape was senseless, too. She had no idea where they were, and the little white whirlwinds at the cave's opening told her that even if she could untie herself, heading out across unfamiliar, snow-covered mountainsides at night would be suicide. Donahue undoubtedly had all sorts of cruel tricks up his sleeve, but he had to keep her alive. So the best strategy was to rest, and hopefully to eat, and to do whatever was necessary to avoid Clancy's wrath.

Were McClanahan and Silas out looking for her by now? Poor Idaho was probably blaming himself for letting her ride to Mount Pisgah—he'd nearly had the wagon loaded when she left the house this morning. Emily ached with the knowledge that once again she'd gotten herself into trouble by heeding her own desires rather than Silas's warning about going anywhere alone. She rolled awkwardly onto her side to try to rest.

When Clancy returned, he was carrying two skinned rabbits that he'd fastened to a stick. He shook the snow from his coat, ignoring her as he rigged up a crude spit. Emily saw blood and clumps of fur still clinging to the rabbits' legs as her kidnapper turned them over the flames . . . she was ready to pass out, she was so hungry, but the smell of burning flesh and hair turned her stomach. Closing her eyes, she tried desperately to think of anything but vomiting.

Not long after that, she heard Donahue's chewing. Emily looked up to see him tearing half-cooked meat from a charred carcass with his teeth. He caught her watching him, and tipped a bottle of whiskey to his lips.

"If you want some of this, you better ask me real nice before I eat it all," he said sarcastically.

Emily shook her head, swallowing the sour bile that was rising into her throat. She turned toward the wall of the cave and wondered if she'd have the strength to eat by the time she was offered something edible . . . wondered what other ordeals and indignities Clancy would subject her to before she could get away from him.

Why hadn't she realized his motives when he'd insisted

on coming to Cripple Creek? How could she have ignored her instincts about this craven, despicable beast who'd been posing as a bartender? McClanahan told her he'd killed Papa . . . the pieces fit, but Emily still couldn't believe a lout like Clancy Donahue had been able to deceive her for so long. And that scared her.

Her captor wiped the grease from his mouth, studying her with a greedy lust. "Ought to yank your pants down and ream you out, little girl," he said with a throaty chuckle. "Soon as this whiskey warms me up, that's exactly what I'll do. What do you think of *that?*"

As his laughter echoed around the cave's walls, Emily realized it had the same mirthless, mindless sound as Nigel Grath's cackle, only it was deeper.

"Hope you're ready for a helluva man, Emily," he continued between swallows of whiskey. "I'm so big and I come on so strong, why the gals at the Rose always serviced me in twos and threes. Too much for any one of them, I was — except for Princess Cherry Blossom. Now *there's* a woman."

Emily cringed at the thought of Grace Putnam being caught beneath Clancy's bulk, faking passion to save her job — perhaps her life. And once again her pregnancy betrayed her: she cried silently, hating herself for it and fearing that she'd get sick at Clancy's first touch. Her face still smarted from when he'd slapped her on the mountainside; her shattered lip stung with the salt of her tears. She heard him stand up, and then step outside to relieve himself.

When he came back, Donahue resumed boasting about the disgusting things he liked his women to do to him. His pants were unbuttoned, and he was taking his coat off. Emily tried to shut him out by imagining Matt's arms around her, and by recalling the times they'd made love in the abandoned cabin, and in the tub, and while riding Sundance in the moonlight. The passions they'd shared were so joyous, and McClanahan's teachings so tender and romantic compared to the vulgar acts Clancy was describing. She wondered if she'd live to feel Matt's body next to hers again — wondered if Matt would *want* her, once Donahue had taken his degrading liberties with her.

The whiskey bottle clattered against the rocks at the cave's entrance, and Emily held her breath. Clancy was lumbering toward her, whistling tunelessly as his green eyes took in her matted hair and shivering body. He knelt beside her, and after a moment of indecision, he reached for her cloak. "Won't need this for long, once we get hot for each other," he said with a low chuckle.

It was all she could do not to throw up. Donahue's dirty undershirt bulged out over his open fly, and he smelled of liquor and sweat and greasy, burnt meat. She forced herself to lie still as he stretched out beside her; she stifled a cry when her hair caught on the arm he slid clumsily under her head.

"You be thinkin' of how you're gonna please me," he mumbled. "Use the best tricks McClanahan taught you, and then I'll show you how a *real* man feels, darlin'. Right after my dinner settles."

Emily waited until he shifted his monstrous body against her, wondering if she — and the baby — would survive even a moment of his rutting. "It . . . it might be better for both of us if my hands and feet were untied," she said quietly.

"Huh?" He looked at her as though her suggestion hadn't occurred to him . . . which, considering the positions and props he'd described earlier, might have been the case. Then he shook with laughter. "Got to give you credit for tryin', little girl. But there's plenty of ways to take my pleasure. Can't wait to see you on your knees, with your bare ass just beggin' me to plunge into it."

She closed her eyes so he wouldn't see her fresh rush of tears. How had she ever considered McClanahan conniving or possessive for merely suggesting what a grand spread their combined ranches would be? Emily vowed that if she made it back to the Flaming B, and if Matt would still have her, she'd spend the rest of her life showing him how she cherished his affection and loved him for the gentle, thoughtful man he was.

The arm Clancy rested on her hip pinched her beneath its weight; his leg felt like a tree trunk as he draped it over hers. Then he let out a long breath . . . and he was snoring.

"Dearly beloved, we are gathered here today — "

"Cut the crap, preacher," Donahue grumbled. "For what I paid you, you ought to be able to marry us in about two sentences."

The gangly minister's Adam's apple bobbed in his throat as he stood in front of them, clutching his book of ceremonies. His gaze fell on Emily as though he suspected she was there against her will, but he nodded and searched the page for a better place to start reading.

Emily licked her throbbing lip, praying for a miracle. Clancy had shaken her awake, untied her, and they were picking their way along the drifted trail on his horse before the sun rose. They'd been camped just a little ways outside of Victor, she discovered, but as the first plans for an escape whispered through her mind, her kidnapper seemed to read her thoughts. One thick arm around her midsection reminded her that he could crush her into submission; she was sore and hungry and tired, and Clancy made it clear that none of those problems would be solved until after the wedding.

"Fifteen minutes," he'd snarled after he shoved her into a hotel room. "You'll clean yourself up, we'll meet with the preacher, and then we're headin' out of town. Damn shame I didn't get my money's worth out of this room, but I can't risk hangin' around here."

Her arms still ached from being tied behind her all night, but she managed to untangle her hair and wash the dirt from her face. Her shirt and pants were caked with mud. Surely the preacher would realize that a willing bride, no matter how embarrassed by an untimely pregnancy, would wear a clean dress to her wedding.

But the scrawny man standing before them appeared to be even more frightened by Clancy Donahue than she was. He began reading again, in a wispy voice that couldn't have carried much farther than the first few pews.

"Repeat after me. I . . . what's your name, dear?"

She shifted her weight, and felt Clancy's hand tighten around her elbow. "Emily," she sighed.

The preacher nodded, glancing warily at the redheaded buffalo beside her. "Repeat after me: I, Emily . . ."

"I . . . Emily . . ."

". . . take thee, Clancy . . ."

". . . take thee, Clancy . . ." she said under her breath. She recalled Silas's soulful outpouring at her bedside, and reminded herself she was going through with this vile ceremony only to postpone Donahue's revenge upon Hughes. It appeared that God wouldn't intervene by sending a thunderbolt through the ceiling, and with each repeated phrase Emily's spirits sank lower and lower. ". . . till death do us part."

The preacher cleared his throat and avoided Donahue's glare. "And now, sir, if you'll repeat after me: I, Clancy . . ."

"You just do the readin', and I'll say yes afterwards," the outlaw replied impatiently.

The little man's pale eyes widened, but he nodded and droned through the familiar passage. It was almost official; a few more words would make her Mrs. Clancy Donahue, and—

Emily stopped listening to the preacher and cocked her head slightly toward the window . . . there it was again: *bob bob WHITE!*

With a strength she didn't know she possessed, Emily wrenched her arm from Clancy's grasp and dashed to the back of the church. Donahue was clumping after her, swearing loudly, but as she burst through the door all she knew was that McClanahan was grinning at her, reaching down from Arapaho to give her a boost.

"Better hustle, rosebud, or—"

"What took you so long?" she gasped as she was hoisted up in front of him. "Just get me the hell out of here!"

Chapter Twenty-nine

Matt dug his heels into Arapaho's ribs and they loped down the main street of Victor as fast as the snow underfoot would allow. Emily was settling herself in his lap, clinging to him with her feet hanging over to one side. "Maybe you'd better ride astraddle," he suggested gently.

"I — I'm not sure I can."

He felt her trembling and sensed it was as much from being held Donahue's prisoner as it was from having no coat. "Unbutton my jacket," he murmured against her hair. "Put your arms underneath it. We're not going far — giddyap, Arapaho!"

Emily burrowed beneath the fleecy lining of his coat as the horse's rhythmic stride rocked her against Matt's solid chest. The saddle horn cut into her backside and she had to hang on with all her strength, but she was so glad to be safe she barely noticed the discomfort. Matt's beard brushed softly against her forehead, and she found herself reaching for him, kissing him so fiercely that her lip hurt and she nearly knocked his hat off.

"Easy, rosebud — save that for when we can do it right," Matt said with a chuckle. He hugged her hard, suddenly choked up to think he'd almost lost her — and their child — again. "I suppose Donahue's chasing us?"

"He just got on his horse," Emily confirmed, and then she rested against McClanahan's shoulder as they cantered past the houses and mine buildings on the outer edge of town.

"How heavily armed is he?"

She thought for a moment. "He was wearing a pistol, but he might have other weapons in his saddlebags. He

. . . he's got his whip, too."

Matt's hold on her tightened instinctively. "Did he use it on you? Did he—"

"No. He slapped me around some, but come time to bed down, he fell asleep," she replied quietly. "Drunk, and tired, I guess."

McClanahan chortled. "You must be losing your touch, Miss Burnham. Or maybe you weren't wearing any of your fancy underwear." When Emily jerked up in his lap to protest, he groaned playfully. "Do that again and you're on your own, woman."

"Sorry, I . . ." She relaxed against him, her heart swelling with love as his arms tightened around her. They were descending into Phantom Canyon now, leaving Victor behind. "Lord, but I was never so glad to see your face, McClanahan," she murmured. "How'd you find me?"

Matt saw that the trail ahead was rough and snow-covered, so he reluctantly slowed their gait. "We knew there was trouble when Sundance came home without you. Silas and I rode out to Pisgah, figuring you had to come down to travel anywhere else, but the hoofprints wound all over the mountain. Was Donahue lost, or was he trying to elude us?"

"I don't know. I was unconscious." Seeing his concerned scowl, Emily added, "I passed out from morning sickness, right after I threw up all over him."

"Serves him right," McClanahan muttered. He brushed his lips over her forehead, not daring to check Clancy's progress for fear he'd dump her out of his lap. "We finally tracked you to the hills outside of Victor—smelled the smoke from your fire. Silas went back to Cripple to get some men. I hated like hell to just keep watch, but I couldn't risk taking Donahue on alone. I was afraid he'd come out of the cave shooting, holding you in front of him." Matt paused to get his voice under control, and to search the canyon ledges and rock formations above them.

"You . . . tracked me through the snow all night, and

then waited out in the cold for me?" Emily whispered.

"Of course I did. I love you, remember?" he answered hoarsely. Then he smiled, and decided she would enjoy hearing the rest of the story. "Actually, I wasn't out in the snow the *whole* time—I heard Donahue's snoring, so I sneaked into the cave. Wanted to rip the bastard limb from limb when I saw him holding you, but I would've wakened him had I gotten close enough to put the bullet through his head without hitting yours."

Why hadn't she sensed his presence? Had she known McClanahan was on guard, she would have rested better. Yet common sense told Emily that her excitement at seeing Matt would have awakened Clancy, too, and his anger could have been fatal to both of them in the confining walls of the low-ceilinged cavern. "I must've gotten more sleep than I thought," she said in a sheepish voice.

"You were probably too wrung out to do anything else, honey," he said gently. "But it was a small consolation to hear my name mentioned in your mumblings."

Emily smiled and snuggled closer to him. They were going at a slow lope, following the same trail they'd searched for signs of Nigel Grath's explosives, but the canyon looked entirely different with snow and icicles hanging off its rugged ridges. She glanced behind them, and saw that Donahue was catching up. "Do you think it's smart to go into the canyon?" she asked nervously. "There's only one way out."

"I told Silas to have Thompson and his men posted so they could ambush Clancy after we led him in here. Arapaho can't stay ahead of him for long, with both of us riding him. Easy boy . . . watch these rocks, now." McClanahan searched the railroad tracks and ledges around them, looking for better footing, and he felt Emily shiver against him. "We've got to get you into one of those abandoned cabins before you catch pneumonia, rosebud."

She nodded, her eyes widening when she saw that Donahue was rapidly closing the gap between them. She turned to face forward again, and spotted Barry Thompson behind a rock formation, and then saw Silas's dark, slender form **behind** a tree, raising his rifle to his shoulder. "There they are, Matt," she murmured.

"Don't let on that you see them," he replied quietly. "There's our favorite cabin, up ahead. Just a few more minutes, and this whole ordeal will be behind us, honey."

As though Clancy had heard them talking, he fired two shots. He was so close now that they could hear his horse's footfalls, and Matt urged Arapaho faster, over the icy railroad tracks and up the little rise toward the weathered shanty. Emily felt his heart beating harder, and she suddenly realized that Silas and Thompson might have to start firing before she and McClanahan were out of their bullets' paths. She clutched his lapel, trying to remain calm. "I — I love you, Matt," she whispered urgently. "First thing we'll do when we get back to Cripple is get married, all right? I was stupid to —"

Matt crushed her against himself, knowing they didn't have a split second to spare if they were to avoid getting caught in crossfire. "I love you, too, Emily. When I stop the horse, we'll make a run for the cabin — and regardless of what *I* do, **don't** come out till we give you the all-clear. Understand?"

She nodded emphatically, determined to follow his instructions this time. Shots were ricocheting around them now, and when Matt wheeled Arapaho in a half-circle so the horse would shield them from Clancy's gunfire, she saw that the outlaw was only a matter of yards behind them.

"Better come back with me, little girl," Donahue hollered in a menacing voice.

Emily gasped when her feet hit the ground too hard, yet she scrambled toward the weathered cabin, running on raw, nervous energy. Matt had dismounted and was returning Clancy's fire, but when she tripped and fell into a snowdrift he was hauling her up immediately. "Come on, rosebud! Hurry now — get inside."

She found her footing, but suddenly the cabin blurred before her, and the gunfire and voices jumbled in her ears. Emily shook herself, gasping as they rushed up to the rough little building. McClanahan was shooting, covering them as he urged her forward, and the last thing she heard as she reached for the handle on the door was Matt screaming, *"Emily, NO! Trip wire!"*

And then there was the sound of a full charge of dynamite exploding as it carried her into the air, along with the splintering logs and shattering windows of the abandoned cabin.

Chapter Thirty

Emily opened her eyes and saw that the soothing warmth circulating in her hand came from the withered brown fingers massaging it. She tried to smile, but the change in Idaho's expression — from a careworn gaze to a startled grin — warned her that something wasn't as it should be.

"Lord, missy, but I wondered if I'd ever see those pretty eyes again! Silas! Mr. Silas!" he hollered toward the door. "It's Miss Emily — she's come around!"

She blinked and wondered why she was in her bed at Silas's . . . must've been a dream she'd had, where she'd been entering Papa's study at the ranch, and he and Matt had looked up from their cigars and talk to smile fondly at her. "Why am I —"

"It's the answer to my prayers, child," the colored man murmured as he lifted her hand to his lips. "Three days I've been begging God not to take you Home just yet. It's a miracle you weren't killed, too."

Emily heard footsteps hurrying up the stairs and then Silas burst into the room. "How are you, sweetheart? How do you feel?" he asked breathlessly.

"I . . . I don't know." Something was wrong. Why couldn't she remember whatever catastrophic event had caused these two men such extreme worry?

"Idaho, bring her some broth. She must be starved," the mine manager said as he eased onto the edge of her bed.

"Yes, Mr. Silas," the cook answered jubilantly. "Lord, it's a miracle! It's a miracle!"

Emily gazed at Silas, searching his intense gray eyes

for answers to the questions that boggled her mind. "Have I really been unconscious for three days?" she mumbled.

"Three of the longest days of our lives," he replied in an urgent whisper. He stroked the hair back from her forehead, his expression turning cautious. "How much do you remember, Emily? Dr. Geary warned us that you might not be able to recall what happened to you, after the nasty bump you took on the head. When I heard the charge ignite—saw you and McClanahan flying into the air—well, I—" Silas looked away. "Here I am babbling like an idiot, not giving you the chance to answer."

Something in his manner told her he'd said more than he intended to, but what could it be? Emily was now aware of how one side of her head and neck ached, and when she glanced down, she saw that her right arm was heavily bandaged. It felt numb and useless. "Guess I must've landed on this side when I fell, huh?" she asked quietly.

"The doctor said he'd put your arm in a sling when you came around. Said that if it hadn't been for . . . well—you could've been *killed* by the force of the blast."

His face betrayed emotions Emily had never seen there, except when she'd first told him Papa had been shot. It was as though something snapped into place in her mind, and she recalled a grueling night in a cave with Clancy Donahue, and the ride into Phantom Canyon on McClanahan's lap. His words of love echoed in her head, and she and Matt had been rushing toward the cabin, where weeks before they'd made love by the fire—

Emily, NO! Trip wire!

She felt the blood drain from her face as the subject Silas was avoiding became clear to her. "It's Matt, isn't it?" she said in a voice she could barely hear. "Tell me what happened. You saw it all, from up on the ridge."

Silas aged visibly as he let out a sigh. "Emily, my concern now is you. There'll be plenty of time—"

"Stop stalling." She stared at the man beside her, her very soul going numb. "He . . . Matt's dead, isn't he?"

Idaho entered the room, his smile fading when he realized what they were talking about. Silas nodded for the old cook to set the tray on the night stand, and placed his hands gently on Emily's shoulders. "When he saw the wire—must've been at the bottom of the cabin's door—he yelled, but it was too late. He was pulling you away from the building, putting himself between you and the blast as he tried to scramble for cover. One of the timbers caught him on the head. He was still breathing when I was on my way to the Victor hospital with you, so I thought it might be just a bad concussion."

"But it wasn't."

Silas shook his head, turning away from her. "Barry Thompson came by with the news that night. Wanted you to know that Matt's last words were about how happy you'd made him—how he wanted to see the . . . I—I'm sorry, Emily," he mumbled. "I know that despite your squabbles with him, you loved him, too."

Silas was doing his best to soften the blow, yet his unspoken message was achingly clear. "The baby . . . I—"

"You'll have other babies, child. Lots of babies to love," Idaho said in a halting voice. When he wrapped his arms around her, she shrugged away almost violently.

"But I won't have *Matt!*" she shrieked. "Without him, there won't be a chance—I couldn't let another man—"

"You're young, sweetheart. Your heart'll heal, even though right now that seems impossible," Silas said as he, too, tried to comfort her in his arms. He turned to Idaho and nodded toward the night stand. "Better give her some of that sedative, Idaho. Doc Geary said she was to be kept calm."

"Like *hell* I will!" Emily snapped as she struggled against his grip. "You tell that doctor—"

"We'd better get him over here, before she hurts herself," Silas said quietly.

With eyes that were liquid brown, the old colored man nodded, handed the bottle to Hughes, and went downstairs. Emily continued to shove at Silas's chest, but with only one strong arm she soon tired. He held her tightly while he unscrewed the cap from the medicine, eyeing her as though she might bite his hand.

"Please, Emily—don't fight me, sweetheart. Nobody's happier than I am to see you conscious again, but this is no time for Burnham stubbornness." His gray eyes were tender yet unwavering. "Now open your mouth and swallow this. If the doctor thinks we can't care for you here, he'll take you to the hospital. I've heard rumors that they tie incorrigible patients' hands and feet to the bedposts there. Think about it."

He wasn't threatening her, exactly, but she refused to be coerced. Emily clamped her jaws firmly shut, gazing defiantly at him until he lowered the bottle. "I'll take that stuff when all my questions are answered," she stated under her breath. "Now what about Donahue? If he lived through this, I'll—"

Silas's expression confirmed her blackest suspicions. "We were all startled by the blast, and our first concern was for you and McClanahan," he mumbled. "Donahue saw that we'd set a trap and just kept riding. Escaped the flying debris somehow."

"That bastard!"

"Emily, swallow this before you—"

"So help me, I'll—" Her sentence was cut short when Silas quickly slipped the bottle to her lips and tipped it up so she had to drink the bitter, burning sedative. Emily coughed, glaring at Silas as he patted her back to settle her choking. "You tell—Thompson—"

"He's got men searching the mountains, and every little town between here and the Springs," he said with quiet urgency. "He's doing all he can, and your job is to rest, Emily. Now lie back for me. Would you like some of Idaho's chicken broth?"

"No!"

"He made tea, too, with—"

"I want Donahue swinging in a noose," she said bitterly. "I won't rest until he pays for killing Papa and—and—" Emily suddenly ran out of words and stared at Silas. "What *is* that stuff?"

331

Silas smiled and eased her back toward the pillows. "Strong medicine, to put that rambunctious mind of yours out of gear so you can rest. Are you sure you don't want some soup? I'll help you with it."

Emily shook her head, a curious sense of lethargy stealing over her as she looked into his kind face. "I've been nothing but trouble for you, have I?" she mumbled as she sank back. "The only reason I let Clancy think I was marrying him was so you could keep running the Angel Claire. He threatened to tell—"

"Shhhhh . . . I can well imagine what sort of blackmail he had in mind." Silas tucked the blankets around her shoulders, his smile wistful. "You rest now. Things will look better when your bruises and sprains start to heal."

But each time Emily awoke from what seemed like an endless nap, she found fewer reasons to go on living. She'd lost her baby, and the only man she could ever love was gone, too. And because she hadn't married Matt when he'd proposed, he had to rescue her from a heartless criminal and had lost his life in the process. It was her fault that McClanahan was dead—her fault that Papa's killer still ran free.

As her skin and muscles mended, she needed less of the pain killer Dr. Geary prescribed. Yet Emily still spent most of her waking hours in limbo, lost between a daze and a stupor. Time had no meaning, now that her life had no purpose. She was vaguely aware that Idaho tried to feed her several times a day, and that Silas fussed over her sling as he tried to draw her into conversations. But she had no interest in Cripple Creek's gossip. Matt was dead. Why couldn't she have been killed in the explosion, too?

Each morning when Idaho raised the window shades, Emily blinked at the bright winter sunshine and ordered him to shut it out. He set bouquets of flowers, baskets of fruit, and numerous trinkets where she could enjoy them from her bed—gifts from well-wishers, he explained.

332

But she glanced at the items without seeing them, and refused to talk with the friends who brought them by. It became a game to see how quickly she could wipe the dogged smile from the housekeeper's face; it fascinated her to watch the flowers wither and die, as she knew she was doing. If only these people would leave her alone, so she could suffer the fate she deserved!

One afternoon, however, Idaho's voice was firm with purpose. "Miss Emily," he said as he sent the window shades flying wildly around their rollers, "Marshal Thompson's here to see you. He's stopped in every day, and he says if you won't go downstairs, he's coming up to your room."

Emily shielded her eyes from the sunlight as she gave him a surly frown. "Forget it. Whatever he has to say couldn't make a damn bit of difference."

The colored man scowled. "I won't have any more of this insolence, Miss Emily. The marshal, and Miss Victoria, and your papa's friends have been worried sick these past few weeks, and you haven't had the decency to even acknowledge their gifts and concerns."

"You'd think they could take a hint. Tell them to save their flowers for my funeral."

Idaho blanched. "Emily Rose Burnham," he said in a strained whisper, "if your father could hear you —"

"Good afternoon, Emily," a hearty voice came from the doorway. "Since you're not able to receive visitors in the parlor, I took the liberty of coming upstairs. Hope you'll excuse my breach of manners."

She glowered at Barry Thompson with all the energy she could muster. "What if I don't?"

"Then you'll just have to tolerate my intrusion," he replied with a good-natured shrug. He filled the doorway, he was so tall, and after glancing around at the mementos crowded onto every table top and stacked in the room's corners, he smiled kindly at Idaho. "I bet you've got some errands to run, after watching over Emily for so long. I'd be happy to look after her while you go."

The old colored man's eyes widened. "Well, I appreciate that, but I don't know —"

"Please, Idaho. Buy whatever she likes best, and fix it for her supper," the marshal insisted. "You know I'd never hurt Emily, or do anything indecent —"

"Oh, no sir. That was the furthest thing from my mind."

"Fine." Barry smiled again and approached Emily's bedside. "I bet a trip into town would be a nice break for you. Silas says you've been here for her night and day."

"We *are* getting low on some things. . . ." Idaho's forehead creased with doubt. "I was ready to bring Emily her dinner —"

"I'll be happy to help her with it. It smelled awfully good from the parlor."

The cook smiled. "Chicken soup — her favorite. And there's plenty for you, too, Mr. Barry."

"Thanks, Idaho," he replied with a dimpled grin. "You run along now, and don't worry a thing about Emily here. We've got lots to talk about."

Emily hadn't enjoyed watching the men discuss her as though she weren't in the room, and the moment Idaho was shuffling down the stairs, she turned her back to the marshal's imposing form. She felt him watching her for a moment, then heard him walk slowly around the room, lifting the various vases and gifts to see who they were from. What right did he think he had, barging in on her this way? Only an insensitive cad would presume to —

"You've made a lot of friends here in Cripple," Thompson commented as he picked up a heart-shaped gold locket to examine it. "And a good number of them seem to be wealthy, eligible men."

Hearing his implication, Emily burrowed her head in her pillow.

"I take it you've given them about as much encouragement and thanks as you've given me. You haven't even looked at this locket I sent, have you?"

She closed her eyes tighter. Why would she care about some dumb locket she'd never wear?

"Actually, I had it delivered as a last favor to Matt," he

continued in a wistful voice. "He told me it was to be your wedding present — had Mr. Mackin, the finest goldsmith in town, create it for you, with little windows inside for your wedding photographs. Mackin can't very well sell it to anyone else, with these initials engraved on the front of it."

Emily held her breath, outraged that the marshal would bait her with such useless sentiment. Why was her heart beating as though it believed him?

"Emily, he loved you very much," Barry said pointedly. "He asked me to look after you if something happened to him, and in the same breath he said you wouldn't need it — that you were as strong and independent as any man. And Doc Geary says your injuries are healed. Personally, I think this binge of self-pity is beneath you, Emily — a thoughtless imposition on poor old Idaho, and an insult to McClanahan's memory."

"So leave," she mumbled. "I didn't invite you here."

"And that's exactly why I came." Without warning, Barry stepped to the bedside and lifted her shoulders from her nest of blankets. "Look at you," he said, shaking his head in disbelief. "Just a month ago the men of Cripple were going to the Golden Rose as much to flirt with you as to see the other ladies — I entertained a few such notions myself. And even before I knew you were E. R.'s daughter, I thought Matt was damn lucky to have a young lady like you crazy for him. But now?"

Emily stared up into Barry's weather-bronzed face, still appalled that he'd dared to touch her. "Now *what?*" she muttered. "Now it's *over.* Clancy Donahue's a free man, while Matt lost his life because I was too stupid to listen to him — or to marry him in time."

Barry studied her for a long while before he lowered her to the mattress. "I'm going to get your clothes out," he said quietly. "And if you're not dressed in five minutes, so we can go downstairs and eat the dinner Idaho fixed especially for you, I'll put them on you myself."

"Like hell you will."

The faintest smile played on his face as he walked to the

dresser. "There's hope yet, since that tongue of yours still has its point. McClanahan used to say you had the frilliest little underthings he'd ever—"

"He told you *what?*" Emily raised up to glare at him, her heart beating with the first stirrings of temper. "He had no business—"

"Men talk, honey. And women are the most fascinating subjects most of us can come up with." Barry lifted a delicate yellow camisole from a drawer, and then pulled out matching pantaloons with a low whistle. "This may be more of a trick than I thought. I'm not used to putting a lady's clothes *on* her."

"So leave, with your dignity and decency intact," she replied brusquely.

"Nope. I came here to keep you company for a while, and I intend to accomplish that. Put these on while I find you a dress." He tossed the lingerie onto her coverlet, and opened her closet door with a playful grin. "You looked awfully pretty in this pink gown at Victoria's party. Thin as you are, it may not do you as much justice now, but it'll put some color in your cheeks."

Emily was still watching him, a slow burn working up her neck. "Put it away, Barry. No gentleman would—"

"Oh, I never claimed to be a *gentleman,*" he interrupted with a chuckle. "And I suspect that's why Silas and Idaho didn't try this days ago—too polite. Now you swing your legs over the edge of the bed, with your back to me, and put those underthings on. Everything'll stay nice and proper unless you don't do as I say."

With a soft, caustic laugh, she slid back under the covers. He wouldn't dare carry through on his threats; it was only a matter of wearing him down so he'd leave her in peace.

But suddenly the blankets were yanked away from the bed and Barry towered above her as she huddled in a knot on the mattress. He was smiling, yet his eyes looked unwaveringly into hers. "McClanahan used to say you were a testy little gal at times, and I'm pleased to see you're living up to that. It means you're no sicker than I am.

336

Last chance—are you going to dress yourself?"

Emily stared at him, still hugging her nightgown around her knees.

"All right, have it your way. I hope you don't embarrass easy, little lady." With one swift scooping movement, Barry Thompson picked her up and then sat down on the bed, dropping her unceremoniously onto his lap. "First the pantaloons—I'll be as polite as I can, by slipping them under your nightie. But come time for the camisole, the nightgown has to go," he said lightly.

Struggling and kicking against the huge hand that was guiding her lacy yellow underwear up her legs, Emily realized how her days in bed had sapped her strength. For the first time she was aware of how thin she'd become—how bony her ankles and knees looked as the marshal bared them. But embarrassment was the furthest thing from her mind. When Barry pulled the pantaloons to her waist and set her down with a smug grunt, she slapped him.

Thompson laughed until he shook. "Do that again—but *hit* me this time, Emily. Then I'll know you can put your clothes on yourself."

"I'm not going to—"

"Fine. Get ready to feel a draft."

Her efforts to slap him again were foiled by his quick lifting of her flannelette gown. Barry hiked it up over her head easily enough, but he had to tug against her struggling arms to remove the sleeves. "You're the biggest, most—"

"I know, sweetheart. All the ladies tell me so," he teased. "And if I weren't such a good friend of McClanahan's, I'd use my *other* method for convincing a woman to see things my way. Now hold still, dammit. I don't want to hurt you."

She gasped at the speed with which the marshal slipped her camisole over her head and arms. "Ouch! That side's still sore."

"I'm sorry, Emily. Now let's just sit quiet for a minute and take stock." He wrapped an arm gently around her

337

middle as he lifted her hair out from under her camisole. Then he leaned her back against his broad chest. "This isn't getting any easier for either of us," he murmured. "So why don't you just cooperate? Stand up and slip into that dress, and we'll eat a nice dinner like good friends. I'm not leaving till we do. Not going to have it on my conscience that a pretty young woman pined herself away instead of living out the good life her father left her."

Emily wanted to rebel against his grip and his words, but she didn't have the strength. Barry Thompson was as big and burly as Donahue, yet he was treating her with utmost care, as though he did indeed feel her welfare was his personal responsibility. Maybe if she gave in just a little — got dressed, but couldn't eat much — he'd think he'd won. And the sooner they got to the table, the sooner the marshal would leave her alone.

She slid off his lap slowly, and when she'd put her full weight on her legs she was shocked at how wobbly she felt. Barry stood to help her with her dress before she could ask him to. His hands were gentle as he buttoned her up the back and smoothed the folds of her soft pink skirts. Then he went to the vanity, and found a hairbrush amid the clutter of presents and flowers on it.

"You probably think I'm as disagreeable as Donahue for bossing you this way," he said as he handed her the brush. His eyes were a deep emerald green, looking her up and down with obvious concern. "I'm not doing this to be mean, Emily. Someday you'll realize how much you have to live for, and maybe you'll consider my rudeness a favor."

As she stroked her hair with the brush, Emily wondered what he was hinting at. Barry Thompson was around Matt's age; a likable fellow — among the favorite guests at the Golden Rose — yet he hadn't found a wife. Was he considering her as a prospect, hoping to be by her side when her grief had run its course? She walked ahead of him to the door, hesitated at the top of the stairs, and didn't protest when the marshal cradled her against his chest as though she were a small child.

But she wasn't giving in — she would *never* stop mourning McClanahan. Barry set her gently on one of the dining room chairs, then talked about the same local happenings Silas had tried to interest her in while he carried hot soup and fresh bread to the table. Emily wavered . . . the noodles and chicken chunks swam in Idaho's rich broth, giving off an aroma that made her stomach quiver with anticipation. But she didn't lift her spoon.

"Terrific bread! Here, let me butter you a slice," Barry said as he chewed enthusiastically. "You'll make old Idaho's day, when he sees you've put on the feed bag again. Maybe I should come around this same time tomorrow — you think?"

Emily smiled feebly, her hands folded in her lap.

Barry looked up from his soup, the sparkle fading from his eyes. "Am I going to have to feed you?" he asked in a low voice. "I will, you know."

She shifted slightly. "I — my stomach must've shriveled up. It looks good, but I'm just not hungry."

"Bullshit." Barry scooted his chair around beside hers and dipped up a spoonful of soup. "Don't make me force you, Emily. Silas says you at least pick at your dinner — probably so he'll leave you alone. That trick won't work with me."

Emily gazed at the large mouthful of noodles in front of her, but she didn't budge.

With a disgusted sigh, Thompson clamped his hand around the nape of her neck, tipping her head back until she had no choice but to open her mouth, and then he slipped the spoon into it. "Now chew 'em up," he muttered. "If you spit them out, by God I'll pour this stuff down your throat. Someday you'll thank me for it, Emily."

She doubted it with every nerve in her body, but she knew better than to push Barry Thompson any further. After another forced bite splattered down the front of her dress, Emily decided to humor him. When she'd devoured the bowl of soup and a slice of bread, not daring to admit to herself how heavenly they tasted, the marshal offered her a damp rag.

"Guess you were hungrier than you thought, huh?" he asked with a gentle smile.

Emily let out a snort as she dabbed at the wet spots on her bodice. "If you think I'll fall all over myself thanking you, you're out of luck."

"I expected as much. At least this first time."

She rolled her eyes, and as Barry chatted about the clean-up progress at the Angel Claire, and Miss Victoria's efforts to find a new bartender, Emily could barely keep from fidgeting. Why didn't this man take a hint and *leave,* now that he'd proven he was stronger than she was?

Barry looked at her as though he'd read her thoughts. "Emily, I'm only trying to keep you abreast of your father's—*your*—affairs," he said earnestly. "Plenty of men here in Cripple follow every detail Silas tells them about you, just waiting for the Burnham businesses in Colorado Springs and Denver to go on the market. They figure you'll sell out cheap, due to your failing health—and maybe because they assume you never knew what your holdings were worth anyway. Is that what you want?"

Emily scowled. "Vultures. All of them."

"Because they have no reason to behave any other way." Barry hesitated, and then he took her hand. "Sweetheart, you've *got* to rally—to show them what Emily Burnham's made of. If your investors lose confidence—"

"I agree completely, Barry. And by God, it looks like she might finally be on her way." Silas was striding across the dining room, his eyes alight as he stopped beside her chair. "I'd all but given up seeing you at the table again. You look wonderful, dear."

"I look horrid, and you know it," she snapped.

The mine manager let out an indulgent chuckle. "I tried my damndest to get you out of that bed, but if it takes having Barry here to work such a miracle, we should ask him to stop by whenever he has a chance."

"We should ask him why he's pestering *me,* instead of tracking Donahue," she countered. "He should've killed that beast the moment he knew Clancy shot Papa."

340

Silas raised an eyebrow and sat down. "Sharper than a serpent's tooth, eh, Barry? Something tells me your afternoon hasn't been entirely pleasant."

The marshal cleared his throat and looked at Emily. "You're right about Donahue, and I apologize," he began quietly. "Even before McClanahan proved the bullets came from Clancy's gun, I had a string of out-of-state charges we could've arrested him for. But Matt wanted to handle it, and out of respect for his expertise, I let him."

Barry slid his chair back and stood slowly, gazing down at her with intense green eyes. "My best deputies are combing the mountains for Clancy, but he's sharper than he looks. So now, also out of respect for Matt, I consider it my top priority to keep his woman from wasting away." The marshal lifted her chin with a gentle finger. "It would've torn him apart to see you acting so hopeless, Emily. And I intend to keep right on pestering you, every day, until you pester me back."

Chapter Thirty-one

The next few mornings, Emily dressed herself and allowed Barry Thompson to help her downstairs for dinner, mainly to spare Idaho and Silas the shock of the marshal's unorthodox behavior. She had no doubts about how Barry would react if he found her still wearing her nightgown, so she valiantly pretended she wanted to eat with him. Idaho loved to watch Marshal Thompson tuck away chicken-fried steaks with mountains of mashed potatoes and wedges of fresh pie, and Barry's sense of humor perked Silas up, too, so Emily made the effort to appear sociable, as penance for the weeks of worry she'd caused the two men who'd cared for her.

But as they chatted with Barry in the parlor after dinner, Emily couldn't help comparing the marshal to Matt and coming up short. He was politely flirtatious — always trying to make her laugh, while being kind enough not to call McClanahan's memory up too often. And he helped with the stretching exercises Dr. Geary had ordered for her right arm; he was careful not to hurt her, yet determined she'd do the full number. It was becoming obvious that Barry was fond of her, and Emily felt terribly guilty about seeing him when she had no intentions of ever loving anyone but Matt. She spent her resting hours fingering the heart-shaped gold locket, gazing at the ornate M engraved between the E and the R . . . Emily Rose McClanahan. And then she'd sigh, wondering how to tell the marshal her soul was sealed off forever.

On his fourth visit, Barry came upstairs with a huge bouquet of yellow roses. He set them on her night stand, where their sweet perfume would drift over her bed.

"Roses for a rose," he said softly. "And with your hair swept up and that bloom in your cheeks, you're as pretty as any rosebud, Emily."

She'd been ready to thank him, but McClanahan's special endearment left her speechless. With a weak smile, she preceded Barry to the door and took the stairs at an agonizingly slow pace, determined not to let him carry her anymore. Silas joined them for the noon meal, with news that nearly half of the Angel Claire's shafts had been cleared of wreckage and reopened, but she hardly heard him. How could she explain to Barry that his gestures were appreciated, but futile?

He was on the loveseat with her, ready to begin her exercises, when a pounding on the door saved Emily from refusing his help. Silas looked thoughtfully over the top of his newspaper, and when they heard Idaho's happy greeting they all turned to see who was coming through the vestibule.

"Richard! Richard Crabtree!" In her excitement, Emily forgot how unsteady she was, until she stood up too fast and fell sprawling over the marshal's lap.

The ranch manager watched her closely as she composed herself, then he shook hands when she introduced him to Barry and Silas. "It's good to see you up and around, Emily. I thought I'd stop by to check on you . . . to pass along my condolences about Matt."

Emily nodded, swallowing the sudden lump in her throat. "Well! Sit down, Richard, and have some coffee. It's a cold day to be riding here from the Flaming B."

"That it is." He hesitated, then sat down and accepted the steaming cup Idaho had poured for him. "I can't stay long. Just wanted to see how you were doing."

The men settled back in their chairs, Silas and Barry smoking cigars as they exchanged news with Richard about the Angel Claire and the ranch. Emily listened closely, but what she saw told her more than what she heard. Crabtree wasn't a man to sit still for long—and he rarely left the Flaming B, except in emergencies—so his clipped phrases and movements stood out like signal flags.

"This isn't just a social call, is it?" Emily asked quietly. "What's wrong, Richard? Are the hands worried about their jobs, thinking I'll die?"

The ranch foreman cleared his throat. "No, ma'am. Nothing like that. Maybe I should talk to Mr. Hughes or the marshal here—"

"The ranch isn't their concern," she replied firmly. "I'm strong enough to hear whatever you came to say. After all, what else can possibly happen to me?"

Richard sighed and leaned his elbows on his knees. "The boys've been finding cuts in the fence, Emily. They figure we might've lost a hundred head this past week, if you count the ones we found shot out in the east ninety."

"Shot?" She sat straighter, gaping at the sandy-haired man across from her. "What kind of a rustler would kill cattle instead of stealing them?"

He glanced nervously at Idaho. "The same kind as would castrate that prize Hereford bull Elliott bought last spring, and leave him to bleed to death," he said in a somber voice. "Probably the same renegade who rode around your house shooting out windows in the dead of night. Shattered most of the ground floor glass and rode off before any of us realized what was going on."

Barry scooted forward on the loveseat, scowling. "Any idea who'd shoot the place up that way?"

Emily didn't have to hear Richard Crabtree's reply— the rapid acceleration of her heartbeat was answer enough. "Clancy," she whispered.

The marshal's face was stern. "Now don't you get any ideas about—"

"I'm here to warn you not to come home yet, Emily," Crabtree said urgently. "You won't be safe there."

"And where *will* I be safe? *Nowhere,* until that bastard's dead!" Standing slowly, Emily clenched her fists and was irritated that she still couldn't close her right one. "He thinks that with McClanahan gone, and with me laid up, he can ride footloose all over Papa's properties. If he'd castrate a bull and shoot out our windows, what's to stop

344

him from—"

"Emily, calm yourself," Silas urged. "You can't—"

"I don't reckon there's much danger of him doing that much damage again," Richard admitted in a quiet voice. "After all this commotion, the hands have taken it upon themselves to ride fence and guard the house full time. They'll shoot an intruder on sight, practically."

"Well, they'd better save Donahue for me," Emily muttered.

Barry reached for her hand, his voice firm. "I'm going with you. You're not fit to travel—"

"I can't let you come home—"

"This is just what Clancy *hopes* you'll do!" Emily silenced the men's objections with her determined glare. "And while you're deciding who's going to protect me, he'll pick you all off—just like he did Papa. He won't stop killing until he has me for his wife."

Silas's eyes widened. "You can't be considering marriage to that—"

"Of course I'm not. But that's my ace in the hole—my only way of luring him out of the mountains so we can put him away, once and for all."

Idaho shook his head nervously. "It's a trap, Miss Emily. The only reason Donahue's shooting up the house is to lure *you* there."

She reached out to stroke his white-sprigged hair, her mind clearer than it had been since before Clancy took her hostage on Mount Pisgah. "But everybody's wise to him now, so he doesn't have a chance. Don't you see? It's the only way we'll be able to live without looking over our shoulders, wondering who he'll shoot next."

Standing tall, Emily gazed at each of the men with a determined smile. "Richard, I want you to go home and protect the ranch as best you can. Come back for me in a week."

"Emily, that's preposterous!" Silas exclaimed. "Your arm's still in a sling and—"

"You couldn't possibly ride that thirty miles," Barry chimed in. "And if you did, you couldn't walk when you got off your horse."

Emily rolled her eyes. "All right, a week and a half, then," she said impatiently. "But no longer! Come in a wagon, Richard, and I'll ride home under a cover so Clancy won't suspect that I've returned to the Flaming B. The only way to beat him is to surprise him."

Silas and Barry exchanged wary glances as the ranch foreman picked up his hat. "I don't like the sound of this, Emily," Crabtree said with a shake of his head. "Not when Sheriff Fredricks and his men are trying to take care of it."

Emily felt her pulse pumping with anticipation as she returned Richard's gaze. "Clancy doesn't want the sheriff. He wants me."

For the next few days, Emily spent every waking moment preparing for the trip home. She walked incessantly through Silas's house, challenging herself on the stairs until Idaho made her sit down.

"You're overworking yourself, Miss Emily," he insisted as he set tea and cookies in front of her. "Rest and food are just as important as all this pacing."

She smiled sweetly—mainly so she wouldn't grimace as she opened and closed her stiff right hand behind her while she pretended to listen to Idaho. Her eye was on the calendar, ticking off the days until Saturday, November nineteenth, when Richard was to come with the wagon. Her every activity was geared toward being physically and mentally ready for a dangerous homecoming, despite Barry and Silas's efforts to dissuade her from making the trip.

But in her mind, she followed a different schedule. Long after Silas and Idaho retired each evening, she was squatting beside her bed, flexing thighs and arms that had grown spindly from lying idle too long. Would she be strong enough to saddle Sundance, and then ride the snowy trail to the Flaming B? Could she gather up food and heavy clothing and a gun, without Silas and Idaho

346

suspecting anything? It took all her concentration during Barry Thompson's visits, but she thought she had him convinced that she was following the plan they'd set up with Richard Crabtree. In fact, it was the marshal who seemed preoccupied, as though he, too, was keeping a secret.

The moon was nearly full Tuesday night, beaming into her room as she exercised. She stood by the window to catch her breath. The neighborhood was quiet; the lawns slept beneath blankets of moonlit snow that glistened serenely under the indigo sky. Emily scowled as a horse clopped slowly down the street. Its rider was heavyset, shrouded in a dark winter coat and hat with a woolen scarf flapping around his neck as the wind picked up. When he turned to look toward her window, Emily's hand went to her throat. "Clancy," she whispered.

The next evening she was so keyed up she went to bed early, so her nerves wouldn't betray her. She undressed, and tugged a pair of Idaho's longjohns over her own underwear. As Emily pulled on her heaviest pants and shirt, she gazed out to the street below, daring Donahue to ride by again. With shaking hands, she fastened the gold locket around her neck and let it drop under her shirts. Finally, she slipped a box of bullets into her coat pocket and tucked the revolver she'd taken from Silas's desk drawer beneath her belt.

She listened for two sets of footsteps to enter the bedrooms adjacent to hers . . . and then she pressed her ear to each wall, to hear the men's quiet snores.

Emily tiptoed down the stairs in her stocking feet, avoiding the creaky spots she'd memorized during her endless trips up and back. She placed a note on the dining room table:

I've gone to the ranch. I can't see getting Richard or Barry shot, when I know Donahue won't risk hurting me. Don't worry — I'm Elliott Burnham's daughter, remember? I love you both. Emily.

Then she put on her boots and slipped out the kitchen door, into the frosty night air.

The walk to the livery stable took longer than she remembered — or was it because she was in a hurry? Sundance nickered softly in his stall as she approached. Although he stood perfectly still, it took her twice the usual time to saddle him. How could she cover better than thirty miles of treacherous mountain trails tonight, when she was already suffering from nervous exhaustion? She swung onto the palomino's back, praying that she had the strength to see this mission through — for Papa, and because McClanahan would expect nothing less of her.

Except for the whistle of a distant train and the whisper of the wind, the night was quiet once she left Cripple Creek. The Gold Camp Road wound around the mountains before her, awash in moonlight and the silvery reflection of the snow. It was the same trail she'd ridden many times — the path she and McClanahan had followed — yet the turns and narrows were taking her by surprise. Perhaps it was best the ride required all her attention: thoughts of how she'd been utterly in love with Matt that week at the ranch, yet had ordered him out of her life, made her eyes sting with unshed tears.

Emily stopped beside Beaver Creek to let Sundance drink and rest. Her hands were cold and numb from gripping the reins. She wrapped her scarf more tightly around her neck, with the eerie sense that she was being watched. Was Clancy out there, planning an ambush? As she swung back onto Sundance, she hoped he was. It was time to declare herself the winner — time to end the threat that hung over every property and employee she was responsible for, so Papa and Matt wouldn't have died in vain.

The miles crept by, because Sundance had to pick his way carefully through drifts and over dark, icy rocks that had slid down the hillsides onto the road. Emily scanned the mountain slopes as she rode. She caught herself checking the revolver in her belt every few minutes, although she saw or heard nothing that frightened her. Then Sundance slipped, and she clutched his neck wildly to keep from falling to the ground. "Easy, boy . . . take your time now," she murmured as he righted himself. They stood in the middle of the trail for a moment, letting both their heartbeats return to normal.

As they rounded the next curves, Emily recognized a rotting miner's shack—the landmark that meant they were about ten miles from home. The building groaned when the wind wailed through it, and Sundance broke into a trot as though he, too, wanted the lonely shanty behind him. His breath came out in puffs of vapor as he dutifully clambered up yet another rise in the trail. Emily patted his back, murmuring encouragements until they reached the summit. Then she tugged on the reins, holding her breath.

Across the valley, on a foothill slightly higher than the one they'd reached, a movement caught her eye. She gazed steadily at the azure, tree-studded horizon, scanning the rough ridges until her suspicions were confirmed. There, in a clearing on the hilltop, a horse and rider were silhouetted against the night sky. "Clancy," she muttered. "I figured as much."

The rest of the ride seemed to take forever. Emily's cheeks were badly chapped, and her fingers and toes ached with cold. She sensed that if she stepped down to stretch her legs, she might not be able to remount, so she rode doggedly on, staying alert by planning her strategy. Donahue could easily overtake her—she was certain he'd spotted her miles ago, and had shown himself only to taunt her. But he'd want to stretch it out, to let her fret over his phantom presence until she succumbed to exhaustion, and then he'd strike.

But would he take her on the trail, or wait until she reached the ranch? The former choice seemed smarter, yet she knew better than to second-guess Donahue's logic. Gripping the pistol in her gloved left hand, she searched the dusky mountainsides with cautious eyes as Sundance trotted on.

The first glimmers of pink glowed in the sky as she approached the Flaming B's front gate. Donahue hadn't shown himself again. He'd wait her out — maybe create a diversion to keep the hands busy, so he could burst into the house when she was relatively defenseless. Emily smiled tiredly. She'd made it this far alone, and by God it would take more than a bullying Irish outlaw to scare her into any foolish moves.

"Go back to sleep, Roscoe," she called out to the cowboy she'd startled awake. He'd looked like an old Indian sitting against the gatepost, a bundle of blankets with a dusty hat perched on top — until he grabbed for his gun. "It's me — Emily."

Roscoe waved her through the gate, staring as she headed toward the stables. Then he burrowed into his blankets again.

She praised Sundance lavishly as she brushed, fed, and watered him. The walk to the dark-timbered house made her muscles ache for a hot soak, and she knew that once she was out of the tub, she'd probably collapse on the first bed she came to. Emily studied the ground-floor windows, pleased to see that the glass had been replaced — and that another ranch hand was watching her from his post on the porch. "Morning, B.J."

"Miss Burnham! We weren't expecting—"

"Don't tell Richard I'm here just yet," she said with a weary smile. "I'm going straight to bed."

"Yes, ma'am," he replied with a nod.

The bottom of the door stuck for a moment, as it always did in frosty weather, and then she was inside. The parlor felt cozy, a welcome haven from the wind, and its early-morning shadows soothed her as she peeled off her gloves and coat. When she'd removed her hat and scarf, Emily shook her hair free and patted her cheeks to warm them. She glanced at Mama's portrait above the fireplace, and then headed toward Papa's study to rest in his musty old chair for a moment before she took her bath.

When Emily reached the doorway, her knees buckled. A dark-haired man was gazing expectantly at her from behind Papa's desk, his beard splitting in a grin as she stared at him. Surely her mind was playing tricks on her — she was exhausted from the ride, and spooked because Clancy was out there somewhere, just waiting to claim her again.

But when the man stood and started toward her, his dazzling blue eyes sending her heart into a frenzied gallop, Emily knew this was no apparition. It was Matt McClanahan.

Chapter Thirty-two

"Emily! Rosebud, I knew you'd come before—"

"You!" She backed away, still unable to believe what she was seeing. McClanahan was laughing as he rushed toward her, and except for a jagged row of stitches along one temple, he was as rugged and handsome as her fondest memories of him. "Silas told me you were dead, and I—"

"He thought I was. It was part of the plan to—"

"—moped in bed for weeks, thinking—*what?*" Emily grabbed his arms before he could wrap them around her. "You put Thompson up to this, didn't you? Told him to—"

"It's the best way to catch Donahue off guard," Matt protested. He gazed anxiously at her, noting the thinness her layers of clothing couldn't hide, and the way her hands trembled as she held him off. "If Clancy thought I was alive, we'd be playing cat-and-mouse till—"

"Matt McClanahan, you're the honest-to-God damndest liar I ever saw!"

He laughed until he thought he couldn't quit, loving the topaz fury in Emily's eyes. "Coming from you, Miss Burnham, I consider that the highest of compliments."

"If you think for a minute that I'm just going to kiss you as though nothing—"

"I think you'll kiss me as though you'll never let me go," he said hoarsely. "It's the only way you know how."

As she gave in to his embrace, Emily's head reeled. He was alive! He'd never stopped loving her, and he was setting himself up as bait for Clancy, just as she was. His lips brushed hers with a desire she wasn't yet able to match. "Matt, you haven't heard a thing I've been—"

"Haven't I told you not to argue with a man when he's making love to you?" He crushed her close, nuzzling her hair and gulping in the scent of her and running his hands over her slender body, unable to control himself. Thanks to Barry—and even to Donahue—she was in his arms again. He gazed into her windburned face, his intense love wiping away the eloquent phrases he'd planned for this moment. He kissed her as gently as his passion would allow, aware that his woman was now as fragile as the flower she was named for.

Emily felt her legs go rubbery, but it didn't matter. McClanahan leaned her against the wall as he kissed her until she thought she'd pass out from the rapture of it. His lips were warm and insistent, flickering from her eyelids to her temples to her earlobes. And when his mouth moved over hers in a declaration of his passion—his possession of her—Emily responded with every ounce of energy she had left.

He felt her strength ebbing, so Matt gave her a final kiss and let her relax against the wall. He stroked her golden hair away from her eyes, aware of a paleness that haunted the hollows of her face. "Do you have any idea what I went through, those weeks when you refused to get better?" he whispered. "Every time Barry came back and said you weren't eating, or even getting out of bed, I almost abandoned my cover and came to see you."

"Why didn't you?" she pleaded softly. "Do you think I *liked* believing my life was over? And thinking you'd died because of my foolishness?"

McClanahan sighed. "I was laid up myself, for a while. When I came to after the cabin exploded, and Barry told me Silas was taking you to the hospital, I asked him to keep me at his place. I'd lost a lot of blood, and I was pretty banged up, so I figured nobody would

353

question it if he told them I'd passed on."

"That's no excuse. I would've kept your secret," Emily whimpered.

"And you would've been trying to flush Donahue out of the mountains and making a target of yourself, before I was strong enough to help you." Matt felt a pang of remorse for prolonging her grief, yet it certainly proved her devotion to him. He smiled and tweaked Emily's nose. "I figured Clancy would get tired of hiding, knowing neither of us was able to come after him, and that he'd return here, to the scene of the crime. And I was right—right?"

"You'll still be scheming when the Devil pricks you with his pitchfork, won't you?" she replied with a shake of her head. "So how'd you know *I'd* be here?"

"Because you won't rest till Donahue's dead. And because you and I usually think alike." Matt ran a gentle finger along her temple, wanting to make love to her immediately yet knowing she needed to rest. "And when Barry told me Crabtree's visit got your spunk up again, I figured you wouldn't wait for him to bring a wagon to Cripple."

Emily smiled tiredly. "So you and the marshal have been in cohoots all along?"

"Yep. He brought me out here a couple days ago, to finish recuperating, and to watch for Donahue." He chuckled. "Richard's eyes about popped out when he saw who was in the wagon, but he's taken good care of me."

She stroked the line of stitches above his cheek and let her fingers wander into his soft ebony beard. Emily was supremely happy that Matt knew her so well and could still love her—what kind of joyless existence would she have faced had he not come back into her life? Yet after all they'd been through, she didn't really know him. "Who *are* you?" she whispered. "You've told me bits and pieces—"

"We'll talk about it later, rosebud. I promise." He

guided her toward the stairs, aware of how heavily she was leaning on him. "Right now you need a hot bath, and two arms holding you while you sleep. Then we'll plan our strategy for when Donahue shows up. I have a feeling it won't be long."

"He knows I'm here, Matt. I saw him on the north ridge about ten miles out, watching me."

McClanahan heard the weariness of the night's ride in her voice, along with a desperation she was trying to hide. The last shots hadn't yet been fired—they both knew that. And as he eased her onto the stool in the bathroom and started her bath water, he hoped the only blood lost this time would be Donahue's. Emily was young and getting stronger, but another brush with death might finish her off.

"I imagine he'll wait till dark, so the hands won't spot him," he said quietly. "But we have to be ready—have to use the element of surprise to its fullest advantage. Let's get these clothes off you."

Emily watched as though from a distance as Matt knelt to pull her boots and socks off. She wanted to respond to his gentle touch, but she was just too tired. Resting her hands on his shoulders for balance, she stood so he could remove her pants.

"Longjohns?" he teased. "What happened to those lacy little temptations Barry described in such detail?"

"I suppose he told you all about how he had to put them on me?"

"Several times. Did me good to know you still had some fight in you, but I nearly slugged him when he sounded like he'd had too much fun at it." McClanahan let her shirt drop to the floor, gazing hungrily at her dainty pink camisole and breasts as he slid the heavy male undergarment off her. "Did you like my roses? Thompson said you didn't make over them much."

"They were from you?" She thought back to the morning Barry had brought the flowers as she stepped out of Idaho's underwear. "I—I loved them, Matt. But I thought Thompson was getting too interested in me, and when he said I looked like a rosebud. . . ."

"I asked him to say that, because *I* couldn't. Didn't mean to upset you, honey." He took her in his arms, savoring her soft sweetness as she rested against him. When he ran a trail of kisses along her throat and felt a delicate chain beneath his lips, his heart swelled. "You're wearing the locket."

"I needed a good luck charm. I thought I'd be facing Donahue without you." When his beard tickled her chest and his tongue teased at her nipple through her silk undergarment, Emily grabbed him so she wouldn't fall over from sheer delight. "Matt, I *want* to want you—it's been so long, but—"

"I'm not playing fair, am I?" he murmured. "Plenty of time for loving you later, when you can enjoy it, too." With a few deft movements, McClanahan finished undressing her and lowered her into the steaming tub. He missed her fiestiness, recalling times when they'd frolicked until the bathroom floor was puddled, yet her languor inspired a fierce protectiveness within him. He rubbed her all over with the soap, and massaged the tight muscles in her back and thighs until he ached from wanting her.

Emily watched, her head lolling against the rim of the tub as McClanahan reacquainted her with the intimate luxury of his tender hands. But when his palm rested on her abdomen she tensed. "I—I guess you heard about the baby."

Matt nodded sadly. "Maybe if I'd landed beside you instead of on top—"

"Don't be ridiculous. You saved my life."

Satisfied that she meant what she said, McClanahan lathered her long, golden hair. "We'll make other babies, Emily. After this showdown with Donahue's over, I don't intend to let you out of my sight—or out of my bed—for very long. It's too hard on both of us."

She let him duck her head gently into the water, and

after he wrapped her hair in a towel, she felt herself being lifted by two strong arms and dried by thorough, loving hands. The last thing Emily heard before she drifted off to sleep was the rustle of McClanahan's clothing falling to the floor. As he drew her against his solid, virile body, all she could think was that she was finally, forever home.

Matt waited until his need for Emily could no longer be denied before he kissed her. Long rays of late-afternoon sunshine turned her hair into a shimmering mass of gold, and once again he was acutely aware of how Emily Rose Burnham could drive him wild without even trying. She needed to eat and to be fully alert before Clancy Donahue showed up, and McClanahan grinned as he thought about how he'd revive her.

Sliding down between the sheets, he suckled each of her pert, enticing breasts until she stirred slightly. He continued on, letting his lips linger on the tautness of her stomach only for a moment . . . he'd have to pamper her, fatten her up so she could carry another child. But all thoughts of food vanished as he settled between her slender legs, crouching near the bottom of the bed to avail himself of the delicacy he craved most.

Emily was aware of a sweet, familiar warmth and she moaned softly. She remembered a grueling ride . . . cold, stiff fingers and a saddle-sore bottom. But the flame now flickering inside her could only be associated with one thing—one man—and as his tongue sent a burst of wildfire through her body, she grinned with the deliciousness of it. "McClanahan, you—come here and kiss me. Give me a chance to catch up to you."

"That's exactly what I'm doing." Chuckling, he delved deeper into her intoxicating warmth. Her moans spurred him on, fueling his own passions until it was all he could do not to crawl on top of her and seek release.

"Matt . . . Matt, I'm going crazy—this is happening too fast!" Emily strained to stay above the waves of heat, coaxing him forward with urgent hands, but it was useless. As the fireworks exploded within her, all she could do was weave her fingers through McClanahan's thick hair and hold on.

He let her rest for a moment, and with a final kiss on her damp thigh he stretched until he was lying on top of her. "Am I too heavy?" he whispered.

"No, but you're a decadent, no-account—"

Matt kissed her firmly, laughing as she tried to wriggle out from under him. She was herself again, rested and playful, and though her passivity had excited him, he felt more keenly virile and alive now that she was responding with her usual energy. Emily Burnham was never meant to be a hothouse flower; she was wild and invincible, like the roses of the prairie, and he intended to be the man who made her bloom again. "You're driving me insane, rubbing against me this way," he breathed.

"*Driving* you insane? Any man who still wants the woman who nearly got him killed is already—" Her words were cut off by a demanding mouth and a tongue that insisted on dueling with hers.

"I love you, Emily," he whispered hoarsely. "Don't you ever forget it."

And suddenly McClanahan's love was all that mattered. She clutched him, pressing her lips to his, and as the passions rose within her again she realized that instead of tiring her, their lovemaking was restoring her strength. His hard, masculine form seemed to be transferring its power to her weakened limbs; Emily wrapped her legs around his hips, rising to meet the need Matt could subdue no longer.

He kissed her hard on the mouth, and in his joy at loving her again, McClanahan rolled them onto their sides. He slid Emily's upper leg higher, deepening his thrusts until her murmurings became as incoherent as his own. As he shot into her, she cried out as though she'd been struck by a fireball, and then he collapsed.

After a few moments, Emily started to buck against him again, satisfying a desire that had lain dormant too long. When he tightened his arms around her, she grinned triumphantly. "Come on, McClanahan," she whispered against his ear. "If you have to quit first, I'll never let you live it down."

Matt felt himself stiffening with her challenge, and quickly rolled so she was on top of him. "Ride on, Miss Burnham," he drawled. "This ole bronc's a long way from bein' broke."

She laughed, happiness flowing through every vein of her body like life itself. McClanahan was grasping her hips and then coaxing her shoulders lower, so he could bury his face in her bosom. She watched him fondle each breast with fervent lips, enjoying the new sensations of seeing and feeling his dark beard on her ivory skin.

He glanced up, his blue eyes sparkling, and then he winked.

"McClanahan, you're the biggest flirt I ever — Matt! You're making us — "

He rocked beneath her mercilessly, aware that they were as close to another climax as they were to the edge of the bed. As Emily's knee slipped off the mattress, she sent him deeper inside her and from out of nowhere he felt a powerful surge of the passion he'd been saving since their last lovemaking. He gripped her arching hips and felt the sheet sliding beneath him as he was carried away by the force of his explosion.

"We're falling! Matt!" Emily tried desperately to shift their weight back onto the bed, but McClanahan's urgent writhing made her forget everything except her own undeniable greed for release. One moment she had the sensation of flying without wings and the next she was sprawling on top of him, caught in a tangle of arms and lacy, white bedclothes on the floor. He was shaking with laughter, and as the sound of her giggles joined his, her body and soul eclipsed and she cried out with the splendor of it.

McClanahan waited a moment, and then shifted so they weren't trapped in the blankets. "Are you all right, rosebud? I didn't mean to—"

"Liar! You knew exactly what you were doing." Emily rose up to stick her tongue out at him, but she broke into a new fit of giggles instead.

"You're a dangerous woman, Emily," he teased. "Half hellcat and half hyena."

"Tell that to Donahue. Maybe he'll think twice before he tries to make me prisoner again." The words swaggered out before she thought about them, and when Matt's smile tightened, she nipped her lip. "Sorry. I didn't mean to spoil our fun."

"You can't help but think about him, honey. We should get dressed—there's something I want you to see before he gets here." McClanahan started to slide out from under Emily and the bedclothes, but she wrapped her arms and legs around him. He chuckled and kissed her nose. "Not again, rosebud. Save it for later."

Emily gazed into his crystal blue eyes and felt a welling up of emotion that nearly choked her. She'd lost this man—twice—and letting go of him, when they knew Clancy Donahue was on his way, was a risk she hated to take. "I love you," she said in a tiny voice.

"I love you, too, Emily." Matt met her lips with a solemn kiss that, for him, was like a covenant: he vowed to cherish and protect her forever, if she'd only love him years from now as intensely as she did at this moment. Her response was sweet and confident, and when she opened her eyes, they were bright with unshed tears. "Go on, now," he whispered.

"What should I wear? I didn't bring a lot of—"

"Pants and a shirt," he replied matter-of-factly. "I took the liberty of picking up your new dresses from Mrs. Andersen, the day after you ordered me off your property. But that low-cut, lacy blue one is the *last* thing I want Donahue to see you in."

Emily smiled wryly, recalling their argument over the revealing gown. "Maybe Clancy would *like* me as a Southern belle. I could distract him while you—"

"I don't intend to let him get close enough to see what you're wearing." McClanahan noted her impish grin and slid resolutely out from under her. "Save those contrary ideas for me, after we've dealt with Donahue. We need to be ready for any tricks he might pull, and I won't have you exposing yourself—in any way."

She watched him dress, and with a last look at his alluring backside as he left the room, Emily pulled herself from the tangle of sheets and blankets. Once again her white, frilly bedroom seemed childish to her—more so, now that she'd made such passionate love here—but she set her wistfulness aside to concentrate on the evening ahead. Clancy would come tonight, as surely as the moon would rise like a gold coin in the sky. She had to prepare herself for a confrontation with a devious, maniacal outlaw whose codes and actions made sense to no one but himself.

Yet Emily slipped into her laciest white underthings and quickly buttoned herself into the provocative dress, just to see how it looked. It was a flattering shade of powder blue, with eyelet-trimmed sleeves, and ruffles in every seam, and a wide velvet sash that tied into a huge bow in the back. As she studied her reflection, she thought of the delicate china dolls that sat on her shelf. Woe to Clancy, if he assumed she was as fragile as she looked right now!

She plaited her long blond hair into four slender braids, which she draped daintily at her crown. Then she fastened the gold locket around her neck, noting that it hung just above the scalloped neckline, right between her breasts. Not even the ladies at the Golden Rose exposed so much skin in public—which was the very reason McClanahan had ordered this dress.

361

She couldn't resist stepping into Papa's study, and Matt's reaction confirmed her theory. He glanced up from the ledger he was reading and let out a long, appreciative breath. "Emily Rose, you look like a cross between a shameless hussy and a Madonna."

"Isn't that what you wanted?" she asked coyly. She turned to show him the ruffled bustle in the back, her color rising as she saw the desire in his eyes. "It's a good thing I lost some weight, or I'd be falling out the front."

"Time and my spoiling you will remedy that, honey." He gestured toward the chair beside the desk, barely able to keep from touching the delicate ivory skin that rose and fell with her breathing. "Let's eat some of this food Crabtree sent over, while it's hot. Then you're changing into pants."

Emily sat down, suddenly aware of how ravenous she was. Matt had set two bowls of beef stew and a half a loaf of bread on the desk, with butter and jam. He cut a generous slice for her, and without bothering to butter it, she tore off a large corner with her teeth. It was soft and chewy, and it was gone before she realized Matt was watching her. "I—you must think—"

"It's good to see you've gotten your appetite back," he said with a soft laugh. "I had a hard time imagining Barry holding you in a headlock, forcing you to eat."

"You must've enjoyed pumping him for every little detail of his visits!" she teased as she reached for more bread. "And Barry! Now *there's* a friend—talked about your death without blinking an eye, as though he were coming to see me in his own interest, rather than yours." Emily chewed for a moment, once again taking stock of her feelings for the man who was sitting across from her. "We've told some real whoppers, haven't we?" she asked quietly. "A pretty untrustworthy lot, the two of us and our friends."

"It's how we've survived, rosebud. You can't always be concerned about etiquette—or ethics—when you're dealing with the likes of Grath and Donahue." Mc-

Clanahan dipped his spoon into his stew, wondering how best to resolve Emily's doubts — how to give her the details she deserved to know, if she was to love him without reservation. He let her eat until she could slow down, while he savored the sight of her flawless face . . . the highlights in her hair, and the way her gaze lingered on him, as though she, too, realized what two heartless rogues could have taken from them.

"I found some interesting entries in your father's records — at Richard's suggestion," he began in a low voice. "I hope you don't think I've overstepped my bounds by looking through them."

Emily glanced at the thick leather-bound books that lay open between her and Matt. One volume was Papa's last journal; the other was yellowed, and it smelled musty. "Of course not. Papa and Richard got together a couple times a year to compare notes on the livestock and the payroll. He often wrote things in his journals, rather than cluttering his ledger with handwriting."

Nodding, Matt carefully turned the older book so she could read her father's small script. "I marked the pages that told about my mother paying back the loan he made her to keep her ranch going, and to start her horse business. And later, he mentions the fire — says he asked Richard and Viry and the men not to discuss it in front of you. You were pretty upset, I guess."

She gazed at Papa's notes, surprised at the emotions and fears his writing brought back. "I had awful nightmares — did my best to keep Idaho from stoking the furnace for several weeks, afraid we'd all be blown into the hereafter." Emily finished reading and looked at Matt with a rueful smile. "I guess this proves what you tried to tell me before. But I still can't understand why, if Papa knew you, he didn't mention you'd returned to run the Wickersham ranch."

McClanahan smiled, pleased to see he'd won a few points. "I'd been away for most of my life. And after the fire, it was easier to stay busy elsewhere than to face that charred foundation." He glanced at the newer journal on the desktop, pointing to a spot on the page. "But those things happened a few years back. It's your father's most recent writing that you'll find . . . especially interesting."

For a moment, the idea that these were some of Papa's final thoughts fogged Emily's vision, but she blinked and skimmed the handwriting she knew so well. Why was Matt sounding so smug, yet so mysterious? She read a few lines and then scowled, flipping back to check the preceding pages.

"This says Papa suspected some rustling way last winter—which is nothing unusual—until April, when he noted his suspicions that Clancy might be involved." Emily stared up at McClanahan. "Why didn't he tell me about this? He made a point of keeping me informed about the problems his businesses were having."

Matt shrugged. "Perhaps it was for your own protection. Clancy might've hinted to him that he was interested in courting you, or—"

"Hinted? Donahue claims my father promised me to him," Emily said with a sarcastic laugh. "Even if they'd had such a conversation, Papa wouldn't have taken him seriously."

"All the more reason for Clancy to resent him, and to start stealing from him. And a very good reason for Elliott not to involve you in it." McClanahan tried to control his smile as he turned to the last few entries in the journal. "I couldn't resist reading further, for more clues. This page might lay some suspicions to rest for you."

Emily looked at the entry he was pointing to, where Papa's words were tiny and tightly packed. "May fourth," she read in a loud whisper. " 'Hired Matt McClanahan to investigate rustling, Donahue in particular'—you *knew!* You suspected Clancy from the start, and you didn't tell me! You—"

"Whoa, there! You could kill a man, pointing at him

that way," he said as he playfully grabbed her hand. Emily was flushed and her amber eyes danced with anger, just as he'd known they would. "I was only on the job a few days before your papa was shot. I didn't see the wanted poster on Donahue till Thompson showed it to me, and then we weren't sure he was our murderer. Look — would *you* recognize him?"

Emily crossed her arms indignantly as McClanahan pulled a folded paper from his pocket and held it before her. The criminal's face was clean-shaven and blotchy; his hair was closely cropped, and the name given was Donald Clancy . . . alias Clarence McDonald, alias . . . a different name for each state that wanted him. The only distinguishing mark listed was a gold tooth. "So?"

"Don't you see?" Matt demanded. "Donahue grew his hair out before he hired on here — grew a beard to disguise his pock-marked complexion. You've said yourself how a little extra hair makes a man look different, and until I knocked his tooth out and proved the bullets in your father were Clancy's, Thompson and I couldn't be sure he wasn't just another rustler on the run."

"But you knew exactly whose mine you were applying at that day at the Angel Claire . . . and you were really in Cripple to investigate Clancy. *Weren't* you?" She rose slowly, feeling foolish and angry because she hadn't seen through Matt's scheme. "Who *are* you? And why didn't you tell me you were already on Donahue's trail the night I hired you, when you found out who I was? Or later? You've had plenty of chances."

"I tried," McClanahan said with a quiet laugh. "But every time we talked about my life — like that day we looked out over Mama's burned-out house — you'd jump to a wild conclusion and shut me off. I got the feeling you wouldn't believe the truth about me unless God himself sent you proof. Finding this journal entry a few days ago was a real piece of luck."

Emily reread Papa's words with a lump in her throat. Her father had hired Matt McClanahan, yet he'd never once mentioned this handsome new employee who was also their neighbor. She chided herself for being so upset about Papa's death that she'd put away his journal without reading it. The answers she'd sought these past weeks were right here in black and white, and they could have saved her months of doubt and weeks of chasing the wrong suspects . . . not to mention the embarrassments she'd suffered because Nigel Grath, Clancy, and McClanahan had pulled the wool over her eyes.

She sighed and looked at the man whose smile was calm and self-assured. "So how'd Papa come to hire you? He required references of all his employees."

"And the Rocky Mountain Detective Agency provided them. I did some work for Wells Fargo, and some investigations for mine owners who suspected their profits were being siphoned off by employees." Matt looked steadily into her wide, golden eyes. "I did some extensive work for Taylor West, too, concerning fraudulent stocks. That's why I know so many of your father's friends in the Springs, Emily."

Dumbfounded, she shook her head. "So you're a detective? That seems like a strange line to go into, with your background in smithing."

"It was work I enjoyed—a way to stay busy without being constantly reminded of the life I could've lived had I come home when Mama first asked me to." He reached across the desk to take her hand. "Believe me, Emily, I've often wondered why Elliott didn't at least *mention* the daughter who was his pride and joy. After I met you, I thought it was because he'd considered me a bad risk, what with turning away from my mother the way I did."

"I doubt that. Papa understood how hard it was to live without the love of a woman." Feeling the warm strength in the hand that held hers, Emily sighed. "I can't tell you how often I've thought about what good friends you and Papa would've been. He admired a man who committed himself to a job until it was finished, yet who wasn't so serious-minded that he couldn't have a little fun."

"The few times I talked with him, I liked your father, too," McClanahan replied gently. "I admired the control he had over his empire . . . respected the way he raised his daughter to fill his shoes. I wish I could've gotten to know him."

Emily nodded, fingering a large chunk of quartz on the bookcase beside her. "But when you found out who I really was, that night at Silas's—and after you got to know me better . . . to love me, you said—why didn't you tell me Papa hired you? It was cruel to lead me on that way, Matt."

"I know. I've kicked myself a hundred times, because I should've been honest with you, of all people." He placed his hands on her shoulders, relieved to see that her anger was mellowing into forgiveness. "I do love you, Emily—more than I can say. But things happened so fast between us, and I wanted to *know* you, inside and out, before I exposed my soul and my secrets."

His face was taut with emotion; Emily saw a tug-of-war between the pain in his past and the new beginning he so desperately wanted with her. "I guess you couldn't let the wrong people know you were a detective, either, so you were disguising your identity, just as I was. You must think I'm pretty obnoxious, always doubting your motives."

"A woman in your position would be foolish not to question a man's intentions—*any* man's." McClanahan gave in to the urge to touch the porcelain hollows above her collarbone, and as he let his finger follow the delicate gold chain to her locket, he smiled in spite of himself. "Maybe, down deep, I didn't tell you your father hired me because I wanted you to love me for who I was—to marry me because *you* thought I was the right man, and not because Elliott Burnham trusted me."

Emily's mouth twisted into a sheepish grin. "Do I put *that* much stock in Papa's ways and opinions?"

"Why shouldn't you?" he asked gently. "His guidance and philosophies turned you into a strong, independent woman . . . a woman who'll make me a fine wife, and an even better friend, for the rest of my life."

His serious blue eyes drove his words straight into her heart: Matt McClanahan had just paid her the highest of compliments. She met his lips fervently with hers, pressing against him as he wrapped his arms tightly around her. Here was the man who would cherish her as no one else—not even Papa—could; who would understand her weaknesses and encourage her strengths. With Matt by her side, she felt able to conquer Clancy Donahue or any other obstacle which presented itself, forever. It gave her a heady sense of destiny, knowing she'd met her true match, and for several minutes nothing else existed or mattered, except the two strong arms that held her and the mouth that was branding her with its fiery passion.

Then there was a commotion outside. They heard boots thump loudly across the front porch, and B.J. was yelling something they couldn't understand. Emily and Matt hurried out of the study and through the parlor.

McClanahan threw the front door open, scowling as he looked out. "What's wrong? What's all the—"

"Fire!" B.J. hollered back at him. "The stable's on fire!"

Emily's first thought was of Sundance and Arapaho, and the horses all the hands depended on. "We have to go—"

"Don't come out till you've changed into pants," Matt ordered. "That dress'll be nothing but a hazard out there. I'll go get Crabtree—"

McClanahan was already down the porch steps, the rest of his sentence lost in the wind. Emily shivered,

staring across the lot at a roof that was suddenly engulfed in flames. The men would be eating their supper
about now, in the mess hall at the far end of the corrals,
she realized, and her blood ran cold. "Matt, come
back!" she screamed. "It's Clancy! He set the fire so—"

But she was too late. There was a thundering of
hooves and a single gunshot, and Matt McClanahan
flew face down into the dirt.

Chapter Thirty-three

Emily rushed into the study and yanked open the top drawer of the desk. As Donahue clumped through the parlor, she gripped Papa's pistol and pointed it at him.

He sneered at her, leaning casually against the doorway. "Put that thing down before you shoot somebody, little girl. I've got one, too, and I'm a helluva lot faster with it than you are."

Standing firm, Emily tried not to think of McClanahan lying lifeless outside. She willed her arms not to shake. The beast before her blocked her view of the parlor, so she was trapped here, by a ruthless, shaggy man who smelled of smoke and kerosene.

Clancy's eyes glittered as he raised his own pistol. "The first thing I'll have to teach you when we're married is to listen to your man. I said to put it down."

Emily wished she *had* listened to McClanahan as the redheaded outlaw took in her revealing scalloped neckline. Donahue looked deadly calm, and since her anger would only give him one more advantage, she laid her gun on the desk. "Why kill my horses and endanger my hands?" she demanded. "Why didn't you just come in after me?"

"Gives me better odds. A smart little gal like you oughtta know that." Clancy holstered his gun, grinning demonically. "Or maybe you're not thinkin' so straight, now that McClanahan's eatin' dirt for the last time. So now it's just me and you, talkin' things over."

"Why should I deal with you? You're nothing but a no-account —"

"Because the killin' won't stop till I get what I want," he growled. "It's real easy to light a rag in a bottle of kerosene and toss it through a window. Next time it'll be the bunkhouse and Crabtree's new place. Is that what you want?"

Emily saw the hard shine in his eyes and the slack in his smile — both reminded her of Nigel Grath — and she knew the bloodshed would continue for as long as this ogre drew breath. She recalled Matt's words about lying to survive and knew she'd have to spin tales to top all she'd ever told. "I want this senseless violence to end," she stated. "I came back to the Flaming B to put my grief behind me and —"

"You came here to meet McClanahan. You knew that story about him bein' killed in the canyon was just a cover — same as all your pinin' and grievin' was," he countered gruffly. Then he leered, his pale green gaze lingering on her chest. "When I saw how he threw you away from the cabin and then fell on you, I knew the explosion wasn't fatal. Figured with him and Thompson bein' thick as thieves, they'd pull such a stunt."

Was it lunatic luck again, or had Donahue been spying on Matt these past weeks in Cripple Creek, just as he'd watched her? It was scary to think he'd seen through Matt's scheme when she hadn't. Emily fought the pounding of her heart as Clancy came over to stand in front of her.

"Nice of you to lose that baby, too," he said with a sarcastic chuckle. "Now you and me can start fresh —"

"You *knew* about the cabin!" she blurted. "You probably wired that dynamite to the door yourself, to —"

Donahue's laughter filled the room. "Grath did that, little girl. Figured you and McClanahan might pay the place another visit someday." After a few more high-pitched chuckles, he looked down at her. "Yeah, ole Nigel and I had lots of time for talk in the jailhouse.

He told me about you and McClanahan goin' at it till we were both half out of our minds. Crazy bastard didn't know when to shut up. He was desperate for a hit on the pipe by then that I promised I'd have some poppy smuggled in, if he'd confess to killin' your daddy. He went loco afterwards, when I told him I couldn't get it, and helpin' him weave that noose was the biggest favor I could've done him."

Emily tried not to blanch. Jumping to a conclusion about Clancy blowing up the cabin had given him another chance to prove how insane he was—and how cold-blooded. He'd orchestrated Grath's suicide so the whiny little blaster wouldn't change his confession. Clancy had a faraway look of pride in his eyes, and she decided her best strategy was to keep him talking. "You should have warned me about the dynamite," she began. "I could have been killed by the blast. And how would you have latched on to Papa's estate, without marrying me?"

"I *told* you to come back, right before you grabbed that door handle. Remember?" He laughed low in his throat, fingering the ruffle on her sleeve with a large, smelly hand. "But with you out of the way, it wouldn't be that hard to steal what I wanted while your daddy's lawyers were figurin' out how to divide the properties among themselves. They would, you know. They might be better dressed than me, but if they had the chance, they'd make most of his money disappear from the ledgers."

He was baiting her, but Emily was determined to control the conversation. "Papa's attorneys earn large retainers," she replied calmly. "And arrangements were made long ago for our managers to assume ownership of his businesses, in the event he and I both died."

Clancy shrugged and made his grimy fingernail sing along the chain of her locket. "I guess none of that really matters, since you survived, and I got you back. What's this little trinket?"

She tried not to wince as he lifted the golden heart

from between her breasts to study it. "McClanahan's wedding present," she said proudly. "I *did* come back here to meet him—to marry him—because I knew you'd be here tonight, sneaking through the dark like a—"

"None of that matters, either. Does it?" he said as he snapped the delicate chain against her neck. He tossed the locket behind him, his expression changing from a mocking grin to a sneer. "He can't come rushin' in to save you anymore, Miss Smarty. And now that you're mine, it's time you stopped makin' the same mistakes your daddy did by standin' between me and what I want."

"Wh-what do you mean?" she mumbled. His paw was curled suggestively around her neck, and Emily was now acutely aware that Clancy Donahue was a deranged man.

His green eyes narrowed as he gazed down at her with a catlike grin. "The first time I saw you I wanted you, Emily," he said in stealthy voice. "Tried to talk to your daddy, but he refused to let me court you. That's when I started cuttin' the fence, lettin' some of my enterprisin' friends help themselves to his Herefords."

It was all Emily could do to hold her tongue. He was stringing her along, trying to catch her up in his rising insanity.

"Then I told your daddy he needed a new foreman—that his old nigger was lettin' his prime stock get rustled," Clancy continued. "He told me to move on if I didn't like the way things were run, so I fed the nigger's horse some locoweed, right before he went out ridin' fence."

She was sickened to think that poor old Idaho had limped and resigned himself to house labor because of Clancy's cruel vengeance. "Why are you telling me this?" she asked stiffly. "You certainly aren't convincing me I should marry you for your—"

"You don't *need* convincin'!" His grip tightened around her neck, and quick as a striking snake he wrenched her right arm behind her with his other hand. "I'm just warnin' you what might happen if you try to cross me again. Now kiss me, dammit. Let me into this dress."

As his mouth crushed hers, Emily's stomach churned. How long would it take Richard and the men to realize she was at Clancy's mercy? The beast was tugging at her scalloped bodice, covering her face and neck with slobbery kisses. There was no doubt in her mind that he intended to rape her right here in the study, and that her only defense was to distract him until help came.

If she'd dressed in pants, as Matt had suggested . . . but it was too late for wishful thinking. Her provocative gown had fueled Clancy's passions, so she'd have to use it as a lure until she could reach the pistol on the desk top. She took a deep breath, and prayed for the strength and presence of mind to become the most charming Southern belle who ever lived. "Mah goodness, but you're passionate," she whispered in an exaggerated drawl.

"Damn right I am. And I don't see any reason to wait for what's rightfully mine, either."

She widened her eyes flirtatiously, but when Clancy pivoted and placed himself between her and Papa's gun, Emily forced herself to think quickly . . . Silas's pistol was still upstairs on the bathroom floor. "What if the hands come in?" she asked breathlessly. "They're not likely to knock, what with the excitement of the fire, and—"

"Maybe they'd like a turn at you," he answered with a laugh. "And maybe I'd like to watch."

Emily felt her supper rising into her throat and fought it back down. "B-but it wouldn't do to let the hands think they can take liberties with your wife, now that you'll be the master of the Flamin' B."

Clancy's eyes shone with a greedy lust as he chuckled down at her. "You might be right about that, little—"

"So why don't we go upstairs, where it's private?" she murmured. She forced herself to stroke his smoke-blackened cheek. "I could give you a nice hot bath, to get the kereosene smell off you, and then—"

"That'll be *after* I—"

Emily kissed him, to give herself time to plan her strategy—which was difficult, with his fat, bearlike body rubbing against hers. Then she pulled away, pretending his kiss had excited her beyond reason. "Clancy, darlin'," she moaned, "do you want to see my naked body, lyin' on the bed waitin' for you?"

Donahue shuddered against her. "That's exactly what I intend to—"

"Then let me go upstairs and get out of all these clothes," she insisted in a breathy voice. "I don't want even my lacy little underthings to come between us, honey. And why not empty our guns and give 'em to me, so we can . . . play with 'em?"

Her captor's lips parted, but his expression was wary. "Not gonna do anything stupid, are you? If you're thinkin' to ambush me at your bedroom door—"

"I'm gonna be spread-eagle on the bed, Clancy. Buck naked, and wantin' you so bad I can't hold still." Emily sucked in her breath to make her breasts heave toward him, and then backed away from his grasp. "You told me in the cave how much fun you and Princess Cherry Blossom had with your pistol, darlin'. I'd like to try it. Really I would."

Clancy released her and reached for his weapon, his arousal apparent. He licked his lips, watching her breasts with utmost concentration as his bullets, and then hers, clattered onto the parquet floor.

"Just think of it," she teased as she took the guns and backed slowly toward the door. "You could plunge into me . . . I'd wrap my bare thighs around you, just like the Princess did. She taught me a few of her tricks, Clancy. You just wait here, darlin', thinkin' about what-all you're gonna do to me, and I'll call you when I'm stark naked. I can't wait. . . ."

Donahue was staring fixedly at her, so she blew him a quick kiss and then hurried toward the staircase. With a last glance to see that he was staying behind, she coyly lifted her hem with a revolver to expose her legs, and then dashed up the steps.

When she turned toward the bathroom, she was suddenly pulled into the shadows by a broad hand clamped over her mouth. Emily struggled against a man who was rock solid and smelled like smoke, until a voice she didn't recognize said, "Goodness but you've grown, Miss Burnham. It was damn hard to stand still, listening to that line you were feeding Donahue, but let's not ruin it for him, all right? When I'm sure you won't scream, I'll let you go."

She tried to rip his hand away, but the stranger tightened his grip.

"Emily, it's me—Sundance," he whispered. "The guy who gave you that fine palomino?"

Her eyes flew open and she collapsed against him nodding.

"I heard about your pa getting shot," he continued in a quiet voice. "And now that the law's not combing this place, I came to offer my condolences. Noticed that fellow throwing fire bombs into your stables, so I thought I'd better help out." Sundance cleared his throat as though it was a strain for him. "I can't keep my hands under control much longer, with you hanging out of your dress this way, Emily. Don't make a sound, all right? And for Chrissakes, don't shoot!"

She nodded emphatically, and when he released her, she quickly laid the guns on the floor so she could tug her bodice back up. The blond man in the shadows was trying to stifle his laughter and keep his pistols pointed away from her as he took in her shocked expression. "What about the horses?" she whispered. "Did they—"

"I shooed them out before most of the straw caught. Saw the firebug's mount tied to your porch, and figured you might need—"

"But what about the man you saw—"

"Shh!" Sundance clamped his hand over her face again, listening. "Our culprit's getting restless. You'd better call him out, so he won't suspect anything. Just say something real juicy, and then stay out of my way."

Hesitating, she wondered if a man as compactly built as Harry Longbaugh could withstand Donahue's enraged, bullish charge if his first bullet missed.

"Go on, sweetheart. Tell him those naked thighs are all a-tremble."

Emily tugged at the top of her dress again and leaned over the balcony railing, forcing the sweetness of a thousand magnolias into her voice. "Clancy?" she called out. "Darlin', I'm waitin'. Come and get it!"

They heard quick, heavy footsteps. "What took you so damn long?" came Donahue's hoarse reply. "I was ready to come bustin' up there—"

The Sundance Kid vaulted neatly over the rail, his hat sailing off as he planted the heels of his boots in Clancy's upturned face. Then the front door burst open, and McClanahan rushed inside, pointing his pistol at the undulating mass of arms and legs on the parlor floor. "Careful, Longbaugh," he called out above their grunts. "He's quicker than you think."

Emily stared at the scene below, too stunned to move. Sundance was pummeling Donahue with his fist and his gun butt, yet the oversized rustler was slowly rolling into a sitting position as though nothing were happening to him.

"Jump back," Matt hollered. "He's not going any-where with my gun in his face."

But before the agile blond could move, Clancy threw him against the doorway of the study with a swat of one huge paw. He glowered at McClanahan, wiping his blood-soaked mustache with his sleeve. "You wouldn't shoot an unarmed man."

"Why not?" Matt countered. "Elliott Burnham didn't have a gun that night you killed him, and it didn't matter *then*." He stood poised to spring away, his arms

377

extended as they clasped his revolver. "Put your hands on your head. Crabtree's coming with a rope, and we're taking you to the sheriff in Colorado Springs."

"Too chickenshit to shoot me?" Donahue taunted.

"A bullet's better than you deserve. Now get those hands up there."

Emily's heart pounded up into her throat as Matt stepped close to Donahue. "Shoot him," she pleaded. "He'll trick you into—"

Clancy's hand darted out and when McClanahan's pistol struck the wall, it fired. Matt jumped away, but not before the red-bearded rustler sprang to his feet and landed a solid right hook in McClanahan's face.

Unable to think or breathe, Emily rushed into the bathroom. Grunts and curses rang out below her as she desperately sorted through her riding clothes for Silas's gun. Grasping its cool pearl handle, she hurried back to the balcony and then partway down the stairs. Longbaugh had joined the scuffle again, but he was suddenly caught by the collar in a chokehold. Clancy then lumbered after McClanahan, tripping Matt as he scrambled toward his gun; the burly outlaw started swinging Sundance as though he intended to bash the two men's heads together.

"Let them go, Donahue! You're a dead man!" Emily yelled above their ruckus.

Donahue looked up at her with a malicious laugh. "Hell, you don't even know which hand to hold the gun in, little girl."

Emily saw blood running from Matt's stitches—reminded herself that Clancy had killed Papa, maimed Idaho, attacked Zenia Collins and Grace, and sent Grath and probably countless others to their graves—and she squeezed the trigger. Clancy's mouth dropped open, and when the bullet whistled past his ear he let go of McClanahan and Sundance, just as she'd planned.

"You ungrateful little bitch, I'll—"

"You'll be wearing a rope collar, if *I* have anything to

say about it," Emily badgered him. And just as she'd hoped, Donahue started toward the stairway, which gave Matt and Longbaugh a chance to prepare for another attack. The outlaw's face was bruised and bloody, and his hideous grin left no doubt in her mind that if he caught hold of her again, she wouldn't live to tell about it.

From the corner of her eye she saw Longbaugh scrambling for their pistols and McClanahan positioning himself in front of the fireplace. "Only an idiot would kill his victim before he got his money," Matt taunted. "Come at *me*, Donahue! Get rid of me, and Emily's yours for the taking."

"She's mine anyway," Donahue grunted. His breathing was labored, and Emily thought he might be seeing double, the way he was squinting at her, but he was only a few steps away from the staircase.

"So fight me for her, man to man," McClanahan sang out. "Any lout who threatens a woman's a *coward*, in my book. A bigger damn coward than Grath was."

Emily was ready to bolt back up the stairs, but McClanahan's words made lightning flash in Clancy's eyes. The brute pivoted suddenly, like an angry bull.

"Shut your damn mouth, McClanahan."

"Shut it *for* me, coward! Longbaugh's out of it—it's just you and me, like it should've been all along."

"You sonuvabitchin'—"

With surprising speed, Donahue lowered his head and charged toward Matt, who was poised before the fireplace to pounce on him. The men suddenly seemed suspended in time, moving toward each other with the fatal finality of two locomotives meeting head-on, and it was more than Emily could bear to watch. Squeezing her eyes shut, she turned away just before a fierce yell filled the room, followed by the sickening sound of the collision.

For several moments the parlor rang with silence. Emily held her breath, not daring to look upon the grisly scene she imagined below her. Had McClanahan been crushed between the burly outlaw and the stone fireplace? Or were there *two* bodies on the floor?

Then Sundance cleared this throat. "McClanahan, you damn near didn't dodge him in time."

"Couldn't have dived any sooner, or he would've figured me out."

As their voices penetrated her frantic thoughts, the pistol dropped from her quaking hand and she leaned heavily against the newel post. Cold sweat was popping out on her brow, and a rankling coppery taste flooded her mouth as she forced her eyes open. Clancy's bearlike body lay sprawling across the hearth, his head cocked at an unnatural angle.

Matt saw her face go white and sat her down on a step. "You were right, rosebud. I was a fool to think he'd stand for being delivered to the law alive. I should've put him away a long time ago, when I knew he killed your father."

Emily stared blankly into McClanahan's face, still unable to fathom what had just happened. "I thought you were dead. Again," she murmured weakly.

"I would've been, had you not distracted him with that bullet," he replied. He wrapped his arms around her shaking shoulders, trying to coax a smile out of her. "Lucky for me Donahue wasn't such a hot shot. His bullet grazed my boot out there, but I played dead to catch my breath. A few minutes later Longbaugh dusted me off, and he slipped in through the kitchen while I covered him from the porch window. I knew you could entertain Clancy till we charged in on him — but it was a helluva shock to see you hurrying up the stairs with your clothes half off."

The hint of indignation in his voice brought Emily out of her stupor. "What'd you think we were doing — playing cards?" she demanded shrilly. "I thought I did damn well, convincing him to wait till I fetched Silas's gun."

"Promised him naked thighs, and tricks some Cherry Princess taught her," Sundance teased. He set the pistols aside, and then picked something up off the rug before he joined them on the stairway. "You better watch out for this woman, McClanahan. She talks dirty, and she plays for keeps."

"I know. I plan to marry her as soon as I can — so the rest of the men in these parts'll be safe, you know."

"I appreciate that."

Emily looked from McClanahan on her left to Longbaugh on her right, noting two sets of sparkling blue eyes in rugged, smudged faces that were creased with mirth. "I was scared spitless that Donahue'd rip this dress off me — a dress I didn't even want," she added in a bitter whisper. "And you two sit here making light of the way I —"

"You saved my life, rosebud," Matt murmured as he tightened his arms around her. "But rather than say gushy things that'll embarrass you, in front of Sundance here, I'm trying to perk you up."

"You looked ready to keel over," Longbaugh added gently. "Even though you saved our shiftless butts, it's still a shock to think about what we just saw. Your pa'd be mighty proud of the way you handled yourself."

"Yes, he would," McClanahan chimed in. "So let's see some sparkle in those eyes and a smile on that pretty face."

"Maybe this'll help. I believe it's yours?" Longbaugh grinned at her — a kind, boyish grin she didn't expect from a notorious horse thief. He pressed something cool and hard into her hand.

"My locket," she said softly. "Damn bandit broke the chain when he yanked it off me."

McClanahan hugged her close and was about to kiss the single tear dribbling down her cheek when the door flew open. Richard Crabtree rushed in with a rope, followed by B.J. and three of the other hands.

"What're you doing — oh." The foreman walked over to Donahue's inert form and stared down at it. "Guess we're too late. You all right, Emily?"

"I — I'll be fine. Thanks, Richard," she replied quietly.

He nodded and looked at the smoke-blackened faces of the hands who'd come in with him. "Haul him out to the yard. Let's hope the sheriff comes in a wagon — he'll need it."

B.J. and the others each took one of Donahue's treelike limbs. As they strained to carry him toward the door, Richard followed them. Then he turned and smiled at Emily. "The horses are fine — spooky, but we got them herded into a corral for the night. Since we owe your friend here a favor, I won't tell Sheriff Fredricks who chased them out of the stable."

Longbaugh stood, nodding his appreciation. "Thanks, Crabtree. I was just leaving."

Emily watched the men stumble outside, bearing the dead weight of Donahue's body. When she looked up into the Sundance Kid's keen blue eyes, she felt her smile returning. "We *do* owe you. It would have taken us weeks to train new mounts for the men, and I guess you know I *couldn't* find another horse like my Sundance."

Longbaugh stooped to retrieve his hat from the corner, and then put it on. And with a perfectly straight face he replied, "Comes a time you need another one, though, I might be able to bring you a mount nearly as good. You folks take care now."

He slipped through the kitchen and closed the door so silently they didn't hear anything, until quiet hoofbeats were galloping into the distance. Matt let out the breath he was holding. "Of all the nerve, to — you know damn well he means to steal that horse from me!"

McClanahan's smudged face grew ruddy as he continued to rail about outlaws' thieving ways, and Emily couldn't help chuckling. Their life would return to normal now: they could marry and have a family, and carry their Colorado empire into the next generation, without the threat of a ruthless, red-bearded killer hanging over them. Yet she knew life with Matt McClanahan would be anything but boring. "It'll still be

382

our horse, you know," she interrupted quietly. "You should be flattered that Sundance recognizes your stock's excellent blood lines and breeding."

Matt looked at her with something akin to wonder. She was really his now, this petite, golden rose whose tawny eyes saw through his schemes and dreams, yet still shone with love. He kissed her lightly on the lips, letting his fingers wander to the warm flesh beneath the scalloped edge of her dress. As always, he felt the stirring that would keep him clinging to her for the rest of his life. Then he chuckled and kissed her again. "I do have a good eye for horseflesh, don't I?"

ROMANCE FROM JO BEVERLY

DANGEROUS JOY   (0-8217-5129-8, $5.99)

FORBIDDEN   (0-8217-4488-7, $4.99)

THE SHATTERED ROSE   (0-8217-5310-X, $5.99)

TEMPTING FORTUNE   (0-8217-4858-0, $4.99)